WEST TO EDEN

EMMA
A fiercely independent, daringly ambitious immigrant, she had the courage to create a new future, but was forever scarred by the painful memories of the past.

ISAAC
Emma's handsome, brilliantly innovative husband. He too struggled against past tragedy, but he would build a business empire—even as his failing marriage led him into the arms of another woman.

ISABEL
Modern-minded and exotically lovely, she fought a hard political battle for women's rights . . . yet gave in too easily to another woman's husband.

HENRY
He couldn't forgive his father's sins, and his vengeance almost destroyed an entire family.

GLORIA GOLDREICH

WEST TO EDEN

AVON BOOKS ⬢ NEW YORK

AVON BOOKS
A division of
The Hearst Corporation
105 Madison Avenue
New York, New York 10016

Copyright © 1987 by Gloria Goldreich
Front cover painting by Robert McGinnis
Published by arrangement with Macmillan Publishing Company
Library of Congress Catalog Card Number: 87-5549
ISBN: 0-380-70601-6

First Avon Books Printing: January 1989

AVON TRADEMARK REG. U.S. PAT. OFF. AND IN OTHER COUNTRIES, MARCA REGISTRADA, HECHO EN U.S.A.

Printed in the U.S.A.

K-R 10 9 8 7 6 5 4 3 2 1

For my daughter Davida

The author wishes to acknowledge, with thanks, the kind advice of Dr. Michael Wechsler of the Columbia Presbyterian Medical Center in New York, regarding medical information; Mr. Ronald Eisenman of Brooklyn, New York, regarding the military history of the period; and Ms. Edith Goldberg of the Beth El Synagogue Library in Phoenix, Arizona, with reference to the history of the Jewish community of Phoenix.

CONTENTS

Amsterdam, 1897

EMMA COEN stood in a circlet of sunlight and listened as her brothers chanted the Kaddish prayer beside their father's newly dug grave. Their clear voices rose in unison, Simon's baritone blending with Emil's tenor. Benjamin Mendoza, Emma's fiancé, rested his hand protectively on her shoulder and adjusted the fur collar of her black cape. His fingers tenderly brushed the nape of her neck and toyed with a tendril of auburn hair. Emma shivered and drew closer to him. It was cooler at Ouderkirk than it had been in Amsterdam. The wind from the Amstel River blew across the open expanse of the Jewish cemetery, scattering the detritus of dried leaves and wilted floral offerings. The bright-headed tulips that stood sentinel at the grave sites swayed and trembled. Emil's voice broke and Simon concluded the prayer alone.

"May He Who establishes peace in the firmament grant peace to us and to all Israel."

"Amen." The mourners issued the response with muted relief, and the beggars who stood at the fringes of the gathering shook their charity cannisters impatiently.

Leonie, the widow, approached the grave supported by her sons. Her pale skin was mottled and her gloved hands trembled. Her lips moved soundlessly as she dropped a handful of earth onto the pale pine coffin. Her mother would not weep before others, Emma knew. Sorrow was private and personal and had to be internalized like the other emotions that intruded upon the ordered calm Leonie prized. Emma had never heard her mother's voice raised in anger, nor had she ever heard her laughter ring with wild abandon. Leonie had shed her tears in the dimness of her curtained bedchamber and then had dressed carefully for her husband's funeral in the long black skirt with its matching swallow-tailed jacket

3

and the sleek seal coat. She had selected her outfit weeks before because Jacob Coen's illness had been a long one and had allowed his wife to carefully prepare for her widowhood.

She stepped back, and Simon and Emil lifted the shovels that stood in readiness and heaved the rich dark earth into the grave. Slowly, Emma moved forward, Benjamin beside her. She inhaled the fragrance of the soft springtime soil and looked up as a flock of wide-winged terns glided through the cloudless sky in ghostly aerial procession.

"Papa," she whispered, and dropped the single white tulip bud she had picked that morning onto the coffin. Her father had preferred the furled bud to the full-blown flower, she knew. He had often worn one in the lapel of his suit and had once threaded a pearl-colored blossom through Emma's thick hair.

Benjamin took up the shovel and added another coverlet of earth, and the other mourners pressed forward. Katrina, the housekeeper, led the small group of servants who stood awkwardly beside the grave, and nodded sadly to the family. Katrina's clumsy body, cocooned in layers of shawls, heaved with grief and she shuffled away, holding a large handkerchief to her face. Friends and relatives, men and women who had worshiped with Jacob Coen at the Portuguese Synagogue on Rapenburgerstraat, who had shared meals with him at his Prinsengracht mansion and strolled with him on Sabbath afternoons in the Botanic Gardens, added their offerings of earth and small stones and offered their condolences to his family.

Emma knew each of them. She knew whose son had married whose daughter, who suffered from arthritis, whose business was prospering, and whose enterprise was failing. The Sephardic Jewish community of Amsterdam was small and tightly knit. She smiled thinly at Mathilde Orenstein, who had introduced her to Benjamin Mendoza. Mathilde inclined her head in sympathy and pressed her lips against Emma's cheek, but her gray eyes were cold. Tall, dark-haired Benjamin Mendoza had been invited to Amsterdam from Antwerp by Henrik Orenstein, and it had been understood that he was to court Mathilde. It had been Mathilde's error to invite Emma Coen to a party during the Hanukkah festival. Emma had lit the fifth candle, and Benjamin Mendoza had remarked that the dancing flame exactly matched her hair, which she wore loose that evening so that it formed a fiery capelet about her slender shoulders.

He had been intrigued by her earrings and necklace. He was a diamond cutter and curious about all gems. They were turquoise, she told him, a gift from her brother Simon, who had recently returned from a journey to the American West. Benjamin Mendoza had observed that they exactly matched her eyes. Was that why her brother had selected them? he asked daringly, and watched her creamy cheeks turn rose-colored.

"Brothers never notice the color of their sisters' eyes," she had protested.

"No one could forget the color of your eyes."

She had laughed then and danced away with Mathilde's brother, who had been dispatched by watchful Madame Orenstein. But Madame Orenstein could not prevent Benjamin Mendoza from calling on the Coen family the next day or dining there on the weekend. Soon Emma and Benjamin were seen walking together in the city, and within weeks Emil Coen, the elder brother, journeyed to Antwerp. When he returned, the engagement was announced, and Mathilde Orenstein confided to her closest friends that she felt a bit sorry for Emma Coen. She had thought Benjamin Mendoza a bit brash, a bit opportunistic.

"Thank you for coming, Mathilde," Emma said softly now, and Mathilde inclined her head and nodded to Benjamin Mendoza.

Leonie extended her gloved hand to the elders of the synagogue and stoically accepted the damp kisses and feeble embraces of their wives. She shivered imperceptibly as a cousin who had traveled from The Hague for the funeral placed his hands comfortingly on her shoulders. She had withdrawn from her own sons' comforting arms that morning and had ignored Emma's touch when the nurse came to tell them that Jacob Coen had not awakened from his afternoon nap and would never awaken again.

Emma, her body convulsed with grief, her tears falling freely, had clutched her mother's hand, but Leonie's fingers had been ice-cold and unbending; briefly a spasm of pain had distorted her face, but she had not wept.

"You must control yourself, Emma." Her voice had been calm and distant.

Even now she stood alone, dry-eyed, as the mourners filed past her. She mouthed the polite response and acknowledged sympathy with requisite grace.

"May you know no more sorrow."

A handful of earth dropped onto the coffin, and Emma stiffened.

"May you be comforted among the mourners of Jerusalem."

The sour aroma of sorrow nauseated her as the rabbi's wife pressed her cheek against Emma's and murmured a blessing in Ladino.

"May the Messiah quicken your father to life."

The beadle's hand pressed her own too hard, but his eyes were moist. Jacob Coen had been a good man, a loyal congregant, and he had always sent the beadle a generous check just before the Passover festival.

The coffin was almost covered now, and Benjamin Mendoza added another shovel-load of earth. He was impatient suddenly for the graveside service to be concluded, for the procession to wend its way northward to the city.

"Come," Simon Coen said, and he offered his arm to his mother. The pale wood was no longer discernible, and they could turn the task over to the professional gravediggers, who had waited patiently for the Jews to complete their rite.

"Emma." Benjamin carefully shook his gloves free of earth before taking her hand in his own.

"Wait." Emma's voice was breathless, her gaze riveted on a woman who slowly approached the grave, accompanied by two young men. She was enveloped in a black velvet cloak, its hood almost concealing her finely chiseled features and the opalescent pallor of her skin. She moved toward the open grave with the slow, dream-bound steps of the somnambulist, her lips moving wordlessly. She looked down and swayed slowly from side to side, and her sons lifted their arms as though to support her.

"Jacob. My Jacob." Grief muffled the words, obscured

the prayer that followed them. The woman lifted the black
lace handkerchief she clutched, and a delicate white tulip bud
glided from its folds onto the earthen coverlet that concealed
the coffin.

Emma trembled and moved forward, but the woman
looked at her briefly and averted her eyes. The taller of her
youthful companions turned and ceremoniously removed his
black dress hat. Emma saw that his hair was the color of
burnished bronze, and she knew that it would glow like fire-
light, as her own did, during the bright days of summer. His
brooding beryl eyes swept across her face, but he turned
away without offering the traditional words of comfort.

"Emma, please." Benjamin Mendoza's voice was impatient. The other mourners were already in their coaches, and
the horses pawed the ground and tossed their manes restlessly so that the black cloth that ribboned their reins fluttered
in the wind.

"All right." She turned from the grave, which would be
covered and level with the ground before the day was over,
and allowed him to help her into the coach where her mother
sat rigidly between Simon and Emil. Almost involuntarily,
she looked back. The woman was climbing into a fiacre
pulled by matching piebald ponies.

"Who are they?" she asked.

"Perhaps a family with whom your father had business
dealings," Leonie Coen said indifferently. "I never saw them
before."

Emma stared at her mother in surprise and then remembered that her family had not heard the woman's strangled
voice, had not seen the pale white flower drift soundlessly
into the grave. She leaned back and closed her eyes. Benjamin Mendoza sighed.

The funeral cortege rolled silently through the ancient
cemetery. It passed the fragile gravestones of the Spinoza
family, the weatherbeaten bricks on which Manesseh Ben
Israel's tombstone rested, the long rows of worn marble slabs
on which biblical scenes had been carved in intricate detail.
The carriage paused briefly before a frieze depicting Tamar,
her hooded cloak drawn closely about her reclining form.
Emma shivered and rested her head on Benjamin Mendoza's

shoulder. Her black beret had slipped off, and her bright hair cascaded across his dove-gray coat. Her father was dead and she mourned his loss, yet she felt strangely peaceful because Benjamin Mendoza sat beside her, his large hand gently covering her own.

The spring sun beamed its way through the French windows and tossed shards of light across the polished floors. The mirrors, which had been covered with sheets during the seven days of mourning, gleamed with refracted brightness. Emma stared at herself as she walked by and was briefly startled by her own face, pale and unsmiling. She glanced across the room at her brothers and saw that their pallor matched her own, yet their faces were relaxed, and Simon laughed softly at something Emil said. Jacob Coen's sons had come to terms with their grief, and they had, after all, been prepared for his death.

Their father had died after a long illness, of a disease which the doctors had declined to name although they had explained it carefully. A tumor had inexplicably formed within his abdominal wall and had continued to grow, cell multiplying on cell until the body could no longer contain it. There was no cure for it, and its progress was excruciatingly painful. The doctors were apologetic but helpless. They assured the family that the disease was not hereditary, and they spoke vaguely of heart failure. Somehow, people found heart failure an acceptable cause of death, they observed. Jacob Coen himself had not been unaware of the prognosis of his disease, although he had stubbornly resisted it. During the early stages he continued to live as he always had, working long hours and sometimes not arriving home until the pale light of dawn crept across the canal, often not arriving home at all.

"He works late and sleeps at the office. There is a divan there which is quite comfortable and his own bath," Leonie had explained when Emma questioned her father's nocturnal absences. Very often Leonie herself did not know whether or not Jacob had come home. They had slept in separate bedrooms for many years, and Leonie, who suffered from recurring sick headaches, seldom came downstairs before noon.

As Jacob Coen's illness progressed, he occasionally did not appear at the Prinsengracht mansion for several nights.

"Where is Papa?" Emma asked her brothers.

Emil shrugged. He appeared dutifully each day at the Coen Emporium on the Kalverstraat and sat on a high stool in the accounting office, studying ledgers and receipts, bills of lading and invoices. But he knew little of his father's activities. He always left as soon as possible, smiling amiably at the clerks who stood behind the wooden counters, endlessly arranging and rearranging their merchandise. The sale of garments and household goods did not interest Emil Coen. The store's huge plate-glass windows, which Jacob had installed with such excitement ("The first in Amsterdam, the very first," he had said again and again), gave Emil no pleasure, and often he did not even look at the displays. He could not understand his father's elation at getting a good price on a wagonload of laces from Brussels or glassware from Italy. He grew impatient when his colleagues discussed their plans for new enterprises, new departments.

Important things were happening in the world, Emil knew, exciting things that had nothing to do with the prices of satin negligees on the Kalverstraat. In Paris, Alfred Dreyfus had been arrested on charges of treason, and Emil had followed the trial avidly. The death knell was sounding for European Jewry, he had decided, no matter how ornate their synagogues, how prosperous their businesses. On that he and the journalist Theodor Herzl were in agreement. Japan had declared war on Russia, and across the Atlantic Ocean, in the United States of America, frontiers were being pushed forward and daring men were seeking gold in a state whose shoreline was licked by the Pacific Ocean. Emil envied his brother Simon, who had journeyed to America and returned with exciting descriptions of the New World with its wondrously named cities and its mysterious mountains and deserts. But then Simon was the younger son, and the future of the Coen Emporium did not depend upon him. He had been free to go to the university and pursue his interest in metallurgy; he had been free to travel.

Her brothers could not explain Jacob Coen's absences to Emma, but after a while there had been no need for explanations. Jacob Coen arrived home one afternoon and never left the Prinsengracht mansion again. During the last weeks of his illness, Leonie moved back into his room and slept on a cot beside his bed.

"It is my duty," Emma heard her say righteously to Katrina. Emma pitied her mother. She would never leave Benjamin Mendoza's bed, once they were married. She could not bear to be apart from him now, and even during the mourning period she had managed to be alone with him in her small sitting room. He had soothed and calmed her then, his hands caressing her, his breath sweet in her ear. He whispered her name. "Emma. Sweet Emma." He whispered his love. "My darling. My own, forever." She quivered at the sound of his voice, at the touch of his hand.

Benjamin Mendoza sat beside her now, although Leonie had initially objected to his presence during the reading of the will.

"He is not family yet," she had maintained. Leonie adhered strictly to the protocols of the Sephardic community.

"But we will be married in six months' time," Emma had protested. The wedding date had been set before her father's death, and it was against Jewish tradition to defer the celebration of marriage once a date had been agreed upon.

"Emma's right," Emil told his mother. It had occurred to him, with a rush of hope, that Benjamin Mendoza might easily be persuaded to assume the management of the Coen Emporium. He certainly spent enough time there, and recently he had made some valuable suggestions. He had suggested that the departments for outer garments be located closer to the store's entry, and within days of the change an increase in sales had been reported. It had also been Benjamin's suggestion that a supply of ladies' silk scarves that were not selling well be distributed as gifts to purchasers of capes. The customers had been delighted, and the sale of capes had more than doubled. Benjamin was even interested in the ledgers, which Emil found impossibly boring. It was true that he had been trained as a diamond cutter, but surely there was more of a future in running the largest department store in the Nieumarket than in carving huge stones into smaller ones. With Benjamin Mendoza in charge, Emil Coen could slip off his high stool and see the world.

Emil smiled. He watched as Benjamin Mendoza adjusted Emma's soft blue cashmere shawl about her shoulders and moved a footstool closer to Leonie.

Emma looked up from the letters she was reading and smiled gratefully.

"Anything important?" Emil asked laconically, glancing at the correspondence that his sister was separating into neat piles.

"Letters of condolence," she replied. "We shall have to write notes of acknowledgment. And a very nice letter from Papa's cousin Greta in London inviting Mother and myself to visit."

"Impossible," Leonie said. She lived according to a rigid agenda, and her traveling was limited to the beaches of the Riviera and the spas of Germany.

Simon glanced impatiently at his watch. It was unlike Daniel Salmon, the family's attorney, to be late. The Coens were valued clients, and Daniel Salmon had always been solicitous of them. It would not do to allow him to think he could deal with the family more casually because Jacob Coen was dead. It would do no harm, Simon decided, to remind Daniel Salmon that there were other advocates in Amsterdam who had expressed an interest in the affairs of the Coen family.

The paneled door opened and Katrina entered, her starched white apron rustling importantly.

"Advocate Salmon is here," she said. She stared disapprovingly at Simon, who had lit a small cheroot and allowed the ash to hover dangerously over the Aubusson carpet. Emma moved swiftly forward and passed a crystal ashtray to her brother, who gave her a conspiratorial wink. Simon had always been Emma's closest ally in the family. It was Simon who knew that calm, efficient Emma, Emma who was always so organized, so self-possessed, harbored mysterious secret dreams.

"There must be more to life than leaving a visiting card at the Polaks and arriving home to find a card from the Orensteins," she had said to him one day. He had seen tears fill her eyes when they attended a performance of Dvořák's *New World Symphony*. His sister's calm did not deceive Simon Coen. He wondered if it deceived debonair Benjamin Mendoza, who busied himself now, helping Emma replace her letters in a ribboned basket.

Daniel Salmon, short and plump, smiled nervously at the family and apologized for his lateness.

"So difficult to cross Dam Square. Everyone seems determined to obtain a visa for South Africa this very morning."

He kissed Leonie's hand, but she withdrew from the sweaty touch of his palm and motioned him toward the large easy chair covered in gold damask that stood before the fireplace. Leonie was accustomed to ordering the seating arrangements of her guests and her family. It was, it occurred to Emma, her mother's only domestic responsibility. Nothing else had ever been asked of her. She had been the beautiful daughter of one prosperous businessman and the gracious wife of another. Her health had always been fragile, and it was Katrina who maintained the household and Emma who administered the accounts and undertook the ordering of provisions. Leonie took excellent care of her clothing and her jewelry, and several times a week she shared her tea with other well-dressed Jewish matrons, who sampled pastries and spoke with great earnestness of projects to benefit the poor Jews in the Houtseeg quarter. Wealth and ritual structured Leonie Coen's life and shielded her from every unpleasantness.

"Our mother needs money as other creatures require air," Simon had said once, and Emma had thought the remark unkind but accurate. Still, Leonie was not unlike the other women of the Portuguese Synagogue, whose lives were molded by their husbands and social positions were defined by lineage and acquisition.

Her own life with Benjamin Mendoza would be different, Emma knew. They would break free of the constraining pattern of Amsterdam life. Benjamin had listened avidly to Simon's description of life in America, and it was Benjamin who had given Emma a small leatherbound copy of the poems of Walt Whitman. "I hear America singing," they had read together, "The varied carols I hear." There were no varied carols in Amsterdam, only a familiar, too often repeated repertoire.

"We will cross the ocean and build our future," Benjamin Mendoza had told Emma, his dark eyes burning. "We would need only a small amount of capital."

He was not a wealthy man, she knew. Emil had ascertained as much during his visit to Antwerp, and Benjamin had confided that an older brother had risked and lost the family fortune in careless investments in the Bourse. She found his confession of poverty endearing. It made him oddly vulnerable, and she assured him that her dowry would suffice to launch them on their new lives. In the dimness of her bedroom she dreamed of long days on the ocean with Benjamin Mendoza standing beside her at the ship's rail, salt spray glinting in his black hair, jeweling the narrow silken mustache that he trimmed with pride and precision. Today, when Daniel Salmon read her father's will, the amount of her dowry would be revealed. It would be adequate, she knew. She had been Jacob Coen's only daughter and his favorite child.

Daniel Salmon untied his oversized leather portfolio, fumbling with its ribboned strings. The legal documents were neatly pinned together, and he leafed through them counting the pages, clearing his throat.

Simon turned from the window where he had watched the spring wind whip the skirts of a pretty nursemaid who strolled down the Prinsengracht supervising two small blond girls. She had appeared every morning at precisely that hour during the week of mourning. Did everyone in Amsterdam follow the exact same patterns each day? he wondered. A familiar impatience gripped him. He had already lost a week's work in his laboratory, and he was anxious to complete his experiments.

"Daniel, perhaps we can dispense with the formalities and you can simply share with us the general terms of my father's will," he suggested.

"That would be best," Emil agreed. "There is no need for my mother and sister to be burdened with legal details that will be meaningless to them."

"It's not quite that simple." The attorney stirred uneasily

and shifted his position in the large gold chair. A small rim of perspiration formed on his upper lip and his hands trembled, causing the sheaf of papers to flutter dangerously. "Your father's estate is not what one might have predicted."

"Let us not quibble," Emil said. "A few thousand guilders more or less is of no consequence to us. Please proceed."

The portly lawyer sighed. "It is not a question of a few thousand guilders more or less. Indeed, all we are discussing, in point of fact, is a few thousand guilders."

A new tension filled the room. Simon turned from the window. Emil leaned forward in his chair, and Benjamin Mendoza's fingers tightened about Emma's shoulders, as though to restrain the sudden tremor that seized her. Only Leonie remained immobile, a regal figure in her high-necked black taffeta mourning dress, the long rope of pearls that Jacob Coen had given her as a silver anniversary gift luminous at her throat. But a new pallor veiled her face, and her hands, which had been loosely folded, were now tightly clenched. A wisp of hair escaped her silver blond chignon, but she did not pin it back.

"How can that be?" It was Emma who asked the question, and the steadiness of her own voice startled her.

Daniel Salmon cleared his throat and toyed with his silk cravat.

"I'm afraid that I have some very shocking news for you," he said at last. "It is true that Jacob Coen was a very prosperous man. The Coen Emporium is a flourishing establishment, and for much of his life his investments were considered prudent. But it required great wealth to maintain two families in the style to which you, my friends, are accustomed. And even greater wealth to provide for the future of two sets of heirs."

"What are you talking about?" Simon Coen asked incredulously. The man was mad. He had obviously confused Jacob Coen's estate and history with that of another client.

"Perhaps Madame Coen should be spared this," the lawyer suggested.

"Please go on. It does not matter. Nothing matters." Her thin lips, drained of color now, barely moved.

"I will be as brief as possible. Many years ago, Jacob Coen formed a friendship with a female employee of his emporium, a widow named Analiese Deken. Their relationship was of a very intense and unconventional nature." Daniel Salmon's face grew red, and he kept his eyes fixed on the papers in his hand. "In short—and I am sorry to offend you—they became lovers and two sons were born to them. Jacob Coen provided handsomely for this secret family. He bought them a house in Osdorp. There was a staff of servants, private tutors for the boys, vacations. This, of course, strained his finances."

"I should imagine so," Emil said drily. He regretted suddenly that he had not known his father better. Jacob Coen's secret life revealed a dimension that intrigued Emil as much as it pained him.

"Yes." The lawyer coughed. "He was, of course, aware of the strain, but the Coen Emporium never faltered and he was a shrewd investor. Given enough time, he hoped to be able to generate enough income to guarantee the future of both his households without jeopardizing his holdings. But then he became ill, and he knew that he would not have enough time. He took a gamble."

"He invested in the South African mines," Simon said flatly. It was an easy guess. The discoveries at Kimberly, the success of the de Beers, had had their influence in Amsterdam. More than one family had been catapulted into bankruptcy. Simon, the metallurgist, had marveled at their naiveté, their foolish greed.

"Exactly." The lawyer seemed relieved that he would not be the one to reveal Jacob Coen's foolishness. "And of course there were no mines. Only bogus certificates. Deeds to non-existent mine sites."

"How much did he invest?" Emil asked.

"Almost everything. He borrowed heavily, using the store and both this house and the Osdorp house as collateral. All these properties and their contents are now forfeit to his creditors."

"Everything?" Leonie's voice was hollow with disbelief. She fingered the carved rosewood arm of the chair on which she sat, bent to move a small ornament so that it would not scratch her inlaid table. Abruptly she dropped her hands to her lap. These things were no longer her property. Jacob Coen, the husband who had, after all, been a stranger to her, had gambled them away. Her mouth was sour and she wanted to leave the room, but she was powerless to rise.

She had not been oblivious to his infidelity. She had chosen to ignore it, to pretend that it did not exist, to deceive herself and thus deceive others. Secretly, darkly, she acknowledged that the secret life that kept him away from home offered her relief, exoneration. They had lived their lives carefully, according to rules understood but unarticulated. But Jacob Coen, whom she had dutifully mourned, had not kept his bargain. Her existence had been invaded, her future violated. She sat very still and listened to the voices of Daniel Salmon and Simon; it seemed to her that their words rustled and scattered like dry leaves in an autumn wind.

"Several thousand guilders which were in Madame Coen's name alone remain," the lawyer said. "Not a great deal but enough for her to live on modestly, prudently."

"And my sister's dowry?" Simon asked. He saw Benjamin Mendoza stiffen, Emma lean forward.

"I strongly advised your father not to touch the money set aside for Emma," the lawyer said in a strained voice. "In fact, I hope that you will believe that I strongly advised him against all these investments."

"I am sure you did," Simon said. "But the result is, of course, that my sister's dowry is gone."

His eyes met Benjamin Mendoza's hooded stare.

"It is of no consequence," the Belgian said, and he rested his hands protectively on Emma's shoulders.

"I shall leave the papers with you," Daniel Salmon said. "You will want to examine them." He fumbled with his portfolio. He felt a sudden urgency. He wanted to leave the house before Leonie Coen's false calm was shattered, before she realized the enormity of her loss and her soft, disbelieving tone was transformed into a wail of agony. He wanted to leave the Prinsengracht and seek refuge in a brown café with a stein of lager while the brothers confronted their rage. He would not blame the family. Indeed, he admired their forbearance. It was not easy to have both the past and the future shattered within a few minutes. Only Emma, the daughter, was safe. Mendoza, to his credit, would stand by her—but then, why shouldn't he? Emma Coen was the most beautiful young Jewess in Amsterdam. Daniel Salmon, whose eyes turned toward the women's balcony of the Portuguese Synagogue all too frequently, had noticed that her hair matched the slender flames of the tapers that illuminated the sanctuary. Her skin was pearllike, luminous, and even from a distance her blue eyes glinted like polished gemstones.

Daniel Salmon was a widower, and it had occurred to him that if Benjamin Mendoza chose to cancel the engagement, he himself might be a suitable husband for Emma Coen. He would ask for no dowry and he would arrange for the purchase of the Prinsengracht house. But of course Benjamin Mendoza had not reneged. Sadly the lawyer closed his portfolio and rose.

"My regrets." He bowed formally to Leonie and then to Emma. "My sympathies." He shook hands with the brothers and with Benjamin Mendoza. Oddly, their grips were firm and their voices unperturbed.

"We don't blame you, Daniel," Simon said, and he was grateful for the words of reassurance. It would damage his practice if word traveled through the Portuguese Synagogue that Daniel Salmon's advice had led to Jacob Coen's bankruptcy.

Simon walked to the door with him.

"I did want to ask you, however, about this other woman—Analiese Deken."

"I know her and I hope you will pardon me for saying so," the lawyer said, his face again suffused with color, "but it is not as you may think. She is a fine woman. A gentlewoman."

"She is provided for in some modest manner?"

"She has a similar amount to that which is available to your mother. Perhaps even more because she foresaw the future and through the years she managed to save a bit on her own. She will not trouble you. She plans to go to America with her younger son. The elder is a medical student in Vienna."

"Her sons thought of my father as their father?" Simon persisted.

"David and Henry are aware of their paternity. Your father was a part of their lives. But now they are bitter against him on their mother's behalf. It is understandable."

"Yes," Simon said. "Of course. They would be." He too was bitter against his father on his mother's behalf. He did not begrudge his unknown, unacknowledged half brothers their anger. He had known of his father's secret life for only a single hour. They had grappled with it all the days of their lives.

It was Emma who walked Leonie up to her room.

"You must rest, Mother," she said.

"What does it matter? Everything is gone. I have nothing. I am nothing." Leonie's tone was flat, and Emma did not argue with her. Deprived of her wealth, robbed of her status, Leonie viewed herself as nonexistent. "Do you know how I feel, Emma? I feel that I have disappeared. If I hold up my mirror, the glass will be blank."

"Nonsense," Emma said harshly. She went to her mother's dressing table and took up the inlaid hand mirror. "You are there." She thrust it in front of her mother, but Leonie closed her eyes and twisted away.

"Nothing," she repeated. "Nothing."

Emma left, closing the door softly behind her. Benjamin waited for her at the foot of the stairway, holding her fur-collared cape.

"Come, Emma," he said and wrapped the cloak about her shoulders. His voice rang with a new authority, and she submitted to it gratefully.

"Are you going out?" Simon asked.

"Yes." Benjamin answered for her. "All this has been a shock for Emma. An outing will do her good."

"You're not tired, Emma?" Emil asked. He himself was exhausted. He had felt all vitality drain from him as the lawyer made his grim revelations. His life, all their lives, had been based on deception. Their past was forfeit, their future uncertain.

"I'll take care of her," Benjamin asserted, and she leaned

against him, rested her head on his shoulder. She pitied her brothers, who had no one to spirit them away from the house of mourning, to comfort them with soft whispers of reassurance, promises of constancy. Her heart broke for her mother lying alone in the dimly lit room. She herself was fortunate. Benjamin was with her. Loving and loyal Benjamin.

"I'll be all right," she assured her brothers. "Look in on Mama." She closed her mind against the thought of Leonie lying across the carefully made bed, staring up at the ceiling, and followed Benjamin out the door. The chill-tinged wind of early spring startled her, and she lowered her head against its impact. Benjamin removed his scarf, a deep gray cashmere weave which she had plucked one wintry afternoon from the haberdashery counter at the Coen Emporium, and wrapped it about her neck.

"I told them I would take care of you," he said.

"I know you will," she replied. The wool of his scarf, redolent with the fragrance of his soap and tobacco, was soft and comforting against her skin.

Hand in hand, then, they walked northward and paused to lean against the wrought-iron rail of a bridge and look down into the smoke-colored waters of the canal.

"This city is like a necklace of islands," Emma said. "One after another. I should like to reach land's end." Her voice was wistful, and Benjamin Mendoza cupped her chin in his hand and smiled.

"If you are ready for an adventure, I will take you to land's end," he said.

"I am always ready for an adventure," she said confidently.

She had always been the most daring girl in her form, leading her classmates away from the marked pathways on school hikes, urging her friends to follow her down unfamiliar streets. The unknown intrigued and challenged her, no less today, she acknowledged with relief, than it had on other days. Her lover's words charged her with new energy, invigorated her, ripped away the enervating sadness of loss and death. She *would* be all right. Benjamin would take care of her.

There was a new spring to her step as they walked to the

canal that spanned the isthmus to the North Sea at Imjuden. There, gulls screamed wildly and vendors pressed toward them, proffering containers of herring salad, cucumbers pickled in brine, loaves of brown bread. She remembered that she was hungry, and Benjamin bought the coarse country food, which they ate at wharfside, washing it down with the dark brown beer favored by sailors. She felt strangely light-headed and yet, on the launch that carried them down the canal to Imjuden, she wept. He kissed away her tears, pressed his cheek close to hers, and licked at the salt spray that settled in nacreous drops on her upturned face.

"I will take care of you," he said again. "Trust me."

A light rain fell as the launch docked, and she shivered, drawing her cape closer, tying the knot of his scarf.

"Come. We must get you warm."

He led her then to the wayfarer's inn close by the docking inlet, and she waited in the small anteroom while he spoke to the innkeeper. A fire burned in the grate, and she held her hands out to it, yet her fingers did not grow warm. Apprehension, uncertainty, chilled her.

"Emma." He stood beside her and untied the scarf, removed her cape. "We'll dry your things. Rest." The concern in his tone soothed her, and she was strangely grateful that he asked no questions, offered no options.

She followed him up the narrow stairway and into the tiny whitewashed room. Silver rivulets of rain streaked the windows, and they heard the crash of the North Sea waves against the jetties that rimmed the cove.

"I love you," he said and then added, as though perceiving the hesitancy that caused her heart to beat too fast, "Nothing matters but that we love each other."

He held her close. His breath was moist against her neck. His heart beat in rhythm with her own. His body sheltered and warmed her. She was desired, protected. All that had been lost would be regained. All that had been shattered would be rebuilt.

She wore a high-necked dress of dark wool, and deftly he unfastened the pearl buttons that held it closed. Like a small girl, she stepped out of it and stood before him in her white lace camisole, her organdy crinoline.

"Come."

His voice was insistent, and obediently she followed him to the large feather bed, its thin blue coverlet faded and sea-scented.

"We will be all right?" she said and was surprised that her words emerged as a query when she had meant them to be a statement.

"We will be all right. We *are* all right. Do you remember these words? 'A garden enclosed is my sister, my bride'?"

"I remember them." The words were from the Song of Songs, and he had been granted the honor of reading them from the podium of the Portuguese Synagogue during the Festival of Weeks only a month previous. She had sat proudly in the balcony among the women, and he had looked up at her as he chanted Solomon's sweet pledge of love.

"*You* are my sister. *You* are my bride." He kissed her fingers, one by one; he knelt beside her and pressed his cheek against her wrist.

She wept at his reassurance, his tenderness. Her own doubt shamed her, and in apology her fingers traced the curve of his cheek, the cleft of his chin, his silken mustache and the dark brows that arched above his almond-colored eyes.

"Benjamin." She whispered his name in relieved submission, in tender affirmation.

Simon and Emil spent the afternoon in the office of the Coen Emporium, where they huddled over the ledgers in Jacob Coen's office. After several hours they closed the heavy leather account books and opened the bottle of Genever which their father had kept in the bottom drawer of his desk. They went home when it was empty and walked down the Kalverstraat, leaning on each other and singing a half-forgotten dance hall tune.

"The picture Daniel Salmon painted was too optimistic," Emil told Benjamin Mendoza that night. He was grateful that his mother had not come down for dinner. "It appears that my father even used my mother's jewelry for collateral. But not Emma's," he added swiftly, arrested by the severity of Benjamin Mendoza's gaze.

"As I told you, this new situation does not alter my intentions,'' Benjamin said. He covered Emma's hand with his own, but she did not lift her eyes. Leonie had not even permitted her to light a lamp and had refused the tray that Katrina carried to her. She lay, fully clothed, on the bed, her hands tightly clenched, staring into the darkness.

Benjamin Mendoza left early, and the brothers and sister sat over their coffee. At last Emma smiled.

"At least,'' she said, "we know now where Papa was all those evenings.''

"Somehow I never really believed that he stayed at the Emporium. The divan was not that comfortable, and Papa did enjoy his comfort,'' Emil said.

"We may be certain that the Osdorp establishment was very comfortable,'' Simon added.

They laughed then with a cynicism that was new to them, and their voices were strangely harsh. They were doubly bereft. Their father was dead, and they knew now that all their lives he had betrayed them.

Emma awakened the next morning to voices that threaded their way through the remnants of her dream. Her nightdress was stained with perspiration, and she hovered between sleep and wakefulness, wafted on the vaporous cloud of her dream. She stood beside a coffin, but she did not wear the dark garments of the bereaved. She was dressed in a diaphanous bridal gown of shimmering white and held a bouquet of white tulip buds. Sorrowing mourners drifted by her, murmuring their condolences, and she strained to hear them because their voices were muted and obscured by the strains of wedding music—the nuptial debka of the Sephardic marriage feast. Yet the voice of her brother Emil rang with clarity.

"Perhaps she will find some peace now,'' he said.

Emil's voice did not belong to her dream. She was awake at last, and she knew that her brothers were talking in the corridor just outside her room. She heard Katrina sob, and she recognized the husky voice of Dr. Beinincke. She seized a robe and opened the door.

"Emil. Simon. What is it?''

Her brothers stood, their faces pale, their eyes dull. It was Katrina who answered her.

"My poor Emma. My poor orphan. First your father and

now your mother. Emma, your mother is dead." Grief muffled the serving woman's voice; her large red hands twisted
her white apron into tortured knots.

"No!" Her scream shrilled with disbelief, with fierce denial. She rushed past her brothers, past Katrina, to the bed
on which her mother lay.

Leonie Coen wore a pale blue silk negligee. Her silver-
blond hair had been carefully twisted into a single coil that
rested on her shoulder. The scent of lily of the valley clung
to her newly powdered skin and mingled with the smell of
rotting fruit. Even her fingernails had been neatly shaped and
lightly polished.

"Mama!" Emma embraced the motionless form, thrust
her face against her mother's breast. "Mama!" She shook
the lifeless body; her fingers pressed against Leonie's cold,
unresisting flesh. Dr. Beinincke moved forward to restrain
her.

"Please, Emma. It was her heart. Her heart was never
very strong. Come, Emma." His voice was gentle, persuasive. He was familiar with grief and its exigencies. His hands
were gentle yet firm as he led her away from the bed. But at
the doorway she turned and saw Katrina lift a small smoke-
colored vial from the bedside table and thrust it into the
pocket of her apron.

"She could not bear it, Emma," Simon said softly. "Try
to understand."

"Can *we* bear it?" Emma asked.

Simon did not reply. He held his sister in his arms until
her wild sobs subsided and her tears no longer seared his
flesh.

The women of the burial society arrived later in the morning, and Emma was composed and dry-eyed as she received
them and thanked them. Her skin was as pale as the stiff
white collar of her black dress, and her bright hair was gathered into a severe bun. She directed the maids to bring them
the warm water they required and instructed Katrina to prepare refreshments for them.

She herself covered the mirrors of the house with stiff
sheeting and then wrapped herself in her cape and hurried
out of the house.

"Emma! Where are you going?" Emil called after her.

"I don't know." She knew only that as she had moved from room to room the walls had seemed to enclose her. She could not bear to look at the matching gold damask chairs that stood before the fireplace or to breathe in the fetid aroma of the dying tulips in the dining room. Death haunted the house of her childhood, and she rushed toward water and air.

"What shall we tell Benjamin?"

"I'll be back by the afternoon."

The women watched her from the window of Leonie's room and nodded sadly. They were mothers and wives, and they feared for their children and for themselves.

"Poor Leonie," the rabbi's wife said. "Her heart, Dr. Beinincke told us."

They did not dispute her but busied themselves with lengths of flannel and basins of warm water for the washing of the body.

"So terrible," she continued. "Only a week after poor Jacob's death."

"Yes, terrible." They looked at one another with sorrowing complicity, grateful that their daughters were not as beautiful as Emma, that their husbands had not been as dashing as Jacob Coen; they wondered if they could sustain sorrow with more fortitude than the woman whose lifeless body they carefully and methodically cleansed for burial beside her husband at Ouderkirk.

Emma walked slowly down the Prinsengracht. She lingered briefly at the small bridge suspended above the canal. The waters were murky and the stone balustrades were stained with age and rime. A small tug maneuvered its way laboriously through the narrow waterway and sounded its horn in mournful warning. Two boys waved at it, but their gesture was desultory. The tug's progress offered no adventure, no drama. Everything about Amsterdam was predictable, Emma thought. It was a narrow city, bounded by water. Its horizons were limited, and its very existence was vulnerable to the vagaries of nature. She walked on, anxious suddenly to leave the city streets behind. She did not want to look up at buildings where housemaids shook the bed linen from elongated balconies and grim-faced men offered perfunctory nods to each other as they edged their way across constricted roadways.

She turned her steps southward, and at the Amstel she boarded a small tram. Its steady movement soothed her, and the river wind cooled her cheeks. The roadside blazed with newly blooming flowers, with rainbow-colored tulips, small clusters of grape iris and tall, pale narcissi. Water fowl drifted on the river, the larger, wide-winged creatures protecting their small, featherless young. A mother sat opposite Emma, holding a small blond girl on her lap. She tied the ribbons of the child's pink hat tighter as a strong wind gusted across the river.

Emma turned away, suffused with sudden sorrow. She remembered how gentle Leonie's fingers had been as she adjusted Emma's scarves, arranged her shawl in graceful folds. She thought of how Jacob Coen had held her hand as they walked to the synagogue, stopping now and again to pull her collar up against the wind. Still, she was not alone. Benjamin Mendoza would take care of her. Benjamin would shelter her always. She leaned back and thought of how his hands had moved across her body in gentle caress, how he had held her close in the shadowed room of the inn at Imjuden.

"We are already husband and wife," he had said softly. "We do not need a nuptial agreement, a muttered blessing. We bless each other."

She should not have left the Prinsengracht house so hastily. Benjamin would worry about her, would perhaps go in search of her. She wondered if he would go to Imjuden, if he would race up the wooden hostelry steps to the little corner room with its soft feather bed covered with the homespun linen that smelled of sunlight and sea. She smiled at the thought and fell into a light sleep.

"Ouderkirk! We are arrived at Ouderkirk!" The conductor's voice, harsh and impatient, jerked Emma into wakefulness.

"Ouderkirk?" She spoke the word aloud. She had selected the tram at random, never asking its destination, yet she was strangely unsurprised to find herself at the Jewish cemetery. She descended the rickety wooden steps, ignoring the conductor's outstretched hand, and stared at the serried rows of graves, the imposing mausoleums. A funeral cortege passed through the iron gates, the horses moving slowly, reluctantly. The windows of the coaches were blackly curtained, lest sunlight intrude upon grief. She had sat behind such a curtain only a week ago, Emma thought with sinking heart. And tomorrow she would ride behind the hearse that carried her mother's body. She shivered and hurried on.

An old woman huddled in a worn plaid shawl at the cemetery gate, hawking flowers which Emma knew had been scavenged from grave sites. She thrust the ragged basket in front of Emma. A single white tulip bud nestled amid the yellowed and wilted blossoms, and Emma lifted it carefully, as though it were a fragile talisman. She gave the woman a coin and dropped another into the charity box at the entry. Swiftly then she made her way across the pebbled pathways that led to her father's grave.

A fiacre blocked the roadway, and a tall woman wearing a dark green cloak stood before Jacob Coen's grave. She held a long-stemmed narcissus, and her lips moved in silent prayer. She turned at the sound of Emma's step. The pale flower trembled but her gaze was steady, and when she spoke her voice was calm.

"You are Emma, of course. Your father spoke of you often."

"And you are Analiese Deken."

"Yes." Analiese held out her hand. Emma hesitated, then took it in her own and felt the slender fingers flutter against her palm. Analiese Deken was a startlingly beautiful woman. Her features were delicate, and her luminous green eyes were flecked with gold. Her silken hair had once been dark, but now it was the color of smoke; she wore it loose about her shoulders in the manner of a young girl. She pulled it back now and deftly twisted it into a neat knot.

"I wore my hair loose today because that is the way your father liked it," she said softly.

Emma closed her eyes, again seeing Leonie lying lifeless on her bed, her hair so fastidiously twisted into a silken coil and tied with a blue ribbon. She felt a sudden faintness and moved unsteadily toward a stone bench.

"Are you all right?" Analiese Deken sat beside her. She unloosened Emma's cape and pressed a handkerchief moistened with cologne to her forehead.

"Yes. Thank you. It was just a passing weakness. This has been a sad and difficult morning."

"Daniel Salmon told me about your mother. I am very sorry."

"Yes. I am sure you are." Bitterness edged her voice. She gathered her cape closer and moved away from Analiese, who put her hand on her wrist.

"Emma, please. I take the liberty of speaking to you so familiarly because I feel I know you. Your father was very proud of you and shared much of your growing up with me. I want to tell you how it was between your father and me. I want you to understand for both our sakes." Tears glinted in Analiese's eyes, but she sat regally erect. She was not a suppliant. She offered explanations, not apologies. She was a gentlewoman, Daniel Salmon had said. A gentlewoman with a gentle voice.

"What does it matter?" Emma asked wearily.

"It matters. The past matters. If we do not understand the past, we carry shadowed questions into the future. We are shackled by doubts and we cannot move forward."

"Did you love my father?" Emma asked abruptly.

Analiese Deken looked up at the cloudless sky, her eyes following two low-flying gulls as they soared toward their nesting places in the tall river reeds.

"We loved each other. We did not seek that love, but it happened and we did not flee it. We were both so used to loneliness that it startled us, took us by surprise."

Her voice was dreamy as she told Emma that she had been a young widow when she met Jacob Coen.

"Your age, perhaps. Married at eighteen, widowed and alone at twenty-one, without family, with very little money."

Jacob Coen employed her to assist him in the accounts department of the Coen Emporium. She was a diligent worker with a passion for accuracy that matched his own. Often they worked late together, poring over ledgers in the deserted office until they were shrouded in darkness and kindled lamps that bathed them in pools of gentle golden light.

"Your father's hair turned bronze in the lamplight," Analiese said, and Emma thought of how Benjamin Mendoza had lit a small lamp in the dimly lit room of the Imjuden inn and trained it on her, passing its light across her body and lifting her burnished hair so that it slid in sheaves between his fingers. "Like bronze," he had whispered. "Like bronze."

Analiese Deken and Jacob Coen had often shared a simple evening meal in a small restaurant on the Kalverstraat. They spoke softly, leaning toward each other over the candle that flickered on the table. She told him of her solitude, of how the rooms of her small flat echoed in silence and how she had difficulty remembering the face of the young husband who had died so swiftly of pneumonia. And he told her of his own loneliness in the large house that he shared with his wife and children. There was no one with whom he could speak of his thoughts and feelings. Leonie's door was closed to him. She had not shared his bed since Emma's birth, and even during the early years of their marriage she had submitted to him with suffering forbearance. She hated being touched, she told him at last. She did not think this unnatural. Many women disliked physical contact. She spoke with absolute certainty in a hard, cold voice. Women spoke of such things, he knew, and he envied his wife and her friends the luxury of their intimacy. The Jewish burghers of Amsterdam discussed their businesses and the affairs of the synagogue. They worried about the influx of Russian Jews fleeing the Czar's persecutions and raised money to help them migrate to America. They did not speak of their yearnings, their inexplicable sadness at the hour of sunset, the joy that overtook them at the onset of spring.

Jacob Coen did not press his wife. She was a good hostess, a conscientious mother. She smiled graciously at his friends and stood beside him each Sabbath to greet their fellow congregants at the Portuguese Synagogue. He was as fortunate as most men, more fortunate than some. He had his children, his business. Still, his heart clenched when he approached the Prinsengracht mansion, and often during the long silent nights he awakened, his body tense, tears streaking his cheeks. Once he rose and turned the knob of his wife's door.

It was locked, and he stood alone in the shadowed hallway, shivering, although the night was not a cold one.

One night when he and Analiese had worked later than usual and then sat over their meal until the candle flame had burned down to a scorched stump, he walked her back to her flat. A light snow fell, and he brushed the flakes from her dark hair. She took his hand and led him inside.

"I was never lonely again," Analiese said. "Nor was he. We had found each other."

"But surely another arrangement could have been made," Emma said. She felt strangely grateful to Analiese Deken, who had eased her father's loneliness, but she felt anger as well.

"No. There was no other arrangement. You know how the Sephardic community feels about divorce. Your father feared that it would destroy the family. He could not tolerate the thought that your future would be ruined, that no man would marry the daughter of a divorced man who had kept a mistress. And besides, a Jewish divorce, as he explained to me, had to be agreed upon by both husband and wife, and your mother would never have consented."

"I know," Emma said. Leonie could not have conceived of a divorce. The word was anathema to her. A distant cousin in Rotterdam had divorced, and Leonie had struck her from her guest lists, walked past her at a family funeral.

"And so we settled for what we had, which was, after all, a great deal. Your father insisted that we live in Osdorp. I did not need the luxury, did not want it, but I think it soothed him to think that at least I did not suffer any physical deprivation. I know that he thought of our sons, Henry and David, as his own sons. They were circumcised and taken to the ritual bath, and they are Jewish although I am not."

"Henry and David." Emma repeated their names in a dream-bound voice. Her half brothers, her father's sons. She wondered if she would ever meet them, and she remembered the brooding stare of the young man at the funeral whose hair matched her own. "And they too accepted your arrangement?"

"It was easy when they were young. They loved him then, although they could not understand why he was not with us always. I made excuses. He traveled. He had business in distant cities. And then one day the need for explanations was gone. Henry followed your father when he left Osdorp. He followed him to the Emporium and then to the Prinsengracht. That was on a Friday, a night your father always spent at the Prinsengracht house. Henry watched your father go to synagogue with your family. He walked arm in arm with your mother. He held your hand. He sat between your brothers in the very first pew and helped them find the place in the prayerbook. Henry watched them from the doorway. He never spoke to him again.'' Her voice was heavy with sadness. ''I tried to explain our situation to him, but he would not listen. He felt that he had been betrayed, that his childhood had been a lie.''

As mine was, Emma thought. She understood Henry's bitterness. It matched her own.

''Still, he came to the funeral. They both came to the funeral,'' Emma observed.

''Yes. For my sake. They are good sons, wonderful young men. Perhaps they will understand when they grow older,'' Analiese said wistfully. ''We will leave Holland and go to America. We will start a new life, Henry and I. David will complete his medical studies in Vienna, and then he will join us. And you, Emma? What will you do?''

''I will marry Benjamin Mendoza. I offered to release him from our engagement, but he would not hear of it.'' She felt a quiet pride in her fiancé's love, his loyalty.

''He must love you very much.''

''Yes.'' Emma closed her eyes and thought of how he had demonstrated that love in the compact room that overlooked the waters of the North Sea. He had affirmed it with the gentleness of his hands, with the pulsating strength of his desire, with the anguished joy of his voice as he shouted her name in triumph.

''I wish you well in that love, Emma. But you will forgive me if I give you a small warning, if I speak to you from my heart because you are Jacob's daughter and, although we have only just met and will perhaps not meet again, I care for you. Retain control over your own life, your own future. All the decisions of my life have been made by men. Like your father, I submitted to social fear, to the narrow judgments of the burghers of Amsterdam. I am ashamed, not because of the way I lived but because the choice was never wholly mine. You must chart your own future. You must decide where and how you want to live. Marry your Benjamin, but decide on the patterns of your life together. Share the truth, the secrets of the night, the sweet trivia of the day.'' Her voice was intense, and her green eyes were bright with unshed tears. She clutched Emma's hand. Her nails carved small arcs into the soft flesh of the girl's palm, but Emma did not flinch.

''I want that too,'' she said softly. She was suffused with new grief for her mother, whose life had been a kind of death and whose death had been a sad surrender. ''We too have spoken of going to America, Benjamin and I.''

She touched the turquoise pendant at her throat and thought of how the smooth blue stone had been mined in the red earth canyons of a vast desert. She imagined walking with Benjamin Mendoza across shimmering sands, in a wondrous wilderness, far from ancient Amsterdam with its narrow bridges and ancient waterways. She would ask Simon to tell her more about the American West. Arizona. Colorado. California. The Indian names intrigued her, filled her with a mysterious yearning.

''Perhaps we shall meet again, then,'' Analiese said.

Together, the two women rose and walked to Jacob Coen's newly covered grave. They dropped their white flowers onto the soft and fragrant earth, and then they turned and, without looking back, went their separate ways.

Leonie Coen's funeral was sparsely attended and there were seldom more than ten men present at the prayer quorum during the days of mourning. It was as though her death had embarrassed the staid Amsterdam community. Her vulnerability had rendered them all vulnerable. People avoided the Coen home as the healthy sometimes avoid the homes of invalids, fearful of contagion, angered by their own impotence. Simon and Emil were weary yet fired with a strange febrile energy. They paced the room and stroked the unfamiliar stubble of the beards they were obliged to grow during the mourning period with the nervous gestures of young men catapulted into new decisions, new responsibility.

Simon would go to America. He had made tentative plans for a return journey months ago. He had been in correspondence with the younger Guggenheim brothers, who had expressed an interest in his ideas for a smelting operation.

Emil's plans changed from hour to hour. He spoke of Palestine. He had recently read Theodor Herzl's *Judenstaat*, and it was clear that the man made sense. On the other hand, an Australian cousin had invited him to visit and South Africa, too, seemed like an exciting choice. In a single conversation Emil traversed the globe. He acknowledged ruefully to Simon that when he left the Coen Emporium for the last time he felt a sense of relief, of liberation.

Emma sat quietly on the mourning stool. Her calm was much admired, although there were those who spoke slyly of her coldness.

"But then she always held herself somewhat aloof, even when we were at school," Mathilde Orenstein said.

Benjamin Mendoza was solicitous, but on the fourth day of the mourning period he left for Antwerp. He had family business to attend to, he told Emma. He shook hands with Simon and Emil and kissed her on the cheek. She felt oddly cold after he left, and she asked Katrina to bring her blue cashmere shawl although the day was unseasonably warm.

The next day a messenger brought a letter from him. Emma read it, sitting beside the yellow candle that would burn in her mother's memory for thirty days. Across the room her father's flame flickered against a light breeze. She stared at the elaborate script on the cream-colored vellum paper, as though it contained a message in a language she could not comprehend. She read it slowly to herself, her lips moving soundlessly. She read it aloud, her voice deadened so that her brothers strained to hear her.

My dear Emma—I now must do what is right and release you from all the vows which you have made. It is consistent with your gentle and generous nature that you have insisted on remaining loyal to our agreement in view of the tragedies which have befallen you and your family. I will not exploit loyalty. I do not want to intrude upon your private time of grief. I do not want to interfere with the many decisions which you and your brothers must now make. I will not bind you to promises you contracted when your life was on a different course. It would be unfair of me to ask you to share the uncertain life I offer. I shall always treasure the memory of our happy times together, and it is my fervent wish that when the clouds of grief have cleared you will walk again in the sunlight of happiness.

> With affection and esteem,
> Benjamin Mendoza.

"The bastard," Simon said. "The eloquent, word-twisting bastard."

"Emma, do you understand what he is saying?" Emil asked. Emma's stillness, her pallor, frightened him. He wanted her to weep, to scream out her disbelief, her anger.

"Of course I understand. He is saying that I have no dowry and that our family is compromised and that he is therefore canceling our engagement."

Her voice was brittle. The tips of her fingers were numbed and cold. Benjamin had lied and she had believed him. He had held his hands out and she had glided into them. She had slept with him in the large sea-scented bed, seeking love and protection. And he had slept with her because she was unprotected and could place no lien upon his love. "Come," he had said and she had followed him. Like Analiese Deken, like Leonie, her mother, she had lost control of her life. But the harsh lesson had been well learned. She smiled thinly at her brothers.

"It will be all right," she said, and now certainty rimmed her words. It would be all right because she would make it all right. A new resolve throbbed within her, struggling against the melancholy. She went to the window. A light rain had fallen that morning, but now a pale sun bathed the wet streets with a fragile luminescence. The fragment of a rainbow danced across the casement window, and, smiling, she placed her hand against the prismed crescent.

Emil, who watched her, saw that she stood straighter suddenly, and he was not frightened when she took Benjamin Mendoza's letter, read it once more, and then fed it, inch by inch, to the flame of the mourning candle. The thick paper curled about the edges and dwindled into blackened ash. She bent her head, and the candlelight turned her hair the color of burnished bronze.

London,
1898

"ARE YOU almost ready, Emma? We don't want to be late. Adele Rothschild told me that their American guest of honor is a very pedantic gentleman. Aline Spenser heard him shout at his poor wife because she didn't have her cloak on when their coach arrived. I suppose it's because he's so short. Short men do have this unhappy way of asserting themselves."

Greta Anspacher stood in the doorway of her young cousin's bedroom and watched Emma adjust the clasp of her necklace. The turquoise pendant nestled at the cleft of her neck, a blue teardrop suspended against the camellian whiteness of her skin.

"I'm almost ready," Emma said. Unhurriedly, she studied herself in the mirror and twisted a renegade auburn curl into place.

"You look beautiful," Greta said. "Turn around."

Emma had fashioned the blue velvet dress herself, from lengths of fabric purchased in Whitechapel. She had sculpted the material carefully so that it followed the subtle curves of her body and fell from her narrow waist in the graceful folds that the crown princess had made popular that year.

"Who is your clever cousin's dressmaker?" Marguerite Henrigues had asked after a meeting of the Jewish Ladies Benevolent Loan Society at which Emma had presented a report from Abigail Nathan, wearing a tailored dress of forest-green wool.

"That's Emma's secret," Greta had replied. Marguerite, who had in all likelihood never even threaded a needle, would have been shocked to learn that Emma Coen made almost all her own clothes. Greta had offered to

37

take her to her own dressmaker often enough, but Emma had always declined with the polite calm that Greta had learned to admire and respect.

"You've done quite enough for me, Cousin Greta."

She had, in fact, done little enough for her Dutch cousin, Greta thought. She remembered Emma's first tentative letter from Amsterdam, two years earlier, acknowledging Greta's note of condolence on the deaths of her parents. Emma had written that she wanted to leave Amsterdam and come to London. She wondered if perhaps her cousin knew of a position as a governess or a companion in an Anglo Jewish household. "You may know that our family's situation is considerably altered. I should like to do some useful work and be able to support myself. I speak English quite well, and I have been told that I have a pleasant reading voice." The letter was understated and dignified. It was not a plea for help. It was a statement of direction.

Greta had written at once, inviting her cousin to come to London. Her own Hampstead home was large, and Horace Anspacher's business often took him abroad.

"I need a companion," she said when Emma arrived. She was shocked by the girl's pallor, the sadness that dimmed her eyes. "You shall stay with me."

"No, cousin." Emma's protest had been calm and firm. "Please don't take offense, but I want to be independent. I have a small legacy, and I want a position where I will earn a small salary and my board. I don't know if I can explain to you how important it is to me to be self-reliant. I never want to depend on anyone again."

"I think I understand," Greta had said. She knew the circumstances of Emma's parents' deaths, and although her correspondents in Amsterdam had been genteelly vague, she surmised the facts behind Emma's broken engagement. "I shall see what I can do."

When elderly Abigail Nathan, whose only daughter had died in childbirth years ago, sat next to Greta and complained of loneliness at a meeting of the Jewish Society for the Protection of Women and Girls, Greta had told her about Emma.

"You will find her a delightful companion," Greta had said, congratulating herself that her late arrival at the meeting had led her to a seat beside the widow. Abigail Nathan, mild and soft-spoken, was connected by marriage to the Mocattas and the Oppenheimers, but there was no trace of snobbery in her gentle manner.

"She is more than a companion. She is like a friend to me," Mrs. Nathan reported only weeks after Emma had taken up residence in her Kensington Gardens home. The girl's quiet manner, her cultivated intellect, and her consistent thoughtfulness intrigued the elderly woman, who had lived alone for so many years. It soon became clear that any invitation extended to Abigail Nathan included Emma Coen. Emma was a guest at the great houses of London's Jewish aristocracy. She went to dinner with the Goldschmidts and the Montefiores, and she spent weekends at the Montefiore home at Ramsgate and the Rothschild estates in the lush Vale of Aylesbury. But she did not forget her obligations. She supervised Abigail Nathan's household, checking the housekeeper's accounts and the linens, interviewing servants and answering the mail. Eventually Abigail Nathan asked her solicitor to discuss her affairs with Emma.

"I don't understand all this talk of pounds and shillings," the old woman said plaintively. "My friend Miss Coen has a talent for it, and she explains it to me quite clearly."

The solicitor agreed with Mrs. Nathan. Emma Coen did have a talent for finances, and she had invested the small sums of money available to her with considerable shrewdness. She bought stocks in a small Surrey knitting mill when she read an article in the London *Times* which reported the mill's acquisition of new machinery that would increase its productivity. She asked the solicitor to forward twenty pounds sterling to her brother Simon in America, for investment in a mining company in a western territory.

"Arizona?" The solicitor frowned at the strangeness

of the name, at the distance of the investment, but Emma
nodded calmly.

"Arizona." The word soothed her, caused her to smile
with a sweet and secret pleasure she had not thought to
feel again.

The two months in Abigail Nathan's home passed
pleasantly for Emma. Like a recuperating invalid, she
marked her progress. She no longer wakened in the night,
her face tear-streaked, her body aching with a mysterious
longing. She was able to describe her Prinsengracht home
to Abigail Nathan without dwelling on her last sad days
there when she and her brothers had watched the furnishings carried away or marked by the auctioneer's un-
derlings. The gray-smocked men had moved through the
house in sullen silence, averting their eyes when Jacob
Coen's children appeared. Emma had watched them carry
her father's inlaid rosewood desk out, and she had stood
in the doorway of her mother's room as two overdressed
women from the new garden suburb of Slatervaart discussed the lack of drawer space in Leonie's mahogany
dressing table.

Walking through Amsterdam, during her last days in
the city of her birth, Greta's letter of invitation to London
in her purse, she saw the gold damask chairs and sofa
displayed in the window of a furniture shop. She wept
then and wept again when she returned to the almost
barren house and her brothers presented her with Leonie's Sabbath candlesticks. Katrina had polished them to
a high gleam, and Emma traced the small Jewish stars
entwined with delicate leaves that had been etched into
the soft metal.

"We bought them from the estate," Simon said. "We
shall all gather at your Sabbath table one day, Emma,
and watch you say the blessing over them."

When? she thought bitterly. *Where?* Simon was leaving for America and Emil for Palestine. In a week's time
she herself would be in London. Still, she kissed her
brothers—tall, handsome Emil, whose bright hair
matched her own, and gentle, scholarly Simon, who
stared worriedly at her from behind his thick glasses. She

wrapped the candlesticks carefully in her blue shawl and placed a sliver of sea glass beside them. The polished green, the color of the canal water, was reflected in their silver shimmer.

She showed the candlesticks to Abigail Nathan, who loved beautifully crafted objects.

"And this is all you brought with you?" the English-woman asked sadly.

"Yes." Emma's voice was strangely calm and unre-gretting. She had shed the restraining wrappings of her Amsterdam life and emerged from the fragile and imper-manent cocoon of her girlhood. A new life stretched be-fore her. Its possibilities intrigued her. Her brother Emil, traveling eastward to Palestine, wrote her regularly, and at night she dreamed of the cities of his sojourns—Venice and Bari, Piraeus and Larnaca. But Simon's letters from America sent her to the reading room of the British Mu-seum. She studied pictures of Indians and whispered their tribal names aloud—Pima, Navajo, Apache. She read of vast deserts and mysterious mountains. Her fingers danced across brightly colored maps. They traced their way north and south, east and west. Soon, very soon, she would be ready to choose a direction. The moment would come and she would recognize it.

In the interim she read to Abigail Nathan and accom-panied her to meetings and dinner parties. She dutifully took notes at meetings of the Jewish Board of Guardians and the Charity Organization Society. Because Greta An-spacher and Abigail Nathan insisted, she went to dan-sants at Highfields, the Cohen estate at Shoreham, and at Mentmore, the Rothschild mansion. She received flat-tering letters of invitation from young David Cohen, to which she replied with a polite note of refusal. He smoothed his narrow mustache with his finger as Benja-min Mendoza had and stared at her too intently.

"I am not yet sure of what I want to do," she wrote to Simon. "I have the oddest feeling—it is as though I am waiting for something to happen."

She did know that she did not want to remain in En-gland. The stratified life of London Jewish society oppressed her, and she experienced again the claustrophobia she had felt in Amsterdam. She drove with Abigail Nathan through the streets of the East End, crowded with pushcarts laden with lengths of fabric, shoes knotted together with lengths of soiled rope, vegetables piled high in dangerous, colorful pyramids. Shawled women argued fiercely over the price of a green pepper, held pale tomatoes up to search for imperfections, studied carrots and onions as though they were selecting jewels. Small children trailed after them, holding the market baskets, their eyes rheumy, their skin blanched with the pallor of poverty. Sad-eyed men, bent beneath burdens of linen scraps, trays of merchandise strapped to their shoulders, disappeared into narrow-windowed buildings. Abigail Nathan covered her nose with a handkerchief soaked in cologne, but Emma watched carefully and wrote the reports that Abigail submitted at her meetings.

There had to be a better way to resettle the refugees from eastern Europe, Emma thought. The exodus from Russia was intensifying, and now the Rumanian Jews were fleeing to London. Surely there were places in the world which allowed children to breathe pure air, men and women to walk on soft earth and feel the ease of space and sky.

"The desert is vast and wondrous," Simon wrote from the American West. Emma thought of his words when Abigail Nathan's coach was halted at a Whitechapel corner by a grim parade as a family moved their possessions from one tenement to another. Two small boys struggled with a mattress, and their sister pushed a battered pram laden with pots and pans.

She was bored by the dinner parties and the country weekends. The guest lists were predictable, and she could anticipate when the conversations would drift from a languid discussion of John Galsworthy's newest novels to the parties still being given to celebrate Queen Victoria's Diamond Jubilee. Alone, she reread her leatherbound copy of Walt Whitman's poems, the only gift from Benjamin Mendoza that she had not returned. She watched her small investments carefully, taking an odd pleasure at their steady growth. Analiese Deken would be proud of her, she thought. She had taken control of her life. When Abigail Nathan died in her sleep two years after Emma's arrival at her Kensington home, Emma had a modest savings account In addition to the small legacy that the widow left her.

"What will you do now?" Greta had asked Emma, who was once again staying with her in Hampstead. The ideal solution, of course, would be for Emma to marry, but while her young Dutch cousin was willing to attend the requisite dinner parties and dansants, she always remained disconcertingly aloof. "The ice maiden," the young English Jews called her. Emma's hands were cold to their touch, and when they danced with her, her body was stiff and unyielding, her replies to their careless banter cautious and curt.

"I blame it all on that Benjamin Mendoza," Greta had confided to her husband. "He behaved disgracefully."

"You have no idea at all how he behaved," Horace Anspacher replied patiently. "I can't see that he had much choice. A man without an income, without prospects, must marry a woman with a dowry." Portly Horace Anspacher viewed the world with the balanced logic of a businessman. Specific economic situations demanded specific personal solutions. Besides, Greta was foolish to worry about Emma Coen; the girl knew how to take care of herself. He looked up now as Greta and Emma descended the stairwell.

"I'm lucky to be escorting two such beautiful women," he said.

Greta, in a silver gown that matched her hair, and Emma, regal in the peacock-blue velvet gown that accentuated the porcelain whiteness of her neck and shoulders, smiled at him appreciatively.

"I'm only sorry the evening won't be more interesting for you," he said as he helped Emma into her fur-collared cape. It was growing shabby, he noticed, and he wondered whether Greta could persuade Emma to allow them to buy her a new cloak. All that independence was admirable, but there was no harm in accepting a gift from a relation now and again. He should like to see Emma in one of those new taffeta coats that the Duchess Alexandra had made popular that season. Jade green would be just the color to offset her fiery hair.

"Why won't it be interesting?" Greta asked.

"No young folk for our Emma, my dear. All older pillars of the Jewish community, like you and me, gathering over champagne and caviar to solve the problems of overcrowding and nutrition in our East End and New York's Lower East Side. We'll eat roast goose and discuss raising funds for a new kosher soup kitchen."

"Please, Horace. We won't need your cynicism tonight. Adele's invited Israel Zangwill, and he, after all, is a professional cynic," Greta said. She adjusted the beaver stole of her wrap and smiled at herself in the vestibule mirror. Emma, she noticed, did not give the mirror a glance, and briefly she envied her cousin's youthful confidence in her beauty. Or perhaps she was simply indifferent, Greta thought, but then women who were unconcerned about their appearance did not fashion evening dresses that gently hugged their bosoms and accentuated their narrow waists.

They were the last guests to arrive at the Rothschilds' Piccadilly mansion. The double doors that led to the dining room had already opened, and men in evening dress escorted women in brilliantly colored gowns to their seats. The table, which stretched the length of the room, was covered with the intricately tatted white lace cloth that had been Adele's gift from the household staff of her Belgian relations. Red and white wines sparkled in delicate crystal goblets, and the gold-trimmed Spode china place settings were flanked by the heavy, highly polished Rothschild silverware embossed with the family crest. The centerpiece was a delicate arrangement of baby orchids and white tulips.

"What beautiful flowers," Greta exclaimed.

"Beautiful," Emma agreed, her voice barely audible. A tightness constricted her heart, and her eyes burned. She had planted white tulip bulbs about her parents' graves before leaving Amsterdam, but who would weed them, she wondered, or clip the full-blown blossoms in the waning days of springtime?

"Emma, I've seated you on Mr. Schiff's left," Adele Rothschild whispered. "Please do your best to charm him."

Emma nodded. She wondered, with a brief but startlingly sharp bitterness, whether Evalina Goldschmidt or Helena Spenser would be instructed to charm the cantankerous American guest, or was that responsibility always delegated to the poor relation? Still, she smiled dutifully and took her place behind her assigned chair as Edmond Rothschild intoned the familiar benediction.

"Blessed art Thou, O Lord our God, Who brings forth bread from the earth."

The response was automatic, emitted with embarrassment and relief, but Emma noticed that Jacob Schiff salted a piece of bread and ate it before speaking. He was a truly religious man, then, this diminutive American with his piercing blue eyes and neatly trimmed snowy-white goatee and mustache. A large gold watch on a thick chain rested on his protruding abdomen, and he glanced at it often, as though assessing the value of each passing minute. His pudgy hands were very small, Emma observed, and his fingernails were meticulously rounded and brushed with a pale lacquer. His wife, a sallow, dark-haired woman, seemed to quiver when he spoke, and she waited until he had tasted his wine before lifting her own glass.

Jacob Schiff spoke too loudly, as short men often do. He emoted rather than conversed, as though uncertain that his stentorian tones would travel the length of the table. His crossing had been a difficult one, he proclaimed. The Atlantic appeared to grow rougher each year; still, he had to make the crossing annually. He was obliged to visit his parents' graves in Germany and to spend time with his brother Hermann and his family in England. He spoke of his brother in the third person, although Hermann Schiff, a prominent banker, sat at the other end of the table and did not raise his eyes when his name was mentioned.

"If you found the crossing difficult in a first-class Cunard cabin, imagine what it must be like for those poor Russian devils who are crammed into steerage," Israel Zangwill observed drily.

The novelist, who was seated on Emma's right, wore a wide, brightly flowered silk cravat, but his dinner jacket was frayed at the cuffs and the buttons dangled with dangerous looseness. His curling hair fell to his shoulders and formed dark ringlets across his high forehead and about his protuberant ears. He adjusted his monocle as he spoke and nervously stroked his aquiline nose. He wore the troubled expression of a man whose thoughts and words gave him little peace.

During her duty tours of the East End, Emma had occasionally seen the novelist walk through the crowded streets, stopping to talk to the vendors who shoved their rickety pushcarts through the narrow thoroughfares, always making notes in his small memorandum book. Small boys, shuffling in oversized shoes, their caps pulled over their eyes, hurried after him, imitating his strutting walk and gesturing with imaginary canes like the one he carried, but he paid no attention to them. When he met Emma, he paused to doff his fedora, and she felt his eyes riveted on her as though he were memorizing her expression, committing her voice to memory. It occurred to her that such concentration enabled him to describe his characters with the piercing accuracy for which he was famous. Zangwill's *Children of the Ghetto* had been the last book that Emma had read aloud to poor Abigail Nathan, and they had both smiled at his penetrating descriptions, his wry insights.

"Apparently, they do not find the voyage in steerage too difficult to discourage them," Jacob Schiff replied. "They arrive in New York in greater numbers each year."

"Fifth Avenue will soon be a *Judengasse* if something is not done," his wife said.

"Poor devils—what choice do they have?" Ernest Cassel asked, plunging his fork fiercely into a thick slab of roast beef and then thrusting it back, uneaten, onto his plate. Cassel, who had made a fortune in railway development, was rumored to be in line for a knighthood, but he had never forgotten that he himself had come to London as an immigrant from Cologne, and his close friendship with the Baron de Hirsch had involved him in concern for the refugees from eastern Europe.

His young associate, Philip Sasson, a slender, gray-eyed man who sat at his left, worked with him on projects to benefit the refugees. It was aristocratic Philip Sasson who often arrived at a social service agency with a much-needed bank draft, a block of steamship tickets. He had beautiful hands, Emma noticed, and she wondered idly if he was married.

A melancholy silence settled over the table. It was almost two decades now since Alexander III had become "the czar of all the Russias" and unleashed pogroms and anti-Jewish ordinances that had sent the Jews of that vast land fleeing across the borders. Hordes of them arrived in London each month, impoverished and untrained. The bewildered men and women spoke too loudly and flailed their hands wildly for emphasis, as though fearful that they would not be understood if they relied on Yiddish and the fragments of English they had scavenged. The English Jews were at once embarrassed and compassionate, as the Dutch Jews had been, Emma recalled.

Leonie Coen had been impatient with them. Their dark, shabby garments, their strange guttural dialect, repelled her. But Jacob Coen had been sympathetic.

"They are, after all, our people," he had said. "Ashkenazim, Sephardim, speakers of Yiddish or speakers of Ladino—what does it matter? To the anti-Semite we are all Jews—foreigners intruding on an established culture."

Israel Zangwill looked now across the table at Ernest Cassel.

"I agree that there are few alternatives. It would be a historic irony if the chosen people had no choices at all," he said.

"Is your Lower East Side as crowded as our East End, Mrs. Schiff?" Pauline Montague asked. She was working on a proposal to the Jewish Board of Guardians that money be advanced to East End Jews who wished to emigrate to Canada.

"It is very crowded," Theresa Schiff said, and Emma strained to hear her soft voice above the clatter of the silver and the chime of glasses being refilled. Why was she so timid, so fearful? Emma wondered. Theresa Schiff was, after all, an heiress in her own right. She would inherit a fortune from her father, Solomon Loeb, a partner in the New York brokerage house of Kuhn, Loeb. But of course Theresa Schiff had as little understanding of her own money as Leonie Coen had had, and her ignorance made her as dependent on her autocratic husband as the poorest serving girl was on an indifferent master.

"But we have made great efforts," Theresa went on. "Jacob is perhaps too modest to tell you how he and his friends have worked among the Jewish immigrants in New York. They have established programs and settlement houses. We sponsor soup kitchens and even summer camps for the children. And of course there is our Hebrew Emigrant Aid Society. But some of them are so difficult—so demanding." Her voice trailed off. She toyed with her long strand of perfectly matched pearls and glanced nervously at her husband. Emma watched her with a mixture of pity and contempt.

Jacob Schiff cleared his throat and smiled approvingly. He was not averse to having his philanthropies discussed.

"Of course, we have tried," he said. "But the problem appears to be insurmountable. Frankly, we worry about anti-Semitism in New York if the Jewish immigration continues and we see no signs that it will abate. You speak of alternatives, Mr. Zangwill. Are you thinking of Palestine, perhaps?" He speared a stalk of asparagus and wondered if the Rothschilds had had the vegetable imported from Belgium. They were careless with their money, allowing their sons carriages, their daughters private maids. His own children had been taught thrift and the virtue of economy.

"I don't think Palestine is the answer," Israel Zangwill replied. He waited for the servants to clear the table and leave the room. "Of course, Herzl is a charismatic figure," he continued, "and there is validity to his concept of a Jewish state. But I visited Palestine myself last year. It is a harsh land, all desert and swamp. We would be sending the Jews from eastern Europe into another disastrous and dangerous situation."

"My brother Emil also visited Palestine, and he found it a fascinating country," Emma said. Emil's letters had been effusive. He had visited the few small Jewish settlements and written exuberantly of the charm of Rishon le-Zion and Petach Tikvah. "Unfortunately he contracted malaria and had to leave," she added. Emil was in America now, traveling swiftly westward, still pursuing the adventures he had dreamed of as he sat on his high stool in the Coen Emporium on the Kalverstraat. Handsome, dashing Emil. A wave of loneliness swept over her. She wanted to see her brothers, to hear Emil's vibrant laughter and listen to Simon's calm and thoughtful observations.

"Oh, it is a fascinating country," Israel Zangwill agreed. "I do not dispute your brother. But I do not think it will solve what my colleague Leon Pinsker has euphemistically called our 'Jewish problem.' And I do think there is such a solution to the problem."

"You are more optimistic than I am," Edmond Rothschild said. "What is your solution, Zangwill?"

"Territorialism." The novelist emphasized each syllable. "Jewish territorialism."

"And what do you mean by Jewish territorialism?" Jacob Schiff asked guardedly.

"We find a particular territory—one that is largely unsettled—and we divert the refugees from eastern Europe to that location. They will settle in large enough numbers so that the territory will become predominantly Jewish. Palestine might be one such territory, but Jewish territorialism would not be limited to Palestine. There are other possibilities throughout the world. Uganda, for instance." Israel Zangwill spoke with tutorial slowness. He was the teacher introducing an unfamiliar concept to a class of reluctant students. Patiently, he waited for questions before proceeding.

"But hasn't Mr. Herzl already broached that concept to the Jewish leadership? I believe he spoke of a Jewish settlement in El Arish in the Sinai," Ernest Cassel said.

"Herzl selected El Arish because it was close to Palestine. It is unfeasible, of course, because of the lack of water. I am suggesting that we look for territories, independent of their location vis-à-vis Palestine where natural resources will not be a problem. A sparsely inhabited African country such as Uganda might be a possibility. South America is a vast continent and Baron de Hirsch is actively involved in settling Jewish immigrants there. And of course, Mr. Schiff, there is your wonderfully wild American West." Zangwill tapped his wineglass with a teaspoon, and Emma held her breath, but the delicate crystal did not shatter. A good omen, she thought, and smiled at him. She felt sorry for him because his cuffs were frayed and his dark eyes blazed with passion. It was dangerous to feel so deeply for either a person or a cause, she knew. Passion disarmed, suspended judgment, made one cruelly vulnerable. *As she had been at the Imjuden inn.* She shut her mind against the memory, aware that Jacob Schiff was speaking to her, asking her a question.

"And what are your feelings on this weighty subject, my dear Miss Coen? Does the American West intrigue you? I ask because I recognize that the stone of your pendant must surely be turquoise and the setting appears to have been crafted by American Indians. My daughter, Frieda, has a small collection of Navajo jewelry."

The other women at the table leaned forward to study Emma's pendant. They wore necklaces of emeralds, glittering diamond chokers, strands of perfectly matched pearls. Adele Rothschild touched the huge sapphire that dangled from her heavy gold chain. Still, they recognized the simple beauty of Emma Coen's necklace, and they understood why Jacob Schiff had noticed it.

"I am interested in the American West," Emma said. "Both my brothers are there, and of course I long to see them. I think Mr. Zangwill's idea for settling Jews there is excellent for a reason which he has not mentioned."

"Indeed? Please fill in the omission, dear lady. I am

always ready to take instruction, especially from such a beautiful tutor,'' Israel Zangwill said. Irritation rimmed his voice, but the women at the table smiled and clapped softly at his words. Emma's cheeks grew hot, but she turned back to Jacob Schiff.

"I think that if Jews were to go to the American West, they would be transformed from refugees into pioneers. I do not think that has happened before in our long history of wandering from one country to another.'' She thought of the family she had seen in Whitechapel, transferring their possessions from one urban hovel to another, and imagined them traveling across a vast desert, fired by a sense of purpose rather than a desperate desire for refuge.

"That is a very interesting point,'' Jacob Schiff said thoughtfully. "Certainly it would banish the stereotype of the ghetto Jew. Where there are no established cities, there can be no ghettos.'' He laughed harshly. "And of course, there are Jews now living in the American West. I have a client, Morris Lasker, who lives in Galveston, Texas, a city on the gulf. He tells me that there is a thriving Jewish community there. Indeed, most of the merchants are Jewish, and there is even a rabbi in the town.''

"There is a railroad there,'' Philip Sasson said thoughtfully. He furrowed his brow. "The Galveston, Harrisburg, San Antonio Railway,'' he recalled triumphantly.

"I have thought of Galveston myself,'' Israel Zangwill said. "The North German Lloyd Line docks there. With its railroad and established Jewish community, it would be an ideal launching place for Jewish territorialism.''

"I say that we must explore this idea further,'' Jacob Schiff said vehemently.

"But of course such a project would take years to develop,'' Edmond Rothschild observed. He had caught Adele's desperate glance. His wife did not want her dinner party to become a boring seminar on the Jewish problem.

Hermann Schiff cleared his throat and spoke for the first time.

"When my brother Jacob seizes on an idea, he manages to work miracles with time. Such a project might take another man a full decade to organize, but I will wager anyone here that my brother will have the wheels turning in half that time."

"I wonder if the citizens of Galveston realize that the future of their city has been altered right here in Piccadilly Square," Helena Spenser said sarcastically.

"I think you are optimistic, sir," Horace Anspacher said to Hermann Schiff. "Your brother cannot work miracles. An organization must be developed. The immigrants themselves must be recruited. Temporary lodging houses would have to be established in Galveston and arrangements made for interim employment."

"Details," Jacob Schiff said. "We shall work out the details. We shall discuss it further, Zangwill."

"It will have to be heavily financed," the novelist said gloomily. He was a prophet with a peculiar aversion to having his prophecy too speedily fulfilled.

"I will advance ten thousand pounds sterling myself if we can discuss something else," Edmond Rothschild said. The dessert had been wheeled in. A huge silver chafing dish was laden with delicate raspberries, over which the footman gravely poured an entire bottle of Courvoisier. A match was held to it, and it burst into flame. The guests clapped—all except Jacob Schiff, who had taken out a small pocket notebook and was now occupied with making an entry.

"You did say ten thousand?" he asked, and Edmond Rothschild nodded.

"Very well, then. Now I shall keep my part of the bargain and change the subject. Theresa and I went to the theater last night. We found your Mr. Bernard Shaw's *Caesar and Cleopatra* quite tedious. Did you enjoy it, Miss Coen?"

Emma smiled. "Very much, Mr. Schiff," she said, and watched his wife lean forward in surprise. No one was supposed to enjoy a play that Jacob Schiff had found

tedious. Across the table Adele Rothschild smiled at her
and lifted her small silver bell. It was time for the women
to adjourn to the dining room and speak of fashion and
the vagaries of the royal family while the men sat over
their cigars and brandy and discussed Kitchener's battle
at the Atbara River and the unfortunate American war
with Spain.

In the Anspacher library that night, Emma took Horace's large atlas down from the shelf and turned to a map
of the western territories of the United States. She found
Texas at once, and after some difficulty she located Galveston. It appeared to be the tiniest of islands, shaped
like a dancing slipper afloat in the Gulf of Mexico. It was
colored turquoise blue on the map to contrast with the
azure used for the gulf waters, and the cartographer's
choice of color pleased her. She saw how it was possible
to sail from the island to the port of New Orleans and
further east to Florida and Cuba. She could travel westward across New Mexico into the Arizona territory. Galveston was a gateway to adventure. She closed her eyes
and imagined great sloops sailing into port, gulls swoop-
ing low across a pale beach, a steamship's shrill whistle
piercing the night silence.

A sudden inexplicable gaiety caused her to laugh aloud.
Horace had said that lodging houses would have to be
established. Her bank account would cover the purchase
of such a house, and her experience with Abigail Nathan
had taught her how to supply a larder, inventory linens,
manage a domestic staff. Of course, of course. It was all
coming together as she had known it would. Excitedly,
she sat down at Horace's desk and began to compile a
list. Her fingers fondled the pendant at her throat, and
her breath came with short happy gasps. She was on her
way, she knew. At last, she was on her way.

Galveston, 1900

SUNLIGHT dappled the clear blue waters of the Gulf of Mexico and trimmed the foaming crests of the gentle inland waves with liquid hems of gold. A flock of snowy egrets lazily circled the harbor, and two pelicans perched on a reef and studied the long queue of immigrants, now and again spreading their wings and circling each other. The weary travelers barely looked up. They clutched the worn envelopes that contained their documents and nervously plucked an occasional frayed sheet of paper and stared at it worriedly. Women whispered admonishments to their restless children, bent to tie a loosened shoelace, adjust a small girl's ribbon. Men counted and recounted their money, thrusting the worn wallets and change purses deep into the recesses of their garments. Two bearded men swayed from side to side as though lost in prayer, and an Italian woman shifted her infant child from one arm to the other and inexplicably began to weep. But Isaac Lewin lifted his face to the soft gulf wind and smiled.

"It's hot," he said in Yiddish to the young couple who stood ahead of him. It had been snowing in Hamburg on the day the *S.S. Kassel* sailed, and he had spent much of the long voyage huddled in his greatcoat. Now he thrust the coat into his canvas bag and loosened his collar button. After four weeks at sea, it was strange to feel solid ground beneath his feet and stranger still to feel himself plunged into the sudden chimerical warmth of early spring.

"Very hot," the young man acknowledged unhappily.

His thin, fair-haired wife nervously twisted her handkerchief. She had been ill during the voyage, and she

57

coughed now; her thin shoulders heaved and tears filled her pale, frightened eyes.

"Next." The uniformed immigration officer motioned them forward, and Isaac stared sadly after them as he waited his turn.

"All right." The officer pointed to him, and Isaac stepped into a large room that had been divided into small cell-like cubicles. An American flag stood in one corner, and a framed picture of President McKinley hung crookedly on the peeling yellow wall. The bespectacled official who sat behind a large oak table did not look up but continued to fill out a form, his pen scratching importantly and his wide brow furrowed, as though the task at hand required deep concentration. Isaac set his bag down and removed the pack he carried on his back, conscious of a new and unfamiliar fatigue. The man looked up, boredom wreathing his features.

"Please sit down," he said and motioned to the hard-backed armless chair that faced him.

"Yiddish-speaking?" He did not look up as he asked the question but blotted the completed form and reached for a blank questionnaire. He dipped his pen into the tall inkwell and frowned as a droplet of blue dotted the golden surface of the table.

Isaac nodded. "Also English," he added, but the official shook his head wearily and dabbed at the ink spot.

"Call Rabbi Cohen," he shouted.

The uniformed guard hurried out, and minutes later a short, bow-legged man entered, wearing a dark suit worn to a sheen at the elbows and the knees.

"Ah, Mr. Buchanan," he said. "You have another Jew for me—just as I was about to cycle home for my lunch."

"It's time for my lunch as well," the immigration official replied. He pulled out his pocket watch and glanced at it. "Past my lunchtime," he added bitterly. "But Graves didn't show today, and I'm dealing with everything myself."

"It's always that way," the rabbi said sympathetically. He extended his hand to Isaac and winked at him. "I'm Rabbi Henry Cohen. We'll have to help Mr. Buchanan by answering his questions quickly and letting him get on with his lunch.''

The questions were perfunctory, and although Isaac understood them, he allowed the rabbi to translate them into Yiddish and offered his answers in the same language. He gave his name, his date of birth, and his country of origin and saw Buchanan glance at the ship's manifest, which all the passengers had filled out and signed before embarkation. It was, he supposed, a precaution against stowaways and illegal immigrants.

"Profession?"

"Shipping clerk," Isaac said in Yiddish, without hesitation. The United Hebrew Charities social worker who had interviewed him in Hamburg had advised him not to say that he was a teacher. "There is no great need for instructors in Jewish philosophy in the American West," the man had said wryly, and Isaac had offered no argument. He had decided that night in Kiev, as he stood amid the debris of the vandalized cottage that had been his home, that he was done with philosophy. He would no longer ponder the mysteries of good and evil, of God's intent and life's meaning. Such questions did not concern a man who had touched the crumbling white spongy mass that had been his small daughter's brain and felt his wife's blood, thick and heavy upon his hands, when he moved her lifeless body.

"The man is a stevedore," Rabbi Cohen said. He winked again at Isaac, but warningly this time.

The immigration officer looked up. The Jew was tall enough. He was broad-shouldered, and there was color in his face. Not like most of the Jewish immigrants, pale and skinny, their teeth rotting and their breath coming in gasps when they lifted their valises. This man could heave a bale, lug a crate, although he did not have the look of a dockworker.

"Why did you decide to enter via Galveston?" It was a new question, sent down from Washington only a week ago and designed to trick those who had been solicited in Europe to sail to Galveston rather than to New York. No one wanted the immigrants coming in with false hopes and unredeemable promises to end up living on public charity. A sure way to stop that kind of activity was to ship a couple of Jews back to Europe.

Isaac answered in Yiddish, explaining that the fare to Galveston had been cheaper than passage to New York, but once again Rabbi Cohen offered his own answer.

"He thought there would be more opportunities for employment here. He wants to work on the docks."

"Let's see his hands."

Isaac held out his hands, and Buchanan studied them, taking note of the callused fingers, the work-leathered palms.

"Looks like he knows what a day's work is," he said grudgingly.

Isaac shrugged. The calluses had been formed as he dug the graves for the Jews of Kiev, for Rivka and Sarah, his wife and daughter. Day after day, he and the other young Jews of Kiev had bent over their spades in the cemetery, and when the last victim of the pogrom had been buried, they had slowly rebuilt the houses that had been burned and gutted. The door of the synagogue had been shattered by steel-bladed axes and booted feet. Isaac had undertaken its repair, felling the timber and planing it down, hoisting the sanded panels into place. He painted the completed door on a day so cold that he had to stir the paint in his pail to keep it from freezing. His hands were hardened then, and as he worked his way eastward to Hamburg, finding a day's labor on a farm or with a logging team, his muscles hardened and his skin was burnished by sun and wind.

"You feel you're strong enough to work on the docks?" Buchanan's own hands were soft, and he held them palms down on his desk.

"Can't you see?" Rabbi Cohen answered for Isaac. "That's the doctor's job."

The examination in an adjoining room was swift. The doctor, a wizened, gray-haired man, wore a soiled and rumpled white jacket. His breath was tinged with alcohol as he bent to listen to Isaac's heartbeat with his stethoscope and asked him to inhale, exhale. Once. Twice. He stared into Isaac's eyes and deftly pulled at his eyelash and forced the lid back for a close examination. He was searching for trachoma, Isaac knew. The hostels in Hamburg were crowded with immigrants who had been turned back because they had the dreaded eye disease. He opened Isaac's mouth and studied his teeth. Isaac willed himself to immobility. He remembered the cattle fair he and Rivka had visited. Farmers had studied horses in just such a manner, pulling at an animal's jaw, bending to touch a flank, to feel the beat of a heart. And, he realized, only four decades past, Negroes had been examined in a similar manner on the Galveston pier when they were offered up for auction. His own humiliation, he acknowledged, was brief and necessary, in comparison.

"All right," the doctor said grudgingly. He signed the form.

Isaac buttoned his shirt and returned to Buchanan's table.

"You have sufficient funds to support yourself in the United States?" he asked.

"Of course." The rabbi did not even wait for Isaac to answer. This was the tricky question. It was not clear how much money was considered sufficient. Men with fifty dollars in their wallets had been turned back, and other immigrants, without a cent, had brazened their way through and gained entry. A bell tolled the half hour. "Twelve-fifteen, Mr. Buchanan. I hope our lunches don't get cold."

"I hope so too, Rabbi." He lifted a rubber stamp, slapped it across his magenta-inked pad and then onto Isaac's papers. "Welcome to the United States of America, Mr. Lewin."

"Thank you," Isaac said. He spoke in English, and Buchanan looked up and grinned reluctantly.

Isaac followed the rabbi through the chain-link fence. They passed an enclosed cubicle sealed by a wire-mesh barrier. The young couple who had stood in front of Isaac on the immigration line sat within it, huddled together on a wooden bench. The woman sobbed, her head pressed against her husband's chest. Mechanically, he stroked her hair, but he stared straight ahead, his eyes dull, his sagging shoulders weighted by defeat and despair. A chalk mark wept its way down the back of the woman's worn, dark coat. *TB* was scrawled onto the fabric.

"I couldn't help them," Rabbi Cohen said. "She had tuberculosis. Even that drunken Doc Gladstone picked it up. The Jewish welfare workers in Hamburg should have stopped the poor devils there and sent them first to Switzerland for a cure and then to the States."

Isaac did not answer. The woman's muffled sobs trailed after them as they left the building and stepped onto the granite jetty.

"May I invite you home for lunch?" the rabbi asked. "My wife's a good cook. I guarantee you that."

"No, thank you, Rabbi. I want to use what's left of today to find a job."

"What? Today?" Henry Cohen looked at him in astonishment.

"Now. Today."

The rabbi glanced at him shrewdly. "What's the real answer to Mr. Buchanan's last question?"

"I have two dollars," Isaac said. "And my gold watch."

The rabbi laughed. It occurred to him that chutzpah and courage were an attractive combination. Certainly it required both for a man to cross an ocean with two dollars in his pocket.

"Well, you're lucky that Buchanan was hungry," he said. "Here, Lewin. Here's ten dollars. It's from a fund that the United Hebrew Charities set up. When you're on your feet, you can repay it. And here's a map of the city. My wife drew it herself. It's not hard to follow." He held out a sheet of paper with each street and crossing carefully etched in pale blue ink. Isaac saw that the streets followed numerical and alphabetical sequence.

"See—you just have to know the alphabet. They wanted to make it easy for you greenies," the rabbi said in his Cockney accent, and Isaac smiled. "Now, here's my house—it's starred. Right on Broadway. You're welcome to spend the Sabbath with us—stay the night.''

Isaac shook his head.

''Is there a boarding house in the town—one where Jews are welcome?'' He was tired of transience and charity, no matter how kindly offered. It had been months since he had departed from Kiev, and he had slept in too many strange beds and eaten too many meals for which he had not paid.

''Well, there's Miss Coen's place. Emma Coen. Show this to her. She had a boarder who left for Milwaukee yesterday. Maybe his room is still empty.'' He scrawled an address on his card and added a note.

Isaac accepted the card and placed it carefully in his pocket with the map and the ten-dollar bill.

''Thank you,'' he said gravely and shook the rabbi's hand. ''I will repay you.''

''I'm sure you will, Mr. Lewin.'' The rabbi looked at him thoughtfully. The tall Russian Jew had an independence and determination that contrasted sharply with the shadowed sadness of his agate eyes. Clearly, he was the sort of Jew that Jacob Schiff envisaged for this western project he and Zangwill had devised. ''Jews who break the ghetto mold,'' he had said in a letter to Henry Cohen, outlining his plan for making Galveston a key port of entry for Jewish immigrants. And of course, it helped that Lewin spoke English, although it hadn't been necessary to let Buchanan know that until the papers were officially stamped. Petty bureaucrats like Buchanan needed their sense of superiority. They felt threatened by a man whose education matched or was even superior to their own. Not much different from the lower-level British civil servants Henry Cohen had confronted in his native England and then in South Africa and in Kingston, Jamaica. And Isaac Lewin had understood that at once. He was shrewd as well as educated—a man who knew where he was going and would waste no time getting there. The rabbi watched as the tall Russian walked up the Strand and paused before the iron-fronted building that housed the Port Isabel Freight Forwarding Company.

Isaac Lewin did not find employment at the Port Isabel Freight Forwarding Company. At his next stop the clerk barely looked up as he told him that there were no positions open. Still, he continued on, his pack heavy on his back, his canvas bag pulling at his arm. At his fourth stop, a sympathetic employee told him the clerk at the New Orleans Exchange had been dismissed that morning.

"He was up to no good. Took a couple of dollars for giving preference to one cargo over another," his informant said. "Bosses catch on to that quick, particularly in citrus season. A shipment can go bad sitting too long on a dock or in a warehouse. They'll be looking for another clerk to start on Monday."

"I'll start today if they want," Isaac said.

Four hours after he had passed through immigration, he had a job. He sighed with relief, acutely aware of his own exhaustion and the approaching Sabbath. He looked upward and watched as a single vermilion stripe stole across the clear blue sky and danced in refracted radiance across the calm gulf waters. The sun, which had blazed relentlessly throughout the afternoon, faded to a muted copper as it sank slowly into the bay. The feathery leaves of the tall cypresses that lined the streets of Galveston were brushed with a golden radiance. The slow seaside sunset had begun.

Isaac removed his pack and leaned against his bag as he consulted Rabbi Cohen's map. Miss Coen's boarding house was on M Street, only a few blocks over. Sighing, he hoisted his burdens again and covered the distance in long strides until he reached the address, a newly painted white frame house set astride stilts, as were most of the houses on the island city. Its bay window was awash with the violet shadows of the waning day. Oleander bushes hedged the neat garden, and the fragrance of the full-petaled blossoms suffused the darkening air. A small girl sat on the porch, precariously balanced on a wicker rock-

ing chair. She studied him with the unconcealed curiosity
peculiar to children. She wore a crisp white pinafore over
a starched pink gingham dress, and her black pigtails
were tied with lengths of matching pink ribbons. She
continued to stare at him, and he lowered his head because her large dark eyes were so like Sarah's and because her feet, like Sarah's, did not quite touch the
ground as she swayed back and forth in her chair.

Slowly he walked up the steps and set his burdens down
on the porch.

"If you're a peddler, you have to go to the back door,"
the child said importantly.

"I'm not a peddler." He smiled and reached into his
pocket. The Jewish social worker in Hamburg had given
him a small sack of chocolates wrapped in tin foil. He
offered them to the child, and she nodded her thanks and
smiled gravely.

"Will you be a roomer, then?" she asked. "We're
roomers—me and Mama and Papa. We have the front
room on the third floor. My bed is on wheels. It pulls
out from under Mama and Papa's bed. Of course, not all
the rooms are as big as ours."

"Of course not," he agreed. "But I hope there will
be a small room for me."

"You'll have to ask Miss Coen. Come. I'll take you
to her." She slid off the chair, and he saw, with sinking
heart, that she walked with a limp, dragging her left leg
behind her.

He followed her into the house, grateful for the shadowed coolness of the whitewashed walls, the touch of a
woven rug beneath his feet. The aroma of stewing
chicken and vegetables, of apple and cinnamon, filled the
air, and he was aware suddenly of his hunger. But the
child paused and held a finger to her lips, cautioning him
to be silent.

A slender young woman stood in the dining room, a
white lace mantilla shawling her auburn hair. As he
watched, she touched a flaming taper to two white candles set in silver candlesticks of intricate design. She
stretched her arms out in a circular motion, as though to

embrace and protect the nascent flames. Then she bowed her head and lifted her hands to her eyes. She murmured the prayer, and again her arms encircled the flames, as though to bring their light and warmth closer to her. She handed the mantilla to another woman, who glided toward her from a shadowed corner of the room. She too covered her head, repeated the small ceremony, and passed the head covering to yet a third woman.

Isaac watched the small tableau, weighted by a familiar sadness. How often he had stood in the doorway of his cottage and watched Rivka bless the Sabbath candles, the tentative flames casting linear patterns of light across her outstretched fingers.

"*Shabbat shalom,*" the auburn-haired woman said, and her Hebrew was oddly accented. He recognized the Sephardic pronunciation that had been favored by his Hebrew literature teacher at the seminary.

"*A guten shabbos,*" the other women replied in the more familiar Yiddish.

He stepped forward. "*A guten shabbos.*" He added his own greeting, struggling against a wave of loneliness. "*Shabbat shalom.*"

They turned to him, their eyes puzzled but their lips smiling—three women wearing their Sabbath best on an island licked by the waters of the Gulf of Mexico, fanned by winds that traveled from the Caribbean Sea.

"May I help you?" The auburn-haired young woman turned to him. She spoke in the cool, careful cadence of a woman experienced at dealing with strangers. Her gaze was steady, and briefly he was ashamed because he was covered with the dust of his wanderings through the city streets and his dark hair was stiff with the rime of the sea voyage.

"He wants a room," the child said. "Just a small room."

"Rabbi Cohen sent me." He held out the rabbi's note. "I am looking for Miss Emma Coen."

"I am Emma Coen," she said, and he looked at her in surprise. He had anticipated an older woman, a faded middle-aged spinster who wore her hair twisted in a tight bun and dressed in dark, serviceable clothing, like the proprietress of his student lodging house. Emma Coen wore a full-skirted gown of polished green cotton, and her bright hair was caught back with a matching strip of fabric. He knew at once who had made the small girl's ribbons and tied them with such delicate precision.

She read the note, as surely she read anything that concerned her, with great care.

"You are Isaac Lewin, arrived only today? You are looking for a room?"

He nodded.

"We do have a small room available. Will you want full board—breakfast and dinner?"

He nodded.

"Is twelve dollars a month an acceptable arrangement?"

"Yes." He felt his cheeks grow hot.

"It is in order that you pay me at the end of the month," she said, and he detected a softening in her voice. Perhaps she suspected that all he had in his worn wallet was that exact amount.

"I begin work on Monday," he said. "I have a position with a freight forwarding house on the Strand."

Her eyebrows arched in surprise, but she asked no questions.

"You will want to wash and change before dinner," she said coolly. "Miriam, will you show Mr. Lewin the room on the second floor? The one Mr. Rabinowitz had. Please give him a towel and show him the washroom."

The child nodded and Isaac Lewin again heaved his pack onto his back and lifted his bag.

"Dinner will be at seven-thirty, Mr. Lewin," she said. "We eat later on Friday evenings because of the Sabbath."

"I'll be on time."

He followed Miriam up the stairs, aware that Emma Coen's eyes remained riveted on him, although the other women had moved toward the kitchen and someone knocked too insistently on the front door.

The others were already at the table when he came

downstairs an hour later, his thick dark hair still damp from the shower, a small slit of blood bordering his mustache because, inexplicably, his hand had begun to shake as he shaved. The child, Miriam, had brought his own small Sarah so clearly to mind. He wore his dark serge suit and white shirt, which miraculously had not lost its folds during the long journey, perhaps because he had sandwiched it between his English dictionary and the leatherbound Pentateuch in his case. He moved to stand beside the empty chair, smiling his apologies.

"Mr. Lewin, I should like you to meet my other guests."

Emma Coen made the introductions with quiet grace, as though she were hosting an elegant dinner party instead of presiding over a Sabbath meal in a Texas port city boarding house. The two women he had seen earlier were Chana Freundlich and Basha Weinglass. Basha and her husband, Avrum, were Miriam's parents. Short, bearded Avrum extended his hand in greeting. Suppurating blisters covered his soft palms. He winced at Isaac's touch.

"You see, that's what happens when a Russian tailor becomes a Texas stevedore. But the best money is on the pier. In six months we'll have enough money to move on."

"Where will you go?" Isaac asked.

"Maybe California. Oregon is opening up. I have a cousin in Denver. I don't know." The short man shrugged and grinned, as though delighted by the vast horizons available to him. "Meanwhile we wait and save—and get blisters."

Moshe Freundlich, lean and thin-lipped, was less optimistic.

"It's not so easy. You think California is next door? You want to cross another desert, like our ancestors did— but this time without a cloud by day and a pillar of fire by night? They say the winters in Oregon are bad. You should think about Miriam. Don't you want her to go to school with other Jewish children?" He smiled at the small girl and tweaked her braids, but his wife looked away, as though he had affronted her by his fondness for another woman's child. "What's so bad about staying in Galveston? Here we have rabbis, synagogues. A Jew opens a business, he works hard, he prospers. Look at the Laskers and the Rosenbergs. Does anyone in Galveston care if we worship on Saturday instead of Sunday? Here a Jew is like anyone else—an American. No ghetto. No narrow streets and secret rooms."

The two single men at the table, Hyman Greenstein and Abner Wallach, glanced at each other. They had fled the riots in Bucharest, the urban pogroms that had left the Rumanian Jewish community quaking and vulnerable. Of course Galveston was safer, but it was always necessary to practice vigilance, to warily assess the scene.

"Such a serious conversation before we have even begun to eat?" Natalya Ackerman, who taught the Hebrew school at Temple B'nai Zion, smiled pleasantly at Isaac. She was a tall woman whose wide mouth and oversized teeth gave her face an equine look, but there was a kindness to her manner peculiar to those who have endured cruelty and rejection.

Avrum Weinglass offered the kiddush, the ancient prayer sanctifying the Sabbath, and Isaac watched the two Rumanians swiftly pluck skullcaps from their pockets and cover their heads. He guessed that in Bucharest Hyman and Abner would have covered their heads at all times, and he wondered how long it would be before they stopped carrying the small satin caps in their pockets. Even Rabbi Cohen had been bare-headed, he recalled.

"Will you do us the honor of saying the blessing over the bread, Mr. Lewin?" Emma Coen asked.

He intoned the blessing and lifted the cloth from the braided golden loaves, tearing a knot of bread loose and pouring salt on it before eating it. He grasped the loaf then and held it aloft.

"Mr. Lewin, *please.*" Irritation laced her voice, and she took the loaves and cut them with a serrated knife, placing each slice on a dish, which she gave to the Indian serving girl, who circled the table with it.

Isaac blushed. The ripping of the Sabbath loaves was a Russian Jewish custom, an expression of the belief in God's generosity and man's right to be casual in the distribution of divine bounty on this day of rest. But Emma Coen, he knew, had perceived it as a coarseness, a lack of etiquette. He watched as she delicately lifted her glass, tasted her wine. The elegance of manner that had pleased him moments before angered him now. Who was she to consider herself superior because her customs were different from his, her Hebrew differently accented?

He spoke little for the rest of the meal, although Avrum Weinglass pressed him for news of the Jewish community in Russia.

"You are from Kiev?" the bearded man asked. "I heard that there was a pogrom in Kiev only months ago. There was a report in the Yiddish press. But perhaps you were fortunate enough to leave before then?"

"No. I was still in Russia, but I had been called away from home." Isaac's answer was curt, and Avrum Weinglass did not persist. He understood that when a recently arrived Jew avoided a question, it was because the answers were laced with pain.

The dinner was delicious, and Isaac's anger toward Emma Coen cooled as he watched her cut Miriam's chicken and spoon an extra helping of sugared carrots and prunes onto the child's plate. Basha, her mother, spent much of the meal in the kitchen, helping Mary, the Indian maid, who smiled shyly as she collected the dishes, her teeth gleaming white against her topaz skin. She moved soundlessly, her feet encased in soft leather moccasins, and when she spoke, her voice was barely audible. A gold cross, strung to a thong of leather, glinted at her neck.

Isaac sat on the porch after dinner, his eyes raised to the sky. The stars were huge shards of glittering silver, their constellations etched across the black velvet nightscape with startling clarity. The moon formed a slender ivory crescent: briefly, it was caught in a net of clouds, its gossamer radiance obscured by the drifting nimbus.

"I would wager that you never saw a sky like that in

Russia.'' Abner Wallach sank down beside Isaac and breathed deeply of the flower-scented air. He removed the celluloid collar that cut cruelly into his neck. ''It took me weeks to grow accustomed to these skies. My first night in Galveston I looked up and thought that I could touch the stars. We had a full moon then. It seemed to me I could reach up, pull it down, and send it back to Bucharest—a souvenir from the *goldene medina*—a moon of gold from the land of gold.''

''When did you come to Galveston?'' Isaac asked.

''Three months ago—two weeks after I cleared immigration in Castle Garden. The welcoming committee in New York Harbor gave me a train ticket and twenty-five dollars. 'Go west,' they said. 'Why do you want to stay in New York? It's crowded and dirty.' But I'm not so dumb. Green I was, but not stupid. I knew what they meant. 'For fifty dollars I'll go west,' I said, and fifty dollars they gave me.'' He smiled wryly.

''What did they mean?'' Isaac asked.

''They meant that too many Rumanians and Poles, too many Russians, were filling the streets of New York. Too many Litvaks, speaking too loudly, embarrassing the fine German Jews of Temple Emanuel, the elegant Sephardim with their fancy synagogue on Central Park West. But I didn't care. I took their train ticket and their fifty dollars, and I'm glad that I did. They were right even if their reasons were wrong. Out here we can do anything. Every frontier is open to us. North to Oregon, Montana, Washington state. West to the Arizona territory, New Mexico, California. Out here we are pioneers among pioneers. Out here a man can build his own world, a Jew can be less afraid.''

''Why is that?'' Isaac asked softly. He would always be afraid. Fear would adhere to him all the days of his life like a shadow.

''Because here Jews battle the desert and the wilderness like all the other settlers. Do you think Mary, the Indian girl who helps in the kitchen, sees us as Jews? She's a Karankawa Indian, converted to Christianity. To her we are settlers who light candles on Friday nights and say prayers in a language that she does not understand. You found a job on the Strand today. A couple of hours off the boat and you're hired. No one cares that you're a Jew. You're a man who can do a job in this country. In New York, in Boston, in Chicago—we're greenies, we're kikes, sheenies. In Texas we're pioneers, nation builders.'' Pride edged his voice, and his eyes followed the path of a shooting star that streaked across the darkness and shattered into dancing florets of silver.

''You've lived here since you came to Galveston?'' Isaac asked.

''Yes. It's a good boarding house. Always a good meal. Miss Coen does the marketing and cooking herself. Now Basha Weinglass is helping her in the kitchen so they can save a little on the room rent. Weinglass has the silver itch. He wants to get some mining equipment and try to get into the fields. Every day he reads me news of a silver strike in Arizona, a copper vein in New Mexico, a new gold field in California. If he can get enough money, maybe he can afford an operation for Miriam, maybe a doctor can do something for her leg.'' Abner Wallach sighed. He had left a small sister in Rumania.

''Miss Coen owns the house?''

''Yes. It was abandoned and run down when she found it, but she has a good eye. She saw what could be done. She had it repaired and painted, bought some old furniture, and fixed it up. One room at a time, they say. She's a good businesswoman—she knows what to charge for each room, and she gives different rates to the transients. She's fair with the linens, the hot water. I never heard her raise her voice. So does it matter that she thinks she's better than the rest of us—that she holds herself apart? Hyman asked her to go with him to the Grand Opera House one night, and she looked at him as though she were the Queen of England and he were a peasant. He went himself—Sarah Bernhardt was there—and there was Miss Emma Coen sitting in a box with the Rosenbergs.'' Abner Wallach shrugged. ''So what? Me, it doesn't bother. I don't need a Sephardic princess. When I'm ready to get married, I'll find me a little dark-haired girl who has some weight on her and laughs when I tell a joke in Yiddish.''

"I wish I had one to tell you now," Isaac said. It had been a long time since he had laughed at a joke in any language. Not since that night when he had arrived home from an academic conference in a distant city and discovered that while he had been delivering a paper on Maimonides' analysis of the gradations of charity, a gang of drunken rioters had swept through his town, battered down the door of his small cottage, and killed Rivka, his wife, and Sarah, his daughter. Sarah had been four then, and her hair, like her mother's, had fallen in black silken waves about her shoulders.

Abner Wallach looked at him with sudden gravity, with certain recognition.

"The laughter comes back, Lewin. First you cannot weep and then the tears come. They burn the eyes and you think that all gladness has vanished. Then, one day, something makes you smile, and for a minute the heaviness on your heart lightens. The tears stop and laughter returns, and you know that the dead are lost and you are alive. I remember how Jewish blood rusted the water in the gutters of Bucharest after the riots. A baby's body floated on a sewer grating. I picked it up. An infant—a girl child, maybe two, three weeks old, her mouth open. She was crying when she died, and the sorrow and pain were frozen on her little flower face forever. I brought her to the burial society, and then I stood in the street and vomited. I thought I could never eat again. And for two days I didn't eat. Then I managed, a cup of tea, a rusk of bread, a teaspoon of cereal. Finally I woke up one morning and I was hungry. I ate a whole meal. I was alive, and living people grieve and then they eat and laugh.''

Isaac did not reply, and the two men sat quietly, lost in their memories of the narrow ghetto streets of European cities, hearing again the children's terrified nocturnal shrieking, the soft weeping of women, as they looked up at the stars that spangled the vast Texan sky. They did not notice Emma Coen when she came to the doorway and stared hard at Isaac Lewin, her knuckles whitening against the book she carried.

She acknowledged then that there was something in the coiled grace of his posture, the sharp lines of his features accentuated by the softness of his silken mustache, that reminded her of Benjamin Mendoza. She had thought herself immune at last to the pain such memories brought her. Her own vulnerability angered her, and when she went upstairs she did not turn to the book she had carried with her but stood for a long time at the window, staring out at the star-spangled sky.

During the weeks that followed, Isaac acknowledged that Abner Wallach's cursory assessment of Emma Coen had been accurate. She ran the boarding house with efficiency and grace. She was always in the kitchen when he came down for breakfast, working with Indian Mary and Basha Weinglass. His lunch was ready, wrapped in brown paper and marked with his name in fine cursive script. Dinners were simple but ample, and Emma sat at the head of the table, always polite and always aloof. The rooms were cleaned and aired regularly, and each evening fresh flowers filled the tall vase in the vestibule and the large bowl on the dining room table.

She arranged them with care, he knew. One afternoon he arrived home early and saw her seated at the dining room table, long-stemmed blossoms spread out before her. She studied them with great concentration and placed them one by one into the vase, alternating delicate pink primroses with long-stalked sea oats. She pondered a cluster of gentian, and Isaac noticed that the tiny bell-shaped flowers matched her long-lashed eyes. Small Miriam sat beside her, arranging the fallen petals in a graceful design. Isaac gave the child a doll he had bought from an Indian woman at the pier. It was carved of the soft bark of the cottonwood tree and dressed in scraps of buckskin. Beads formed its mouth and eyes, and a fragment of fur covered the head. Miriam gasped with delight and ran off to show it to her mother.

"Your flowers are beautiful," Isaac said to Emma. "I look forward to seeing them each evening."

"Thank you." She blushed with pleasure. "They are very different from the flowers in Holland. One day, perhaps, I will plant tulips and narcissus bulbs in the garden here. I have asked friends in Amsterdam to send them to me."

"Holland? I thought you had come to Galveston from England."

"I lived in England for only two years," she said curtly.

"Your family is in Holland?" he persisted.

"No." She pursed her lips, and he felt rebuffed, chastened.

"I did not mean to intrude."

She did not reply, and he left the room, suffused again with the embarrassed anger he had felt that first night.

But he had little time to brood about Emma Coen. His workday was long and tiring. He arrived at the Strand office early and checked the bills of lading. By midmorning he was on the wharf, where bales of cotton were heaved from dray wagons onto the docks. He assigned specific shipments to specific barges, learning quickly to estimate which craft could most economically be utilized for a given load.

He relished the activity and excitement on the docks of Galveston. Black men from Louisiana and the West Indian islands shouted to each other in patois French as they worked. Sweat darkened their brightly colored shirts and dripped down their faces, but they did not break pace. They moved the huge bales, the oversized barrels and crates, with rhythmic dexterity, graceful dancers in an intricately choreographed saraband. The white stevedores who worked beside them knew their dialects, sang their songs.

Brokers in dark suits, boiled white shirts, and string ties moved about the wharf, notebooks in hand, fanning themselves with their soft dark hats. They bent to examine the contents of a barrel, a crate; they lifted clots of cotton from the bales and watched with thin smiles as the gulf breeze scattered it like droplets of snow. They spoke urgently to each other and clasped hands as deals were agreed upon, commitments guaranteed.

Cargo vessels dropped anchor in the harbor, and the wind whipped the bright flags at their masts. Sailors of every nationality crossed the granite jetty, flushed with excitement at their shore leave. Young Italians, wearing bright red berets, argued with good-natured intensity. French ensigns in ill-fitting pale-blue uniforms lifted their caps politely to a group of Karankawa Indian girls who held out baskets overflowing with bright beaded necklaces and bracelets, strips of tooled leather, oddly shaped talismans carved from the prong horns of antelope, the antlers of prairie deer. Dusky-skinned Lascars grinned and smoothed their hair. Italian lire, French francs, and English sterling floated from hand to hand. The Indian girls pulled their serapes close about their shoulders and smiled shyly as they studied the notes, counted the silver coins.

Isaac checked the warehouses each day to make sure consignments were shipped on time, that inventories reconciled. He devised a system to relay shipments to Port Isabel in the south and to pick up return cargo so that both voyages showed a profit. He was given a raise and an office with a window that overlooked the Strand.

"Not bad," Abner Wallach said when Isaac told him. "Maybe you'll start your own company yet."

Isaac shrugged and paced the length of the porch. Emma Coen sat in the living room reading, her hair luminous in the lamplight. She turned a page, lifted a finger to her lips.

"Maybe I will," he said in answer to Abner.

"Is that what you want?"

"I don't want to work until I'm dropping to make another man rich," Isaac replied.

"Maybe you want other men to work so that you'll get rich," Hyman Greenstein said sourly. In Bucharest he had been a member of the Young Socialist League. He subscribed to the socialist journal *Der Arbeiter Tseitung* and read aloud to them from the poems of Morris Win-

chevsky and David Edelstadt. The plaintive Yiddish
sounded strangely alien against the background of cica-
das chirping and the scent of oleanders that permeated
the Texas night.

> The sufferer's every sigh
> Resounded in my breast
> And turned into a battle cry
> Revenge for the oppressed.

Hyman read the poem with restrained passion. He was
a short, sandy-haired man who paced the porch when the
other men sat quietly and nervously tapped his fingers
as he read his journals and newspapers. His fiancée had
been killed during the Bucharest riots, and he spoke her
name aloud in his sleep. "Lonya. Lonya." The name
of the murdered girl echoed through the quiet halls
of the boarding house, causing the others to stir rest-
ively.

"And how are you going to avenge the oppressed?"
Isaac asked mildly. It was a quiet question, posed in the
probing tone of the well-trained teacher. Just so he had
addressed his students, skillfully leading them from
question to answer in the days when he had thought that
reason ruled the world.

"By building a better world," Hyman replied. "Why
not a socialist society here in the West? A community
that offers real equality. Why shouldn't the world that
we are building be better than the world we left behind?"

"I do not quarrel with you. In theory you are right.
This is a new and different world. A new landscape, a
new language. Even a new system of government—a democracy. The first time Jews have lived in a democracy.
But are the people any different, Hyman? Do human beings change because the conditions of their lives, their
systems of government, are altered?" The czarist mon-
archy had not killed and raped Rivka, crushed little Sarah's skull. That had been the work of men, not of a
system.

"Perhaps. Perhaps they do change, Mr. Lewin."
Emma Coen's voice wafted toward them from the doorway where she stood listening, an oleander blossom as
pale as the low-hanging moon circling her slender wrist.
She went inside, slamming the door behind her, and the
men sat on, wreathed in silence. Her own words, teasing,
challenging, surprised her. Why should she seek an argument with Isaac Lewin? She rebuked herself yet smiled
because she had startled him, unnerved him.

Isaac walked down to the beach that night and watched
the wine-dark waves rush up to the shore. Moonlight
carved a silver path across the gulf waters, cast an argen-
tous glow across the pounding surf. Two great blue herons swooped down and danced toward each other, their
wings beating the waves. Their mating call pierced the
night, shredding its stillness with the repeated melodic
plea. They circled each other, wing brushing wing, tal-
ons arched in desperate reach. Isaac turned away, choked
with loneliness, and gazed out toward the breakwater.
Emma Coen stood poised on a reef, wrapped in a pale
blue shawl. She too watched the herons as she shredded
the oleander blossom. The pale petals sailed across the
waves and shimmered briefly on the shell-studded shore.
He left the beach, walking swiftly, lest he shatter her
solitude, and his own.

"Are you going to the dance tonight, Miss Emma?" Little Miriam Weinglass stood in the doorway holding her
precious Indian doll.

Emma looked up from the letter she was writing to her
cousin Greta Anspacher, who was a faithful correspondent and worried when Emma's replies were dilatory.
Greta's own letters were full of news of her English
friends and family. She had bought a black velvet ball
gown for the Rothschilds' gala. There had been a round
of parties for Jacob Schiff and his dowdy wife, who were
again visiting London. The American financier had remembered Emma and asked after her, expressing pleasure when he heard that she was in Galveston. "I blame
myself for taking you to that dinner party. If there hadn't

been all that talk about Jewish territorialism, you'd still be with me,'' Greta wrote. ''I shall never forgive Israel Zangwill—oh, by the way, he's written a new play—deadly boring, they say.'' Perhaps Emma remembered Philip Sasson. He had married his childhood sweetheart.

Emma smiled. She missed Greta and Horace, but London seemed so far away, and she had scarcely thought about her life there since her arrival in Galveston. She had loved the Atlantic crossing—the scent of sea air, the sun bright on the rolling waves. She had even relished the two-day storm that had sent the ship rocking dangerously from side to side as sailors scurried to secure the flapping canvas, to pull ropes into taut banisters. She had walked the deck alone and remembered that she had once thought to cross this ocean at Benjamin Mendoza's side, to brace herself against his strength in just such an imagined storm. She had managed well enough alone. The sailors doffed their caps at her, saluting her courage, her fortitude.

Greta had written to tell her that Benjamin had married the daughter of a wealthy Rotterdam merchant family and contentedly managed one of their enterprises in that city. Emma had wondered then if there had ever been any validity to his dream of coming to America. Had he ever meant to leave the security of Europe, the established business he anticipated claiming as his wife's dowry, or had he merely uttered the phrases she had wanted to hear—the skilled suitor matching his words to her moods, his aspirations to her desires, deftly evoking gratitude and submission? He had robbed her of her trust, betrayed her innocence. Still, she owed him a perverse debt of gratitude. She would never again be so vulnerable, so credulous. His weakness had generated her strength. She had survived his betrayal, forged her own life. Her mother would not have approved, she knew, but Analiese Deken would have understood. She would have comprehended Emma's pride in her ability to withstand the waves alone, her confidence in her own fortitude, her own tenacity.

Emma wondered if she would ever again see the sad-eyed woman who had loved Jacob Coen, and smiled at

the naiveté of the thought. America was vast, a huge
continent stretching from sea to sea. How could she ever
hope to find Analiese, and did she even want to? The
confrontation at the Ouderkirk cemetery had acquired a
dreamlike quality, and sometimes she was not even certain that it had occurred.

Alone, Emma had disembarked at Galveston, organized her luggage, and gravely submitted to the immigration procedure. "Does she have enough money to
support herself?" The question embarrassed the immigration official. It was awkward to ask a stylishly dressed,
beautiful woman of obvious cultivation such intimate details. Still, without embarrassment, she showed him the
bank draft Horace Anspacher had executed, transferring
her English earnings to a Galveston bank.

"And I have two brothers in the United States," she
added.

Miraculously, Emil and Simon were waiting for her on
the dock. Horace Anspacher had written to them, his
tone worried and severe. "You must arrange to meet your
sister in Galveston even though she foolishly insists she
can manage on her own." In Victorian England women
seldom left their houses unescorted, yet Emma Coen insisted upon crossing an ocean by herself.

Dutifully, they had met her ship and accompanied her
to Rabbi Cohen's study on Broadway. Sitting in the rabbi's book-lined study, Emma looked fondly at her brothers. Simon was leaner than she remembered and deeply
tanned. He had lost his solemn scholar's gaze. Behind
his wire-framed spectacles, his amber eyes glinted with
a new alertness. He had spent time in Arizona advising
mine owners of the potential of newly discovered veins,
evaluating ores and mineral deposits. He had learned that
the miners hauled the ore to distant locations for smelting.

"When I asked them why, they told me there was no
fuel," he said. "How could they feed a smelting fire in
the desert? I experimented with mesquite. Made a terrible stink, but worked fine. I built a smelting plant, primitive but operative, and fueled it with mesquite. And then

I sold it to one of the Guggenheim brothers. Arizona's beautiful, Emma, but still, I wanted to go out to California with Emil."

"The very word *Arizona* always intrigued me," Emma said.

"Marvelous country," Simon agreed. "An odd thing happened when I was out in the territory. Someone told me that a Dutchwoman had settled there. They remembered only her first name because it was so unusual— Analiese. She'd staked a claim in the valley."

Emma and Emil stared at each other.

"Did you try to find her?" Emma asked.

"I asked about her when I was in Gila. She had died, they said, and her last name had not been Deken. I can't remember it now. Still, it would have been too much of a coincidence." Simon sighed, recalling with a twinge of shame that he had been relieved to find that the woman named Analiese had vanished from the Gila territory.

"And now we're off to California," Emil said contentedly.

"But why?" Emma asked.

Emil laughed. "There's an ocean there I haven't seen yet." His eyes were dreamy, as they had been in Amsterdam. He had crossed the Mediterranean and Adriatic seas. He had sailed down the Rhone and drifted across the Seine. His Atlantic crossing had been undertaken at the height of winter when huge blocks of ice glinted with diamond brightness in the dark and violent waters. He had steamed down the Mississippi River to the Gulf of Mexico, and a sailing ship had carried him across the gulf waters to Galveston Island. But it was the Pacific Ocean that drew him. The very name enticed him. Pacific. Peaceful. Restless Emil Coen was certain that he would find peace at the shores of the great ocean that bordered the United States at its most western frontier.

"It's my own manifest destiny," he said laughingly. "The God of my fathers, the God of Abraham, Isaac, and Jacob, has commanded me to go west."

"The inspiration comes from God, the maps from Fremont, and the directive from Greeley," Simon said wryly. "But I think Emil is right, Emma. California is the place to be—America's last frontier. Her window to Asia."

"What will you do there?" Emma asked.

The brothers glanced at each other.

"We want to set up an export business," Simon said. "Metals. Minerals. The Pacific ports are going to be busier than Galveston harbor. Ships from the east and the west docking and embarking, and we'll be filling their holds with our cargo. Silver from Arizona. Tin from New Mexico. California gold. There's magic underneath the earth in Texas—the Indian black gold—petroleum. Everything will have to be marketed, shipped, and we'll be there at the beginning." Ideas converged upon him as he spoke. America's last frontier would guarantee their fortune. He understood the mineral deposits, and Emil had initiative, imagination. The skills he had developed in the Kalverstraat accounting office would at last be useful. He understood a ledger page at a glance, calculated interest rates without pencil and paper. The combination would guarantee them success, prevent them from duplicating their father's failure.

"Come with us, Emma," Emil said.

"What would I do in California?" Her brothers' fierce ambition frightened her suddenly. She noticed how Simon paced the floor, that Emil's hair was thinning and his skin had a jaundiced cast. The malaria he had contracted in Palestine had taken its toll. He was tired, wearier than he knew.

"You could keep house for us," Simon said. They would have a home overlooking San Francisco Bay, and Emma would manage it as she had managed their Prinsengracht home. He wanted to see his sister again seated at a gleaming rosewood table, arranging freshly cut flowers in a tall cut glass vase. They would take care of beautiful Emma, he and Emil. They would compensate her for their father's betrayal, for Benjamin Mendoza's defection. Simon's lips curled when he thought of the Belgian. A friend in Rotterdam had written that Mendoza's wife was overbearing. "A cow," Simon's friend had written cruelly, adding that it was rumored that Mendoza kept a photograph of Emma in his desk drawer.

"You don't understand, Simon. I don't want to keep house for anyone. I want to make my own way." She tilted her head proudly. "I have money. Money that I earned myself."

"But what will you do, Emma?" Emil asked.

"I wrote you about my meeting with Jacob Schiff in London. There was talk of making Galveston a key port of entry for the Jews of eastern Europe, and Mr. Schiff said then that there would be a need for hostelries here, to house the immigrants. If I can keep house for my brothers, I should be able to keep a boarding house. I don't think it will be very different from running our Prinsengracht home or Mrs. Nathan's London town house. What do you think, Rabbi Cohen?"

Henry Cohen, who had been listening with interest to the exchange between the brothers and their newly arrived sister, nodded.

"I've had letters from both Schiff and Zangwill. They are very optimistic, very determined. But even if their project does not succeed and we are not overwhelmed with immigrants, there is still a need for a lodging house. Some Jews have always found their way to Galveston—otherwise I wouldn't be here. So why not, Miss Coen, why not?"

Her brothers had not argued. The set of Emma's chin, the glint in her eyes, was familiar to them. Even as a child she had seldom resorted to tears and tantrums. A calm determination remained her strongest weapon. Besides, their sister was a woman now; they sensed her subtle wisdom, her gentle certainty. She was a beautiful woman, determined to have her own way.

She waved to them when they set sail, and when they arrived in California her letter awaited them. She had bought a house on M Street—an old house in a state of disrepair, but she had paid a reasonable price for it and was overseeing its repair and repainting herself. She stitched upholstery and curtains, and rose early to sand the floors herself, working alone with the shutters bolted so that no one would observe her involvement in manual labor.

Six months later the house was newly painted, its roof repaired, its wooden floors polished to high shine. She relished the running of it, the small mercantile triumphs when she arranged for a discount by buying meat and produce in quantity, the bartering with itinerant boarders. A Lithuanian glazier, en route to Montana, fixed her windows in exchange for room and board. A carpenter from Cracow lived rent-free until all the doorjambs were repaired. Basha Weinglass darned linen and worked in the kitchen in exchange for Miriam's board.

Emma enjoyed life in the port city. The established Jewish families were quick to welcome her. She occasionally dined with the Rosenbergs and spent Sunday afternoons with the Laskers. She rode through the countryside with the Laskers in their phaeton and gasped at the wild beauty of the East Texas landscape, the outcroppings of chaparral and the giant cacti with their cruel spikes and delicate florets. That first summer in Galveston there was even a sailing party to New Orleans in Emmet Greenberg's tall ship. In the fall Anna Pavlova was the guest star at the Grand Opera House.

"Don't you find it difficult being a single woman among your bachelor boarders?" Louise Lasker asked her teasingly as they watched Pavlova transform the stage into a fairyland.

"No. Not at all," she had answered honestly, vaguely surprised by the question.

She liked the young men who conversed energetically and laughed heartily at her table; they passed their plates for second helpings and painstakingly practiced their English. They were ambitious, exuberant. They studied maps of the United States, speculated on the opportunities available in the Arizona territory, in California, Colorado. An independence of spirit had led them to opt for Galveston. They were not men who would be happy in the ghettos of New York and Chicago, in the immigrant warrens of Boston and Philadelphia. Some of them arrived outfitted with packs of merchandise from the Baltimore Bargain House, Fine and Sons, H. B. Claflin, and set off on foot to peddle ribbons and needles, lengths of fabric, tools and medicine. They wore sturdy boots and soft hats as protection against the harsh sunlight and the sudden rains. Although the packs were heavy, they walked briskly as they left Emma's house. They were on their way to their future. There were those who managed to buy two-wheeled surreys. "Stores on wheels" they called themselves, and they rolled across desert and prairies, stopping at ranches and farmhouses, displaying ribbons and cutlery to lonely women in dusty mining towns.

Emma listened to their stories, always interested and always cautiously aloof. Politely she rejected their invitations to the dances on the village green, the concerts at the Grand Opera House, the teas that followed Friday night services at B'Nai Israel. Gradually, they stopped asking her. They told each other that she had a misplaced notion of her own superiority and noted that she sat by herself at synagogue services and turned the pages of her own Sephardic prayerbook. But of course, there were similar separations among those who attended Friday evening services. The German Jews sat in pews in front of the small sanctuary, and the immigrants from eastern Europe clustered together in the rear pews. The intonations of the prayers differed, and occasionally there was a brief atonal competition as one group tried to drown out the chanting of the other. But Emma Coen prayed silently and alone.

Isaac Lewin had never invited Emma to the Grand Opera House. He fell silent when she joined the group of young people who gathered on the boarding house porch during the quiet spring evenings. Still, she felt his eyes drift toward her, and his most casual glance filled her with a strange unease. There was a brooding intensity in his agate gaze, a coiled energy in his lean, muscular body that threatened, frighteningly, to spring loose. He was a tall man. Once, when she strained to reach for linens on the top shelf of the hall closet, he shoved her gently aside and easily reached the pile of sheets. She had quivered at his touch, but her voice had been cool when she thanked him. He was newly showered, and his blue-black hair curled in damp ringlets. She thought of Benjamin Mendoza, who had stood bareheaded on the Imjuden barge as the North Sea wind moistened his blue-black hair. Isaac Lewin had reminded her of Benjamin Mendoza from the first. Perhaps that was why she had spoken to him on that first Sabbath evening with a harshness that she had regretted minutes later but could not retract.

The other boarders often spoke of their pasts, as though they feared that if they did not speak of absent family and vanished landscapes, memory itself might wither and fade. Isaac Lewin remained silent. But Rabbi Cohen, from whom no Jew in Galveston had a secret, had told Emma that the Russian Jew had been a teacher of philosophy. He had been married and had a small daughter. The rabbi had seen a photograph of a dark-haired fragile-featured woman and a small girl with huge dark eyes. His wife had wanted to leave Russia, but the forged papers, the steamship tickets, the money to bribe the border guard were beyond the means of a teacher. Besides he wanted to finish his thesis. They were a loving couple, but they fought over his decision to stay in Russia. After one such argument he left to attend a learned conference—a symposium on the nature of good and evil, the efficacy of charity and righteousness. A group of drunken muzhiks had swept through Kiev. Eleven Jews had been murdered, among them Isaac Lewin's wife and small daughter. He had blamed himself for their deaths and cursed himself because he had stood at a podium and argued polemics and abstractions while his wife was raped and murdered and his child's head bludgeoned to a pulpy mass by a muzhik's ax handle.

Emma had shivered. She understood then why Isaac Lewin had abandoned his studies and turned to commerce. She understood the ambition that drove him, that led him to ask searing questions of the other boarders. He searched for new and different ways to make money, to increase profits. He would not long be a shipping clerk in a freight forwarding house. It was not that he had recognized the power of money, but he had seen the impotence born of the lack of it. She felt a curious kinship with the tall Russian, but it did not erase the tension between them, the odd constraint that caused her to drop her eyes when they met by chance, to turn a corner when she saw him approach.

Often, in the evening, a lingering sadness overtook Emma. She walked down to the beach then, and the rhythm of the rolling waves soothed her and the scent of the sea assuaged the nameless, aimless misery, the lingering sense of loss that weighted her heart and slowed her steps. She loosened her hair, removed her shoes, and waded into the sea, welcoming its icy touch against her skin. On a night when the two great blue herons winged their way toward each other, she sat on a reef and thought of wading toward them. She would hold her skirts high and the waves would curl and retreat about her legs, leap up to drench her breasts. It would be a release, a relief, to surrender to the gulf waters as she had surrendered to Benjamin Mendoza. The wild, inexplicable thought frightened her. The curtain of loneliness had lifted, and she had briefly seen the stage of madness.

Her throat grew dry, and she turned her gaze from the wild waters to the beach and saw Isaac Lewin silhouetted in the moonlight. He had seen her, she knew, and had chosen to ignore her. She shivered, oddly wounded, oddly grateful, and watched him leave the beach. When she returned to the house on M Street, she saw a light in his window. She imagined his dark head bent over a philosophy book, but she knew that he had not been reading but only waiting for her step upon the path.

Now, as she pondered her letter to her cousin Greta, she thought of writing about Isaac Lewin (yet what would she say? ''There is a new boarder here whose gaze makes me uneasy, whose face flashes before me at night''?). Miriam's question had interrupted her thought, and impatiently, she crumpled the sheet of writing paper and turned to the child.

''Aren't you going tonight?'' Miriam asked again.

"You know I never go to the dances, Miriam," she said severely.

"But you could go once. Maybe you would like it. Natalya has such a good time when she goes. I hear her singing when she comes home. Besides, my mother said that if you went I could go with you. She won't let me go with anyone else," Miriam said.

Emma smiled. She understood Basha Weinglass's over-protectiveness toward Miriam. The child was so often ill, her violet eyes shadowed by circlets of pain. She dragged her left leg as though it were an awkward encumbrance, mysteriously and uselessly attached to her body. She had been crippled by a treacherous and frightening illness.

"She ran a fever," Basha had said. "Her skin was on fire, and we thought that she would not live, but God spared her. He saved her for us. Avrum has heard that there is an operation that can make her leg straight, give it back some strength."

"I hope so," Emma had replied. It was, of course, the crippling disease that struck children and adults and often left them paralyzed. Poliomyelitis, the doctors at the Medical Center in Galveston called it, and they cautioned children against swimming in the bay waters or playing among the palmetto trees where huge mosquitoes darkened the air. Avrum and Basha guarded their child with grim vigilance, keeping her safe until the magic day when the mysterious operation could be performed. At the hint of a breeze Basha ran forward with a sweater. Avrum watched the child eat, hovered over her sleeping form, called her name as he walked up the street each evening.

"Do you really want to go so badly, Miriam?" Emma asked. Her heart turned in sorrow for the small girl, who would perhaps never be able to glide across a dance floor but who wanted to watch others move with grace and ease to the strains of the fiddle, the melodic invitation of the accordion.

"It's the best dance of the year—the Juneteenth dance," Miriam said plaintively.

Juneteenth was the nineteenth day of June. It marked
Emancipation Day in Texas, the day on which all slaves
had been granted their freedom. There were fireworks
and speeches and performances by the various civic
groups in Galveston. Emma remembered now that Rabbi
Cohen had been asked to speak, and the children of the
Bernard de Galvez School were to put on a play. It would
not be fair for Miriam to miss it—she missed enough of
life as it was.

"All right, I'll take you," Emma said. "But we may
have to leave early. I still have the household accounts to
pay."

She glanced at the small pile of bills, pleased with the
knowledge that this month the boarding house would
show a reasonable profit. She even thought of adding another wing to the house. Three more bedrooms would
enable her to accommodate six more boarders, but she
would have to go into debt for the construction, and the
thought frightened her. It was debt that had ruined Jacob
Coen—debt coupled with duplicity. She associated one
with the other, and although she understood her father,
she would not emulate him. She would wait. Perhaps
when Jacob Schiff and Israel Zangwill succeeded in their
plan for intensive Jewish immigration via Galveston, she
would add the wing—if indeed she still wanted to remain
in the port city. She was newly aware of a yearning to
move on, to travel across the desert and the prairies. Each
letter from her brothers brought a new restlessness. They
wrote of the beauty of San Francisco, where their business was prospering—of their business trips throughout
the West. The Indian and Spanish names had a lyric ring:
Santa Cruz, El Mirage, Geronimo.

She dressed carefully for the Juneteenth dance, selecting a white georgette gown that she had fashioned from
remnants a peddler had offered in exchange for a night's
lodging. It was full-skirted, its neckline artfully scooped
and rimmed with lace. She strung the turquoise pendant
across a narrow strip of grosgrain ribbon and tied it into
a bow at her neck. She put up her hair and then, impul-

sively, she brushed it loose so that it fell in red-gold swirls about her face.

"You look beautiful," Miriam gasped. "Like a bride."

Emma smiled and struggled against the strange melancholy that the child's words had evoked.

The town green was crowded when they arrived. Men and women dressed in their best greeted each other exuberantly. Young girls carried baskets of oleanders and smilingly offered them to new arrivals. Negro youths wearing snow-white shirts walked arm in arm, now and again breaking into song. Juneteenth was not an ordinary holiday for them. They lived with grandparents who had been slaves, bought and sold on the Galveston pier. They understood freedom because they had lived with the specter of slavery.

American flags and red-and-gold Lone Star banners festooned the gazebo and draped the podium that dominated the green. Emma greeted the Rosenbergs and the Laskers, the Kaplans and the Ginsbergs. Her own boarders stood together—Hyman Greenstein and Abner Wallach, tall Natalya, and Isaac Lewin. Isaac said something that made the others laugh, and Emma felt strangely excluded, isolated from their intimacy, their easy exchange. She turned her attention to the podium. A tall, gray-haired Negro spoke, his voice husky with emotion.

"We are in a new century," he said. "The year 1900 marks the beginning of a great era for these United States, for the Lone Star state of Texas, for the white people and the Negro people, for our Indian neighbors—for all who would work together for our great democracy. We are, all of us, linked in a fellowship of pioneers, of nation builders. We do not celebrate June 19 as the day that slavery ended. We celebrate it as the day that freedom began."

Shouts of acclamation and wild applause greeted his speech.

"That was Norris Wright Cuney," Emma told Miriam. "He's the head of the Negro Longshoreman's Association."

She had heard the aging Negro leader speak from Rabbi Cohen's pulpit. He was a staunch advocate of education for his people, and he had implored the Jewish community of Galveston to work with their Negro neighbors.

"You have known slavery and we have known slavery. We have passed through the darkness of the past into a land that at last guarantees all of us freedom. We can hold our hands out to each other and help to build that land together," he had said earnestly. The sparsely populated West would welcome them, would absorb their energy, their talents. The children and grandchildren of slaves, the immigrant Jews, refugees from ghetto and pogrom, were united in a shared effort. The American West was the proving ground of their newly gained freedom.

The mayor spoke next, and his remarks were brief and optimistic. The new century would be a turning point for Galveston. Harbor trade and traffic were increasing. There were plans to build a land bridge that would connect the island with the mainland.

"We have great hopes for the future," he concluded, but even as he spoke he lifted his eyes worriedly to the skies. There had been rumors of a norther—the sudden and devastating storm that rushed in from the north. Briefly, a sharp, cold wind had banished the heat of the spring afternoon and dark clouds had rimmed the northern sky. Housewives had scurried to collect their wash from clotheslines and had rushed their children inside. Only a year ago the hurricane-force wind of a norther had carried a small boy aloft. He had been found miles away, his back broken, his stricken face wind-bruised. Men had moved porch furniture inside and braced sandbags against the walls of their houses. But they had been fortunate. The temperature had risen and the black clouds had drifted away. The wintry wind had been replaced by the sweetly mild gulf breeze, laced with the fragrance of the oleanders. The men and women of Galveston set their fear aside with the wondrous resilience that enabled them to live in the unpredictable gulf climate year after year.

"Northers are like pogroms," Rabbi Cohen had said

wryly to Emma. "Once they're over, you tend to put them out of mind—until the next one."

Now the musicians struck up the Texas Two-Step, and couples danced across the green in time to the lively music. The women artfully crooked their arms, and the men bent and swayed as they lifted their partners high, clicking their heels and effortlessly picking up the beat.

Isaac Lewin watched as tall Natalya Ackerman joined the line dance for Cotton-Eyed Joe. With her dark hair swept up in a gleaming coronet and the excitement of the dance flooding her face with color, the schoolteacher looked almost pretty. Awkward in her ordinary movements—she loped rather than walked, fumbled her parcels, and her students imitated her clumsy, self-conscious motions with the indifferent cruelty of the young—she was wondrously graceful when she danced. She held her dark skirt demurely high, curtsied coquettishly to her partner, and laughed as she whirled up and down the line with the young women of Galveston, who whipped their bright skirts and displayed layers of ribboned petticoats and crinolines, patterned stockings that hugged their calves and ankles.

"You dance well," Isaac said as Natalya sank down beside him, breathless and bright-eyed, loosening the top button of her high-collared white blouse.

"I never danced before I came to Galveston," she said. "Oh, yes, with other girls and women at weddings. But I am a rabbi's daughter. It would have been unthinkable for me to dance with a man."

"Where is your family now?" he asked. "Still in Lithuania?"

"No. My parents and my brothers are in New York. I have a married sister in Chicago."

"And you are in Galveston. Why?"

She tossed her head defiantly.

"Because I didn't come to America to re-create the world I had left behind in Europe. In Vilna my father had a small *shul* and my mother assisted a wigmaker. In New York my father has a small *shul* on Grand Street and my mother works for a wigmaker on Ridge Street. In Vilna we lived huddled together in a courtyard. In New York we huddled together in a tenement. We had come to this enormous country, but we ourselves had not found space. We elbowed our way through crowded markets, we walked down narrow streets. I worked in a factory so close to the table of the next girl that our arms touched as we worked. This was America? At the settlement house, in the evening school, we learned a song—all about purple mountains and amber waves of grain. I saw soot-covered buildings, garbage floating in gutters. I went to the public library on East Broadway and looked at books with pictures of the mountains and the deserts. Granite hills cut into the earth, rolling prairies. The photographs gave me a feeling of freedom, of excitement.

"I studied a map. Oklahoma, New Mexico, Colorado. Texas. That was America. There I would find the purple mountains, the amber waves of grain. My parents sent me to visit my sister in Chicago. I think they thought there might be more Jewish bachelors there, but I wasn't looking for marriage. I read an ad in the *American Israelite*. Here, in Galveston, they needed a Hebrew teacher. Well, I had taught a class of small girls in my father's *shul*. I decided that that made me a teacher. So I wrote to Rabbi Cohen, and he sent me a train ticket. And *nu?* Here I am."

She smiled, and he smiled back, moved by her courage. The accordionist struck up a Cajun waltz, and he rose to invite her to dance, but Abner Wallach stood before them.

"Will you dance with me, Natalya?" the young Rumanian asked. His cheeks were dappled with patches of red as he danced her across the green.

Isaac watched and saw them pause to greet Emma Coen and little Miriam Weinglass. Emma's presence at the dance surprised him. She looked beautiful, almost bridal, in the white dress. He had watched her stitch its seams during the long spring evenings as they sat on the porch. Miriam looked sweet in her best pink dress with long ribbons looped through her dark curls. The crippled child clapped her hands to the music and looked longingly at the dancers. Impulsively, he strode across the green and bowed elegantly before them.

"Good evening, Miss Coen."

"Good evening, Mr. Lewin."

"May I have this dance, Miss Miriam?"

He held his hand out to the shyly smiling child, and before she could answer he lifted her in his arms and danced away. He circled the green with long sweeping steps. The crippled child seemed weightless in his arms. Her soft hair brushed his cheek, her laughter trilled and trembled. Just so he had danced with Sarah, his small daughter, holding her aloft in his arms, the lightest and loveliest of burdens.

"Am I too heavy, Mr. Lewin?" Miriam asked.

"Of course not." His tone feigned indifference, and he showed her that he could hold her with one arm, swaying in an intricate step that made her laugh yet again. She was breathless and bright-eyed when he carried her back to Emma Coen. The next dance was a Viennese waltz. Emma smiled as she recognized the tune. She had danced to it in Amsterdam and in London. She swayed to the music and closed her eyes, surrendering briefly to the luxury of memory. Isaac Lewin's strong hands encircled her waist.

"Wait here for us, Miriam," he instructed the child, and he danced Emma away.

Her body was supple beneath his touch. She followed as he led, her steps magically following his own as though they were long-practiced partners, skilled at anticipation, emulation. The music was a narcotic that released them from all uneasiness, all trepidation. He whirled her about the green, a confident, controlling captor. A smile played at her lips. Her flesh glowed rose-gold against the bridal whiteness of her dress. Small drops of perspiration jeweled her brow, her neck, but her feet moved with chimerical lightness.

She tossed her head, and her red-gold hair whipped about her face. She felt his strength, his deft control, and her body moved as one with his. She laughed as he spun her about, releasing her and claiming her with effortless grace. How wonderful it was to dance beneath the open skies, to entrust herself once again to strong and certain arms. She lifted her glowing face to the music, to the soft gulf breeze, to the forgotten joy of her own youth and yearning.

The fiddler broke into one last crescendo, whipping his bow against the strings, and Isaac danced her about in an ever-decreasing circle until the music stopped. Dizzied, she clung to him for support, breathless, her fingers tight against his arm. He held her so that she would not fall and led her back to the wooden bench where Miriam waited for them.

"That was wonderful," the child said. "You looked so beautiful, Miss Emma. Everyone was watching you."

Emma blushed. The child's words had thrust her back into reality. Isaac Lewin stared down at her, but she did not look up to meet his eyes. She had sensed a new recognition in his gaze, as though she had revealed a mystery to him as they danced.

"Thank you, Miriam. I'm very thirsty, Mr. Lewin."

"I'll get you both some lemonade."

But when he returned from the refreshment table, holding two tumblers of the thick, sweet drink that the women of Galveston had made from the lemons that grew in profusion in their gardens and groves, Miriam was asleep, her head resting on Emma's shoulder.

"Too much excitement for her, I'm afraid," Emma said.

"No need to waken her. We'll take her home." Gently, he lifted the child, as he had so often lifted his own daughter when she had fallen asleep and he had carried her to bed, as he had lifted her and placed her in the pine coffin, so small that it looked like a child's toybox. He drained one glass of the lemonade, and Emma drank the other. A sliver of citrus clung to her lip, and he thought to brush it away but did not.

They waved to Abner and Natalya, who were dancing yet again, and walked home, the breath of the sleeping child warm and sweet against his neck. The streets of Galveston were dark, but chandeliers sparkled in the windows of the turreted Victorian mansions that lined Broadway. The great maritime families held their own dances on Juneteenth. The children and grandchildren of confederate soldiers were not yet comfortable with the descendants of slaves, with the new generation of pioneer immigrants.

A young couple stood on the balcony of the stately

Gresham home and leaned against the delicate wrought-iron railing. The girl was petite, blond. She wore a white dress, and her laughter was hauntingly musical. The young man with her encircled her waist with both his hands and bent to kiss her.

They passed the plazas where the *lavanderas,* the laundresses, set up washtubs converted into cooking pots and sold their spicy chili to foreign sailors on shore leave, merchant seamen from Port Isabel, Port Bolívar, Corpus Christi, in Galveston for the celebration. The men scooped up the beef and beans with tostadas and told each other of other cities where the women were more beautiful, the *salsa picante* even sharper. The *lavanderas* laughed and told stories of their own. But they fell silent as Isaac and Emma passed, in deference to the sleeping child.

"*Buenas noches*—good night, beautiful family," one of them called softly, and although the men laughed, the *lavendera*'s voice was tender, almost wistful.

Isaac glanced at Emma, but she averted her eyes and they walked on, across the quiet avenues where the gaslit lamps cast golden cornucopias of light. When they reached the house on M Street, he surrendered his tender burden to her. The child stirred but did not awaken. Emma carried her inside, but he remained on the porch. He heard the murmur of voices, saw the light in the Weinglass room glow briefly.

He was tired, and the next day was not a holiday. A schooner from New Orleans was scheduled for an early docking, and he wanted to be on hand to check its manifest, to speak with its captain. Still, he did not go in. The stars, huge and discrete, hovered close, and an aureole rimmed the moon with a hazy circlet of golden light. The door behind him opened and closed.

Emma Coen stood beside him, the soft blue shawl draped about her shoulders, her eyes lifted to the wondrous night sky. He moved toward her, grasped her shoulders, and kissed her. Her hands reached up to touch his face; her fingers fluttered like butterflies across his cheeks, tremblingly traced the curve of his mustache. He held her closer, murmured her name, and then suddenly, she slipped out of his embrace. The door slammed behind her, and he stood with his arms still outstretched and watched the cypress tree's feathery crown rustle against the impact of the newly forceful wind.

Emma lay awake that night breathless and trembling, like a fugitive who has narrowly escaped entrapment. She had been dangerously close to submission. How deceptively simple it had been, during those magical starlit moments on the porch, to forget the lesson she had learned so painfully that distant afternoon in Amsterdam. In the darkness, she saw again her mother's lifeless body and remembered Analiese Deken's monitory words. She would not allow herself to be as passive as Leonie, as vulnerable as Analiese, as naive as the girl she had been when Benjamin Mendoza whispered lying endearments and pressed his body against her own. Always, she vowed anew, she would retain control over her own life. She would resist the magnetic sway of Isaac Lewin, whose blue-black hair shimmered in the darkness. She could not, she would not, risk another betrayal, another loss.

Down the hall, in his own small room, Isaac stretched out on his bed and smiled into the darkness. Abner Wallach had been right. Slowly, imperceptibly, remembered miseries were assimilated, and it became possible to smile again, to laugh, to thrill to the touch of a woman's hand in his own. How beautiful Emma was, how sweet her laughter as he whirled her across the green. Gaiety had sparkled in her eyes as they danced, and later, as they stood together on the porch, he had sensed a yearning that matched his own. Magic had trailed them that starlit night, and music and laughter had surrounded them. He looked at his watch and counted the hours that must pass before he would see her again at the dinner table. He fell asleep at last, still smiling, bemused that happiness had come to him again.

He was disappointed the next night when Emma did not come down to dinner. He had thought to walk to the beach with her, to show her the cove where sea oats and Spanish daggers grew in wild profusion. He would speak softly to her and calm the fear and uncertainty that had caused her to flee the previous evening. She was young, inexperienced, in need of reassurance. But Chana Freundlich explained that

Indian Mary had fallen ill and Emma had taken her to her family's hogan in Maison Rouge.

The following afternoon he bought a nosegay of verbena and primroses from the cross-eyed Irish flower girl who haunted the docks. Emma was on the porch when he reached the house, and he offered them to her, bowing low from the waist, imitating his own gestures at the Juneteenth dance, as though to invoke the mood of that evening. She stared at him coldly and did not extend her hand to accept his gift.

"I thought you would like these," he said awkwardly.

"Did you? What do you know of my likes and dislikes?"

He flinched at the coarseness of her words, the harshness of her tone.

"If you give them to Basha Weinglass, she will put them in water. She's in the kitchen," Emma added indifferently.

He did not reply but placed the fragrant bouquet on the porch railing and went inside, fury glazing his eyes, curling his lips.

She did not turn, but her heart sank when he slammed the door behind him, and she tied her handkerchief into angry little knots. Late that night, she stole into the kitchen and plucked a sprig of verbena from the gay bouquet. She tucked it beneath her pillow, and its teasing fragrance wafted its way through her brief and turbulent dreams.

Isaac left the boarding house after dinner. He paced the beach, pausing now and again to hurl a polished rock, a length of driftwood, into the roaring surf. His own naiveté angered him. She had toyed with him for a single evening, and he had allowed himself to dream of a new life. He stretched out at last on the clammy cold sand, exhausted by his own exertions, the darkness of his disappointment.

"Bitch," he thought. "Bitch!" His fingers clenched and unclenched about a fragile shell until it snapped in half in his palm.

He had never used such an epithet before, and its utterance startled and frightened him. He shifted position and listened to the mating shrieks of the herons, the soft nocturnal cooing of the mourning doves.

* * *

Miriam Weinglass sang softly to herself as she sat on the porch that first Friday in September. Carefully, she placed the Indian doll on the small table and surrounded it with her collection of clothespin dolls. Emma Coen had given her the wooden pegs and taught her to fashion minuscule dresses out of scraps of fabric and bits of ribbon. It had been Natalya's idea to paint the faces, and Abner Wallach had carefully cut up bits of antelope pelt, which served as hairpieces.

The boarders had a special affection for small Miriam, the only child in a household of transient adults. She restored to them a sense of normalcy, of established domesticity. She reminded Natalya Ackerman of her brother's daughter in New York, of her sister's dark-haired twins in Chicago, and the schoolteacher told Miriam the stories she would never share with her distant nieces. She was the younger sister Abner Wallach had kissed goodbye in a Bucharest doorway. His mother had gripped his shoulders in a farewell embrace, but she had been dry-eyed, firm featured. "Of course, you must go," she had said. "There is no future for you here." But Abner's little sister had clung to him and wept, the moisture of her tears dampening his shirt front. Once, Miriam, hobbling down the stairs, had slipped and scraped her knee. She had wept, and Abner, lifting her, pressed her head against his chest, felt the heat of her tears, and saw himself again on that narrow street in the Bucharest ghetto, holding his sister in his arms.

To Chana and Moshe Freundlich, she was the small daughter who had died only four days after their arrival in America. Like many immigrant children, she had developed dysentery during the Atlantic crossing.

"It is no mystery that she died," Chana Freundlich said bitterly. "The miracle is that *we* survived."

The boarders did not disagree. They remembered the steerage crossing, when they had traveled below deck, packed so closely that there was no space between their bunks, the women and children separated from the men. They had eaten the greasy food in dishes that were washed in water on which slime floated in dark pads; they had endured the stench of vomit and excrement, of their own unwashed bodies. It

seemed to them that even their fear and loneliness had ex-
uded a sour, putrescent odor.

Chana Freundlich could not forget that while her child lay
ill she had been obsessed with worry over whether the illness
would prevent the family's entry into America. She had
pinched the sick girl's cheeks to give them color, and when
the ship rolled into Galveston harbor, she had combed her
hair carefully, covering the little frock she wore with layers
of petticoats to disguise her gauntness. Miraculously, they
had passed through immigration, but within the week the
child was dead. Chana Freundlich was certain that the death
was a punishment from God, Who had read her selfish
thoughts, her misplaced anxiety.

"*Sha,*" her husband whispered to her comfortingly in the
darkness. "How could it be your fault? We will have other
children. We will have a house. Our American children will
grow up in sunlight and freedom." He had saved enough for
a down payment on a grocery store. The American dream
was within their grasp.

But meanwhile they had Miriam Weinglass—Miriam who
seemed to understand their sadness and their need, who allowed Chana Freundlich to braid her hair and Moshe to take
her for walks, matching his steps to her limping slowness.
The Freundlichs bought her a bag of sweets each Friday, and
Chana saved the leg of the chicken and roasted it for the child
in a honeyed sauce. The small girl who had died in her arms,
her lost daughter, had relished that Sabbath delicacy.

Miriam basked in the warmth of their affection. Her limp
limited her activity with the other children who lived on M
Street. She could not jump rope or play ball, although they
sometimes allowed her to keep score. All that summer she
had stared longingly after them as they walked in groups to
the piers and the beach. She waved and they waved back.

"Hi, Miriam."

"Ain't it hot, Miriam?"

That very morning they had called to her on their way to
the school where they would rehearse for the opening-day
ceremony. Miriam had wanted to join them, but Basha, her
mother, had adamantly refused.

"Look—already a wind is blowing and the sea is dark. There

might be a storm and you have a cold. Today, stay home. Miss Coen expects two new boarders—'passers-through.' ''

Miriam liked the itinerant boarders who told her stories, taught her limericks. They reached into their packs for secret treasures, spools of gem-colored threads, gilt barrettes, candies wrapped in paper that crinkled at her touch. The ''rolling storekeepers,'' peddlers who had managed to buy a surrey or a buckboard, always remembered to bring her a book or a puzzle. They were lonely men who traveled across the plains, made their way across the desert. Often their own children were in distant cities or even in Europe, awaiting the arrival of a steamship ticket. They spoke to Miriam in Yiddish, their eyes misty.

The boarders and Emma Coen were Miriam's friends and companions. Emma Coen taught her to weave flowers into intricate patterns and showed her how to arrange them in tall vases and deep bowls. Isaac Lewin played checkers with her and held her on his lap when he played chess with Abner Wallach or Hyman Greenstein.

''Teach me to play chess,'' Miriam pleaded.

''Next year,'' he promised. ''You're too young.''

He closed his eyes, remembering that he had tried to teach small Sarah the opening moves and had grown angry when the child could not grasp them. ''You ask too much of her,'' Rivka had scolded. ''You ask too much of both of us.'' She had been right, he knew now. He had asked them to wait until his thesis was completed, although their wiser neighbors were selling off their possessions and their businesses and leaving the town. Those small businesses had brought them steamship tickets, survival; his scholarship had earned his wife and daughter despair and death.

Miriam played with the chess pieces, told herself stories about the horse and the king and the queen. Sometimes she set the pawns up in orderly procession, white alternating with black, and marched them about the table. Across the room Emma watched her and smiled. Isaac Lewin might lift a bishop and cause it to strut. But if his eyes met those of Emma Coen, he put the chess piece down and turned to his newspaper.

''Don't Miss Coen and Mr. Lewin like each other?'' Miriam had asked her mother. Their long silences that summer had confused her. She remembered, still, how beautifully they had danced together during the Juneteenth celebration.

"A foolish question," Basha had scolded. "They like each other, but they are very different. Miss Coen is a lady—a Sephardiah. Even her prayerbook is not the same as ours. And Mr. Lewin is one of us—very educated, it is true, but still he is a *shtetl Yid,* and our customs are different from hers. Understand something, my Miriam—oil and water don't mix. They never have and they never will."

What did oil and water have to do with it? Miriam wondered. She turned to Indian Mary.

"Do you think Mr. Lewin and Miss Coen like each other, Mary?"

The Indian girl laughed and fingered her beaded bracelets. "They like each other too much, I think. Like the doe and the stag who hide from each other in the chaparral." She briskly flipped a thin mattress. "Like the doe and the stag," she repeated and moved on to the next room, chanting softly in the language of her people, the secret knowledge of the native American glinting in her gold-flecked eyes.

"You are still playing with your dolls, Miriam?" Mary asked now as she stood framed in the doorway.

Miriam nodded and looked up. Mary wore her best blue dress and a brightly woven rebozo. Her black hair was freshly oiled and plaited into thick, glistening braids, tied at the ends with turquoise-studded bands of leather. She carried a leather pouch that bulged with a length of scarlet satin, which she had bought for a good price from a peddler.

"Are you going away, Mary?" Miriam asked.

"Yes. My brother came this morning. My father wants me to come home to Maison Rouge. He read the stars last night and he saw danger coming to the city. I will go with my brother until my father is comforted. He is an old man, ill and full of fears."

"Do you know how to read the stars, Mary?"

The Indian girl did not answer. Her eyes were lifted to the sky, which had grown imperceptibly darker. She pulled her rebozo closer as though anticipating a sudden chill.

Miriam studied one of her clothespin dolls. She had

dressed it in a scrap of silver cloth and set it on a sliver of blue-painted bark.

"Do you like her? She's my mermaid. But I need seaweed for her hair."

"Green hair?" The Indian girl smiled.

"Mermaids have green hair," Miriam explained patiently. "They need it so that they blend with the sea."

"The sea today is very dark, I think."

"Still, I want green hair. I'll go down to the shore and get some."

"You must ask your mother," Mary said.

"She's not home. She's working today at the dry goods store. No one's home. Besides, she won't care. It's cool, and they only worry when it's hot and there are so many mosquitoes and they're afraid I'll go into the water." Carefully, Miriam put her dolls in their cardboard box, which Mary placed on the high shelf Isaac Lewin had built that summer.

"Have a good time at Maison Rouge, Mary," Miriam said.

One day, she hoped, Mary would take her to her family's hogan near the inlet where Jean Lafitte, the notorious buccaneer, had built the fortress, dominated by the legendary red house, from which he had ruled Galveston Island for four terrible years. Mary's family lived there peacefully now, but the elders of the tribe had told her the stories of the battles between Lafitte's pirates and the Karankawa Indians. The Indian girl had told the tales to Miriam, who trailed behind her as she did her daily chores. Graphically, she had described the kidnapping of a squaw by Lafitte, the tribe's retaliatory raid, and the bloody battle at the place called Three Trees. There was pride in her voice as she spoke, and Miriam listened with wonder in her eyes. Her classmates told her that the Karankawas had been cannibals, but Miriam did not believe them. Mary was good and kind, and she went to mass each Sunday morning at Saint Mary's Cathedral.

Mary watched Miriam as she limped to the corner. Again, she looked up to the sky and held her hand out, as though to test the air for heaviness. She sighed, straightened a porch chair, and walked swiftly and soundlessly to the plaza where her brother waited for her.

* * *

Emma Coen moved through the market square, completing her Friday morning purchases more swiftly than usual. The sky was slowly darkening, and she worried that she had not closed the front windows.

"Such a swift change in the weather, Emma." Rabbi Henry Cohen, his own market basket overflowing with vegetables for the huge Sabbath lunch he and his wife hosted, smiled at her and doffed his Stetson.

"Another storm, I suppose," Emma said, looking at the darkening sky with only mild concern. "Let's hope it will be swift."

She had experienced three northers since her arrival in Galveston, and she was somewhat shamed that the violent storms filled her with excitement and awe. There was mystery in the roaring wind, challenge in the silver swirls of rain. The houses of Galveston, astride their stilts, trembled, and children gathered on the high steps, which were unconnected to the houses. The children leaped from their porches to the serried parapets of safety and called gaily to each other, their high-pitched laughter masking their fear. Emma understood the children's excitement, their daring glee. They were small heroes as they balanced themselves with curious grace on the dangerous precipices; they challenged the elements and braved nature's inexplicable fury.

She herself had been caught outside during the last storm. She had dashed home, her face lifted to the stinging shafts of water, her body thrust against the powerful breath of the storm. Exhilarated, she had jumped over fallen branches, danced her way across storm-vanquished flower beds, even stooping to gather a soaking cluster of oleander blossoms. It was the risk that invigorated her, she knew. She welcomed the test of her own strength and daring. Just as she had crossed an ocean alone and launched the boarding house, so she braved the storm. The raging wind was a hymn to her hard-won independence, and her laughter vied with its roar. When she arrived home, her clothing had been drenched and the chill seemed to have penetrated the very marrow of her bones, but still she had felt herself quiveringly alive, fiercely and unashamedly proud.

"I don't think this one will be swift," the little rabbi said, worriedly studying the sky. "It isn't like an ordinary norther. The wind is still mild and there are no clouds, no chill. But the sun set so strangely last night."

"Yes. I remember."

She had stood on the porch and watched the sun plunge into the bay with the suddenness of a fireball. Isaac Lewin strode up the street, his face bathed in that strange fiery glow of lambent light. Quite suddenly, he stood beside her.

"The lamps will have to be lit early tonight," he said in that strained, cautious tone in which he had spoken to her since the night of the Juneteenth dance.

"Yes. I'll tell Mary." Her own tone had been equally guarded.

They stood together for a moment, awaiting the onset of darkness, and then abruptly he turned and went inside. She had not entered the house until she heard his step upon the stairwell.

"And this morning I watched the sun rise," the rabbi continued. "A pale sunrise for the Gulf of Mexico in early September." He had been haunted that morning by the thought of the sun as it fought its way free of the mists, only to remain a penumbral orb hovering over the dark seawater.

"Mary, the Karankawa girl who works at the boarding house, left for home today. Her father sent for her," Emma said. "He did not like the stars last night."

The rabbi smiled. "Ah, yes. I have always said that we Jews and the Indians have much in common. We worship a God Who has made peace in the firmament, as they do. 'Our God has many stars,' the Karankawas say. We both hold worship services at the seasons of harvest. They too bless the new moon and study the message of the rising sun."

"Does today's pale sunlight send us a message?" Emma asked.

"You know, Emma, I had a pulpit in the Caribbean—in Kingston, Jamaica. I saw such a spectral sunrise there only once, on the day that a tropical cyclone hit the island. It was a small cyclone, the natives said, but it uprooted our little synagogue from its foundations. It began very quietly." He was silent, as though waiting for something to happen. "Listen, Emma."

She stood very still and heard the wind gather momentum now, and then the soft musical patter of raindrops falling on the canopies of the market stalls.

"It is beginning," she said.

The rain hit the tin roofs of the market stalls with staccato taps, and even as they stood, its tempo increased subtly. The downpour reverberated like ominous drum beats, and the vendors hurriedly gathered up their merchandise and scattered, running across the plaza and shouting to each other above the tympanic cacophony of the storm. Bushel baskets were lightly lifted by the newly swirling wind, their contents tossed across the cobblestoned paving. Sun-colored lemons, bright oranges, bolts of gaily patterned cloth rolled about beneath their feet. A palpable fear swept through the crowd. Women clutched their children's hands, held their babies high on their shoulders.

"I only came out to buy a lettuce," a young mother repeated again and again, as though apologizing to the frightened infant she carried in her arms. She looked wildly about as though uncertain which direction to take.

"You must go to the buildings on Broadway," Rabbi Cohen shouted. "The high buildings. Emma, show them which way they must go."

"This way. This way!" She forced her voice to rise above the chaotic raucousness. She motioned with her arms, and they followed after her, women screaming, children crying, men cursing and impotently shaking their fists at the sky.

"I'm going to Rosenberg and to Lasker," the rabbi called after her. He struggled to keep his balance against the wind. "Their carrier wagons are the largest, the heaviest. We must evacuate the people who live closest to the sea." He disappeared then, hurrying toward the Strand through the sheets of blinding rain, and she turned in the opposite direction.

"Follow after me," Emma shouted. Her voice rang with authority, and the crowd trailed after her, waiting as she stopped before each house that had not been built on stilts or did not extend beyond a first floor. Imperiously, she knocked at doors, urged frightened women and children to wrap themselves in tarpaulins and follow her.

"I must stay here," a young pregnant woman protested. "I will be all right."

A gleaming piano stood in her small living room. She had been playing it when Emma knocked. The sound of the slow concerto defied the rapid beat of the rain, the insistent rush of the wind.

"You must come with me," Emma insisted. The house had not even been built on stilts, and it had no separate high steps on which she might seek refuge.

"But the piano." The woman's voice was plaintive.

"Never mind the piano!"

Still, Emma waited while the woman closed the keyboard and draped a blanket over the instrument. In the street, she bent her head and went forward. Wagons clambered by, the rain flashing through the spokes of the great wooden wheels in whirling spangles of spray. Many headed toward the small bridge that connected Galveston to the mainland. Briefly Emma wondered whether she should counsel her cortege to go in that direction, but she rejected the idea. The bridge would be too vulnerable to the storm, and it was dominated by a railroad track, with narrow roadways on either side. She would not trust it under the impact of so many frightened people.

At one house, she ripped a white cloth off the table and draped it over a broomstick. She held it aloft as she led the crowd, so that they would not lose sight of her in the darkness. At last they reached the great Victorian mansions in the heart of the town. She stopped at the Trube house and pounded on the thick oak door. Patrician Mrs. Trube opened the door and stared out at Emma.

"Mrs. Trube, we're afraid the water is going to rise. Can you shelter some of the women and children on your top floor and in your attic?"

The Trube mansion was renowned for its beautiful Oriental carpets, its crystal chandeliers and inlaid tables. The mistress of the house was known to be scrupulous in her invitation lists and solicitous of her possessions. But without hesitation, she flung the doors of her home wide open. The storm had shattered all protocols, all barriers. There were no blacks and whites, no Gentiles and Jews in Galveston that day. There were only human beings confronting the violence of nature and offering each other comfort and refuge. A black woman held a small blond girl in her arms and spoke to her softly.

"Soon you'll be dry, my darlin'. Soon we gonna be out of this bad ole rain."

A Karankawa Indian boy clung to the skirts of rotund Mrs. Levi, who ran the trimmings store. She reassured him in English laced with Yiddish, reached into the pocket of her voluminous skirt, and found a sucking candy for him.

Emma counted heads and allowed fifty of her followers to troop into the mansion. Then holding her banner aloft, the drenched linen dragging at her arm, the rain blinding her, she trudged on.

The gate to the Landes mansion was already open, and a team of men were nailing boards across the front windows to prevent the glass from shattering, and piling sand bags against the front porch. What was happening to her own house? Emma wondered. Had the boarders known what to do? None of them had ever experienced such a storm before, but surely Isaac Lewin would organize them. The thought of Isaac moving through her house, struggling to protect it, was oddly reassuring.

"We'll take the smallest children and their mothers," aristocratic Mrs. Landes said. She directed them to the upper stories.

"Go as high as the attic," she called above the sounds of their weeping and their bewildered questions.

"Mama, Mama, where's Papa? Is Papa safe?"

"What will happen to our house?"

"Will the rain ever stop?"

Some shouted above the sounds of the intensified downpour. Sheets of silver rain fell relentlessly from the slate-blue sky. The wind gathered momentum, whipping the cypress trees, shattering the fronds of the palmettos. The thick leaves of the oleander bushes were sodden sponges glinting with oily malevolence. The rain flowed through the streets in rivulets, accumulated in small pools. Emma's high-buttoned boots were soaked through, the wet leather cutting into her flesh. At the Gresham house she unlaced them and then tucked the muddy edges of her skirts up, securing them with her hatpins

Mr. Gresham stood on his balcony and directed the remaining wanderers into the house. Emma looked up at the wrought-iron banister and remembered how she and Isaac Lewin had watched a young girl and her lover lean against it. Now the rain cascaded over the balustrade and the black barrier gleamed wetly, as though it were newly soldered. The French door shattered as the wind briefly changed direction, and glass flew through the air and fell in slivers onto the muddied earth.

Emma rushed to the synagogue. Natalya Ackerman and Mrs. Cohen, the rabbi's wife, were in the communal kitchen filling cartons with food that had been prepared for a bar mitzvah the next day. Emma marveled that they had thought of the food, but then they were Jewish women who had been educated to cope with disaster, to confront calamity with organized practicality.

"Emma—you're safe." Natalya embraced her.

"I was worried about the children."

"They're at the Rosenberg house. On the third floor. The children from Saint Joseph's Church are there too. We're lucky that most of them were together, rehearsing for the opening-day ceremony at the school." Natalya went back to work. Her dark hair hung damply about her face and she brushed it back impatiently.

"Was Miriam with them?" Emma asked.

Miriam had wanted to go to the opening-day rehearsal, but Basha had been reluctant. The child had coughed in the night, and the impending storm worried her. When Emma left for the marketplace, Miriam was still arguing with her mother.

"I didn't see her," Natalya replied. "But surely she never would have left the house, so she's safe. But have you seen Abner Wallach?"

"Yes. He was helping to put slats across the windows at the hospital. And he asked me if I had seen you," Emma recalled. Natalya smiled.

"I'm sure Miriam is fine, Emma," she said again.

"Probably." But still, doubt taunted her. She shivered in her wet garments, twisted her hair into a single coil, and pinned it back. She was startled to discover that her hands were shaking. "I'm going back to the house to check."

"Emma, no. It's blocks away, and the wind keeps growing stronger," Natalya protested. "Don't go. Stop her, Mrs. Cohen."

"Emma, believe me, it's too dangerous." The rabbi's wife's voice was laced with knowledge, authority. She had endured a tropical cyclone in Kingston, and she recognized this storm that had come upon them on the eve of the Sabbath and caught them unaware and unprepared. It would grow worse before it diminished, she knew. The waves of the sea would soar to mountainous heights, and the streets of Galveston would turn into rivers on which the smaller houses would float like fragile boats, inadequate vessels built for calmer waters. In Kingston their synagogue had been carried away into the ocean, and an entire family had vanished forever, swept from their sugar cane fields into the raging waters. A Jewish family from Antwerp. Her husband had said Kaddish for them, tears streaming down his cheeks, and she had never known whether he wept for them or for the inexplicable natural cruelty that had claimed their lives.

"I must go," Emma said.

She raced out, and they watched from the window, saw her fall almost to her knees. She wore the white tablecloth as a shawl about her shoulders. It would provide her with some visibility against the unnatural darkness. She braced herself and pressed forward. The storm was an adversary, an enemy that pursued her, threatening physical assault, personal violation. The wind tore at her clothing, ravaged her energy. Still, she struggled on. The two women watched her from the window. Mrs. Cohen, whose father had been a Hasidic rabbi, suddenly remembered a tale he had told, of flames that had burned steadily through a fierce rainstorm, leaving at last damp embers that retained their fiery glow. Surely the remnants of that tenacious fire must have been the color of Emma Coen's hair as she plunged into the heart of the storm.

* * *

Isaac Lewin was at his desk when the rain began. He looked through his window onto the Strand and then across to the docks. The sky had turned a menacing dark blue, and the stevedores glanced warily northward as they heaved the bales and barrels from the two newly docked tall ships. Aboard the craft, sailors scurried about the decks, battening down hatches, lashing lifeboats with coils of rope, carrying what they could below deck.

Norris Wright Cuney, the head of the Negro Longshoreman's Union, burst into Isaac's office. He was a tall, powerful man who moved vigorously despite his age. Both blacks and whites deferred to his opinions. He and Isaac had had some dealings together, and they liked and respected each other. He wiped the rain from his face with a large handkerchief.

"I think we ought to stow whatever's on the docks into the warehouses, Lewin," he said. "The sea is rising, and the wind ain't going to get any gentler. We don't want to risk the merchandise, and we sure as hell don't want to risk the men."

"You're right," Isaac said. He stared at the heavy British steamship in the harbor and saw that sailors in rubber rainwear were lowering the Union Jack. Seamen read the waters and the wind with instinctive accuracy. "Let's close down."

"I'm going to advise my people to try and get themselves and their families to the mainland now, while they can. That damn bridge may not be any good much longer, and by nightfall no ferry will be able to set sail. Now there's still a chance." Norris Cuney buckled his yellow raincoat.

"Wait, Norris, I'll come with you."

Hurriedly, Isaac locked the safe and carried the account books to the upper floor and placed them on the highest shelf. It occurred to him, with bitter amusement, that he had automatically thought of securing the firm's treasures. It was his own wife and child whom he had not sequestered, whose lives he had not secured.

"The ferries will have to carry as many passengers as possible. And someone will have to police the traffic across the bridge. We don't want a panic." He shouted above the crescendo of the storm.

"The ferries will make as many crossings as they can. But I'm worried that the bridge might collapse."

"We have to organize people to leave their homes and go to the higher buildings."

"Our higher buildings don't stand too high," Norris Cuney retorted. He had argued in town meetings for higher buildings, for a sea wall, but always he had been voted down. Galveston had always weathered its storms, his opponents claimed. It would survive in the future as well. The Negro crossed himself and hoped that they were right. "Anyway, your friend Miss Coen is doing just that in the town. Gettin' people out of their houses into safer buildings."

"Emma Coen?" Isaac asked.

"Yes. I saw you dancin' with her at the Juneteenth celebration."

Norris Cuney had been pleased to see Isaac Lewin waltz across the green with the beautiful auburn-haired Dutchwoman. It was not good for a man to be alone, without a woman at his side. And Isaac Lewin was too often alone, solitude and sadness etched across his face, liquid in his eyes. The black man had noticed that Isaac and Emma had danced with ease and grace. A good-looking couple, he had thought, she in her dress of bridal white and the mustachioed Russian Jew so lean and muscular, his thick dark hair brushed back but still an unruly mass of curls.

"I live in her boarding house," Isaac said shortly.

"I thought you might be friends. You're alike."

"Alike?"

"She's a take-charge person, your Miss Coen. She had people following after her from house to house, listening to her."

Isaac was relieved that the noise of the storm obviated the need for a reply. At the dock, the two men separated. Norris Cuney organized the storing of the cargo in the warehouses that bordered the port and the Strand. Shipments of produce would have to wait.

"Stow the furs and skins on the top lofts!" he shouted. The most valuable cargo would be given priority.

Isaac stood at the embarkation pier, organizing the ferry evacuation, cautioning those who went by foot on the bridge to walk single-file so that too much pressure would not be placed on the wobbly structure. It was clear that there would not be enough boats to carry all those who waited to the mainland.

"Room for two more."

"We can squeeze in a couple of kids."

Isaac assessed the crowd, matched passengers to boats, and watched the valiant little flotilla set sail for the mainland. A small girl waved to him and held her Indian doll up. *Miriam.* His heart contracted suddenly. Where was Miriam? Her parents were away, he knew. Basha worked at the dry goods store on Fridays, and if Emma was in town, then Miriam was alone. Would she have the sense to climb up to the attic? He organized the sailing of the last small craft and found Norris Cuney.

"I've done all I can here," he said. "I'm heading for Miss Coen's boarding house to check on things there."

The black man nodded. "The wind's building up to gale force," he said. "It's time for everyone to be heading in. Men!" He raised his voice with the same ringing authority that had caused the strikers to set aside their fury and listen to him during the famous confrontations. "We all got to find shelter now. Head for the high places, as high as you can get. We got to outfox this storm." Even as he spoke, the surf pounded in ferocious cacophony.

The men on the dock turned as one and looked out at the sea. The waves leaped higher now, and the frothy spray danced wildly to meet the steady rain. A bolt of lightning split the sky in two, shearing it with treacherous radiance, electrifying the darkened waters with shards of kinetic light. Gulls shrieked wildly, their primeval fear shrill and piercing. Three pelicans stood on the pier, bewildered by the wind and rain that threatened their peaceful habitat. They arched their rain-weighted wings awkwardly, and their wails of fear were frighteningly human. The men fled then and ran toward the city, to the shelter of houses that trembled on uneasy stilts and quivered in the wind, lit by candles that flickered tremulously in the unnatural darkness.

* * *

Isaac ran the distance to Emma Coen's house, pitting himself against the columns of rain and the wind, which in its increased strength had assumed an almost corporeal power. Panting with exhaustion, he reached the wide-porched house at last and saw with relief that a lamp burned on the second floor and a small light glowed in the attic window. Someone was there, then. Miriam was safe, and in all probability Emma Coen was with her. He hurried up the steps, wading across the flooded porch. The wicker chairs on which they had sat through long, peaceful evenings as they looked up at the huge stars were afloat. Someone had left a book on the table, a copy of Walt Whitman's poems, and although its pages were sodden, Isaac plucked it up and placed it on the high shelf. Startled, he saw the shoe box that contained Miriam's clothespin dolls and the Indian doll that he had bought for her. He frowned. Why hadn't the child taken her precious playthings inside with her? He thrust open the door.

"Miriam!"

His voice echoed through the house, but there was no answer. He bounded up the stairs. Hyman Greenstein met him on the landing, worry lines streaking his forehead.

"Miriam isn't here, Isaac. I thought she was at the school with the other children."

"I don't think so. Basha didn't want her to go to school today." He sank down on the steps, overcome suddenly by his exertions, and wiped his face dry with the kerchief Hyman handed him. "But is there someone in the attic? I saw the light on there."

"Indian Mary and her brother. The storm caught them before they could reach the road to Maison Rouge."

"Mary!" Isaac shouted.

The Indian girl and her younger brother came to the top of the stairs. They stared down at Isaac; their almond-shaped eyes, deeply set above their high-planed cheekbones, glittered with worry. They had seen other storms whip across their island during the treacherous equinoctial season. They had watched trees snap like matchsticks and irrigation canals flood over with water and silt. They knew that sand reefs had been hurled across the beach and that tents of meeting had become the wind's playthings, to be tossed about in a wild turbulence. Their father and their grandfather had told them of storms that uprooted citrus groves and of the storm that had carried strong men out to sea, less than three decades past. The white men did not understand the storm's fury.

Divine rage bellowed in the awesome wind; the unrelenting rain expressed a primordial and unrestrained sorrow. The new settlers, the white men and the black, had played havoc with the landscape that belonged to the gods. They had carried great boulders from the granite hills of Texas and built a jetty into the peaceful waters of the Gulf of Mexico. They had carved roads through the wilderness, felled trees that had endured through the generations. Now the anger of the gods would destroy all of them. Indian Mary touched her cross and prayed soundlessly to the ancient deities of her people. She thought of her father, an old man, whose death had already formed in his stomach. He was in pain, alone in his hogan; the storm kept his children prisoner in the white man's city.

"Mary, have you seen Miriam?" Isaac Lewin's tone was harsh, anxious.

"Much earlier. She played with her dolls. She wanted to gather some seaweed, and she walked to the beach. But that was before the storm. I would not have let her go if the rain had been falling. Surely she came back and found shelter somewhere. I am sure she returned."

The Indian girl began to cry. She loved the small white girl who dragged her poor leg behind her like a wounded animal. She should have cautioned Miriam against going toward the sea, but the child had been so determined and she had so little freedom. The Karankawas, who prized their hard-won liberty, had been taught not to interfere with the freedom of others. Karankawa children roamed the beaches and the groves of Galveston without restraint. Nature was their automatic monitor. But she should have realized that Miriam was not like the wing-footed children of her tribe. She would never forgive herself. She clenched her fingers and pressed her fists to her eyes so that the white men would not see her weep.

"I'm going to the sea," Isaac said grimly.

"Isaac, if she went down before the storm and hasn't come

back yet . . .'' Hyman Greenstein's voice faltered. He did not want to articulate the thought that weighted his heart.

"She may have fallen."

Isaac imagined the crippled child lying helpless on the beach. Perhaps she had stumbled as she walked across the sand or climbed a sand bar. He had to reach her before the tide rose, the terrible tide that would transform the sea into a violent aquatic monster assaulting beach and overgrowth.

"I'll go with you." Hyman Greenstein reached for his rain gear.

"No. You stay here. People may come seeking refuge. Take them up to the attic. And put these up there on the highest shelf." He wrapped Emma Coen's silver candlesticks in the white cloth she used to cover the Sabbath loaves. "Try to brace the front windows with wood and carry as much food and water as you can manage to the upper floors."

He ran out, slamming the door behind him. The wind had intensified, and he knew that within a short time it would reach gale force. No more ferries would leave Galveston Island for the mainland, and the fragile bridge would support no more refugees. Those who remained on the island were captives of the storm, isolated on this narrow strip of land, this "hand of Texas outstretched in greeting." He increased his pace and sped toward the beach, running as though he would outstrip the wind itself, his heart pounding. Small rasping sounds rose from his throat, and he realized that he was sobbing.

Emma Coen also felt the renewed strength of the wind as she reached the beach. Monumental waves sailed over the esplanades, rising above rock and reef, crashing against boulder and barrier. The rush of surf, when they broke at last, was thunderous. The spent waves churned shoreward with belligerent strength, claiming the white sands, shattering the ghostly dunes.

"Miriam!"

Emma pitted her voice against the sonority of the wind, the cacophony of the ocean.

"Emma!"

A voice answered her, came toward her, a human sound triumphing over roar of wind, crush of water.

"Over here."

She waved the white cloth, lifting the sodden fabric with difficulty, as though it were a banner of surrender. She heard the frailty of her own voice. She had been battling the storm for hours now, it seemed, and its strength had increased while her own had been dissipated. The pale, wet sand stretched before her like a counterpane across a bed. If she sank down upon it, she could rest, sleep. Perhaps, when she awakened, she would discover that the storm was a bad dream, that she had imagined the violent wind, the torrential rain. She would be home, and Miriam would knock shyly at her door and enter, carrying a tray with a cup of coffee, a freshly baked apple cake. Sweet little Miriam. The name jerked her back into reality.

"Miriam!"

Her shout was lost in the whirling breath of the wind, and she knew that she had dreamed no dream. The nightmare was real.

She struggled toward the sea and stumbled on something. She bent and picked up a shoe. It was a child's black boot, its heel built high, the leather muddied by sea water. Miriam's shoe. Emma sank to her knees and crept forward. Her searching fingers grasped a scrap of pink ribbon entangled with a length of seaweed. Tears seared her eyes. Miriam had been here. She had been caught and overpowered by the storm. Perhaps she was here still, lying helpless on the sand. She moved on, the white cloth shawling her shoulders. A hand covered her own. Isaac Lewin sank to his knees beside her. He had found her by following the white cloth as it moved through the darkness.

"I found Miriam's shoe, her ribbon. She was here. At this very spot."

"They could have been blown here by the wind."

"No, she was here. She must be nearby."

He did not argue with her but pulled her to her feet. Hand in hand they walked slowly toward the sea, but it was Emma who saw the small figure lying so still on the shoreline. She broke free of Isaac and rushed toward the fallen child.

Miriam's eyes were closed. Her pale face, so strangely peaceful, glistened wetly, and the salt of the sea jeweled her dark hair with sequined radiance. She was fine, Emma thought. She had fallen and had lost consciousness, but she would be all right. Relief flowed through her, banishing fatigue, filling her with new energy.

She brushed the child's forehead with her lips, but Isaac lowered his head to her heart, placed his hand upon the child's slender wrist.

"She's gone, Emma," he said. Grief deadened his voice.

He lifted the child, and although her clothing was sodden, she was still the lightest of burdens in his arms. He remembered the night of the Juneteenth celebration when she had slept against his shoulder and he had carried her home through the streets of Galveston, her breath sweet against his neck. Then, too, Emma Coen had walked beside him. "Pretty family," a *lavandera* had called after them, and then, for the briefest of moments, he had felt himself again part of a family, linked to the child and the woman who shared the mysterious spring night of freedom with him. No one called after them now. Only a gull shrilled mournfully from its sentinel post on the rock barrier. The great waves throbbed and broke, as though spilling forth an endless and terrible grief.

Emma trailed after him, swaying from side to side. She could not walk much farther, he knew. Desperately, he searched his mind for a possible nearby refuge and remembered the shorefront warehouse. Its loft was as high as any building in Galveston, and it was only yards away. He led Emma there, his hand linked to hers, as though she were blind and he were her sighted companion, her guide and her protector.

"Only a little farther." He urged her forward as once again they endured the wind and the rain.

They reached the warehouse at last. He paused at the small shed that stood beside it and gently placed Miriam's body inside. The dead child looked oddly peaceful. Gently, he removed a streamer of seaweed from her dark hair. When he touched her hand, he was startled to see that her fist was clenched. He pried the small, slowly rigidifying fingers loose and saw that a transluscent sea shell, striated with veins of violet, nestled in her palm. Its rim had cut an arc of blood into the child's tender flesh. He put it in his pocket and hurried out to Emma, who stood leaning against the warehouse. He guided her inside and up to the storage loft.

"I can't go any farther." Her words came in an exhausted gasp, and she sank to the floor, her eyes closed.

Her wet clothing clung to her body, and her face, framed against her hair, the color of mahogany now, was dangerously pale. Grief and exhaustion had robbed her of consciousness. He touched her wrist and recognized the weakness of the pulse. He had to get her warm and dry, he knew.

He took his knife and cut the wet clothing loose from her body. A pile of gunny sacks stood in a corner, and he used one to wipe her skin dry. Slowly, he passed it across her naked body. Her skin glowed lunar white in the darkness of the loft. Her long lashes spanned her cheeks, strands of spun copper thickened by rain and tears. He draped another sack over her and carried her to the pile of buffalo hides and pelts which he had caused to be stored there.

Only then did he remove his own drenched garments and rip apart another sack and cloak himself in it. Then he too stretched out on the high mattress of animal skins. Briefly, he lay there and listened to the roar of the wind, the terrible tympanic chorus of the unrelenting rain. Then his eyes closed and he slept.

The storm raged, the ocean roared, but he dreamed of a town at the edge of a forest, of a small shingle-roofed house and a sweet-singing woman.

"Rivka," he whispered and he moved in his sleep, his arm circling Emma Coen's bare shoulders, his eyes, unseeing, turned toward hers.

Emma wakened to a cannonade of thunder. A bolt of lightning streaked past the narrow dormer window of the loft and turned the sky a canescent silver. Her own nakedness startled her, and instinctively she pulled the gunny sack tighter, remembering the storm and Miriam's body sprawled across the surf. The rain had not abated, but above the roar of the wind she heard piercing screams, the shattering of glass and the sounds of crying children.

"What is it?" Isaac lay beside her, but his voice was muted by the turbulent clamor of the raging tempest.

"Something terrible is happening," she whispered.

They lay still, listening, as though hypnotized by the sounds of the storm. Suddenly, the pounding of the waves seemed so close that they might have been standing at the shore at riptide. Isaac rushed to the narrow window.

"My God." Awe and terror rimmed his voice. "The ocean is unleashed. It's a tidal wave, Emma."

She went to stand beside him and saw that the ocean had claimed their island for its own. Water rose almost to the window where they stood. They saw a child's bed bob up and down on the waves; ludicrously, a small doll perched on an embroidered pillow. Emma thought she saw small boats floating down the Strand, but she realized they were houses, small dwellings wrenched from their foundations. They had not been built on stilts and so had no resistance to the storm, no redress from the rising waters. There had been people in those houses, small children whose lungs had filled with water, whose bodies had been broken and shattered. Bloated corpses would float down streets become rivers, and parents would search for their children, brothers for their sisters.

"No!" she cried out. The images overwhelmed her with their terror, but the reality, she knew, would be beyond her imagining.

"I know." Isaac Lewin encircled her in a comforting embrace. Two lone survivors, they gazed out at the devastating destruction from the precarious parapet of their own fragile ark. The waters continued to rise, and he led her away so that she would not see how perilously close the ocean came to their window, so that the triumphant trumpet of the warring wind would be muted. Gently, he covered her with a buffalo hide and lay down beside her. The heavy fur was smooth as satin against their bodies and redolent with an odd, elemental scent. Yet still they shivered, and in the darkness she moved closer to him. They sought out the warmth of each other's flesh, the reassurance of warm breath and touch. His lips came down upon hers, and they felt the beating of each other's hearts, and clung closely, their limbs entwined, united against the threatening danger.

He rode her body, rising and falling, wave against shore, their tears mingling. She dug her fingers into his shoulders, claiming him as invader and defender at once, matching his rhythm to her own. They would not, could not, speak of it, yet it relieved them both that she had known love before. This was not a night for gentle initiation. Demons of memory and desire swirled as the winds raged and they clung together, united against the storm's mysterious fury.

They lay quietly at last, in their bower of fur. The storm did not abate, and throughout the long night, rain streaked the window, although mercifully the ocean no longer threatened. They understood, with their newfound calm, that the greatest danger had passed.

The tidal wave had subsided, had withdrawn to its oceanic depths. Her head rested on his shoulder. Her eyes were closed, yet he sensed her wakefulness and stroked her hair, sea-scented and storm-dampened. He kissed her forehead, then took her hand and pressed it against his lips as though he would have her fingers feel the words that he spoke in a soft yet strangely reverberant voice.

"Set me as a seal upon thy heart, as a seal upon thine arm. Love is strong as death. Many waters cannot quench love. Neither can the floods drown it."

"The Song of Songs," she said, her words a trembling whisper.

He held her closer.

"All in these few hours. We have known death and we have known love. We have had the many waters and the flood." Outside the rain continued to fall, steadily, rhythmically.

She shivered and stiffened in his arms.

"And have you set me as a seal upon your heart?"

He felt her tense against him, heard the ironic edge that rimmed her question.

"Why do you doubt me?" He searched her face; her eyes were closed, and she was very pale. "I have given you no cause for doubt."

She turned her head away. She did not want to tell him

that once before, in a room near the sea, she had looked through a rain-streaked window and listened to a man softly speak a verse from the Song of Songs.

At last she turned and looked at him in the milky half light. She saw the strong set of his jaw, the intense, velvet darkness of his eyes.

"You are right," she said. "You have given me no cause for doubt."

His arms tightened about her, and now she relaxed in his embrace. She had been wrong to compare him to Benjamin Mendoza, who had fled at the first sign of danger, of economic and familial hazard. There was no cowardice in Isaac Lewin, who had plunged through wind and rain to search out a child. The man who held her tight in his sinewy arms had thrust her from the dangers of the storm and carried her to the safety of this stark haven. And she was no longer the young girl who had watched the rain streak the windows of the seafarer's inn at Imjuden.

Isaac lifted a lock of her hair. They lay upon a pile of red fox pelts, and he marveled at how the fine silken furs matched the mahogany hue of her storm-darkened hair.

"I would understand," he said, speaking slowly, carefully, "if there are times when you find me distant. I carried many memories across the sea with me. I had a wife in Russia. Rivka. I had a child. Sarah." His voice broke when he spoke their names, and she put her fingers to his lips as though to silence him, to stop the words that caused him pain. Still, he continued, and she lay still and listened, her heart stirring with compassion, pierced with his pain.

In a strained voice, then, he spoke of Rivka and Sarah and of the sweetness of their lives in the cottage at the forest's edge.

"You loved them very much," Emma said. He heard the wistfulness in her voice and pressed her hand to his cheek.

"I did not love them wisely," he replied. "Others saw the dangers, the escalating anti-Semitism, the pogroms, and left. I studied Jewish history and I said, 'This too will pass.' I gambled with their lives, but it was they who paid the price."

Bitterness seared his words; a patina of grief glazed his dark eyes. He shivered, and she held him close.

"When I picked Miriam up today, it was as though I again held my daughter, Sarah, in my arms." His voice quivered and broke. Always, he knew, he would carry with him the shadowed memory of those small girls, of the terror and inequity of their deaths. "Miriam died because her parents did not have enough money to take her away from Galveston, to pay for the operation. Sarah and Rivka died because I didn't have enough money to get us out of Russia before it was too late. In my arrogance I thought historic perception outweighed reality, that a life of the intellect took precedence over money. It is a mistake I will never make again. Does that sound too harsh and calculating to you?"

"Not harsh. Not calculating. Only realistic. Wealth is irrelevant only to those whose futures are secure. Once I had that luxury, but it was lost." She closed her eyes and thought of herself as a young girl dashing through her father's emporium, plucking a cashmere scarf from a counter and playfully, teasingly, presenting it to her lover. The rich man's daughter, gay and careless.

"How? How was it lost?" he asked gently. He wanted to know her, to understand her. It was not sufficient that he loved her.

She told him then of her father, the man of wealth and passion, who had led two lives and ruined two families.

"What happened to Analiese and her sons?" Isaac asked.

"We don't know. My brothers heard that a Dutchwoman named Analiese had settled in the Arizona territory, but nothing came of their inquiries. I would guess that they have vanished from our lives." She felt again the vague sadness she experienced when she thought of the woman her father had loved, of the half brothers she would never know.

"So many people have vanished from our lives—yours and mine," he said, his voice so soft that she strained to hear him.

Tragedy had twinned them and fortune had coupled them. He kissed her, his lips barely brushing hers, his hands caressing the soft rise of her shoulder.

She turned to him and smiled because a shaft of milky light danced across his face, silvered his mustache. She was astonished anew that she had ever thought that he resembled

Benjamin Mendoza—posture and feature had deceived her, and fear had veiled her perception. Benjamin Mendoza belonged to another world. She had crossed an ocean and reached a new continent of frontiers where men and women forged their own fortunes, accepted challenge and risk. Isaac Lewin looked back at his past, plucked lessons from his pain, and planned his future.

"You will not mock me now if I tell you that I have set you as a seal upon my heart?" He posed the question with the certainty of one who knows the answer. He lifted her hair and allowed it to fall in radiant sheaves through his fingers.

"What are you saying, Isaac?"

"I am asking you to marry me."

Tears seared her eyes but did not fall. Sorrow and joy commingled. She struggled for words, and when she spoke her voice was barely a whisper.

"Because of all that has happened to me—"

She hesitated, and he rushed to block her silence.

"Emma, share with me only what you will." He would stake no claim to her vanished past, to the love that had preceded his own. It was not the daughter of the Amsterdam merchant he courted, but the fierce young woman who lay beside him on the pelt that matched her fiery hair.

"But it is of sharing I want to speak," she said, and the new firmness in her voice startled them both. "To me marriage would be sharing—in all things." Unbidden, Analiese's graveside admonition sprang to mind. *Marry . . . but decide on the patterns of your life together. Share the truth, the secrets of the night, the sweet trivia of the day.*

"I understand." His voice was grave. He would nurture her trust, soothe her sad unease. "We will build a life, a good life."

"Together." The word was at once assent and troth. He felt her lips soft against his arm. She too had set her seal, had made her pledge.

He pulled her toward him, rough suddenly, his fingers biting into her shoulders, his lips hard against hers. She clung to him, thrust for thrust, breath for breath—lovers and secret sharers, promised and betrothed, they came together again, while outside their refuge the spent wind whimpered and breathed its dying gusts.

Lazily, then, in the aftermath of the weathered storm, they spoke of the future, of their future. Circling gulls shrieked querulously in the new calm. Fire bells sounded clamorously. Voices drifted up to them, the shouts of men, the moans of women. The city was surveying its losses, monitoring its options. Grief quivered in the vagrant wind; the palmetto trees were bent low with sorrow.

"I do not want to stay in Galveston," Emma said. She understood suddenly why she had not added another wing to the boarding house. She had been summoning her strength, preparing to leave. Now they would leave together. She smiled in wonderment that she was no longer alone.

"Because of the storm?" he asked.

"Partly. But I think I always knew that I wanted to go farther west. When I was a girl in Amsterdam, I dreamed about the desert. My brother Simon had visited Arizona, and he told me about sands the color of amber and stretches of wilderness shadowed by mountains. He gave me a turquoise pendant." She smiled dreamily.

"I have seen it," Isaac said. "It matches your eyes." His finger rested on the high curve of her cheekbone and was brushed by her long copper-colored lashes.

"Yes. It matches my eyes." Benjamin Mendoza had held the pendant to the light and marveled at the match. But she could not tell Isaac Lewin that she and Benjamin had spoken of Arizona, that they had repeated aloud mysterious Indian names as they walked along the canals and paused on narrow bridges to watch pale, wintry sunsets.

"Arizona," Isaac repeated thoughtfully. "I have been thinking and reading about Arizona. It interests me because it is still a territory. Wild country. Desert and mountain. Settlers are drawn to it, despite the heat, the barrenness. There are riches beneath its earth which the miners already begin to claim. Copper and tin. Gold and silver. Men will pry wealth out of the land and look for ways to spend it. Their wives will want pretty dresses, nice furniture. Cities will rise on the sand, and eventually statehood will come."

She listened, her head resting on his shoulder. His words echoed her thoughts.

"And remember," she said, "the desert is a passage to California, and those who journey there need supplies, provisions."

"I have not forgotten. A good businessman could do well in the Arizona territory," he said.

"We will do well there," she replied.

He smiled at the certainty of her tone, at how swiftly she had translated speculation into decision. He took her hand in his, and they lay very still as the pale, fragile light of dawn drifted through the room. They were reluctant to stir, to shatter the new calm that suffused them. Their silence was an acknowledgment that they had reached an undefined border but that they would press on. The future trembled before them; their pasts would be reconciled. They watched as two mourning doves flew in tandem and briefly perched on the crown of the palmetto tree just beyond the warehouse window.

"An omen," he said.

"For good or for evil?"

He did not reply but held her close as though to shield her from the storm-shattered world beyond their fur-strewn bower.

They wanted to be married as quickly as possible, but they turned their attention to the needs of Galveston. Emma comforted the Weinglasses and made arrangements for small Miriam's burial. The pale pine coffin looked like a child's toy, and it was so light that Isaac carried it alone, as once he had carried the sweetly sleeping child.

The tidal wave had claimed six thousand lives, and there was no room on Galveston Island to bury the dead. In desperation, the corpses were loaded onto barges, which were carried out to sea. Within hours, the bodies were washed back to shore, bloated and stinking.

The American Red Cross sent a contingent of helpers, headed by Clara Barton. Emma walked down to the shore with the veteran nurse and listened as the older woman spoke of the Johnstown flood and the hurricane that had wrought devastation along the coast of South Carolina.

"Children were orphaned overnight—men and women widowed. Tragedy upon tragedy." The nurse spoke in a clipped tone. She had known war and disaster. The vagaries of nature, the aggressions of men, were beyond her control. The survivors worried her, absorbed her energies. She did not weep over the dead as she surveyed the water-logged bodies, picked up a single shoe and dropped it again. She brushed a clump of mud from the pocket of her white apron and held a handkerchief to her nose.

"The bodies must be burned," she said. "There will have to be mass cremations. Otherwise we will have disease, epidemics."

She met no arguments. Grief was a luxury the islanders could not afford. Isaac Lewin, who had helped to bury the dead of Kiev, now helped to burn the dead of Galveston.

Emma worked with Clara Barton's Red Cross team distributing food and clothing. She helped Natalya organize a school in the basement of the synagogue. Each evening she returned to the boarding house and looked despairingly at the wreckage of the storm. The tidal wave had battered her home. Only a few pieces of furniture were salvageable. She attempted to wring out her linens, but the seawater had been corrosive and discoloring, and there was no fresh water to wash out the silt that clung to every sheet and coverlet. All her savings had been invested in the house. She was, she realized, in exactly the same position she had been in when she had first arrived in England. Most of her painfully accrued savings were gone.

Isaac showed her his own bankbook. Less than a thousand dollars.

"Abner Wallach asked me to lend him two hundred dollars. He and Natalya want to marry and go to Colorado. He has a cousin in Cripple Creek," he said.

"What did you tell him?"

"I told him that I would speak with you—that we had agreed to decide such things together."

She smiled and he realized, with a slight stirring of anger, that he had passed a test of a kind.

"Of course, we must lend them the money," she said. Natalya's happiness thrilled her. The awkward young woman who had always thought of herself as plain was aglow with happiness and moved with a new grace, new assurance.

Emma found an unsoiled length of organdy and sewed her friend a bridal peignoir. She showed her handiwork to Clara Barton, who admired it and lifted the soft fabric wistfully to her weathered cheek.

"It is good to plan for the future," she said. The victims of Johnstown and Hatteras had recovered. The people of Galveston would also rebuild their island and their lives.

"But you too will soon be married. Why don't you make such a garment for yourself?" she asked Emma.

The auburn-haired young woman smiled sadly. Trousseaus were within the province of the innocent. Still, alone at night, she danced before the mirror in Natalya's peignoir, pleased at the glow of her skin against the sheer material. She wore it still when Isaac knocked at her door to say good night.

"How beautiful you are," he said, his voice husky, the fingers that touched her face trembling.

He worked now with the teams of assessors who estimated the damage done to the island. Twenty-six hundred structures had been totally destroyed. The remaining buildings had suffered structural damage from the wind and the sea. Most of the cargo stored in warehouses and lofts had been destroyed. The second floor of Emma's house was unusable and irreparable. The living room and dining room became sleeping areas, and they ate their meals in the kitchen. She worried over accounts but refused her brothers' offer of assistance. They were still struggling to establish their business.

"We will manage," she wrote to them. "We will manage," she said to Isaac.

"Yes."

Plans spun about in his head, and he juggled them— dropped one and plucked up another. He estimated the cost of the journey to Arizona and read through the catalogues of the Baltimore Bargain House and H.B. Claflin. It would take a fair investment to stock even a small store, and he wanted to avoid buying on credit and paying interest.

Late one afternoon he walked through the business district. Meyer Weissman, the gray-faced proprietor of what had been Galveston's leading dress shop, stood outside his establishment. His entire stock of velvet and brocaded dresses were piled beside him. The rich fabrics were faded and water-streaked. Isaac touched them, and the stench of their dankness clung to his fingers.

"What can I do with them, Lewin?" the shopkeeper asked. "They're worth thousands—they can be salvaged—but the shop is condemned. The flood damaged the roof. I cannot store them, and my wife wants to leave Galveston at once." The Weissmans' small son had drowned in the tidal wave.

Angrily, he kicked at a pyramid of gowns and turned away. His tears shamed him.

"I suppose I can ship them," he muttered. "More trouble than they're worth to me now."

Isaac looked at a green velvet ensemble. How beautiful Emma would look in such a color. A sudden thought struck him. Wouldn't frontier women crave the small luxury of a beautiful dress, the softness of velvet, the smoothness of satin and silk? The dresses could be refurbished, restyled. He did a series of swift mental calculations. Emma had given him the remainder of her savings the previous evening—six hundred dollars, two hundred of which they would lend to the Wallachs. His own funds would suffice for the journey and their initial expenses.

"I'll buy your entire stock for four hundred dollars," he said.

"I must have the money today." Meyer Weissman did not look at him as he spoke. "My wife wants to leave Galveston as soon as possible."

"Of course. In an hour's time."

He hurried back to the boarding house. Emma had placed the money in a small tin box and then concealed the box beneath her handkerchiefs.

"Emma!"

She was not at home, but he went at once to her room,

found the box, and counted out the money. Four hundred dollars exactly. He replaced the box and returned at once to Weissman's store, carrying a large valise so that he might begin to transport the dresses. He walked swiftly, proud of his daring, his insight. He had seized the moment, the opportunity. He had gambled, but the odds were with him.

It was early evening when Emma returned home. She had spent the day at Red Cross headquarters, unpacking cartons of supplies and directing their distribution. The floodwaters had formed stagnant pools outside the shack where she worked, and the air within was fetid. She blamed that sour dankness for the headache and nausea that had nagged her since the late afternoon. She would feel better if she rested for a half hour before dinner with a damp handkerchief across her forehead. Her mother's remedy, she recalled, and, as always when she thought of Leonie, a wave of sadness washed over her. Impatiently, she opened the drawer and saw at once that the neat pile of handkerchiefs had been disarranged. She opened the tin box. It was empty. Shock and despair paralyzed her, but she willed herself to calm. She opened her door and went out to the corridor, where Mary stood sorting the linen they had managed to salvage.

"Mary, have you seen Mr. Lewin?"

"He went out before carrying his big valise. The brown one."

She went back to her room, closed the door softly behind her, and sat down on her bed. Fear dizzied her, soured her mouth. The minutes passed. She clenched her fists and her fingers dug into her palms. The clock struck the quarter hour. She heard the front door open and close.

"Emma. Emma!" His voice rang through the house, excited, almost exuberant.

She felt weak with relief, and yet her voice, when she answered him was strangely calm.

"I'll be down in a moment, Isaac."

She brushed her hair, staring at herself as though fearful that those brief moments of terror had somehow scarred her.

When she came downstairs, he was kneeling beside the

open valise, unpacking the gowns, pleased because the storm damage was less than he had anticipated.

"Look, Emma," he said. "We worried how we might stock a store, and now it's solved."

"What's this?" She picked up the green velvet dress, ran her fingers across a burgundy moiré skirt.

"Meyer Weissman's stock. At least part of it. I bought it with the four hundred dollars that was left after I gave Abner the loan we promised him. You weren't home, and Weissman wanted the money today. Lucky, I knew where you had put it."

"Four hundred dollars." She allowed the green velvet dress to slip soundlessly to the floor and stared at him through narrowed eyes. "Do you realize how little that leaves us with?"

"Enough," he said brusquely. He wanted her to rejoice at his daring. He was unprepared for her apprehension, for the anger that iced her voice.

She bent to pick up the fallen garment and averted her head. It was her own vulnerability that angered her, her swift and easy surrender to a fear that she had thought vanquished.

"We had an agreement—an agreement to share. In all things." The words she had spoken as they lay in each other's arms formed a remembered litany, but he had negated them and loosed her terror. She had trusted him, and he had betrayed her.

"Emma, an opportunity presented itself. I took it. Would you have me consult with you on every such decision?" His anger matched her own. He had wanted her to approve his acumen, to share his enthusiasm. He had not anticipated her dismay and her veiled distrust.

She sank down on the sofa, and he saw that her face was drained of color.

"Emma, are you all right?" Concern muted his ire, negated his disappointment.

"I have a headache."

Her voice was plaintive as a child's, and he sat down beside her. Gently, he pressed his fingers against her temples and stroked them with a rhythm that at once soothed and numbed. Silently, he acknowledged that he had comprehended neither the source nor the breadth of her need. He would be more careful.

"It will be all right," he said softly.

"Yes." She closed her eyes and sat motionless as, with tender touch, he subdued the throbbing pain. She would be more vigilant.

They remained together then, in the gathering darkness, until Indian Mary padded into the room carrying a lamp that surprised them with the brilliance of its light.

A week later Emma and Isaac were married in the sanctuary of Shaarei Tefillah. The room was filled with flowers, but even three weeks after the flood the stench of putrescent bodies and the acrid odor of charred and burning flesh lingered.

Isaac bathed carefully for his wedding, lathering his body with carbolic soap, shampooing his thick dark hair with furious fingers. He did not want to smell of death when he stood before his bride. He went to the morning prayer quorum and wept as he prayed. He had not thought to find happiness again, yet now he was once more a bridegroom and life was no longer a struggle to survive but an adventure.

Emma wore the white dress she had fashioned for the Juneteenth celebration. She had washed it again and again to rid it of the sea salt it had absorbed when the tidal wave swept over the house. Only her mother's candlesticks, which Isaac had placed in the attic, had remained magically untouched by the storm.

"How pale she looks," Natalya whispered to Abner.

"Yes." Abner's voice was worried. It disturbed him that Emma's eyes were downcast through the brief ceremony. Natalya had looked up at him at their own wedding, her face aglow, her eyes sparkling. Still, Isaac's voice was strong and firm as he placed the plain gold wedding band on his wife's finger.

"Behold, with this ring, thou art consecrated unto me, according to the laws of Moses and of Israel."

With one stamp of his foot he shattered the glass goblet that the rabbi placed on the floor. The broken glass, he knew, was the symbol of the Temple destroyed, of a desert folk scattered. For him, it was a symbol of a city destroyed, a mark of his embarkation into the desert of his chosen land.

That night he gave Emma the violet-hearted shell he had taken from small Miriam's hand. She placed it in the tiny box that contained her turquoise pendant and the sliver of green sea glass she had plucked from the Prinsengracht walkway. Her candlesticks and that box were in the portmanteau she carried when they left Galveston for the Arizona territory. Sunlight spangled the clear blue gulf waters, but Emma and Isaac Lewin turned their eyes westward, their hands outstretched but not quite touching.

The Journey West, 1900

EMMA AND ISAAC LEWIN planned their journey from Galveston to Phoenix carefully. They traveled across Texas by coach and rail and then planned to continue on to New Mexico. It was fall, and the fierce heat of summer had abated. The evenings and mornings were cool, and although their conveyances were not uncomfortable, Emma, who had walked the deck of the Karlsruhe on the storm-tossed Atlantic, felt ill from the onset of the journey. Her pallor and the sudden bouts of dizziness that overcame her frightened Isaac. Twice he insisted that they break their journey across Texas, but although she reluctantly agreed, she was anxious to reach the Arizona border.

"I'm fine. It's just the aftereffect of the flood," she insisted, and it was true that she was still haunted by the memory of the rising waters, the floating corpses, the wails of frightened children and agonized parents. One night she dreamed of small Miriam, her hair beribboned with seaweed, dressed in a fragrant shroud of oleander petals. She awakened to the sound of her own sobs and Isaac's arms enfolding her, his own face wreathed in sadness. Why was it, she wondered then, that they came together without restraint only during times of danger and sorrow?

In Lubbock, a Jewish family invited them to dinner. The ritual slaughterer had visited that week, and the family roasted a flank of beef in an open barbecue pit. Slowly, they rotated the bloodied meat and allowed it to drip onto the glowing mesquite. Emma left the small group hurriedly. The scent of the charred meat and sizzling fat nauseated her, and she walked unsteadily to the house, fearful suddenly that she might faint.

"It's the odor," Isaac explained to their concerned hosts.

They nodded sadly. The Lubbock newspapers had written of the bodies burned on the funeral pyres of Galveston. It was a fearful thing to burn the dead, a violation of the holy Torah, of the laws of Moses. But they knew, too, that there had been no choice. The basic tenet of their faith was the preservation of life. It was better to burn the dead than to allow the putrefying bodies to contaminate the living.

The woman of the house set the table and then sought Emma out. She offered her wet cloths and smelling salts and unbuttoned her dress.

"When did you have your last monthly, my dear?" she asked conspiratorially. She herself was the mother of four children, and she was fond of noting that each had been born in a different state as she and her husband had made their trek westward.

"I'm all right," Emma insisted. "I'm fine."

The woman's intimation was clear, but stubbornly she denied it. She could not be pregnant. They had been cautious, almost constrained, she and Isaac, since that night when they had looked down at the flooded streets of Galveston and clung to each other in desire and despair. Never had they spoken of children, of family. They had other priorities. Their first joint purchase had been a leatherbound ledger book, and the first entry, in Emma's spidery script, had been the four-hundred-dollar purchase of Meyer Weissman's velvet and brocade ball gowns. Somehow they would rend a profit from that purchase. She no longer pondered the wisdom of the investment. It was done. But it had become an emotional landmark, a signal post, a violation of what she had considered to be a condition of their marriage.

"It is not that important," Isaac had insisted.

"To me it is important."

She would not explain again the fear that gripped her when she felt her voice stilled, her options ignored. A small breach had opened between them, and neither of them had moved to close it. A new wariness unsettled them, but they did not speak of it.

Emma refused the offer of smelling salts and washed her face, brushed her hair, and applied rouge to her cheeks. She forced herself to eat the roasted beef, aware of the woman's watchful gaze, of Isaac's worried glance. She danced with wild abandon after the barbecue, and the fiddler stepped up the tempo to match her swift steps during the contra line dances. She whirled through a dizzying polka and stepped high for "Cotton-Eyed Joe." She was not pregnant, she assured herself, exhilarated by the music and the movement. She still controlled her body, her life. Her independence was inviolate.

But in Santa Fe she fainted as they waited for the train that would carry them from the New Mexico territory into Arizona. Isaac carried her to the surgery of a German doctor, who examined her and smiled at them benignly.

"It is not at all odd that you should have fainted, my dear Mrs. Lewin. Pregnant women often do, although I have never read of a good explanation for it. Still, you are in perfect health. I see no reason why you should not continue your journey into Arizona. But be cautious. God breathes with the strength of a furnace in these desert territories." He removed his glasses, as though wondering now what had possessed him to move from the spired Bavarian city of his birth to this sand-bound enclave.

Isaac stared at Emma and took her hand into his own. The heat was intense, the sky streaked with veins of molten gold, but her fingers were cold as ice upon his palm.

"You knew, didn't you?" he asked and cursed his own stupidity.

She did not reply. She hesitated to tell him that she had been frightened and unsure. He had taken a partner who would work beside him, not a woman who trembled with uncertainty and wakened, weeping, in the night. She would not betray their bargain.

"I suspected but I was not sure."

He turned away and allowed her hands to drop. She lifted them to her eyes. His mouth was sour with disappointment. She had not trusted him enough to tell him of her hope, her fear. She had not cared for him enough to share the tremulous knowledge that together they had created life, that out of that night of death and destruction, of horrific loss, a child would be born. He, who had lost a child, had been granted another. A tear trailed down his cheek, but because her eyes were shielded, she did not see it. In silence, then, he paid the doctor, and in silence they returned to the station and boarded the train. The gaslit lamps in the parlor car flickered as they journeyed southward to Albuquerque and at last crossed into the Arizona territory.

Emma leaned back in the horsehair seat and studied the landscape she had dreamed of as she walked along the canals of Amsterdam. Always she had conceived of Arizona as a desert territory, but the terrain through which they passed was mountain country forested with thick-branched ponderosa pines, leafy junipers, and sky-stretching aspens. The mountains flanked gentle valleys, and the face of the country changed with such rapidity that she kept her eyes fixed to the isinglass windows, which the conductor cautioned the passengers against opening except when he confirmed that there would be no danger.

"You're in Indian and outlaw country now," he said, and they did not argue with him.

All the passengers had read newspaper accounts of railroad piracy, and there was not a family in the West who could not recount a personal tragedy resulting from Indian violence. Wagon trains were consistently raided, and scalping and stoning were standard forms of Apache revenge on the white men for their invasion of the mountains and deserts that had been Indian strongholds for generations.

The Hopi and Navajo Indians, who roamed the mountain country through which the Southern Pacific railroad had carved its tracks of steel, believed that their gods dwelled amid the yawning crags and snow-crowned peaks. The white men had violated not only their earthbound lives but their eternal destinies.

"You can't blame them for thinking so," Brother Timothy, a slender Catholic priest who had boarded the train at Albuquerque, told the Lewins. He was on his way to a mission school in the Chino Valley.

Isaac nodded. "One feels that this country was touched by God," he said.

It was the sunset hour, and the sky was streaked with splashes of carmine, fringed with gold. Purple clouds crowned the mountains, and at last, as the slow darkness triumphed, brilliant stars emerged and lit the immense void through which they traveled. In the starlit darkness, the tree-ribbed ranges assumed a luminous amethyst hue; night owls called mournfully to each other from their lofty perches atop majestic firs and spruces. Emma fell asleep as a flock of smoke-colored quail streaked past the window. She was drowsily aware of Brother Timothy, in the seat opposite her, reading his hymnal while Isaac turned the pages of his Bible. When she awakened, Isaac's eyes were closed, and she saw that he had been reading from Psalms. She covered him with her own cloak and gently removed the open book from his hand. His fingers stirred at her touch and he smiled, but his eyes remained closed. She was startled to see the glint of silver in his thick dark brows, and with her finger she traced the gentle arch.

"Rivka," he murmured, and her heart turned. He felt her touch but spoke the name of the woman who had been killed in a Russian hamlet. She rose, then, careful not to disturb Brother Timothy, who slept with his cheek pressed against the window, and went to stand alone on the narrow platform between the cars. The night wind whipped her face and she swayed to the rhythm of the endlessly rolling wheels.

The long train journey carried them from forested mountains to sere deserts. They had arrived in a land of contrasts, of fallen forests turned to stone and living forests turned to thorn. The train shrilled to a halt at small station stops where mail was deposited and collected and fresh water taken on. Indians, who had come to the station store to barter jewelry and blankets for staples, stared at the passengers, their faces solemn, their dark eyes guarded. Some touched the train with tentative gesture. "The iron horse," they called it, and Emma understood that they distrusted it for both its passengers and its cargo. Its harsh whistle was, for them, a funeral sound, signaling the death of their way of life.

"They are as frightened and as fascinated as we are," she said to Isaac.

He nodded. She smiled at an Indian boy whose thin body was draped in an oversized rebozo. Shyly, he smiled back until his father spoke sharply to him and he turned his back. He ran to where a group of Indian women with tattooed faces stood. They huddled into their blankets as their men did the trading.

The standard greeting of the Southwest was shouted at every stop.

"¿Cómo está, amigo?" "How's it going, my friend?" This was a country where men acknowledged their aloneness and courted each other's friendship.

The train whistle signaling departure echoed across desert swells of amber sand, wafted across gullies and arroyos.

"Adiós—go with God." They blessed each other at leave-taking, wary always of the unsettled and desolate landscape.

Whose God? Emma wondered. The God of Brother Timothy, Who had sent him into the American desert to save the souls of Indian children? The God Whom she and Isaac worshiped, Who had handed down His Law in a desert as awesome and beautiful as the one through which they traveled? Perhaps they offered their parting benediction to the gods of the Indians, concealed amid the sheltering mountains and the secret caves?

The train carried them from mountain to plain. Columbines and fairy fern grew in feathery splendor beside a spring that trickled with sudden chimerical brilliance from a silver-grained granite ledge. Gentians and violets blanketed the roots of the paloverde, and lavender-hued ironwood turned regal purple at the sunset hour. Hummingbirds hovered above the wands of crimson flowers that shot out of the thorny ocotillo, and white-winged desert doves plucked up the fruity carmine seeds of the saguaro cactus. Occasionally the train slowed to a halt, and they waited for a team of workers to repair a length of track. Ocher sand caked the faces of the diminutive Chinese workers. Their black braided hair was slick with sweat, and their gray uniforms clung to their bodies. They moved swiftly, their hammers triggering sparks as they pounded the steel rails that gleamed silver in the sunlight. Emma walked along the tracks, studying the cactus flowers and the tiny blossoms that hid from the sun in the shelter of earth-colored boulders.

"You will not miss flowers in this desert country," Isaac said, recalling the pleasure in her face as she arranged her flowers in the Galveston dining room.

"Will tulips grow here?" Her tone was wistful, and he struggled to think of words that would comfort her, but she had set the flowers aside and returned to her work.

Since their departure from Galveston, she had busied herself with the long ball gowns. As the train carried them down mountain slopes, across cliff and canyon and into the reaches of the upland desert, she snipped at embroidery that had been discolored or damaged by the floodwaters, and reconstructed facings and hemlines. She transferred beading from the sleeves of one gown to the bodice of another. Isaac watched her as she severed the sleeves of a green velvet gown, waterstained and mildewed, from an otherwise undamaged blouse, which she converted into a sleeveless jacket. She ripped the skirt free and stripped it of its decorative lace fringes.

"We can sell this as a lady's suit. It can be worn to business with different-colored blouses," she said. Natalya had fashioned such outfits to wear to school. She wondered if Natalya and Abner had reached Cripple Creek yet and wished again that they had decided to seek their fortune in Phoenix rather than in Colorado.

Isaac nodded, admiring the swiftness of her thoughts, the deftness of her fingers. Her needle and scissor glinted in the sunlight, which bathed her face with a liquid radiance, concealing the pallor of her skin. The long journey and the lingering malaise of her pregnancy had fatigued her. Violet circles rimmed her eyes, and she moved slowly, as though conscious of her own fragility. Still, he thought her beautiful as she bent over her work in the sunlight, but hesitated to tell her so.

She threaded yet another needle and tried to think of who would buy gowns of velvet and brocade, silk and satin, in this desert country where energy was concentrated on survival rather than frivolity. Still, women always craved a bit of luxury, a touch of beauty. The splintered tables of the meanest hovels in London's East End had been spread with an embroidered cloth. The poorest woman in Amsterdam's Houtseeg district had a bonnet trimmed with feathers and ribbons. She had to hope that Isaac's instinct would prove correct.

At Prescott, Brother Timothy left them, and they were

sorry to see him go. They had grown fond of the thin, pale priest, who spoke with impassioned fervor about his mission. He was, he told them, following the tradition of a seventeenth-century Jesuit, Father Eusebio Francisco Kino, who had crossed the sands of Arizona and founded missions at Tumacooria and San Xavier del Bac. It had been Father Kino, Brother Timothy told them, who had traced the origin of the blue abalone shells to the Pacific shore and proved that Baja California was not an island. He had trained Indian cowboys and was responsible for introducing the cattle industry into Arizona. He had protected Indians and produced a map of the Southwest that settlers followed for years afterward.

"He made his life matter," Brother Timothy said passionately.

They understood the depth of his feeling. They had exchanged personal histories with the swift intimacy of traveling companions. The young priest was the second son of an Irish family. His father had scraped the unyielding earth of a Killarney farm and had died in poverty. An older brother had inherited the meager patrimony and now replayed the grim scenario of the father's life, one generation following the tragic example of another.

Their lives had counted for nought, Brother Timothy said in his musical brogue, and their deaths for even less. The land was exhausted, the country itself tired, riddled with fatigue. A local priest had rescued him from the farm and sent him to a seminary. There he had learned about the work of Father Kino and about the American West—a new country thriving with energy, a land of infinite resources. In such a land his life would matter. His journey to Arizona, his work among the Indians and the pioneer settlers, was a bid for immortality. Perhaps one day others would remember him as he remembered the legendary Father Kino.

"And your lives, too, will matter—will make a difference," Brother Timothy added. He admired the handsome young Jewish couple. Their courage moved him. He wanted to speak to them of Christianity, but he did not. Their own faith, he knew, was firm, and like himself, they believed in one God—a God Who had revealed Himself in a desert not unlike the one through which their train hurtled. Isaac had tried to teach him the letters of the Hebrew alphabet, and together, as the train crossed the majestic mountains and hovered over valley and gorge, they had repeated the psalm of thanksgiving in English: "To Him that stretcheth out the earth above the waters; for His mercy endureth forever."

Together they had stood beside the train at nightfall and watched the first brilliant stars of evening emerge. Softly, then, Emma had spoken the words of David, the desert king, the poet of her people: "To Him who made great lights—the sun to rule by day and the moon and stars to rule by night."

The psalmist's words merged the separate deserts, linked their hopes and dreams. The Jesuit priest from Ireland and the Jews from Kiev and Amsterdam linked hands in farewell at Prescott.

"Come to see us in Phoenix," Isaac said. "I will teach you Hebrew yet."

Brother Timothy laughed. "I will," he promised. "Write to me when the child is born." He was unprepared for the look that flashed between them, the sudden wariness, as though a secret had been betrayed. "I guessed," he said, fearful, suddenly, that he had invaded their privacy.

He did not wish them success. Their prosperity was guaranteed, he knew. They were too determined, too imaginative and diligent, not to succeed. But they would need more than success.

"I wish you peace," he said instead.

Emma watched him as he descended, lifting his soutane so that its hem would not drag across the dusty station platform. She wondered how he had sensed the unarticulated furor that smoldered between Isaac and herself.

They drew closer to Phoenix. She set aside her sewing, anxious now to absorb the landscape that would become her own. She stared out at the wrinkled, lovely land, at the patterned earth which changed color almost imperceptibly, drifting from sandstone red to subtle ocher, from pale sandy stretches to sere plateaus fringed by micaceous boulders. She saw the many-armed saguaro cactus, its thorny branches laden with bright flowers, and the paloverde tree with its promise of springtime blossoms the color of sunbeams.

At a water stop they sought the shade of an earth-hugging Joshua tree, its fern-studded, yearning branches greenly defying the barren landscape. Isaac plucked a prickly pear for her from a giant cactus. The fruit was concealed, like a hidden treasure, amid protecting thorns and crimson-hearted flowers. He peeled the rough, needled skin and passed the moist, bright fruit to her. He had cut himself on a thorn, and a ruby drop of blood spurted at his fingertip.

She ate the painfully harvested fruit, savoring its juice and sweetness, cognizant suddenly that the simplest mechanics of life in this desert land would require a disproportionate expenditure of effort, a letting of sweat and blood. Still, she was not discouraged; the beauty of the land enchanted and its challenge intrigued.

She was excited now and pressed her face to the window. Two large sand lizards scurried beneath the shade of saguaro. "Look," she called, like a small girl, her voice high-pitched and joyous.

Isaac smiled, amused by her wonderment, pleased by her gaiety. She had dropped the green velvet gown on which she had been working, and he held it up now and draped it over her shoulders. Almost shyly, she turned to him, and together they stood at the window and watched the desert skitter by.

Near Phoenix a brief and sudden rain fell, and the cooled air was redolent with the pungent scent of the creosote bush. Drops of water glinted on creamy sprays of yucca blossom, and in the near-darkness, the pale flowers resembled slowly burning candles. Isaac took her hand, and they disembarked at last in the small city they had chosen as home.

They took rooms at the Phoenix Hotel, a one-story building in the shape of a hollow square. The sun had baked and cracked its pale stucco façade and sheer heat had caused painted wicker furniture to peel. Their room was small, dominated by the large bed. A ceiling fan revolved slowly, persistently, and golden dust motes danced between its rotors. White dotted-swiss curtains hung at the narrow window, its shade drawn against the penetrating brightness of the sun. Emma pulled it up and looked down at the busy intersection of Washington and Third streets. She watched bonneted housewives make their way from the butcher shop to the bakery, from the greengrocer to the dairy. The women paused to chat in the shade of the palm and tamarisk trees that lined the narrow streets. The fragrance of orange blossoms floated on the heat-heavy air. Men in work clothes stopped at Mike's Brewery and held cold mugs of dark beer and pale ale to their cheeks before drinking deeply. At Hancock's Store, small children shared glasses of lemonade, and a fortunate few paid a few pennies for a plunge in the hotel swimming pool, which was shielded from the searing sun by a canvas roof. The water, the hotel proprietor had told them proudly, was pumped in from a nearby irrigation ditch.

Water, Emma realized, was the secret of Phoenix's success. The Hohokum Indians, who had so abruptly and mysteriously vanished from the Arizona desert, had prospered because of their engineering ingenuity. They had dug a network of canals, and farms had flourished in the valley. Brother Timothy, who had studied Indian folklore, had told them that the peaceable Pima and Maricopa Indians who still lived in the area spoke reverently of La Ciudad, an ancient city on the site of the modern enclave which the white men were developing in the heart of the Salt River Valley.

The Hohokum, in fact, had been indirectly responsible for giving the new city its name. A colorful English adventurer who called himself Lord Darrel Duppa had studied their mounds and canals and had suggested that the city be named for the mythical bird that was consumed by fire and rose in resplendent glory from its own ashes. The wife of a local barkeep had embroidered Lord Duppa's extravagant prediction in needlepoint, and her handiwork hung on the tavern wall: ''A city will rise Phoenix-like from these ashes of the past.''

Isaac studied the legend as he stood at the bar, nursing a weak whiskey and listening carefully to the gossip of the town. The phoenix, he recalled, was said to be consumed by fire every five hundred years. He wondered if the pioneering townspeople fully understood the myth they had embraced as their own reality.

Still, there was no premonition of doom in Phoenix during those hot, bright days of the first autumn of the new century.

Business was booming, the men said as they downed their beer and held their glasses out to be refilled. The new electrical systems, which would soon span the country, needed copper, and the territory's mines were working at top capacity, with new strikes reported every day. The Lesinskys of New Mexico had expanded their operations and were mining veins in Arizona. In Solomonville, Isadore Solomon was shipping out wagonloads of ore, pulled to railroad crossings by mules and burros. He had even started his own bank.

"Trust the Jews to get in on the ground floor of a good thing," a tall miner said. Isaac stared at him hard, but there was no malice in the man's words. They rang with an ungrudging admiration. "It's a damn good thing to have them in the territory."

Initiative and hard work would be welcomed here, Isaac knew. Western pioneers had little energy to expend on active anti-Semitism. The same harsh jokes and latent prejudice were probably there, but they recognized that the forces of nature and hostile Indians were their true adversaries. Jews and Mormons, visionary altruists like Brother Timothy, and adventurers like the fabled Lord Duppa were all accomplices in the exciting and hazardous adventure of pushing the frontier farther westward and building a metropolis on the desert sands.

Isaac returned to the hotel armed with the knowledge that he had been right to select Phoenix as their home. The small city would formally become the territorial capital in February, and he predicted that from that time on it would be the most important city in the Southwest. The men in the tavern had spoken of statehood. McKinley was opposed, but then McKinley would not be president forever.

Emma listened to his assessment and nodded. She herself had observed the vitality of the city. Besides, letters from her brothers had awaited them in Phoenix, and their evaluation of Phoenix conformed to Isaac's impressions.

Emil and Simon Coen were guarded in their congratulations on her marriage. "We wish you happiness, but it would have been well if you had consulted with us," Emil wrote cautiously. He himself was engaged to a young woman from a prosperous family. They socialized a great deal. He had even met Jacob Schiff at a dinner party.

"He remembers you still," Emil wrote, "and he, for one, was delighted to hear of your marriage. He sees you and your new husband as the vanguard of a new breed of Jewish pioneers. He is a bit of a romantic for a tycoon who has a stranglehold on America's railroads."

Isaac frowned as he read the letter.

"What does he mean when he says, 'he, for one'—he implies, I suppose, that he does not share Mr. Schiff's pleasure." Abstractly, he understood that a penniless Russian Jew was not the Coen brothers' idea of a suitable husband for their sister, who had been the belle of the Sephardic Jewish aristocracy of Amsterdam. But still, their coolness wounded him, and their assumption of superiority stirred his anger.

They were men who, from earliest childhood, had accepted luxury and cultivation as their due. Like Emma, they had always been at home in carpeted rooms lit by crystal chandeliers. They dined easily at tables covered with damask cloths and set with fine china and sterling silver. The financial reverses they had suffered at their father's death had not undermined their feeling of entitlement and privilege. They considered themselves different from the struggling Jews who had poured out of the ghettos and shtetls of eastern Europe— Jews like himself and the Weinglasses and the Wallachs, desperate to escape poverty and persecution.

"How did you describe me to your brothers?" he asked suddenly. Emma shrugged and did not look up from her sewing. She was embroidering a square of fine linen with her initials. The women of Phoenix wore gingham and calico kerchiefs, but his wife stitched a lace-trimmed square. Even in this small gesture, she emphasized her separateness. An unfamiliar rage gripped him.

He strode across the room and gripped her at the shoulder with one hand while drawing the window shade with the other. Sunlight pressed against it still, and he moved her out of the path of its invasive brightness and thrust her toward the bed with the strength of his anger, the need of his love. His lips silenced her protest and proclaimed his majesty over her; his body arched and pounded in fierce struggle for her surrender. In the heat of the Arizona afternoon, he claimed her as his wife; he passed his hands across the slope of her abdomen *(his child within, his child)* and remembered the night of raging wind and rising water when he claimed her as his love.

"Emma. Emma!" Her name was a whisper; her name was a shout.

They lay together on the narrow hotel bed, until at last the window shade was shadowed by the first darkness of evening. He slept then, but her eyes remained open, and she struggled against her own fatigue. She had felt his anger and his strength. It had aroused and excited her, yet filled her with trepidation. How simple it was to be caught off guard, to surrender vigilance, to submit. She lay rigid in the encroaching darkness and struggled against his love and her own vulnerability.

They explored the city in search of a home and a location for their business. They looked admiringly at the Victorian mansions on Monroe and Adams streets and paused before the home of the Rosson family, which reminded them of the stately Gresham dwelling in Galveston. Emma stared at the house as though memorizing the curve of the belled roof that deflected the sunlight, the sleeping porch contrived of wood and canvas. He would build a house like that for her one day, he promised himself. They would not always be on the outside looking in.

Women stood on the porches that girdled the larger homes and created small breezes with elegant fans of ostrich feathers. Her cousin Greta had written her that such feathers were now fashionable in London, and Emma took careful note of them.

They visited the capitol building, which was being readied for its official dedication in February.

"We have only four months in which to establish ourselves," Isaac muttered. He would launch Lewin's Emporium as the city itself took on its new historic role as territorial capital.

Indian workers scrambled across the copper roof and

climbed the great dome, polishing the metal to a high glow with chamois cloths. They moved, in their moccasined feet, with casual grace, betraying no fear as they made their way across the shining sheets of metal.

"They say that Indians are not afraid of heights," Isaac said musingly.

"Perhaps it is because they are so used to the mountains," Emma replied.

She wondered if she would ever grow accustomed to the beauty of the mountains that surrounded Phoenix. Each street revealed a new vista of graceful range and soaring height. Toward the north, Squaw Peak towered in purple majesty; the undulating ridges of the Camelback Mountains were etched against the horizon, curving and rising, as though battling the encroaching desert. At twilight the mountains became velvet sculptures against the darkening skyscape, and always, in the east, the rocky panorama of Four Peaks was silhouetted, its jagged crown thrust against the endless expanse of sky. Here, the landlocked world of mountain and desert seemed to go on forever. Emma remembered the narrow, canal-bordered streets of Amsterdam, the slender buildings on land scavenged from the water. She had been right, after all, to yearn after this limitless landscape, these spacious skies.

They discovered, with grim finality, that there was not a single vacant store in all of Phoenix that they could afford to rent. They did, however, find an adobe house, although Emma's heart sank when she looked at the dirt floor and the clay walls. Still, an olive tree grew in the garden, and the rubbery leaves of a eucalyptus tree provided some shade. The roof was fashioned of round logs, *vigas* covered with stick and brush and plastered with mud.

Isaac hoisted himself up and saw that it had been carefully constructed. It would shield them from the rainfalls of winter, which were sometimes intense enough to cause flash floods. An open lean-to adjoined the house—a flimsy construction covered with branches and supported by posts. The canvas cot that had been left on it sagged sadly in the center. The previous occupant, a failed miner, had surely slept there during the brutally hot nights of summer. The sourness of the man's despair clung to the small enclosure, and spiders crawled out of the empty liquor bottles ranged in a corner with disturbing precision. Isaac saw how the lean-to could be brushed clean and lit with the soft light of a naphthalene lantern. They would be able to sit out there at night, as they had on the porch of the Galveston house; they would see the stars through the branches and feel the wisps of evening wind against their faces.

"What do you think?" he asked Emma hesitantly.

She held a stick in her hand and etched a design in the earth that would be her living room floor. She drew the flowered pattern of the Aubusson carpet in the drawing room of the Prinsengracht mansion. She remembered its soft thickness on the polished wooden floor. She turned to Isaac, and her eyes were dangerously bright.

"We have no choice," she said. Her voice was so low that he bent close to hear her.

They moved in the next day, furnishing the small house with secondhand chairs, a battered bed and bureau. Isaac fashioned a table from a plank of wood stretched across two barrels.

"How is that?" he asked apprehensively.

"It's all right," she assured him. She covered the rough wood of the table with a white linen cloth and set her silver candlesticks on it. He had forgotten that it was the eve of the Sabbath, but she had remembered.

She watched as he affixed a mezuzah to the doorway of the adobe house—a narrow wooden shield containing a strip of hand-inscribed parchment that testified to the sovereignty and oneness of God—the same mezuzah that he had removed so carefully from the doorpost of the cottage on the edge of the Kiev forest. Snow had fallen as he had pried each nail loose on that day of his leavetaking; the desert sky was threaded with filigreed strands of gold and violet as he hammered each nail into place and murmured the blessing for his new home.

"Amen," her affirmation echoed his own. She reached up and touched the mezuzah, its wood worn thin by another woman's touch.

He watched, in turn, at the sunset hour, as she lit the

Sabbath candles, her bright hair covered with the same white mantilla she had worn that first evening in Galveston. They stood together then, as the last vestige of daylight faded, in the candlelit room so newly become their home.

There was no vacant store to be rented in Phoenix, but there was an empty plot of land on West Adams Street, near Melczer's liquor store. The Jewish liquor merchant advised Isaac that the location was an excellent one.

"Land like that is going to skyrocket in the next couple of years. Grab it now and you'll have the perfect place to do business when we get the capitol dedication ceremonies in February. Believe me, they'll swarm in from every part of the territory and from the New Mexico territory too, to celebrate. They'll come with money in their pockets and gold dust and silver nuggets in their wagons, and here is where they'll come to spend it. This will be the heart of Phoenix."

Isaac looked up and down the street. Wagons pulled by teams of horses tossed up clouds of dust as ranchers deposited produce and beef to be sold and picked up their own provisions. Women lingered in the shops that sold ribbons and trimmings, bolts of cloth and household wares. They studied their weather-worn faces in the gleaming bottoms of pots and pans and craftily adjusted a vagrant curl. Other women rode their bicycles with large shopping baskets affixed to the handlebars. They hoisted their skirts to shield them from the spokes of the wheels, and their broad-brimmed straw hats shadowed their faces. They chained their bicycles to the newly hewn poles of the electric company as they made their purchases. The more prosperous matrons made their rounds in canopied phaetons, their horses moving at a languorous pace through the heat.

"I agree with you," Isaac told the liquor merchant. The street was the focus of nascent Phoenix. It would be the major thoroughfare of the developed capital. "I could manage to buy the land, but even if I had the money to build the store, I'd never get it up in time for the dedication."

"You have merchandise?" Melczer asked. "Something special maybe to bring in the ladies?"

Isaac nodded. Emma was working on the last of the dresses

and ball gowns, and her brothers had offered to send a shipment of dry goods and a draft against additional purchases.
He felt no unease about accepting their help. It was a temporary loan and would be duly recorded in the ledger. The
Coen brothers, for all their reluctance to accept him, were
after all his kinsmen now, linked by ties of marriage and
bonds of faith.

"If you have merchandise, you have a business. Lease or
buy the land, get yourself a tent, and hang out a sign. Poof—
you're in business. I did it myself." The liquor merchant
waved proudly at his glass-fronted, brick-walled establishment. "I began here with a tin shack and a half a case of
bourbon. All you need is a little bit of chutzpah, Lewin, and
if you didn't have chutzpah, you wouldn't be in the Arizona
territory."

Emma agreed with Melczer. "We must take a chance,"
she said.

A week later they hoisted a tent on the empty plot. Isaac
built a floor, using lengths of lumber. He carefully cut and
sanded a thin plank and carried it to a sign painter.

"Make it simple," he said. "Nothing fancy. I don't want
to scare away the customers." His trade would come from
farmers and miners, from families passing through Phoenix
on their way farther west. He did not want them to be intimidated.

"No one will be scared away from a tent store," the sign-
maker said sourly. Still, he was a skilled craftsman, and he
painted the legend on the pale wood with glossy black
enamel paint. *Lewin's Emporium*. Isaac paid him a dollar
and looked at it with satisfaction.

"It won't hang on a tent for long," he said.

The sign was affixed to the ridgepole where the tent's flaps
were pulled back. A board stretched across two packing cases
became their front counter, and cigar boxes contained their
cash and receipts. Their merchandise was so sparse that there
was no need to worry about the lack of a door. Each evening
they loaded their stock of ready-to-wear children's clothing,
cotton housedresses, and men's work clothing onto a buckboard wagon and carried it back to the adobe house. There
was no interest in the ball gowns, and they remained unsold,

although every woman who came into the tent store lingered to touch the soft velvet, the fine brocade.

"They're not buying now, but they'll remember them," Isaac told Emma.

"We'll see."

Isaac noticed that the miners who came into Phoenix wore cotton bib overalls, which wore out quickly at the seat and the knees. He wrote to the Levi Strauss Emporium in San Francisco and ordered a hundred pairs of the work pants that the enterprising Bavarian immigrant had fashioned out of the tent canvas from Nimes, France. Isaac did a brisk business in Mr. Levi's denims, but for the most part business in the tent store was slow and he was haunted by doubt. If the tent store failed, how would he support Emma and the child who would be born in a few months' time?

Throughout the long nights, he tossed and turned. He thought up merchandising schemes and discarded them. Their fate, their success or failure, rested on the February festivities. He left their bed and walked through the darkness to the leaf-roofed lean-to. Emma kept bottles of water in the desert cooler—a wooden frame covered with burlap, set in the shade of the eucalyptus tree. The upper edges were immersed in pans of water that dripped down through the burlap. The desert breeze and the low humidity combined with the evaporating water to lower the temperature sufficiently so that perishables remained cool in the makeshift container. Isaac drank deeply of the cold water and looked up at the stars. The beauty of the night stirred him, renewed his courage. He thought of waking Emma, so that they might look up at the heavens together as they had the night of the Juneteenth celebration in Galveston. She had come to him then, wrapped in her soft blue shawl, her fiery hair caping her shoulders. But he dared not wake her. Her pregnancy was not an easy one, and he worried over her health, was bewildered by her moods.

She struggled against her increased weight, the impact of fatigue, as though to deny her body's dominance over her spirit, her will. Often in the morning, noting her pallor, he begged her to stay home and rest, but she rode to the tent store beside him in the buckboard and busied herself at the counter, arranging and rearranging the meager stock. They spoke of orders and deposits, he riffled through catalogues and asked her advice. He would not repeat the mistake he had made in Galveston of making an investment without consulting with her. They discussed the possibility of printing handbills for distribution in the mining towns before the February festivities, of running advertisements in the *Arizona Miner,* the *Phoenix Gazette.* But they did not speak of their uncertainty or of their loneliness. The articulation of their fears might endow them with a reality they were not prepared to confront.

Autumn drifted into winter, and the days became cooler. On Friday nights, Isaac occasionally went alone to the Sabbath eve services that were held above the Donofrio store on Washington Street. Emma was always too tired. A handful of Jews gathered in the dimly lit room. They shared the few prayerbooks, passing them from hand to hand. There was no rabbi in Phoenix, but Max Goldstein, a grocer, and Harris Gruenstein, a leather merchant, vied for the honor of giving the Torah commentary. Isaac winced at their sophomoric interpretations but hesitated to reveal his own training. A scholar might be distrusted as a businessman. Funds had been collected for the purchase of a Torah, and a small ark had been crafted for it.

"Henry Stern paid for it," Emanuel Melczer told Isaac. "He hardly comes himself, although he is always here for the High Holy Days. But then, he's a busy man—a banker. You'll meet him one day."

After services, the Jews of Phoenix lingered. A copy of *The American Israelite* was passed from hand to hand. They argued about an editorial by a prominent Reform rabbi in New York which advised Jews to keep a low profile, to become Americanized.

"That's what they have to worry about in New York," Max Goldstein scoffed. "Here in Phoenix we already have a Jewish mayor for five years."

He beamed at the mayor, Emanuel Ganz, a bald and wide-jowled man who had served for five consecutive years.

"Who else wants such a job?" Ganz said. "Maybe when Arizona becomes a state things will be different, but for now, what are we?—a small city in a territory. In Washington they think we speak Spanish.''

''They should only know that we speak Yiddish,'' Melczer quipped, and the assembled Jews laughed. They were comfortable with their non-Jewish neighbors, but here, at Friday evening services, they relaxed, linked by shared history and their own peculiar in-turned humor.

They spoke of the Fourth Zionist Congress, which had met in London that summer. In the desert city in the American Southwest, they argued Herzl's dream of a nation reborn in the desert land of Judaea. Some called the Viennese Jew a lunatic and others a visionary, but when a youth from California stopped in Phoenix en route to a Jewish settlement in Palestine, they all contributed to a collection toward his passage.

Isaac and Emma drove to the outskirts of the city and passed an ostrichery. Emma looked at the long-legged birds, which strutted regally about their pens, their colorful feathers spread in dazzling fans. That night she opened the *Ladies' Home Journal* and stared at the photographs of models in feathered hats. She reread a letter from her cousin Greta in London: ''I have bought myself a cloche with a cunning ostrich feather. Everyone is wearing them.'' If such hats were stylish in London and New York, they should certainly be popular in Arizona, where ostriches were raised. The next day she returned to the ostrichery and made a purchase. That night she began to fashion feathered hats to match the unsold ball gowns.

''It's a gamble,'' Isaac said. They watched every penny now, and although the draft from her brothers had been generous, their capital had dwindled.

''Didn't you gamble in Galveston?'' she asked.

He did not answer. When would she stop treating their marriage as a page in her ledger book, looking to see whether debits and credits were evenly matched? One indiscretion balanced another; accounts were endlessly reckoned.

She worked on, her fingers bruised by the thick needles, the sharp spines of the long feathers. She was finished just in time. In February advertisements in every Arizona gazette announced the availability of ''fashionable ball gowns and

specially styled millinery'' at the Lewin Emporium on West
Adams Street in Phoenix.

A febrile excitement gripped Phoenix during the last weeks
of January. Houses were repainted, and the municipality
planted young tamarisks along the streets of the city. Shop
windows were washed and counters rearranged. Emma and
Isaac decorated the tent store with red, white, and blue bunting. Streamers hung from the canvas folds, and Isaac bought
a huge block of ice, which he placed in a barrel filled with
water. Dippers and cups were ranged on a nearby table.
"Lewin's Emporium Invites You to Refresh Yourselves,'' a
sign over the barrel read. The store was guarded by two
dressmaker dummies attired in the most elegant of the ball
gowns and matching hats. One papier-mâché model wore a
royal-blue taffeta gown trimmed with elegant gold brocade
and a hairpiece of ostrich feathers. The other wore the green
velvet skirt and sleeveless jacket that Emma had fashioned
as the train rumbled through the hillocks of Texas.

The night before the dedication of the capital, Emma and
Isaac slept on the floor of the tent store. They opened the
flaps at sunrise, prepared for the custom of the celebrants
who already milled about the streets of Phoenix.

The rooms of every hostelry were booked, but still wagons
rolled toward the city. Miners and ranchers from Prescott and
Maricopa Wells, from Tombstone and Flagstaff, from Arcos-
anti and Scottsdale, arrived by train and buckboard. Homesteaders and their families made the journey in farm wagons
pulled by slowly moving field horses. The railway scheduled
additional cars and extra runs. Brother Timothy led a group
of neatly dressed Indian boys from his mission school, who
lifted their feet cautiously as though their new leather shoes
hobbled them. Soldiers from Camp MacDowell, the buttons
on their blue dress uniforms polished to a high gleam, smiled
shyly at dark-haired Mexican girls in brightly embroidered
cotton dresses.

Lemonade stands sprouted at street corners. A troupe of
actors set up a tent and announced performances of a play
written especially for the dedication of the capitol. Gaily
dressed clowns executed comical somersaults in front of

Hancock's Store, and a band assembled on Washington Street and played for hour after hour, alternating dance music with patriotic tunes. A bagpiper offered a concert of his own and attracted an audience of wide-eyed children.

Mexican guitarists strolled the streets, mischievously serenading the staid matrons of Phoenix. Indians dressed in beaded buckskin, draped in bright rebozos, squatted on the ground, and spread their wares on lengths of blanket. Pins and pendants crafted of silver and turquoise, kachina dolls carved from soft cottonwood and willow roots and painted in the likeness of masked gods, leather belts strung with conchos, formed small pyramids. The Pueblo Indians sold their *bayetas,* blankets of red-dyed, finely spun wool, and the Navajos flapped their geometrically designed rugs, their colorful serapes.

Handbills announced a public dance in front of the capitol, and visiting dignitaries had been invited to a grand ball given by Governor Brodie and his wife in the rotunda. There would be private dinners as well. The banker, Henry Stern, had invited prominent business people to a small dinner at his home, and the Chamber of Commerce sponsored a luncheon at the Phoenix Hotel.

The governor's wife had already purchased a ball gown for the evening gala in San Francisco, but she paused in front of the tent store and stared hard at the royal-blue taffeta gown on the mannequin. She entered and bought it at once. A half hour later, legislative wives, laughing and chatting, followed her. They carried the ball gowns into the sunlight to study the color of the fabrics; they changed into them, giggling nervously in the darkness at the rear of the tent, and modeled them for each other, playfully swirling and curtsying. They bought gowns for themselves and for their daughters and left the tent store with the feather hats perched on their heads.

Thirsty children headed for the Lewin water barrel, and their mothers trailed behind them and remained in the tent store to study the available merchandise. A weary miner's wife wearing a sun bonnet and a cotton dress, faded to the ocher tint of the desert sands, smoothed a red moiré skirt. Her work-worn, callused fingers stroked the smooth fabric, and she lifted it to her cheek. She paid for it with a bag of silver nuggets and smiled shyly at Emma.

Two women argued over the green velvet suit that Emma had thought to sell for a hundred and fifty dollars. It went to the florid-faced wife of a rancher, who paid for it with ten crisp twenty-dollar bills pulled from the pocket of her blue-and-white gingham skirt.

A heavyset miner from La Paz bought three of the ball gowns and gave Isaac heavy gold nuggets in exchange, plucking them from the small leather bag that dangled at his belt.

Emma and Isaac worked steadily, reaching across the improvised counter to extend merchandise and accept payment. Their arms ached, and smiles were frozen onto their weary faces. Cigar boxes filled with cash and ore were emptied into a gunny sack, and the empty containers were replaced on the plank counter. Emma helped a young girl to adjust a pink organdy gown. The girl preened before the narrow mirror they had borrowed from Mina Melczer.

"You look beautiful," Emma assured her truthfully. She caught a glimpse of her own reflection and turned away from the haggard, pale woman who stared back at her. The child she carried stirred and shifted. She rested briefly on an overturned barrel and returned to the counter.

The loose blue dress she wore was dark with sweat now, and her hands trembled with weariness, but still she worked on. The water barrel was empty, and the splintered shelves and packing barrels were depleted. By midafternoon every item in the tent store had been sold.

Isaac carried the gunny sack of receipts to the bank and heaved a sigh of relief as the clerk counted the cash and entered the amount in his passbook, blotting the numbers carefully. Within five hours he had made several thousand dollars, and the assayers had yet to give him a price on the nuggets and the ore he had taken in payment. He and Emma had gambled, and they had won. Their stake in Phoenix was guaranteed, their future in the territorial capital ensured.

Now they themselves were celebrants, and they followed the crowd to the capitol building, where the official ceremony was just beginning. A huge American flag was suspended at the entryway, and the outer walls of Arizona malapai, granite, and tufa were brushed with sunlight. A sculpture of the Winged Victory crowned the zinc and copper dome, her torch of liberty and her wreath of triumph ignited by the desert sun. Fathers held their small children on their shoulders as they strained to hear the message of congratulations from the Congress in Washington, D.C., and President McKinley's carefully phrased greetings.

Governor Brodie's proclamation was simple and eloquent.

"Today we dedicate this great capitol building in the territory of Arizona, in the city of Phoenix. Once before, a city stood here, and now a city has risen again in wondrous testimony to man's faith in this land blessed by God. We have followed our destiny here. This desert has become our oasis, these mountains our fortress. We have raised a city on a shoreline of sand. The future is ours, and on this great day we lay claim to it!"

Firecrackers exploded and the band struck up "The Battle Hymn of the Republic." Children blew horns and whistles. Women hugged each other and men clapped. The crowd surged forward toward the capitol building, moving closer to the music and the laughter, to the energetic vortex of history in the making.

Emma Lewin also moved forward, as though propelled by an unseen hand to an amorphous destination. She waved to Brother Timothy as two Indian boys hurtled past her, barefoot now, their shoes hung by their laces at their shoulders. The liquor-tinged breath of a bearded miner mingled with the fragrance of his wife's overly sweet eau de cologne. The Ferris wheel whirled above her head in a dizzying pattern of mobile light. Band music pounded in her ears, competing with the staccato explosion of firecrackers. A child screamed in panic, and the crowd pressed about Emma, blacking her vision, forcing her to struggle for air. She fought a wave of nausea, but still the ground slid away beneath her feet and a strange darkness dimmed her eyes.

"Emma!" Isaac's voice was harsh, but his arms about her waist were strong and sustaining. He cradled her, supported her, breaking the fall of her faint.

An hour later she stirred to wakefulness in Dr. Cantwell's whitewashed surgery. The shades were drawn, and she lay very still and listened to the murmuring voices behind the white screen that encircled her cot. Isaac and the doctor spoke softly, but she heard them clearly.

"The child will be all right?" Isaac asked, and his voice trembled with anxiety.

She pressed her hands across her abdomen, felt its gentle swell and, then, magically, the slow movement of the child.

"The child will be fine." The Scots doctor's voice was calm, reassuring.

She waited for Isaac to ask another question. His silhouetted figure sailed across the screen. How tall he was, how thick his dark hair, how finely carved his profile. She hoped he had not been frightened by her faint. She was not ill, only tired, so tired. He had asked anxiously after the baby. Now she waited for him to ask about her. He lifted his hands to his eyes. Was he weeping? she wondered.

"And your wife will be fine," the doctor continued. "See that she rests more. She is a strong woman, but even a strong woman must rest at such a time, in this climate."

"Yes, of course."

Why didn't he come to her? Why didn't he hold her and comfort her? She turned her face to the wall, startled by the unshed tears that stung her eyes, by the heaviness that had settled on her heart.

She slept then, and when she awakened Isaac was sitting beside her, his hand resting lightly on the bright hair that always caused his heart to turn. She moved her head and smiled bitterly up at him.

"I'm fine," she said. "Fine." The word, twice repeated, was at once an assertion of her independence and a denial of his support, his comfort. She ignored his extended hand and lowered herself from the bed. Her voice was cool, almost detached, as she thanked Dr. Cantwell and apologized for the inconvenience that they had caused him on Dedication Day.

Three months later, as workmen heaved the plate-glass window into place on the simple wooden structure that was the new Lewin's Emporium, an Indian boy ran up to Isaac to tell him that Dr. Cantwell had sent for him. Isaac handed a workman the wooden sign that he had removed from the tent store and was about to affix to the new building, borrowed Melczer's horse, and rode with wild speed to the adobe house. His heart hammered and his throat was dry. Small prayers formed in his mind. *Keep her safe. Keep them safe.* His wife with the red-gold hair. His child, light as a cloud in the strange dreams that invaded his nights.

A group of women sat beneath the eucalyptus tree, talking softly as they folded white squares of cotton, lengths of flannel. Diapers and swaddling clothes for the infant, he realized, and steeled himself against the memory of a similar layette hand-stitched by Rivka, his wife, for Sarah, his daughter.

The women stared at him with narrowed eyes and turned away as Emma's scream pierced the air. They waited then, their own breath coming in shallow gasps as they rode the crests of remembered pain. He moved to enter the house, but Mina Melczer, a tall, capable woman, moved toward him.

"Not now," she said gently.

She led him into the loggia and poured him a glass of root beer from the pitcher in the desert cooler. He accepted her ministration, obedient as a child, and listened to his wife's agony, his teeth clenched against his lips until he tasted his own blood. The wrenching shrieks and the low, submissive moans rose and fell, and his heart turned. He cradled his head in his arms, closed his eyes. Death adhered to him, trailed him. He saw again, in memory, Sarah and Rivka, broken and bloodied—pale Miriam with seaweed in her hair. *Keep her safe. Keep them safe.* The prayer became a hypnotic litany, but he was not calmed.

"Now—yes—now!" Emma's voice rang loud and clear in her native tongue. Triumph rimmed the words, joy surpassing pain. The strong burst of an infant's wail trembled on the heat-heavy air, and the women smiled at each other and touched hands.

"Go to her now," Mina Melczer said gently.

He opened the door to their bedroom. Emma lay very still, her pale face glistening with sweat, her hair spread in a fiery fan across the white rise of the pillow. She looked up at him, and her blue eyes blazed with a febrile intensity. She inclined her head toward the infant, wrapped in white swaddling and nestled in the crook of her arm. He saw the feathery patch of dark hair that matched his own and the wondrously small, perfectly formed face.

"A girl," Dr. Cantwell said. "A bonny baby girl."

Isaac breathed deeply and touched the tiny fingers curled about a moist tendril of Emma's hair. He had buried one daughter and fathered another. A second chance had been given to him. Beneficent ghosts hovered over his beautiful newborn daughter, and he wept as strong men do, allowing the tears to course freely down his cheeks. His lips moved, but no voice came.

Emma watched him and held her daughter closer. He had wanted a son. He had told her so one night as they lay together in the darkness.

"Do you want a boy or a girl?" she had asked—an idle question asked in an idle tone.

"Every man wants a son."

Now his tears betrayed his disappointment and stirred her anger.

"Are you all right?" His voice was very low.

"Fine. I'm fine. But now I want to sleep."

"I'll take the baby." Mina Melczer lifted the infant and wondered that Isaac Lewin did not kiss his wife, did not take her hand in his.

"Leonie. We shall call her Leonie," Emma said. "For my mother." She turned to Isaac and he nodded.

"Of course." He wanted to take Emma in his arms but he knew how weary she was. The infant girl, his daughter, cried lustily. The child, born in the adobe house in a desert city, would be named for the woman who had taken her own life in the great stone mansion on Amsterdam's Prinsengracht.

"Leonie Lewin," Dr. Cantwell repeated in his pleasant brogue. "It has a ring to it."

Isaac took the child from Mina and carried it outside. It was the hour of sunset, and he showed his newborn daughter how the violet shadows stole across the slopes of the Camelback Mountains and formed mysterious patterns on the smooth amber sands of the desert floor.

"Leonie." His voice was a whisper, her name a benison.

It was the assault of the heat that awakened Natalya Wallach her first morning in Arizona. She stretched out her arms as though to free herself from the suffocating blanket of desert air that had settled over her and realized that her white nightgown was soaked with sweat. The hot oven breath of the southland wind wafted through the narrow windows of the Lewins' adobe house, and the brilliant sunlight of dawn penetrated the dark blue curtains, which Emma had warned her to draw closely. Natalya stirred uneasily and closed her eyes, weary still from the long journey, but she knew that she would not sleep again. She heard the murmur of voices and sniffed the scent of newly brewed coffee and freshly baked bread. Of course—wherever Emma lived, there would be fresh coffee served in china cups and thinly cut bread, artfully arranged in a basket covered with a snowy napkin. The cultivated routines of Amsterdam and London prevailed in the Arizona desert.

Natalya was aware suddenly of another presence in the room. She opened her eyes and smiled at the child who stood in the doorway, her small flower of a face framed in petals of soft brown hair.

"You must be Leonie," she said.

The child smiled shyly, and her turquoise-colored eyes, fringed by thick dark lashes, glinted with a gemlike brilliance.

"You are Natalya." She enunciated each syllable carefully. An attentive child who scavenged adult nuances, always listening, always learning—Natalya, the teacher, recognized her at once. Occasionally she grew fond of such children. More often, she disliked them.

She got out of bed and held her hand out, enfolding Leonie Lewin's small fingers in her own.

"I have a present for you," she said, and she went to her portmanteau and removed the silver bracelet studded with rough-cut turquoise that she had purchased at the Papago trading post in Santa Fe. She slipped it on the child's wrist and was pleased when Leonie pressed it against her cheek and moved it, with artful vanity, up her arm.

"A small girl won't appreciate something like that," Abner had argued. He had wanted to buy the child one of the small dolls that the Indians fashioned out of corn husks, but Natalya had resisted. She remembered, too well, the Indian doll that Isaac had bought for Miriam on the Galveston dock, and she did not want her reunion with the Lewins to be haunted by the penumbral ghosts of the port city.

Four years had passed since the Lewins and the Wallachs had parted. Abner and Natalya had traveled to Colorado on the strength of a letter from a cousin of Abner's who spoke of the opportunities in Cripple Creek. Gold was being mined there, and a man could make his fortune in a few years' time.

"It's hard work," the cousin had written. "But think of the opportunity." *Opportunity.* The word had a magic ring, demanding optimism and energy. Abner tried to translate it into Yiddish and found that he could not. Perhaps the very concept was alien to the Jews of eastern Europe.

Abner and Natalya journeyed to Cripple Creek only to find that the cousin was dead, the victim of an ore house explosion. His widow stared at them with a dead-eyed gaze. She was a young woman who had grown old in the gold fields of Colorado. She would travel now to New York, where her sister worked in a shirtwaist factory and she herself had the promise of a job.

"Let God protect me from 'opportunity,' " she said bitterly.

Natalya made Abner promise that he would never go down to the mines. "We saw enough death in Galveston," she said. "I am tired of pitting myself against nature."

They had miraculously escaped the floodwaters of the Mexican gulf—she would not allow him to risk his life in the bowels of the earth. They had, instead, opened a small general store in the dusty mining town where they sold staples and supplies to those who came to Cripple Creek with dreams of prying riches out of the earth. They stocked the narrow shelves with bolts of cloth, gleaming tins of paraffin and cooking oil, cannisters of sugar and coffee. Sacks of cornmeal and grain leaned against the walls. But although they knew how to stock their store, they never learned how to refuse credit.

"I must have cornmeal for the baby," a gaunt miner's wife said, "Put it on the book. I'll have money next week I'll pay then."

Kind-hearted Natalya measured out the cornmeal and made a notation in the ledger, often adding a lump of sugar or a stick of licorice for the child to suck on. Too often, the next week did not bring a payment but instead a request for additional credit or, frequently, the news that the miner's family had left the area, their ore bags empty, their eyes blank with despair.

"Some of that pretty cloth. A few yards for my little girl's first dress," a man with work-scarred hands pleaded, and Abner cut the fabric loose from the bolt, his heart heavy with the knowledge that he would not receive payment for it. Often he slashed at the air with his razor, angry because he could not resist the pleading in a father's voice.

By the time the mines of Cripple Creek enjoyed a boom, wholesalers would no longer supply Abner Wallach with goods. *Chispas*, heavy gold nuggets, were wrenched from the earth, and the small saloons of Cripple Creek were filled with revelers who paid for their drinks with fingerlings of ore. But Abner Wallach's ledgers were full of promises, and his resources were exhausted. He and Natalya closed their store for the last time on the day a letter from Isaac Lewin arrived describing his enterprise in Phoenix and inviting the Wallachs to help him manage it.

"The business expands, and I plan now to build a new store in Phoenix with branches in other towns. I will need your help, and Emma would be glad to have Natalya nearby again. It has not been easy for her here in Phoenix."

Abner had wondered shrewdly whether it was his business prowess or Natalya's friendship with Emma that had motivated Isaac to make the offer, but he did not ponder the question for long. He would do a good job for Isaac Lewin, he knew, and it was clear that Phoenix, with its access to transcontinental railroad branches, was fast becoming both the commercial and political center of Arizona. Natalya, who studied maps and geography books with an odd intensity, pointed out that Phoenix was now within a week's journey of every trade and manufacturing center in the nation. Arizona would not long be a territory. Despite resistance, its statehood was inevitable, and Phoenix would then be the capital of one of the largest and richest states in the union.

Natalya and Emma had corresponded regularly during the years of their separation. Their letters had assuaged the loneliness of their new lives and compensated for the lack of a community with whom they could share Sabbath meals and holiday celebrations. The Jewish community of Phoenix was slowly growing, but it was still very small, and the services were sparsely attended. The men missed the ritual, but the women yearned for a sense of community.

"I light my Sabbath candles and watch the last streaks of daylight melt into the desert," one of Emma's letters read. "I think of you doing the same thing in Cripple Creek, murmuring the same prayer, and somehow I feel just a bit less lonely."

Natalya imagined her friend standing before her silver candlesticks, her face radiant with the glow cast by the newly lit flames. She understood the solitude that Emma felt at such an hour. How alone they all were on this vast frontier, far from homeland and family, and how vulnerable were the small and valiant Sabbath beacons that flickered in desert and mountain winds. The acknowledgment of that loneliness created a unique closeness between Abner and herself, a renewed will to endure together in the world they had chosen for their own. They recognized that Cripple Creek had been a failure and a disappointment, but they sought new paths and made each other laugh by exaggerating the vagaries of their neighbors and repeating the pithy comments they heard each day in their store.

"All this country needs is less heat and more water," one miner said to another as they waited for Abner to pack their purchases.

"That's all hell needs," his neighbor replied.

"What's a mine?" Abner asked.

"That's an easy one, 'Jewsie'—a hole in the ground owned by a miner." The men laughed easily, openly. Abner did not wince at the nickname. "I'll begin to worry when they use it behind my back," he told Natalya.

But there was no hint of joy or spontaneous frontier humor in Emma Lewin's letters. They were permeated by a sadness that was unrelieved even by her descriptions of the varicolored beauty of the Sonoran desert and the awesome dignity of the surrounding mountains. The only hint of lightness came with a mention of little Leonie.

"She has a rare and gentle beauty," Emma had written, and Natalya, watching the child toy with the bracelet, saw that Emma's words had not been the subjective exaggeration of a proud mother. The small girl who stood in her doorway was beautiful, with her dark hair and gem-colored eyes. The silver bangle gleamed against her rose-gold skin. She left the room as quietly as she had entered, and Natalya saw that she did not have a child's playful clumsiness but moved with a fluid grace.

Why weren't Emma and Isaac happier, then? Their daughter was beautiful and their business had prospered. They were both enthusiastic about Arizona and optimistic about their future there, yet an odd reserve had grown between them, a careful, almost fragile politeness.

The water in the pitcher that stood on the washstand was lukewarm, and Natalya used it sparingly on the cloth that she passed across her parched skin. She passed the damp cloth across her breasts, noting with pleasure their new fullness. Her pregnancy had been her own sweet secret, concealed even from Abner until their arrival in Phoenix the previous evening. Natalya had miscarried twice before, once during the journey from Texas to Colorado and once during their first bitter winter in Cripple Creek. She had feared that if Abner knew of her condition he would refuse to proceed to Arizona and the opportunity to work with Isaac Lewin would be lost. Isaac had stressed the importance of Abner's arrival in Phoenix in time to help him with the special sales he planned in conjunction with President Theodore Roosevelt's visit to the territory.

Still, Abner had been joyous and forgiving when she confided in him. "I am glad, Natalya, but you must not keep secrets from me. Secrets shadow and scar a marriage." They had been silent then, thinking of Isaac and Emma Lewin in the room down the narrow passageway. They had been guests in the adobe house for only a few hours and shared only a late supper, yet they sensed the strange tension between Emma and Isaac, the silence and constraint redolent of words unspoken, feelings unshared.

Natalya recalled Emma's words when she had first told her that she and Isaac had decided to marry.

"We are in agreement about how best to live our lives," Emma had said.

"And you love each other," Natalya had added.

She herself had been newly betrothed, and she smiled at herself in the mirror as though mystified by her own reflection. She was a plain young woman made beautiful because she loved and was beloved. Surely Emma, so soon to be married, was aglow with similar feelings, similar dreams. But Emma had not spoken of love, although her breath quickened when Isaac entered the room and there was a softness in her eyes when she looked at him.

That softness was still there, Natalya had noticed, the previous evening, but only, it seemed, when Isaac was unaware of Emma's gaze. And although Isaac had spoken proudly of Emma when she was not in the room—telling them of her fortitude during the journey west, her tenacity during the days of the tent store despite her pregnancy and the unfamiliar heat ("No other woman could have done what she did," he had said, love and admiration mingling in his voice)— when she entered, his tone changed and he spoke with dispassionate neutrality. It was as though the Lewins played an elaborate children's game of hide-and-seek with their feelings—at once yearning for discovery and yet fearful of betrayal.

"No one loses in this game," Natalya had once advised a crying child, and she wished that she could dispense similar counsel to her friends.

She sighed and carried the china bowl that contained the residue of her washing water into the kitchen, where Emma sat plaiting Leonie's dark hair into a single silken braid.

"Good morning," she said and poured the water into a

pail so that it could be used to mop the floor and ultimately tossed onto the struggling shoots in the kitchen garden.

Emma smiled.

"You learn the secrets of living in the desert quickly, Natalya," she said. "When we first arrived in Arizona, I made the mistake of actually tossing away the washing water."

"I have a good teacher, Emma," Natalya replied. "I watched you last night. Perhaps you didn't have as efficient a welcoming committee when you arrived in Arizona."

"I don't like to think of our arrival in Arizona," Emma said harshly, and Natalya stared at her in surprise, noting the new sharpness in her friend's features, the delicate lines about her eyes. Some few silver strands glinted in her hair, but her skin had lost its pallor and assumed the amber sheen of the sun-washed desert. Her hand trembled as she passed Natalya a cup of coffee. The tenacity and strength that Isaac had described so proudly had taken its toll.

"Was it very difficult for you, Emma?" Natalya asked softly.

"It was not easy," Emma replied. She turned away, but Natalya saw the sadness in her eyes. Deftly, Emma changed the subject. "How far along are you, Natalya?"

"Only three months." Natalya blushed. Emma had discerned her secret at once, but she could not tell if her friend's glance betrayed sympathy or joy. "Abner is very pleased," she added, "as Isaac must have been."

"Our children will be born at the same time, then," Emma said. "I too am pregnant." There was no joy in her voice, only restraint and resignation. Isaac had wanted another child and had spoken of it from the time Leonie began to walk. He wanted a family, brothers and sisters who cared for and about each other. He did not want Leonie ever to be alone, as he had been.

It was a plea she could not deny, had not wanted to deny. Still, she had waited for him to add that he wanted another child conceived in love mingled with desire, a child born of their commitment to each other and to their chosen life in this land. He had not spoken, fearful as always of betraying the compact she had forced upon them. She punished him for his silence with a cool bitterness, which even her brothers remarked on, when they visited from California.

Simon held Leonie in his arms and marveled at the child's beauty.

"A dark-haired version of you as a small girl," he told Emma. "Now she needs brothers to admire her as we admired you." Simon's wife was pregnant for the second time, and Simon had always operated on the assumption that what he did should be emulated by others.

"A woman needs to decide things for herself," Emma had retorted. "Encourage Emil to marry before you interfere with my life."

Her brother Emil worried her. His success in California had not calmed his restlessness. The Coen brothers served as brokers for mining companies throughout the West. They arranged for export and managed sales and shipments to the Far East and Africa. They leased cargo ships and arranged for contracts.

"Business is a game," Emil said. "You toss the dice and move a marker. If you're sufficiently skilled, you know when to forego your turn and when to slant the board. And since Simon and I make the rules, we win more often than not."

The cynicism in his tone frightened Emma. Emil kept a mistress, a Mexican singer. "I'm not interested in marriage," he said when Emma offered to introduce him to the daughter of a Jewish family in Phoenix. "I have the example of my parents' marriage."

Isaac, who was holding Leonie on his lap, looked at Emma. Their child would have the example of their marriage—a carefully controlled partnership, deftly balanced, each word and gesture weighed and measured. Emma turned away, ignoring his silent plea.

"You should think about joining us in California," Simon Coen said to Isaac.

His sister's husband had impressed him. He had imagined Isaac Lewin to be a provincial shtetl Jew, not unlike the Yiddish-speaking peddlers who drifted into California where they inevitably opened small stores or even saloons. Simon thought it ironic that they had fled the ghettos of eastern Europe yet seemed intent on building their own ghettos in the cities and towns of California. His coreligionists, he acknowledged regretfully, embarrassed him, and he was grateful for the community of cultivated Sephardic Jews with whom he worshiped at Temple Emanuel. But Isaac Lewin was an intelligent and educated man who perceived the developing West with a rare insight.

"These territories will be the focus of energy for the United States in this century," Isaac said gravely. "New Mexico, Arizona, Texas. We are in the new age of electricity, of horseless carriages, railroads. There are men who dream of flying machines. This will be an era of speed and light. The world will need the resources of these states so that they can fire their generators, fuel their vehicles, thread their cables."

"Exactly," Emil said. "All the more reason for you to join us. We're exploring new markets in Asia—shipping more copper across the Pacific. You're not a miner, Isaac. You're a businessman with a sense of history, a vision of the future."

Isaac smiled. "Your business is too amorphous for me. You send telegrams, sign contracts. You negotiate your agreements without knowing what your shipments look like. I like to see my merchandise arrive and fill my shelves. I like to see my customers come in and touch a garment, smile at a toy for a child. A bride purchases her first set of cookware. A miner makes his first strike and comes to Lewin's Emporium to buy a coat for the wife who for three years wrapped herself in thin shawls. Emma and I have plans for the Emporium. Soon, very soon, we will expand. My friend Abner Wallach is coming to help me manage the store in time for President Roosevelt's visit. We have plans for a whole new line of merchandise, special displays. We anticipate more visitors to Phoenix than we have had since the dedication of the capitol."

Isaac had obtained photographs of the Roughrider president which would hang over every counter. Handbills announcing the Lewin Emporium Presidential Sale had been printed and distributed. He had calculated his profits and estimated that with the anticipated income and a substantial loan, he could undertake the construction of a new store, a four-story structure, the largest in Phoenix. The architect's plans were in his drawer with the contractor's estimates. He was prepared to submit them to the banker Henry Stern, whom he had now met several times at Friday evening services. Stern had made it known that he was amenable to advancing loans to expanding businesses. He, too, had a commitment to the future of Phoenix.

"I wish you luck, then," Simon Coen had said. "And remember, if this Henry Stern does not give you the necessary financing, Emil and I are ready to help you." The brothers' initial loan to Isaac for the launching of the tent store had been repaid with interest. That loan had been based on fraternal obligation. Now they believed in Isaac and Emma's demonstrated business acumen.

"I should prefer to do it on my own," Isaac said cordially but firmly.

"Yes. It would be best if we were to proceed on our own," Emma had added, enunciating each pronoun carefully. She would not allow her husband and her brothers to discuss her future while she sat quietly in a corner, rising occasionally to refresh their glasses of iced tea.

Emil and Simon had glanced at her and then at each other, but they had made no reply. They had lost arguments with Emma too often in the past. They did not see Isaac stiffen, nor did they observe the bitter smile that played across his lips.

And now at last the Wallachs had arrived, and the president's visit was imminent. Emma reached for Natalya's hand.

"How wonderful it is to have you here," she said. "I hadn't realized until you arrived how lonely I've been."

Natalya smiled at her, as she sometimes smiled at the small girls in her classroom when she comforted them against the waves of inexplicable sadness that caused them to separate themselves from the other children at play.

"It will be all right, Emma," she said, and her own words of reassurance mystified her. She sensed her friend's melancholy, but its source eluded her. They sat quietly, then, in the sun-swept, clay-walled kitchen as the child Leonie played with her turquoise bracelet and a mockingbird perched on the silver-leafed branch of the olive tree and sang with heartbreaking sweetness.

* * *

Isaac Lewin had always regretted that he was not yet an American citizen during the election year of 1900 because he would have wanted to cast a ballot in favor of William McKinley. It was not the presidential candidate who intrigued him but his running mate, the bespectacled and mustachioed former Secretary of the Navy, Theodore Roosevelt. When McKinley was assassinated less than a year after his inauguration, Isaac was saddened, but he did not share the consternation of most Americans. He was certain that Theodore Roosevelt would be a great president for the entire nation and especially for the Southwest.

Isaac had read Roosevelt's thoughtful biography of Thomas Hart Benton. The biographer and his subject were curiously linked by their mutual appreciation of the importance of the expanding American frontier. Brother Timothy had sent Roosevelt's four-volume *The Winning of the West* to Isaac. The books were a gift of appreciation for a shipment of clothing that Isaac had solicited from other merchants for the mission school in response to his friend's heart-rending description of the needs of Indian children.

"We have taken away their land, their way of life, their ancient gods. We must offer them in return at least basic protection against the environment—food and clothing to match our lofty words. We disparage their tents and hogans, but we do not offer them houses."

Brother Timothy's words echoed the complaints of Johnny Redbird, the slender Hopi Indian whom Isaac had hired to assist him in the store. It was Johnny who had told Isaac that the traditional Hopi blessing was a prayer for long life, healing, rain, and fertility. The Indian had smiled when Isaac read the same prayer in Hebrew and translated it for him.

"We are not so very far apart, then, your tribe and mine— your god of the desert and my gods of the mountains."

Like the Jews, the Hopis traced descent through the maternal line, and when Johnny's father died, a rent was made in the mourner's buckskin vest as a symbol of loss and mourning. Isaac remembered still the sound of the rabbi's razor severing the cloth of his jacket that wintry day when his own wife and daughter were buried. Just as the Jews lit a remembrance candle on the anniversary of a loved one's death each year, so did the Hopis hold a brief fireside ceremony. The Indians, too, considered themselves a single family, each tribe linked by ties of blood and heritage. Their circle dances were not unlike the festive horas of the Jews.

Accounts of Indian violence and hostility frightened Isaac but were not incomprehensible to him. He understood the rage of the uprooted and the persecuted; always he had been sympathetic to the Indians. The Lewin Emporium was the only store in Phoenix that allowed Indians to try on shoes and clothing.

"I shall not continue to shop here if you allow that," an irate Phoenix matron had once told Isaac. "I shall take my custom to a store that knows how to deal with Americans."

"Who is more American than an Indian?" Isaac had retorted.

He had not abandoned the practice, and he noted that within two months time that woman resumed her patronage. The Indian problem would not go away, he knew, nor did he foresee how it could be solved.

Roosevelt perceived the Indian problem, but he could not identify with it and he thought that palliatives which the government offered were superficial and self-serving. The Bureau of Indian Affairs was laced with corruption, and the reservation lands were often confining and unsuited to the Indian pattern of life. It had been necessary to contain Indian violence, but Isaac was troubled by the cruelty of that containment.

Perhaps it was necessary to have experienced persecution and dispersal, racial cruelty and economic and spiritual deprivation, in order to understand the Indians—the fear that bred violence, the pride and tenacity that caused them to reject compromise and assimilation. Certainly, Isaac and Brother Timothy, both of them fugitives from poverty and rejection, felt an instinctive compassion for the natives of the land they now called their own. Roosevelt, by contrast, was the Harvard-educated son of an established and wealthy Dutch family. Could he be expected to understand the despair in Johnny Redbird's voice, the sadness in his eyes?

Still, Theodore Roosevelt understood other aspects of the

Southwest. He loved the rugged, dramatic landscape, and the wilderness intrigued him. He had hunted in Minnesota and operated a ranch in the Dakota Badlands. He was known to be sympathetic to the concept of statehood for New Mexico and Arizona, but unfortunately he linked the two territories as McKinley had. Still, this visit to Arizona could change that. Surely Roosevelt, the historian and concerned naturalist, would recognize the inefficacy of joining the enormous territories. Their size, coupled with their cultural and historic differences, made such a linkage impractical at best, inoperable at worst. That was a lesson the president would surely learn in Arizona.

Isaac Lewin and Abner Wallach worked long hours before the president's visit to Phoenix. An American flag draped the plate-glass window and a large portrait of the president on horseback stood in the window itself. Placards throughout the city and the surrounding towns announced that the store would remain open for extra hours in honor of the nation's first citizen and that free lemonade would be served.

"We make progress," Isaac observed wryly. "Three years ago we dipped water out of a barrel in front of a tent. Now we offer lemonade in glasses on a polished counter."

Emma served the lemonade, and Natalya presided over the neighboring counter, which displayed the only selection of "teddy bears" west of the Mississippi. The jocular stuffed animals had been designed by Richard Steiff that year and named for the president, who had immediately purchased one for the White House. Isaac had telegraphed his order to the manufacturer as soon as he learned of the president's impending visit, and the cuddly animals disappeared from the counter at a rapid rate.

"You may have been a student of philosophy, but you do have the instinct for merchandising the right product at the right time," Abner Wallach said wonderingly. He had not thought that the stuffed animals would prove so popular.

"It's all based on a pragmatic perception," Isaac retorted. "You must read William James, Abner."

"Oh, I intend to. Tonight. First thing. Do you have a Yiddish translation?" Abner asked jokingly. He was too weary in the evening to do anything but scan the newspapers and skim through the catalogues. The pace of life at the Emporium left him exhausted, but Isaac sat up late into the night reading history and philosophy. Did Emma lie awake waiting for him? Abner wondered. Certainly, Natalya never closed her eyes until he slid into bed beside her.

Again, as the president drew closer to the territorial capital, a holiday spirit prevailed in Phoenix. Visitors poured in, hoping to catch a glimpse of the hero of San Juan Hill. It was said that Roosevelt had been accessible to the crowds during his visit to the Grand Canyon. He had kissed small children and affably shaken hands before making a speech that was widely quoted in every Arizona newspaper the next day. The beauty of the Grand Canyon had to be preserved, the president had stated unequivocally. It could not fall victim to those who might exploit it. A national park system would have to be established to protect the natural beauty of the land.

The Arizonans were optimistic. This president appreciated their land; he would support their aspirations for statehood. Certainly Governor Brodie, who had been Roosevelt's comrade during the Cuban campaign, would exert some influence on the president.

Isaac, however, was cautious. "It will not be so easy to sell the concept of separate statehood for Arizona. The president is a politician, and he has a politician's debts. It is Brodie who owes Roosevelt the favor for his appointment as governor, not Roosevelt who owes Brodie."

"Why must you see everything in terms of debit and credit?" Emma asked irritably.

"I'm a businessman," Isaac replied. "You know that."

"I grow more aware of it each day," she said.

Abner and Natalya looked uncomfortably at each other. The brief bitter exchanges between Isaac and Emma embarrassed them. Their own marriage seemed to them to be a precious gift, an opportunity that neither of them had thought possible. Contentment had softened Natalya's sharp equine features, banished the stark and haunted look in Abner's eyes. Their failure at Cripple Creek had brought them closer to each other, renewed them. What would such a failure do to

Emma and Isaac? Natalya wondered. Could their marriage sustain loss and disappointment?

Isaac had not underestimated the flow of business that day. Twice during the morning the home furnishings counter had to be replenished. All through the territory, newly prosperous miners were building houses, and they seized on the president's visit as an excuse for a shopping holiday. Phoenix itself was rapidly expanding, and new communities developed in its environs. The housewives of Scottsdale and Fountain Hill, of Tempe and Mesa, wanted carpeted floors and upholstered sofas and chairs. Curtains had hung limply on the narrow apertures of the meanest adobe huts, but the new wide-windowed houses would have draperies as protection from the onslaught of desert sunlight.

Isaac stacked a pile of fabrics and decided that the new store would have an entire department for home furnishings. He would even hire someone to do the purchasing and oversee the displays. And the counters would be much expanded, the aisles widened. He studied the narrow passageways, aware suddenly that the store pulsated with new excitement.

"The president's coming! The president's coming!" a small boy shouted excitedly. "He's coming right into this store. He's outside now, looking in the window!"

Emma and Natalya looked at each other in amazement. It had never occurred to them that the president would enter the Emporium. Hastily, Emma removed the lemonade glasses from the counter, and Natalya rearranged the much diminished selection of teddy bears.

"Leonie," Emma called, and the child ran to her, dark curls flying, her face radiant with excitement.

Isaac hurried to the door and opened it himself for the presidential entourage.

"Mr. President, I welcome you," he said, and Theodore Roosevelt smiled at him and extended his hand.

"I couldn't forgo a visit to an establishment that named its sale in my honor, now, could I?" the president said. His voice was deep and jovial, and his hazel eyes glinted behind his thick glasses. He toyed absently with the black satin ribbon that dangled from his rimless spectacles and smiled amiably. The president was not an exceptionally tall man, but he stood with a practiced erectness that gave the impression of height. His muscular body strained against his well-tailored dark waistcoat, and his fleshy neck seemed constricted within his starched white collar. An impeccably knotted silk cravat matched his chestnut-colored mustache, and his skin had the ruddiness peculiar to fair-complected men who spend a great deal of their time out of doors.

"You are Isaac Lewin?" the president asked. "The proprietor of this establishment?"

"I am, Mr. President," Isaac said. "And I have the honor to introduce you to my wife, Emma Lewin."

Theodore Roosevelt looked approvingly at Emma Lewin. He was partial to auburn-haired women, and the storekeeper's wife had a natural grace and dignity. Her dark blue dress with its white collar and cuffs was adroitly tailored to conceal the gentle swell of her pregnancy. Her hand when he took it in his own was calloused and work-roughened. Clearly, life in the American West had not been easy for her, yet the enterprising Lewins were infinitely more fortunate than their coreligionists in Europe. Only weeks earlier the president and his secretary of state, John Hay, had attempted to prevail on Russian authorities to halt pogroms like the one that had occurred in Kishinev that spring. The Russians had adamantly rejected the president's intervention and accused him of interfering with internal Russian matters. Yes, the Lewins had been fortunate enough to find refuge in the American West, and the West in turn was fortunate to have such pioneers.

"I am delighted to meet you, Mrs. Lewin," Theodore Roosevelt said. "May I enlist your assistance in making my purchases?"

"It would be my honor, Mr. President."

"I noticed in your advertisement that you have a number of ladies' hats with ostrich feathers available?"

"We do."

"My wife designs the hats herself, and the feathers are from Arizona's ostricheries," Isaac Lewin interjected.

"Ah. I should like you to show me some of your creations. I promised gifts that were uniquely Arizonan to my wife and my daughter, Alice." He glanced at the display of teddy bears and smiled. "I imagine you will find enough purchasers for my namesake, Mr. Lewin."

Emma led the president to the millinery counter and held her most stylishly fashioned hats up for his consideration. The crowd moved respectfully back and watched the conqueror of San Juan Hill ponder his purchases. Gently, Emma encouraged him to buy a gray cloche plumed with a matching feather for his wife. Edith Roosevelt dressed conservatively, she knew. A peacock-blue feathered bonnet was selected for Alice, who was known to have more daring tastes. Theodore Roosevelt beamed with the satisfaction of a man who has accomplished a difficult task successfully.

"I congratulate you for establishing your store, Mr. Lewin," the president said to Isaac. "And I advise you to expand. Arizona has a great future. It is a beautiful territory."

"We should like to see our territory become a state," Isaac said daringly. "We should like to see her star added to the flag of the nation."

The presidential aides glanced at each other nervously. The president had spoken of Arizona's potential and its beauty, of the need for preserving its natural assets. He had made a point of avoiding mention of its statehood, and now this Jewish shopkeeper would embarrass him into making a statement fraught with political danger.

Theodore Roosevelt whipped off his spectacles and fixed his gaze on Isaac Lewin.

"Would it not be more practical to join two great territories into a single state, my friend? It would be eminently reasonable to have New Mexico and Arizona enter the union as one state with Santa Fe as a joint capital. You are a businessman. Is it not more sensible to consolidate one's enterprise and control it from a single location? Why have two headquarters when one will suffice?" The president smiled, pleased with the parallel he had so spontaneously drawn.

"With all due respect, Mr. President, I must disagree with you," Isaac said, and the crowd gasped at his temerity. Mina Melczer clutched a letter she had received from her sister who lived in the Russian pale of settlement. There, a Jew who complained mildly about a tax question had been killed by a constable who claimed he would incite the community. Yet here, in Phoenix, a very recent immigrant could argue openly with the president of the United States. Mina drew closer and saw President Roosevelt twirl his spectacles and smile benignly.

"That is the great thing about this country of ours, isn't it, Mr. Lewin? Here we have the freedom to disagree with each other."

He held his hand out to Isaac, who grasped it in a strong clasp and turned to Emma, who held Leonie in her arms.

"Your daughter, madame?"

Emma nodded.

Theodore Roosevelt leaned forward and flashed an engaging grin at the beautiful dark-haired child. In turn, she playfully pulled at the black satin ribbon and jerked the president's spectacles from his nose. The crowd laughed, and Emma pried the ribbon loose from Leonie's fingers.

"My apologies, Mr. President," she said.

"No harm done. Your child will be an awesome young woman, I think, determined to get what she wants." The president smiled. He had enjoyed his brief visit to the Emporium. A man whose English was still tinged with the gentle accent of eastern Europe had bravely argued with him, and the playful fingers of a beautiful small girl had been soft against his skin.

The store teemed with activity for hours after the presidential party left Phoenix. Word of the president's purchases had spread, and within an hour the millinery counter was stripped of hats and Natalya was occupied with taking orders. After the stock of teddy bears was exhausted, every other plaything in the store was sold. Purchasers drifted from counter to counter, and twice that afternoon Abner Wallach rushed to the bank to make deposits. The talk everywhere was of Isaac's exchange with the president.

"Only in America," Max Goldstein said to the former mayor, Emanuel Ganz, who nodded. They would never cease to be amazed by the country they had chosen for their own.

A portly man left a note for Isaac. "As an Arizonan and a Jew, I am proud that you told the president what he did not want to hear. If you are ever in Solomonville, please come to see me at the Gila Valley Bank.'' It was signed Isadore Solomon, and Isaac placed it in a closed cubby of his rolltop desk.

That night he studied his ledgers carefully.

''I think our estimates were exact,'' he told Emma. ''We have enough on hand to build the new store—with one large loan. I shall arrange an appointment with Henry Stern tomorrow.''

''My brothers would be willing to arrange it,'' Emma said. She had never met Henry Stern. She did not attend the Friday evening services, and the banker had not been at services she attended during the holidays. He worshiped with his wife's family, some said, in California.

''No.'' Isaac's tone was firm. This new enterprise would be his own. He would negotiate its financing himself.

She stood beside him and studied the ledger.

''We will go to see Henry Stern together, then,'' she said. Her eyes locked his in a solemn stare, a reminder of the agreement on which their marriage was based.

''All right.''

He turned from her, his shoulder slumped, as though he had suffered a small defeat. Her trust would mean her surrender, her acceptance of his love, a demonstration of her faith in him. But she would not grant him that, and he could not wrest it from her. When would she relax her vigilance and understand that his love was her protection? He went outside to sit in the loggia. Alone, he stared at the Camelback Mountains, draped in the velvet blackness of the night.

The Salt River Bank was housed in a small brick building on Jefferson Street, near the warehouse of the Wormser Company, a firm that supplied sharecroppers with seed for their crops and the tools and water rights with which to cultivate them. Henry Stern had shrewdly chosen his location, Isaac thought. The bank was sufficiently distant from the more established commercial banks and close to mercantile activity of the Hispanic community. He noticed that the signs were all translated into Spanish and that a Mexican girl sat at the wooden table that served as a reception desk. She smiled cordially at the Mexican farmer who had entered before the Lewins. The man's face was gaunt, his skin the color of dried ashes. His espadrilles were worn, and he twirled his straw hat nervously.

"*¿Préstamo?* A loan. Money to pay for the crops?" His voice was low, his eyes downcast. His poverty shamed him. The farmers of Arizona had just weathered a season of drought. Their winter harvest of wheat and barley had parched in the fields, and few of them had enough cash on hand to purchase seed for the summer crop of vegetables.

"*Sí. Préstamo.*" She nodded and directed him to a small cubicle. "Señor Gómez will help you," she assured him. The farmer's shoulders straightened, and he smiled. Her small courtesy, her knowledge of his language, had restored his dignity.

"I am Isaac Lewin of Lewin's Emporium. My wife and I would like to see Mr. Henry Stern."

The girl's smile was dazzlingly brilliant, her reply pleasant.

"I will tell Mr. Stern you are here," she said and disappeared into an office.

Isaac and Emma sat on a wooden bench and watched the farmer confer with Señor Gómez, who toyed nervously with his black string tie as he listened. The farmer gesticulated wildly; he pointed upward as though to describe the relentless sun and the lack of rain. He ground his feet on the floor to demonstrate the worthlessness of the few kernels he had harvested. He nodded sagely as the bank clerk made some notes on a sheet of paper and asked him a question. Minutes later he stood at the teller's cage and grinned broadly as a small sheaf of bills was counted into his outstretched hand.

Isaac watched the transaction thoughtfully. The Salt River Bank had acted swiftly and wisely. The farmer was a good risk, a hard-working man who had been defeated by the elements for a single season. His demeanor mingled energy and pride. Had he come into the Emporium, Isaac would have extended credit to him. The loan had been swiftly negotiated so that the man would have money on hand to sow his seed in season. In turn, he would come to the Salt River Bank in better times to make deposits, and he would tell his neighbors how he had been treated. An investment had been made with only a small risk taken. Other banks might have delayed the loan, asked more questions, investigated further, but Henry Stern's reputation was built on swift intuitive judgment, and clearly, his well-trained staff followed his direction.

Isaac relaxed. Their own loan would surely be swiftly negotiated. He smiled at Emma. She looked especially beautiful today in a loose black dress of polished cotton, her bright hair spilling out of a wide-brimmed black boater hat.

"Mr. Stern will see you now," the Mexican girl said and motioned them to the office.

"Good morning, Mr. Lewin, Mrs. Lewin."

Henry Stern rose to greet them, his tone affable, his voice tinged with an accent. Of course, Emma had heard that he, too, was an immigrant Jew who had worked in a European bank. A file was open on his desk, and she recognized the familiar handbills and advertisements they had distributed for the now famous Presidential Sale (it would be an annual event, Isaac had decided, and she agreed with him) and the newspaper story in the *Arizona Miner* describing Theodore Roosevelt's visit to the Lewin Emporium. She smiled at Henry Stern, a man who did his homework carefully. He was younger than she had imagined him and of a slender build. His chestnut-colored hair was thick, and a carefully trimmed goatee emphasized his finely chiseled features. But it was his eyes that startled her. Thick-lashed beneath heavy brows, they were lapis-hued, the color of polished turquoise. Eerily, when Henry Stern looked at her, it was as though her own eyes were mirrored in his intense stare. Her heart beat faster and she gripped the arm rests of her leather chair.

"I have heard a great deal about your establishment," Henry Stern said. "In fact, I was one of your earliest customers. My wife purchased one of your gowns for the governor's ball when the capitol was dedicated. She has worn it many times since."

"I am glad," Isaac said. "We take pride in our merchandise. My wife worked very hard on those ball gowns."

The banker glanced at Emma, but she averted her gaze and stared out the window. The Mexican farmer stood outside the Wormser warehouse loading his burro with sacks of seed. The animal stood with stoic patience as the farmer carefully knotted the cord at the throat of each sack. The precious seed must not be allowed to spill during the journey back to his plot of land. It was no easy task to wrest growth from the desert, to live in this arid territory of mountain and desert where treasure was concealed beneath earth and rock, in rushing waters and sloping hillsides. Her heart turned with pity for the farmer, who had been born into this landscape, and for herself and for Isaac, who had chosen it.

"Of course, you have expanded since then," Henry Stern said.

"Naturally. We no longer do business in a tent. But now we have outgrown our store, and I have plans for a larger establishment." He undid the ribbons on the folder he carried. "These are some sketches which an architect made according to my directions. I want a building of brick, rising to at least four stories. The merchandise will be organized into separate departments. Children's clothing in one place, women's apparel in another, and so on. One complete floor will be devoted to home furnishings. I do a very brisk business in draperies and materials for upholstering," Isaac explained, his fingers moving rapidly across the drawing as though to show where each department would be placed.

"Yes. This is the age of home building for Arizona. Adobe houses and miners' shacks will disappear, and the children who were born in them will not remember the feel of a dirt floor or the smell of a clay wall after a rain," Henry Stern observed. "They will search for carpets and sofas with soft cushions. You have your hand on the pulse of the territory, Mr. Lewin. But still your plans are ambitious, very ambitious. Do you have trained personnel to staff such an establishment?"

"My friend Abner Wallach and his wife have moved here from Cripple Creek, Colorado, at my invitation. They had a store there, and Abner will help me manage the Emporium."

"Mr. Wallach's undertaking in Cripple Creek was not very successful," the banker said.

Isaac was surprised and impressed. He had expected Henry Stern to familiarize himself with the history of Lewin's Emporium but he had not expected him to investigate Abner's background. Where had the man been born? Isaac wondered, and he regretted now that he knew so little abut the president of the Salt River Bank. He had heard it said that he had come from Portugal and that his Hebrew accent, in prayer, was similar to Emma's Sephardic intonation.

"We all have our own talents, Mr. Stern. Abner Wallach is an excellent buyer with a good sense for merchandise, a gentle way with customers. Unfortunately, he is often too generous, and that is why he failed in Cripple Creek. I am a fair man, Mr. Stern, but not a foolish one. I will not fail, and my friend will help me and not hinder me. He is essential to my plans." Isaac's voice was firm. He had made a commitment to Abner, and he would not betray it.

"I did not mean to imply that I was uncertain of your success. I have, after all, heard of the special festivities at your Emporium on *el cinco de mayo* and *diez y seis de septiembre.*" The banker's Spanish pronunciation was natural and effortless.

"Those are very successful days for us," Isaac said. "I must tell you that they were my wife's idea."

Rosa, the Mexican girl who helped Emma in the house, had told her that the Mexican community traditionally celebrated May 5, the anniversary of Mexico's victory over France, and September 16, when Mexico gained its independence from Spain. Emma had suggested that they decorate the store with Mexican flags and invite the children to a piñata party. The Mexican community of Phoenix had flocked to the Lewin Emporium to watch the blindfolded children shatter the hollow piñata and scramble for the favors that poured out of it. They had stayed to make their purchases. The *"gringo"* store that had once intimidated them became familiar territory, and now they shopped there regularly and were always cordially welcomed.

Again Henry Stern looked sharply at Emma, and again she experienced an overwhelming sensation of elusive recognition.

"How much money would you require, Mr. Lewin?" he asked.

"Ten thousand dollars." The coolness in Isaac's reply matched the tone of Henry Stern's question.

"Ten thousand dollars is a very large sum for my small bank."

"It will be repaid with interest. I think you know that," Isaac countered.

"I should like to believe that. Your only collateral is your home and your current establishment—neither of them properties of significant value."

"I count my good name and my talent as collateral," Isaac said. He struggled to contain an irrational anger. The banker had the right to ask questions before he gambled ten thousand dollars on a loan. Isaac asked questions of farmers and miners who wanted credit enough only to buy a pair of overalls or a naphthalene lamp. Still, the supercilious tone in the banker's voice was grating and offensive.

"Ah, yes, your talent and expertise as a merchant. Were you a merchant *in der heim*—the old country—Mr. Lewin?"

"No. In Russia I was a teacher and student of philosophy." As always, when he spoke of Russia, Isaac's voice grew hard, and he stared out the window at the dusty street as though he saw again the thick foliage of the forest land that surrounded his native village.

"And you, Mrs. Lewin—it would appear that you are a great help to your husband."

"We are partners," Emma replied stiffly. She saw the color rush to Isaac's face. She had angered him. A moody satisfaction gripped her. She welcomed his rage; it justified her own slowly smoldering anger. She only asked her due, yet always she felt his resistance, his reluctance.

"Perhaps you had experience in the running of a store in Russia?"

"I am not from Russia, Mr. Stern. But my father was a merchant, the proprietor of a large emporium not unlike the one we plan to build in Phoenix."

"And where was this establishment?" Henry Stern stared at her hard, and his voice took on a new intensity. He leaned toward her, his pen clenched so tightly in his fingers that she saw the whiteness of his knuckles.

"In Holland. In the city of Amsterdam."

"Amsterdam," he repeated as though mesmerized. He pronounced the word as she did, correctly emphasizing the last syllable. He was Dutch. She had recognized the accent at last and was surprised now that it had taken her so long. Perhaps she had not wanted to recognize it, just as she had not wanted to look into the eyes that matched her own.

"Can it be that you are the daughter of Jacob Coen?" Disbelief edged the question, harshness framed the name.

She nodded, her mouth dry, her back rigid. Her hands clutched the leather arm rests. If she released them her fingers would tremble, flutter uncontrollably like the petals of a flower tossed earthward on a windswept day. She saw again the white tulip petals falling onto the newly dug grave, and she knew where she had last seen Henry Stern. She remembered the exaggerated gesture with which he had removed his top hat, his mocking gaze, as they stood together at the Ouderkirk cemetery. He was the son of Analiese and of her father. It was her own half brother who sat across from her in this desert city named for a bird destined to be reborn in flame.

"And you are the son of Jacob Coen? You are my brother, then?" The question was gently asked, but her voice trembled and her eyes burned. Isaac turned to her and rose from his seat; he stood beside her as though to shield her, but she ignored him. She needed no protection from this man whose eyes matched her own, whose mother had sat beside her and revealed the secrets of her heart.

"I am the son of Analiese Deken. I have no sister. I had no father." His face was very pale, and he sat with an odd rigidity, as though he feared that if he surrendered control he might fall.

She understood the bitterness that laced his words. Everything that Analiese had told her was indelibly etched in her memory. Henry had been the boy who followed Jacob Coen one Friday and trailed him to the Portuguese Synagogue. He had watched the man he called his father stand beside another boy and point out the correct psalm in the prayerbook (it must have been Emil, who always lost his place). That boy who had stood in the shadow of the synagogue portal, had grown to manhood. But so many years had passed, and they were in another country now.

"Your mother told me that you were very angry—and very slow to forgive," Emma said softly.

"My mother is dead," he said, and his face melted. His sorrow surpassed his bitterness.

"I'm very sorry. We spoke only once—your mother and I—but what she said was very important to me. She was a very wise woman. I wondered always if I would ever see her again," Emma said.

Silence grew between them. The light musical laughter of the Mexican receptionist floated into the room. Señor Gómez opened the door to ask a question, but Henry Stern waved him impatiently away. The bells of the mission church tolled the noonday hour.

"Are you sorry?" Henry Stern asked at last, his voice flat. "Yes. Perhaps you are. But your sorrow does not help her. She died alone as she had lived alone. A woman without a name, without a husband, without a life."

"She had you," Emma said. "And your brother."

"We were boys. Stupid, selfish boys. We never understood. We could not comprehend what she endured. I curse myself now because I spent my youth locked in anger against her. We were ashamed because she was not like other mothers, our home was not like other homes. She was alone, always alone. No one came to our house. No friends, no relatives. David and I talked too loudly to fill the silence. We shouted our names aloud in an empty garden. I was a small boy when she became pregnant with David. She never went out of the house. *He* came bringing flowers and candy. Expensive toys for me, beautiful robes for her. The servants did the shopping and whispered to each other in the kitchen. It took me years to realize that she did not leave the house because she was ashamed.

"Five years ago my wife, Abigail, became pregnant with our first child—our son, Jesse. I walked beside my wife during that pregnancy. I held her arm, circled her waist. I was so proud of her, and she was so proud of my pride. We lived then in Las Cruces, New Mexico, a small mining town with narrow planked streets. She sailed down that narrow street, and I was never far from her side. The sun was so bright—the future ours to grasp, our unborn child a pledge, a promise between us. But in the night I remembered my mother, a prisoner of her pregnancy, laughed at by servants, scorned by neighbors who were never deceived by the grand house the Jewish merchant had built for his mistress and her bastards. The only comfort I find is that in the end, that house, that way of life, beggared you and your brothers and cast you down as always we had been cast down.'' Henry Stern's voice rose to a dangerous pitch and spittle foamed at the corners of his mouth.

''Why should that have given you comfort? Why should you hate us?'' Emma cried. She had passed from pity to anger. She and her brothers had done nothing to wrong Henry and David Stern and Analiese, their mother. They, too, had been victims of their father's passion, their mother's passivity.

''It was because of you that she was forced always to live in the shadows. It was because your father had plundered her life that she died alone as she had lived alone.''

''You speak without reason, Henry Stern,'' Isaac said. He spoke in the firm tone of the patient teacher, reprimanding a student who could not grasp the essence of a lesson.

''These are not reasonable things we speak of, Mr. Lewin. Was it reasonable for my mother to die thousands of miles from the land of her birth among strangers who did not speak her language? The doctors said that her heart failed her, that she was too weak for life in the Southwest. But I say that life failed her—that her heart was not weakened but broken. It was your wife's father who killed her,'' Henry Stern retorted.

''My wife's father was your own father,'' Isaac said. Again he was the forbearing instructor, waiting for frustration to subside so that learning might begin.

''*I* have never claimed his name. I took my mother's maiden name, Stern, as my own. I have a new name, and I have created a new life. The only thing I have not surrendered is my hatred for the Coen family and for the hypocrisy and falsehood which they represent.''

''How are we hypocritical and false?'' Emma asked. ''And how will hating us accomplish anything? I do not defend my father, Henry Stern, but it was your mother who asked me to try to understand him and forgive him. I have tried. Can you not make a similar effort? Can we not be brother and sister instead of enemies?'' She spoke the last words in Dutch, the shared language of their separate childhoods.

Henry Stern strode to the window and turned his back to her.

"We are not brother and sister." He spat the words out with staccato harshness. "Thieves and victims cannot befriend each other."

"Who is the thief and who is the victim?" Her question was anguished. She sensed defeat. Analiese's son was wedded to his fury, chained to his bitterness. Yet she persisted. Henry Stern was her father's son. His eyes, like her own, glinted with cerulescent brightness; in the glow of lamplight, his hair, like hers, like their father's, would turn the color of polished bronze. Perhaps he, too, dreamed of Jacob Coen's whimsical smile, of the canal-edged walkways of Amsterdam and the pale wintry sunsets that turned the still waters of the Amstel a melancholy violet.

But Henry Stern's reply was swift. He would not be appeased. He had hugged his anger too closely to surrender it.

"You and your brothers stole my childhood, ruined my mother's life. That cannot be forgiven. I am no Joseph, embracing the brothers who betrayed him in Dothan and appeared before him as suppliants in Egypt."

"My wife and I are not here as suppliants, Mr. Stern," Isaac said evenly. "We came here without knowing of this link between our families, to offer you the opportunity of joining with us in our new enterprise. A business proposition drew us here. We do not intend to become involved in your personal vendetta against the Coen family, brothers and a sister who meant you no harm, ever, who suffered as you suffered. We would welcome you as a brother—and I speak now for Emil and Simon Coen as well as for my wife. You may reject our kinship, but we in turn reject your enmity."

Henry Stern wheeled about. His face was very pale and etched with anger lines.

"You do not deceive me with your calm words, Isaac Lewin. I reject your friendship, and you will find that my enmity will pursue you."

"Come, Emma." Isaac took no further notice of the man who stood before them, trembling with rage.

Emma rose, and he felt her body sway. He supported her with his outstretched arm. They left the Salt River Bank without looking back, their heads held high. But when they reached the shade of the Wormser warehouse, Emma paused. Two Mexican workers who squatted on the dusty road to eat their lunch of tortillas stared curiously at the pale *gringa* in the elegant black dress who vomited in an irrigation ditch. They nodded sagely as her husband gently wiped her face with his large white handkerchief. That was how it was with women. They suffered discomfort in the bearing of children and pain at their birth. It was the will of God—*el poder de Dios*. They wiped the golden crumbs from their chins, crossed themselves, put on their sombreros, and walked slowly back to their jobs. Emma and Isaac walked in the opposite direction, their footfalls creating small clouds of dust on the unpaved road.

Henry Stern's threat had not been idle. Isaac applied for the loan to two other banks in Phoenix and then turned to bankers in Tucson. Everywhere, his application was dismissed. It was a difficult time, he was told. The simmering conflict between Russia and Japan had created uncertainty in the financial community, and even small loans were being carefully examined. It was true that Lewin's Emporium had an excellent reputation, but after all, they had been in business for only three years—not long enough to warrant a loan as substantial as the one Isaac was demanding. Besides, there was some doubt about the concept of a department store. Was the concept a valid one? Didn't people like to shop in specialty stores? Women liked the adventure of going from shop to shop. Would they want to do all their purchasing in a single establishment?

"They do it now," Isaac replied drily, "only we call it a general store."

The bankers were sympathetic but reluctant. Perhaps Mr. Lewin would consider delaying his plans. Perhaps things would be better in two or three years' time.

"I don't have two or three years," Isaac replied. "I have now."

Natalya and Abner Wallach had moved to Phoenix on the strength of his expansion plans. His own family was still living in the adobe house. He had obligations to fulfill, and besides his concept was solid.

It was Emanuel Melczer who told him that Henry Stern had cautioned the bankers against extending the loan.

"It's a whisper campaign. He knows something that they don't know. You're a bad risk. It's a deep, dark Jewish secret, and if they give the loan he'll call in some notes that he holds because their business judgment will be suspect. It's a rotten business, Isaac. What does he have against you? He always had a reputation for being fair, but this isn't fair. It's not even reasonable."

That night, as Isaac cleared out the cubbies in his rolltop desk, he found Isadore Solomon's note. The next morning he packed a reticule and began his journey through the Superstition Mountains and across Christmas River to the small city in the Gila Valley called Solomonville.

Isadore Solomon was a legendary figure in the Arizona Jewish community. He had migrated from Poland to America when he was only seventeen and settled in Towanda, Pennsylvania. His wife, Anna, had relatives in the New Mexico territory, and when they suffered financial reverses in the East, they journeyed to New Mexico and then to the Arizona territory. They had prospered, seizing every opportunity and working at each enterprise with energy and imagination. Isadore ran a charcoal business, a haulage company, and the Solomon Commercial Company. Anna was the proprietress of a hotel. The town had been named for the family, and it had seemed only natural that they founded a bank to accommodate the expanding needs of the settlers in their region.

Isaac checked into the Solomon Hotel and went at once to see Isadore Solomon. The banker listened patiently to Isaac's plans for the expanded emporium. He was silent as he studied the architect's drawings that Isaac spread across his desk. He sat back and toyed with the gold watch chain that dangled from his waistcoat, and stroked his mustache.

Isaac grew increasingly uneasy. The Gila Valley Bank was

his last chance. He had stubbornly resisted Emma's suggestion that they apply to her brothers. The Coens had done
enough for him. It was time that he prove himself. He felt a
rush of fury at Henry Stern, who had placed him in this
position of doubt and uncertainty. He would pay the bastard
back. The vindictiveness of the thought frightened him. He
had never been a man to pursue grudges, yet this assault was
one he could not forgive. His mouth clenched in a bitter
smile as he awaited Isadore Solomon's decision. At last the
banker sighed, and Isaac's heart sank.

"How much did you say you needed, Lewin?"

"Ten thousand dollars," Isaac said. The amount had not
seemed large when he applied to Henry Stern. Now, after
weeks of rejection, it seemed exorbitant.

"Ten thousand dollars. Not a small amount of money. I
remember once going to Phoenix on the old Black Canyon
Stage. I was coming from Fort Whipple with two thousand
dollars in government drafts from the quartermaster, and
bandits stopped us just at the Agua Eria River. They took the
Wells Fargo box and robbed the passengers of all the cash
and jewelry they carried. We couldn't give them the money
fast enough. That day the two thousand dollars seemed like
nothing because we got to Phoenix alive. Do you see what I
mean, Lewin? Sometimes ten thousand dollars is a lot of
money, and sometimes it's like a penny."

"To me, it's my future," Isaac said. He liked Isadore Solomon. He had been interested in the tale of his escapade,
but he was impatient for a reply.

Isadore Solomon opened a large black leather book. He
dipped his pen in his large copper inkwell and laboriously
made an entry, which he blotted twice.

"You have your loan, Mr. Lewin. A Jew who isn't afraid
to disagree with the president of the United States and can
recognize the opportunities in this territory doesn't have to
show me contractor's estimates. This is a new era for the
Jewish people, Mr. Lewin. Here in this desert, something is
happening that has never happened before. Here we are not
newcomers, refugees coming into a land settled by others.
Here we are pioneers, like the others. We share the adventure, and where there was nothing, we build something.

Where there was no bank, I built a bank. Where there was no store, you built one. Before I came to this town it was called Pueblo Viejo—a hamlet where a few farmers scratched the earth for a living. We built Solomonville. Pueblo Viejo was changed, but it did not suffer. It will not suffer. I read in *The American Israelite* that Jacob Schiff and Israel Zangwill spoke about the Jews in the American West. 'The new Jews,' they called us. I call us the new Americans.''

Isaac smiled. ''And our Gentile friends have other epithets for us,'' he said.

''Let them call us what they will. I've heard it all. Kike. Sheeny. Christ killer. Shylock. *Nu?* We know what we are. Build your emporium, Mr. Lewin. And include a bridal salon. My daughters will need wedding gowns.''

He laughed and brought out a bottle of whiskey and two shot glasses. The day had drifted into the twilight hour, and now the flame-red sun plunged through the slowly darkening sky. They lifted their glasses, filled to the brim with amber-colored liquor.

''L'chaim,'' Isadore Solomon said.

''L'chaim,'' Isaac Lewin replied.

The liquor seared his throat, but he drained his glass.

''To life,'' he repeated.

He drank to his life and to Emma's, to Leonie's life and that of the child who would be born in a few months' time. Henry Stern had lost and Isaac Lewin had won, but the victory had been hard-gained. A sudden weariness overcame him, and he sank into a chair and watched the Gila Valley disappear into the darkness of the desert night.

Phoenix,
1912

A LIGHT TAP sounded on the frosted glass of his office door, and Isaac looked up irritably. It was early in the day, but he felt the weariness of accumulated fatigue. The previous day's journey had exhausted him, and the few hours of sleep on the cot bed in his office had done little to refresh him.

"Come in," he called, his voice forbiddingly low.

"I wonder if I could speak to you for a few minutes, Mr. Lewin."

He stared at the petite young woman whose dark hair formed a sleek cap that hugged her head and fringed her high brow. He struggled to remember her name. It was Spanish, he recalled, and fairly unusual. She had repeated it twice for him during their brief interview several months earlier. He recalled the musical lilt in her voice, the slight blush that had turned her skin rose-gold as she sat before him then, her portfolio open on her lap. He had hired her to help with the display cases and to execute the drawings for the advertisements that Lewin's Emporium ran regularly now in the *Phoenix Gazette* and other territorial journals. She had undertaken the new catalogue as well, he remembered now, and at once her name came back to him. Isabel Cavalajo. He smiled at her, pleased that his memory had not betrayed him.

"I am rather busy just now, Miss Cavalajo," he said. "I haven't been in Phoenix for several days, and a great deal of work has piled up."

"I understand." Her voice was regretful, but she made no move to leave.

"I am sure Mr. Wallach can help you. He's familiar with every aspect of the store," Isaac added.

"It is not on store business that I came to see you," she

said, and again he saw the rush of color to her cheeks and noticed the amber flecks in her hazel eyes, the tiny golden hairs finely sprouting on her earth-colored arms.

The phone on his desk emitted a harsh double ring, and he answered it, careful to avoid her gaze but aware suddenly that the tiny buttons of her starched white shirtwaist matched the magenta cotton of her high-waisted skirt.

"I'll have the figures for you tonight," he said into the phone, pulling the instrument close to him and speaking too loudly, as though skeptical still of its powers of transmission. "It's a question of whether to remain open at all in Yarnell. The mines aren't producing that well, and if they close down, the handwriting's on the wall. Arizona will have another ghost town, and the Yarnell branch of Lewin's Emporium will be a ghost store. On the other hand, if there's a big strike, we'd be giving up a good location. I want to think about it some more." He hung up abruptly, annoyed with himself because Isabel Cavalajo's presence had interfered with his concentration.

"As you see, Miss Cavalajo, I don't have time during business hours to discuss anything that doesn't relate to the Emporium," he said, his voice steel-edged now.

"Then perhaps we can discuss it outside of business hours," she countered. "Please don't think I'm being too forward, Mr. Lewin, but this is very important to me—and I think to you as well."

The openness of her smile countered the mystery in her words, and he was intrigued.

"I see. Will tomorrow at noon be agreeable, then? This important business of yours will endure until then?"

She smiled, the satisfied, full-lipped smile of a woman who has gotten her way without undue effort, and he felt briefly uneasy.

"It will," she said and slipped out of the door, closing it softly behind her.

He phoned Emma then, clutching the earpiece too tightly. Gregory, their youngest son, had been ill when he left for Yarnell. It was only a summer cold, the doctor had assured them, but Isaac was worried. It was odd that Joshua and Samuel, the older boys, and Leonie seldom suffered even a slight fever, but sturdy Gregory, with his nut-colored skin and chubby cheeks, the largest of their children at birth, was so prone to illness.

"He's fine now," Emma assured him, her voice crackling into the receiver. "Although he asked for you last night. We were sure you would be home, and he struggled to wait up for you."

"I slept at the Emporium," Isaac said. "It was very late when I reached Phoenix, and it just seemed easier."

"Yes. I'm sure it did," Emma said, and he winced at the coldness in her tone. He imagined her standing rigidly erect, her lips pursed, the tension of her stance and expression constraining her anger.

They had quarreled before he left, keeping their voices very low and controlled as always, so that the children would not hear. Arguments between Emma and himself hissed like slowly smoldering fires and dissipated into the gray ashes of a sour silence. He had thrust his clothing into his bag with angry movements and left drawers and closets open as he stalked through the room. She knew full well that his journey to Yarnell and the other stores in the outlying areas was imperative. It could not be put off until Emma could accompany him, and she could not leave a child whose racking cough made it difficult for him to breathe, whose eyes glittered with a febrile brightness.

Their quarrel had an echolalic quality—it had been so often repeated. As always, Emma wanted to be a full participant in any decision he made. As always, he had discussed the entire situation with her. A smaller store might benefit from expansion, and he wanted to scout locations in the town. The problem in Yarnell had to be resolved, and there was the possibility of opening a store at a new railroad crossing. Inevitably, her persistent questions had exhausted his patience.

Emma had never been comfortable with the concept of branch stores. She had resisted Isaac's arguments from the outset, and even her brothers' remonstrations failed to reassure her.

"Isaac understands how merchandising must work in this country," Simon argued. "A large parent store in a centrally located city spawns smaller stores in suburbs and outlying areas. It makes sense in such an enormous country—in an age of telegraphs and telephones, of motor cars and railroads.''

"The wives of ranchers and farmers love their wish books," Emma countered. "They line up at the post office the day the new Sears Roebuck and Montgomery Ward catalogues arrive. They won't travel for miles to a tent store when they can order by mail."

"You're wrong, Emma." Isaac spoke softly, firmly. "They would much rather touch a piece of fabric, try a sweater on a child, see themselves in a mirror in a new dress, a blouse, than turn the pages of a book. Oh, they'll order from the catalogues as well, but we'll get our share of the business. And what's to prevent us from doing a catalogue?''

In the end he had prevailed. During the years that followed the opening and the immediate success of the enlarged Emporium in Phoenix, Isaac and Abner Wallach had traveled the length and breadth of the Arizona territory opening branches of Lewin's Emporium in remote areas. Wherever a mineral strike was declared, from Bisbee at the Mexican border to Rainbow Flat, where the stateline of Utah encroached, Isaac and Abner journeyed. They estimated the number of miners who were drawn to the area, the size of their families, the richness and depth of the vein. Occasionally, they began with a tent store similar to the one Isaac had first opened in Phoenix. More often they decided on a cabin-type structure, which they furnished with merchandise from the Phoenix Emporium.

Isaac had swiftly discovered that even if the small stores in the outlying territories failed, that failure was covered by the discounts he obtained from suppliers when he made his purchases in quantity. The stores were able to maintain a low inventory and supply each other with necessary merchandise by sending telegrams. The miner's wife who came into a Lewin's Emporium in Cottonwood for a length of pink muslin might not find it on the shelf, but the storekeeper could easily send a telegram to his counterpart in Winona and obtain it for her in a few days' time. It was such services that drew custom to Lewin's and guaranteed its reputation.

Still, Emma was not convinced. During the early days she had often traveled with Isaac, with Leonie perched beside her and the infant Joshua asleep in her arms. She had stood with him at deal tables as they studied balance sheets, checked inventory sheets and ledger pages. Always his eyes were narrow, his lips pressed firmly together as he watched her peruse the figures. He said little but answered her questions with an ironic courtesy that caused the store managers to avert their eyes. Still, they had to admit that Mrs. Lewin made valuable suggestions. It was she who suggested that the ribbon wheels be placed on the counter where they could be seen by customers as they paid. "Oh, give me a yard of that blue instead of the change," a housewife would say. "Let me add a dime and take some of that nice gold moiré." They had sold a great deal of ribbon that way. And she was such a fine-looking woman, her hair the color of flames, her eyes the same shade as the turquoise that the Indians called their desert diamonds.

Still, they were not sorry when she stopped coming after her two younger sons were born. Her presence stirred up an odd unrest, raised questions they did not want to answer. More recently, Isaac traveled alone or with Abner Wallach and Johnny Redbird, his Indian assistant. Emma had the children to look after and the large new house on MacDowell Road to manage. But Emma resented her exclusion, and each departure, for even the briefest of journeys, was prefaced by anger and argument.

"Do you think I want to go alone?" he had asked just before leaving for Yarnell. He wanted to tell her how often he thought of her when he was away, how he missed consulting with her, but he feared her derision.

She had not answered, and it occurred to him that more and more often they offered each other silence, as though fearful of the words they dared not speak. He longed for the release of anger. She offered him the containment of courtesy.

"I'll be home for lunch, and I'll stay for the rest of the afternoon," he said now, in a more conciliatory tone.

"Natalya and the children are here." Her voice, too, softened, and he felt a surge of hope. It was possible for them to reach a separate peace, to speak with each other openly and calmly. They could not live always on the edge of anger, weighing each phrase, arbitrating each action. Too often during the dozen years of their marriage, he felt himself an acrobat, negotiating the high wire of their strained relationship, taking each step with concentration and caution, as though fearful that the slightest shifting of weight, the minutest miscalculation, would presage disaster. He had become adept at setting his moods to match her own, of outlining his ideas in cool and reasoned tones lest his passion disarm and frighten her.

Sometimes it seemed to him that it was only when loneliness overwhelmed them—when a desert owl hooted with resonant melodic trill or a falling star streaked a silver path through the cavernous desert darkness—that they abandoned the studied caution, the intricate balance of their shared life. They were impelled then to reach out to each other, wordlessly moving closer through the dense blackness of the heat-swathed night.

They came together then in a surge of passion that denied tenderness, each separately triumphant. They slept always, in the end, with their faces turned away from each other, although their bodies were linked by silver bands of moonlight. Once, at such a time, he awakened and saw that tears streaked her cheeks.

"Why are you crying?" he asked. His own voice broke with sorrow, throbbed with urgency, but she did not answer him. She feared to tell him that it was the wall of silence between them that saddened her and that she longed to scale it. She wanted to laugh with him as Natalya laughed with Abner. She wanted to rush into his arms when he arrived home each evening, and she wanted to sleep enfolded in his embrace. The wall had been of her own building, she knew, but he made no move to help her destroy it. More and more, she could feel that he distanced himself from her. She felt herself alone in the moonlit room, as she had ever been alone wandering across the canals of Amsterdam, the beachhead of Galveston.

She tried to speak but could not, and he took her silence as reprimand, and he felt again that familiar defeat that had trailed him since that distant morning in Galveston. Her grief was private; she would not reveal it to him. Always and forever she would be at a remove from him. She had not wanted a husband, this proud Sephardic woman who shared his life. It was a partnership that she had sought. Yet too often, he thought, they were adversarial partners—she thin-lipped, examining the accounts he proffered; he tight-voiced, advancing an argument, validating a decision.

Weary now, Isaac replaced the receiver and turned back to the business on hand. Abner had completed the inventory, and Isaac noted with pleasure that the home furnishings department had enjoyed a successful season. The few sofas still in stock could easily be sold at the branch stores, and he would arrange to have the large leather settee shipped to Brother Timothy's mission school. A glance at the figures told him that they had done well with the Buster Brown line of children's clothing, but they would have to expand the ready-to-wear women's department. Emma, who still made her own dresses or went to a dressmaker, resisted the idea that women were increasingly drawn to the larger selections newly available from manufacturers. The new cutting and sewing machines had made size gradations and a variety of styles easily and inexpensively accessible. Customers at Marshall Field in Chicago and the Sanger stores in Dallas headed for the ready-to-wear racks, and Isaac knew that the women of Phoenix would do similar shopping at Lewin's Emporium. He would show Emma the actual earnings and his projected estimates. Swiftly, he tallied the figures, and his pencil snapped in his tightened grasp. Damn it! He was tired of arguing every issue with her, of discussing every decision. They would have to arrive at a new understanding of this mythical partnership of hers.

He turned his attention to the drawings for the new catalogue. Isabel Cavalajo was a clever artist. Her drawings were reminiscent of Charles Dana Gibson's work in *Scribner's* and *The Century*, but whereas the Gibson girls were pale and fine-featured, their hair neatly swept into soft chignons and flawless pompadours, Isabel Cavalajo's models reflected the rustic life of the West. Their hair was windblown, their eyes blazed with teasing excitement, and they wore their shirtwaists with a western flair—a bright neckerchief tucked beneath the collar, a small silver pin of Indian crafting on the lapel of a suit jacket or centered on a lace jabot. "Lewin's Lasses," she called these creatures of her brush and pen. Isaac repeated the phrase aloud and then crossed it out. "The Lewin Look," he wrote in its stead and felt a rush of certainty. The phrase would catch, he knew, and it could be applied to every department in the store. Pleased, he initialed the catalogue and wrote out a print order. This new edition would be larger than previous publications. Emma had been right in that perception. Women still loved and treasured their wish books.

He made his rounds of the store, walking from department to department, his notebook in hand. Johnny Redbird had spoken of underutilized space in the accessory department that he wanted to discuss with Isaac. The tall, lean Indian met him in the corridor, and together they walked down to the third floor, weaving their way through crowds of customers.

"We're busy today," Isaac said.

"Back-to-school time. We outfitted the entire lower form of the Phoenix Indian School today," Johnny said.

"Good."

It had been Johnny's idea to prepare small gifts for each schoolchild who made even a small purchase at the Emporium. The previous year they had given out pencils, but this year they had distributed brown paper book covers embossed with a drawing of the sign that had originally hung on the crossbeam of the tent store. That placard, faded and splintered, had been cemented onto the front of the new building. Emma had repainted it herself, etching each letter carefully.

"What do we need that old sign for?" Leonie had asked.

"So that we won't forget," Emma had replied, her eyes meeting Isaac's. They were united, at that moment, by their memories of the journey westward, of those early days beneath the canvas when each small sale had been a triumph and they had struggled against the specter of defeat.

"Forget what?" Leonie had asked impatiently, but she had skipped off without waiting for an answer.

The reproduced sign had become an insignia for the store,

and it hung in every Lewin outlet—the tent and cabin stores in the boomtowns and the small brick buildings in the suburbs of Tucson and Flagstaff.

"Do you see what I mean about this space?" Johnny Redbird asked, pointing to an area that was used only for the wrapping of packages.

"Another department could easily fit in here," Isaac agreed. "What did you have in mind, Johnny?" Johnny did not make casual observations, he knew.

Johnny Redbird had worked for the Lewins from the day Isaac opened his first store. The lithe Indian youth had glided up to Isaac the morning he arrived to move the merchandise from the tent store to the newly constructed building. Without saying a word he had helped Isaac empty the shelves. Silently, he had trailed behind him, watching as Isaac stacked the items on the shelves and then helping him.

"Do you want to work for me?" Isaac had asked him at the end of the first day.

"Yes."

"I can't afford to pay you very much."

"You can teach me."

Johnny came from a tradition of bartering. The Hopi Indians had long ago traded their pots and baskets, their intricately designed blankets and woven garments, for livestock and seed. This was simply a new kind of barter—Johnny Redbird's services for Isaac Lewin's knowledge. Isaac had taught the Indian to read and write using primers borrowed from Brother Timothy. He had explained the business to him and learned to carefully consider Johnny's ideas. He had listened to Johnny's stories of Hopi life and told him of his own life in Russia. Johnny's eyes had widened when Isaac told him of the pogroms, of the deaths of Rivka and Sarah.

"They killed your wife and daughter without reason?" Johnny had asked incredulously.

"Many have been killed without reason," Isaac replied bitterly. He thought of the Apache raids against wagon trains, of Geronimo's war of vengeance and the punitive retaliations against innocent tribes; he remembered nature's random acts of violence—small Miriam's rain-drenched corpse washed up on a beach, ribbons of seaweed in her hair.

"The word *Hopi* means peace." Johnny's voice was grave. "Hopis do not kill. We flee from the killers."

Johnny's family had fled the marauding Apaches and built a pueblo village on the rock tip of a coal-black mesa. They had sought refuge, but they had not surrendered either their lives or their ideals. They had planted peach trees in the arid earth and harvested the juicy, plump fruit, whose brightness mocked the sere desert floor that gave it flower. They herded flocks of mountain goats and captured the colors of the ever-changing desert in their sand paintings, their weaving, and their pottery. Their baskets were handsome, although not as sturdy as those of the Pima and the Apaches, but that was because they were not a tribe of wanderers nor of warriors. The fierce Apaches needed baskets to carry on their forays, tightly woven so that they could be used to hold water or grain yet light enough to be easily stored. The domestic Hopis crafted pots and clay bowls and strung bright peppers out to dry. They were a peaceful and stable people, unafraid of possession and permanence.

"They are not men who submit to their environment," Brother Timothy had pointed out. "They conquer it and rise above it. In that, they are not unlike your people, Isaac. Like the Jews, they turn adversity to their advantage."

"How so?" Isaac had asked.

"Johnny is a case in point. The white men came to his land. He could have submitted to them or fought them as the Apaches did. He did neither. He decided to learn from them. Just as his father learned to plant peach trees on the mesa and to live on a rockbound parapet, Johnny came to you and learned to live in a white man's city—in a world as potentially hostile as the mesa itself. He changed his thinking, Isaac, as you yourself did when you came to America. You left one life behind and saw another. You saw the future. Johnny, too, saw the future. But you did not abandon your religion or your people, and neither did Johnny abandon his."

There was sadness in Brother Timothy's voice. He had come to the New World to save the souls of the Indians, to capture them for Christ, yet he admired their tenacity, their fierce sense of history. His perceptions were too often at cross-purposes with his ministry. He was not a good mis-

sionary, he told himself, and he took on tasks and penances
as punishment. Often when Isaac visited him at the mission
school, his soutane was stained with dust and grease and his
eyes were red-rimmed with fatigue.

"Always listen carefully to Johnny," the priest had advised his Jewish friend. "You have much to learn from each
other."

Isaac listened carefully to Johnny now. The heavy-browed
Indian spoke slowly, fingering the bright blue strand of beads
that fell gracefully to the midriff of his embroidered chamois
shirt.

"Every year more and more visitors come to Arizona to
see the mountains and the desert. Travel is easier now. We
have the trains, and soon there will be flying machines. The
tourists come to our store looking for something to take home
with them to the cities in the East and the North, to the new
cities in the West. They ask me about my beads—and the
embroidery on my shirt, my buckskin vest. They stop the
Indian children on the street and ask them where they can
buy our kachina dolls, our blankets and jewelry. Some of the
Indians sell them their own things, sometimes charging too
much, sometimes charging too little. Others take them to the
hogan of a potter or basketmaker. Some run from them because they have fair skin and pale eyes. They run although
they need the white man's money and would gladly sell to
them. But if we had a place here where we could sell the
crafts of my people, it would be good for the customers,
good for the Indians, and of course, it would be good for the
Emporium. The tourist lady who comes to buy a bracelet of
silver and turquoise will pass through a department that sells
dresses. Surely she will need a new dress to show off her
new bracelet, her brooch. And a new dress means a new
hat." Johnny smiled wisely. He had proven himself an apt
student, utilizing Isaac's tutelage to prove his point.

"You are proposing we open a department of Indian hand-
icrafts?" Isaac asked.

"Indian. Native American. Perhaps we can call it the Arizona Heritage. We will find the words to describe it."

"It's certainly something to think about," Isaac agreed.
"I shall have to discuss it with Mrs. Lewin, of course."

"Of course."

Johnny was one of the few Lewin employees who did not find it odd that Isaac discussed major decisions with Emma. Even faithful Abner Wallach occasionally grew impatient when Isaac deferred to his wife's judgment. But the women in the Hopi tribe were responsible for each family's inheritance because property was matrilineally controlled. Johnny's parents had always conferred over the sale of a lamb, the acquisition of a goat. Johnny thought it only natural that Isaac consult with Emma. His possessions were hers. She had worked beside him. It was her future and her children's future that were affected by his decisions.

It was fortunate that Isaac Lewin's beautiful wife thought so well, acted so prudently. Johnny admired Emma as he admired all women who worked hard and considered their words before speaking. Her thick hair was the exact color of the flame-hued blossoms of the dwarf cactus bush, and the Indian thought it sad that Leonie, their only daughter, had not inherited it. Still, Leonie's dark hair was beautiful, and she had her mother's wondrous eyes. But she was not a happy child. She seldom laughed, and often when Johnny passed the school yard during a recess, he noticed that pretty Leonie Lewin sat alone while the other children played circle games or chased each other in endless rounds of tag. She had, he supposed, inherited her father's moodiness and her mother's ingrained sense of privacy.

There were people like that in his tribe, who preferred being alone—men and women who sought solitude in the darkened underground kivas where the Indians built small shrines to their deities—children who herded their flocks on the loneliest stretches of the mesa. Johnny's own daughter was addicted to solitary nocturnal strolls. "Lonely Star," the young braves of the tribe called her. The young men would find a similar name for Leonie Lewin, he knew.

"Then we will talk about this tomorrow?" Johnny persisted.

"Yes." Isaac had detected a note of urgency in Johnny's voice. "It's a new idea, Johnny. Surely, we don't have to act on it at once."

"I should like to go forward on it. I have worked for you

for more than ten years, and I have learned a great deal. Now it is time for me to build something of my own.''

''What will you do if I decide not to open this Indian crafts department?'' Isaac asked carefully.

''You know that the people of our tribe have been well treated by the Salt River Bank. I, too, have an account there, and I often speak with Mr. Stern, who has always been a good friend to the Hopis.''

''I know that is true,'' Isaac said. Henry Stern had long been an articulate advocate for the Indians. He argued on their behalf in the Arizona legislature and advanced them funds for seed crops during the years of drought. Like Isaac, he respected their traditions and recognized the injustices they had suffered.

It was ironic, Isaac thought, that he and Emma's half brother, sworn enemies, were so often on the same side in issues of importance to the territory and to the Jewish community. They both advocated the establishment of a synagogue, and both had contributed generously to a fund for the relief of victims of the new outbreak of pogroms in eastern Europe. They both sought employment for the Jews who now came westward in greater numbers. Jacob Schiff had at last established a Jewish Immigrant Information Bureau in Galveston, and jobs were constantly being solicited for new arrivals. Yet despite such affinities, tensions between the Sterns and the Lewins had increased throughout the years.

They nodded to each other when they met occasionally at the religious services held in the makeshift synagogues above the Jewish shops. Isaac discouraged his own contacts from doing business with the Salt River Bank, and he knew of at least two suppliers who had denied Lewin's Emporium favorable credit because of Henry Stern's intervention. Emil and Simon Coen had also encountered difficulties with the banker. They had been denied a loan at a crucial time because Henry Stern had scattered stories about their imprudence and impropriety in a business community where much rested on reputation.

Emma was not asked to a meeting of the newly organized Daughters of Zion because Abigail Stern was on the board. It was an unspoken rule in Phoenix that the Sterns and the

Lewins were not to be invited to a musicale or a dinner party together. The source of their enmity was not known, but it was rumored that Emma Lewin and Henry Stern had been lovers in Amsterdam.

"I spoke with Mr. Stern of my plan," Johnny said. "He told me that he would be glad to make an investment if you were not interested."

"I would imagine that he urged you to go ahead on your own without giving me the chance to make an offer," Isaac said drily.

"Yes," Johnny admitted, "but that I would not agree to. Still, if you decide against it, I will speak again with Mr. Stern."

"We'll talk about it in the morning," Isaac said curtly.

Damn Henry Stern, he thought. He probably knew full well that another floor would have to be added to the Emporium for Johnny's venture. That small space near the accessories would not suffice. And he knew, too, that Isaac had overextended himself with the branch stores. Too many of the boomtowns were turning into ghost towns, and others, like Yarnell, had an uncertain future. It was true that the Phoenix store was doing a brisk business, but Lewin's Emporium as a whole was experiencing cash-flow problems. Bankers talked to each other, and Henry Stern would have inside knowledge that Isaac had made inquiries about short-term loans. Still, he would speak to Emma. They would have to find a way to accommodate Johnny Redbird, and the idea was an excellent one. It would transform Lewin's Emporium from a conventional department store into a unique Arizona experience.

The children were playing on the steps of the large white-columned house on MacDowell Road when Isaac drove up. As always he felt a rush of pleasure, a stirring of pride, when he saw his home. He had modeled it on the mansions of Galveston, and at his instruction the architect had designed wide verandas and balconies of fretted ironwork. There was a *viga*-roofed loggia and sleeping porches built of wood and canvas that gave them refuge from the searing heat of summer that invaded even the belled roof of the house. Emma had insisted on the use of an earth-colored stucco, and the dark carved wooden doorway was studded with brass in the Spanish fashion.

Inside, the polished white plaster walls reflected the dazzling sunlight, but the gray slate floors, covered with thin, bright rugs of Hopi and Navajo design, were cool beneath their feet. Always, flowers filled the ceramic pots on the low mesquite tables—dogwood and magnolia from the trees that Emma had planted so close to the house that their shadows patterned the pale stucco and cooled the rooms within. There were sprays of orange blossoms in season, cut from the trees that grew in the small grove near the outbuildings where the children's ponies and Emma's mare were kept. Each fall bulbs arrived from Holland, and Emma carefully planted them, but although an occasional tulip or narcissus shoot thrust its way through the sandy soil, the tuberous roots did not flower. Instead, Emma and Leonie rode into the desert and filled their saddle panniers with clusters of columbine and long wands of Spanish dagger.

Emma sat with Natalya on the porch, her head bent over a basket of flowers. The two women wore the long white linen skirts and the wide-collared blouses that Gibson had made so popular that spring.

"It's Daddy!" Nine-year-old Joshua abandoned the game of hide-and-seek that he and his brother Samuel had lost to the Wallach twins with distressing consistency all morning. Their copper-colored hair, sticking out above creosote bushes and around the curve of the citrus and magnolia trees, too easily betrayed them.

Samuel, too, rushed forward, and the boys hurtled into Isaac's outstretched arms. Leonie, however, put her book down on the porch glider and walked toward him more slowly. Her lips were velvet-soft against his cheek, and he lifted her in his arms and twirled her about.

"Isaac—the child is getting a bit too old for that." Emma's voice held a warning note, and he saw the rush of color in Leonie's cheeks and noticed for the first time the gentle swell of breasts against her schoolgirl's gingham dress. She had been a grave-eyed child, and she would pass too swiftly into womanhood. Gently he set her down and watched her walk slowly back to her seat, apart from the other children.

She was so unlike lively and active Joshua and Samuel, who were always organizing games and clamoring for parties and outings. Even Gregory, when he was not ill, joined his brothers in their boisterous sports, acted in their impromptu porch theatricals. But Leonie was happiest with a book or riding her pony out into the desert.

Isaac frowned and turned his attention to Gregory, who stood beside Emma. The child had lost weight, and his color had faded so that his lucent cheekbones pressed against his pallid skin. His mahogany-colored hair clung to his scalp in damp curls. He smiled listlessly at his father, who touched the child's brow with his lips.

"He feels warm," Isaac said to Emma. "I thought the fever had gone."

"It comes back in the afternoon with summer colds," Natalya said in her reasonable, reassuring voice. "There's nothing to worry about, Isaac. Come, children." She clapped her hands—the schoolteacher's authoritative gesture translated into maternal summons. Joseph and Reuben, the twins, and Rachel, her daughter, laughingly rushed to join her.

Motherhood had rounded Natalya's gaunt figure, softened her features. She laughed easily and often. She approached each day with the astonished pleasure of a woman who, much to her surprise and against all perceived odds, has found happiness and contentment. Her good fortune amazed her. She had a husband, children, and a home that was at once spacious and sheltering. Undulating mountain ridges and a heart-stopping expanse of desert vista were framed in her windows. She who had fled the narrow ghetto streets of Vilna, the teeming warrens of the Lower East Side, looked out at a wondrous and unmarred landscape, breathed the clear, dry air so lightly scented with the breath of citrus, the tang of juniper.

Isaac and Emma watched her leave. They were generous friends. They reveled in Abner and Natalya's happiness. Still, a bittersweet envy edged their joy.

They had an early dinner in the formal dining room. Emma frowned when Samuel shoved the Stafford chair that she had imported from England across the slate floor. She spoke sharply when Joshua dropped a fork on the long Mexican refectory table.

"Must I tell you again to be careful, Joshua?"

The boy blushed and then scowled.

"It was an accident," Isaac said.

"It is necessary that we maintain standards," Emma replied. The house and its furnishings, the pattern of their lives, were important to her. They represented bastions of security after so many years of insecurity and uncertainty.

"This is not the Coen mansion of the Prinsengracht, after all," Isaac said. He had reached for levity, but in the end his words were laced with bitterness.

The children looked away. Such brief, harsh exchanges between their parents bewildered them. Samuel ate too quickly. It was his fault that his mother and father were angry with each other. He should have been more careful with the chair. Joshua spread the butter too thickly on the freshly baked black bread and took very large bites despite his mother's disapproving stare. Who cared about the table anyway? Why did they have to eat every night with this fancy silverware and china? He had liked it better when they lived in the adobe house and ate in the clay-walled kitchen.

"Is having proper decorum during dinner and using utensils carefully so difficult for you? And why must you bring the Prinsengracht into this conversation?" Scorn masked her hurt. He knew how the magic world of her girlhood had been betrayed. Couldn't he grant her some of the understanding he seemed to dispense so easily to others?

He did not reply. She had, in fact, he decided, re-created her parents' home. Just as her mother had withdrawn from her father, so Emma had withdrawn from him. It was not necessary to sleep behind a locked door, as Leonie Coen had done, to seal one's self away. Emma and he shared a room, but she had removed herself from him. He turned to his children.

"Did you do your Hebrew lessons while I was away?" he asked. He had taught them Hebrew himself, and now he was instructing them in the cantillations of the prayers. Joshua would be of bar mitzvah age in a few years' time, and the son of Isaac Lewin, who had once dreamed of being a scholar, would be properly prepared. The absence of a rabbi in Phoenix did not deter him. More and more Jews were coming into the territory, and their numbers would increase when Arizona was granted statehood. One day there would be a synagogue and a Hebrew school in the city. There was talk of it already. But in the interim he would instruct his children and prove that they could survive as Jews even though they were distanced from the sources of Jewish authority. The challenge intrigued and invigorated him.

Leonie and Samuel nodded. They had studied together. But Joshua shrugged.

"I didn't get to it," he said.

"Then do a double portion tomorrow," Isaac said severely. "I will listen to you before dinner tomorrow evening."

"He's only a boy," Emma said when the children left the table after dutifully replacing their napkins in the tooled silver rings.

"You have your standards and I have mine," Isaac replied coldly.

He carried Gregory upstairs and put the child to bed. The fever had subsided, but Gregory was listless. His voice was almost a whisper when he spoke.

"Don't go away, Papa."

"I'm just going downstairs to speak to Mama."

"Leave the door open, then."

"All right."

He bent to kiss the child, and Gregory's arms reached up. He pulled his father close, his arms entwining Isaac's neck like thin and fragile vines.

"I get so scared sometimes," he whispered. "I get so scared when it's hard to breathe."

"Don't be frightened, my son," Isaac said gently. "I am here. I'll always be here."

He went downstairs and joined Emma at the table. She stirred her coffee moodily as Rosa, the Mexican maid, cleared the table. He poured himself a fresh cup and told her of his visit to Yarnell.

"I looked at the figures when you were away," she said. "It is best to close that store."

"You are right," he agreed. Still, he was annoyed that she had been in his office during his absence and studied the ledgers. "You could have waited until I returned. We could have gone over the figures together."

"Does it make a difference?" She would not tell him that she had gone to the Emporium to divert herself from her anxiety over Gregory. The columns of figures engaged her concentration, absorbed her, freed her of thoughts of the sick child, whose illnesses recurred with distressing frequency. The boy was of school age now, but the doctor had advised her to have him tutored at home. And he was such a sweet child, always so gentle, so eager to please—the most vulnerable and the most affectionate of her children. He sang softly to himself in his bed at night, and she lay awake and listened to the piercing sweetness of her small son's voice. Other children wept when they awakened in the darkness, but their Gregory sang.

"No. Of course not." He would not ask her yet again to trust him. He told her then of Johnny Redbird's proposal.

"It makes sense." A wisp of hair escaped her neat bun and looped her neck, forming a collar of flaming tendrils. He resisted the impulse to stroke the bright strands, to claim her by seizing them. "But there is something about it I do not like."

"And what is that?"

"Johnny would want control of that department. I assume that he would select all items for sale—jewelry and ceramics and woven goods?"

"Yes. He wants complete responsibility."

"How can we be sure of the quality of what would be sold if we entrust it entirely to Johnny? We don't want Lewin's Emporium to become a cheap tourist attraction. The name of the store must be protected. Already, I have heard talk that there are some who do not bring us their custom because they are uncomfortable with the kind of patrons we attract. The ready-to-wear departments have brought us a different class of customer. When my sister-in-law Thea visited from San Francisco, she told me, in all frankness, that we were becoming somewhat déclassé. That is not what I would want for our store." She did not meet his eyes as she spoke but studied her coffee cup as though she might discern the future in the dregs that clung darkly to the translucent china.

"Thea is a goddamn snob," Isaac countered angrily. "And you, Emma, are speaking nonsense. Anyone who wants to make a purchase at Lewin's is welcome and will be treated with courtesy—your sister-in-law and the wife of a panning miner—Mrs. Solomon or a Pima squaw. Haven't we given everyone equal service since the days of the tent store? All our merchandise has always been of good quality. Everything we sell is worth what we charge for it—the inexpensive items as well as the expensive ones. If such a policy does not appeal to Thea, let her shop at Magnin's where the salesladies will kiss her backside. We don't need customers like her. Johnny will do as we have done. His inexpensive beads will be worth the price he sets, and the silver and turquoise will be worth what he charges. Lewin's Emporium is a store for the people, for all the people: those with ten dollars in their pockets—which, my fine lady, is as much as I had when I got off the boat in Galveston Harbor—and those who can write a check for a thousand dollars without blinking an eye." His voice thundered as he spoke, and Leonie, who had wandered into the room searching for a book, glanced at them nervously and hurried out.

"I don't need a lecture on democracy, Isaac," Emma said coldly. "But perhaps we ought to think of setting a direction for the store."

"That is precisely why I am enthusiastic about Johnny's idea. Such a department will make Lewin's Emporium uniquely Arizonan. Besides, if we don't undertake it, Henry Stern will. He has already offered to underwrite Johnny."

She stiffened, and color flooded her cheeks. Only that afternoon Leonie had come home in tears because she was the only child in her grade who had not been invited to a birthday party for Barbara Stern. Emma had felt a new infusion of anger. Henry Stern had tried to poison their lives in Phoenix, and now he reached out to harm their children. If he wanted Johnny's enterprise, she would fight him for it.

"Can we afford to open such a department?" she asked.

"It would be a strain," he admitted. "The branch stores aren't holding their own."

"I warned you."

"Ah, but you are always warning me. Look, I am very tired. The journey was exhausting, and I slept very badly last night." He pushed his chair back and went upstairs, taking the steps two at a time. The discussion was over. Their verbal war had ended, but the victory was, as always, insubstantial and bitter.

Emma, her head in her hands, heard him open the door of Gregory's room and imagined him kneeling beside the child's bed. How tender Isaac was with the children—how gentle his hands when he touched them, his voice as he spoke to them. Yet he denied her that same gentleness, that same tenderness.

"He doesn't offer it because he is afraid you will reject it," Natalya had told her that afternoon as they sat in the loggia. They had spoken, as always, with the intimacy of women who have a shared history and are unafraid of revealing their deepest fears, their most fervent yearning.

"He knew when we married how important my independence was to me," Emma had protested.

"You can have both your independence and his love." Natalya spoke with the calm assurance of a woman who had both and struggled for neither. "You must meet him halfway, Emma, or you will both travel so far from each other that no meeting will be possible."

Emma remembered her friend's words as she sat alone in the darkened dining room. Rosa came in to wish her good night. The children wandered upstairs to bed, but she sat on, staring at the pale magnolia blossoms that shimmered whitely in the gathering darkness. She rose abruptly and went upstairs, moving swiftly, determinedly, as though she had at last arrived at a difficult decision.

In her dressing room she stood naked for a moment before her full-length mirror. Her body was supple, her breasts still high and firm. She slipped on a white lace nightgown, and her skin glowed golden through the intricately tatted pattern. She brushed her hair until it fell to her shoulders in radiant folds. She smiled at herself, as she might to a shy stranger, and saw the fear that darkened her eyes, muting their beryl brightness. Softly, she opened the door to their bedroom. He was fast asleep, his breathing rhythmic and deep.

She drew close to him and touched his shoulder.

"Isaac." Her voice was a whispered caress.

He moaned but turned away from her, still submerged in a heavy sleep.

"Isaac."

She rested her head on his chest, caping his body with the fiery folds of her hair. He stirred. His eyes were closed, his breath still even, but his hand encased her arm, pressed her heated flesh.

"Mama!" Gregory's voice shrilled through the darkness.

She eased herself free of Isaac's grasp and hurried to the child. He was feverish again. She bathed him with cool cloths and fed him a mixture of Seidlitz powders and lemon juice, grateful that he breathed without effort.

"Don't go away, Mama. Please don't go away."

"I won't," she promised.

She slept for the rest of the night on the daybed in his room and awakened to the whistle of the Santa Fe express as it plunged southward to Tucson. The vestige of a dream clung to her. Somehow she had missed a long-awaited train, and she stood, trembling with disappointment, on a desert platform. She shivered and passed into wakefulness.

She was draped in a light blanket from her own bed. Isaac had covered her before leaving for the Emporium. Her body ached with a sudden and unfamiliar emptiness, and she gasped desperately to free herself of the sorrow that constricted her breath.

Isabel Cavalajo sat opposite Isaac Lewin in the dining room of the Commercial Hotel. In her pink wide-collared middy blouse and navy blue serge skirt, she had the look of a schoolgirl, and the businessmen who greeted Isaac as they passed smiled at her indulgently.

"Good afternoon, Miss Cavalajo." Henry Stern paused briefly and doffed his hat. He nodded coldly to Isaac. The banker looked gaunt, and the eyes that so closely matched Emma's were shadowed with worry. Isaac had heard that morning that his wife was ill. The desert sickness, it was said, a tenacious and recurring malaria. Isaac raised his hand, an indifferent gesture of acknowledgment.

"*Buenos días*, Señor Stern," Isabel Cavalajo replied, and Henry Stern moved on to join a colleague at a table across the room.

"How do you know him?" Isaac asked.

"He is a friend of my father's. They study together."

"What do they study?"

"The Talmud." She smiled at his surprise. "You did not realize I was Jewish, Mr. Lewin?"

"It hadn't occurred to me," he confessed.

"My family's story is complicated."

"I like complicated stories." He smiled at her encouragingly. A dimple cleft her chin and she clasped her hands on the table as she spoke, just as Leonie did.

She told him then that her family had left Spain during the Inquisition, one step ahead of expulsion. They fled to Mexico, and it was said that they had held a land grant to the Kingdom of Nuevo León issued by King Philip. Some became cattle ranchers and others settled in Mexico City. They wrote to their relations and other Marranos, or "secret" Jews, crossed the ocean, and it was rumored that by the end of the sixteenth century there were more Jews in Mexico City than Catholics. Some posed as Christians, but when the hand of the Inquisition reached the New World, they knew that they were again in jeopardy. Many crossed the Rio Grande into West Texas. Others became part of different *entratas*. To many, their religion was a matter of indifference. They circumcised their sons and did not eat pork, although they also observed Christian rituals.

Isabel Cavalajo's grandfather went to church every Sunday at a West Texas mission. A piñata hung in his house at Christmas, the family celebrated Easter, and a calendar marking the days of the saints hung in the kitchen. But every Friday night, in a corner of the house where there was no window, his mother lit candles and his father murmured an incomprehensible benediction over a silver beaker filled with the sour red wine of the region. In the fall, his father opened a leather-covered book whose pages had yellowed with age. They could not read the words, which were written in an elegant and unfamiliar script, but the book was passed from child to child, and each, in turn, touched the pages, resting their fingers on the strangely formed letters. They bent their heads then although they knew no prayer.

The book and the silver beaker had long been in the family, passed from father to son, wrapped always in a frayed woolen shawl decorated with oddly knotted fringes. In the spring the family ate the flat bread tortillas of the Mexicans and hard-boiled eggs sprinkled with a bitter herb that grew in the desert. "This is the season of our freedom," they repeated after the father who told them that when the cactus flower bloomed they must eat no risen bread for a week. He did not know why, but he taught his sons the lessons of his own father.

Isabel's grandfather adhered to the strange tradition, but he was a curious man and widely read. He found a book about the Jews and learned that they lit candles each Friday evening and celebrated the new year in the season of autumn. He read that they ate unleavened bread during Passover, which came in the spring. He understood then that he was a Jew, the son and grandson of Jews. Years later he came to Phoenix, and he went to a Jewish prayer service held above one of the shops, carrying with him the beaker and the prayerbook, wrapped in the tattered shawl. The shawl was a *tallith*, used for praying, the men there told him, and there was no doubt that he was a Jew—in all probability, because of his name, a descendant of Don Juan de Cavajal, one of the first Jews to settle in the New World. He wept then. The mystery of his life and his family's life had been solved.

Slowly, he learned to read the pages of his prayerbook. They taught him the blessings to say when the candles were lit and the wine consecrated each Friday evening. They welcomed him and embraced him.

"Yo estoy en casa," he said that night. "I am home with my people." He raised his son, Moise, Isabel's father, as a Jew and sent him to study in Chicago where there were Jews who could teach him Torah and Talmud. Moise Cavalajo found a Jewish bride, studied mining engineering, and returned to the West, carrying his Hebrew books from en-

campment to encampment. It was not easy to find a Talmud study partner in Phoenix, and Isabel's father and Henry Stern had been happy to discover such a shared interest.

"I was not aware that Henry Stern had such a deep interest in the Talmud," Isaac said drily, and Isabel Cavalajo blushed and dropped her eyes as though she had stumbled into dangerous conversational territory.

"I did not come here to discuss religion, Mr. Lewin," she said.

"I did not think so."

The Chinese waiter set their food on the table, and he took note that like himself, she had ordered only tostadas and vegetables. He wondered vaguely if she observed the Jewish dietary laws.

"What did you come to discuss, Miss Cavalajo?"

"Politics." She smiled at his surprise. She took a secret pleasure in catching people off guard, he recognized.

"I'm not very politically oriented." He drenched a tostada with guacomole and dropped it deftly into his mouth.

"People still speak of your exchange with President Roosevelt."

"That was almost ten years ago," he said, startled to realize that a decade had flashed by since the Roughrider had lifted small Leonie in his arms, pressed his hand in a powerful grasp. So much had changed and so much had remained the same. He had been lonely then, and he was lonely still. He thought back to his exchange with Emma the previous evening, of how he had slept alone. Their marriage had assumed the ambience of the Arizona landscape, where living forests turned to thorn and fallen forests turned to stone. Their mutual guardedness had drained it of life and vitality.

"But the same problem you discussed with him ten years ago persists," she said. Her voice quivered with passion, and her golden eyes flashed. "Arizona still has not achieved a separate statehood. We are still not part of the union. We are a stepchild of the United States—our citizens disenfranchised, our borders uncertain."

"Statehood is inevitable," Isaac said. "President Taft signed the Enabling Act, and he will give careful consideration to the new constitution."

"You must know that he will veto it. He is firmly against referendum and recall. The only way we can make progress is if a delegation goes to Washington to argue with him, to bargain with him. Not a delegation of politicians who will seek their own end and argue their own interests, but an envoy of Arizonans who love their land and are prepared to fight for its future."

"You have made this your cause?" Isaac asked. "Why?"

"Because I love this land and I believe that Arizona has earned its right to statehood. Why should we stand on the threshold of the Union and be denied entry? Arizonans fought for their country in the Spanish-American War, but they cannot vote for their own commander in chief. I have known all my life what it was like to be on the outside looking in—a tolerated guest but not a participant. I have known because I am a woman and I am a Jew. Prejudice has operated against women and Jews, and prejudice has kept Arizona out of the Union. They say in the Congress that there are too many Mormons in this state, too many Spanish-speaking Mexicans, too many Democrats. Arizonans are too liberal. We will upset the balance. Therefore they fight to keep us outside the Union."

"You do not easily accept being an outsider?" Isaac observed.

"I do not accept it at all," she retorted. "*I* will never light Sabbath candles in a hidden basement. *I* set my menorah in the window for all to see. I proclaim my Jewishness. And I have traveled to Montana to march beside Jeannette Rankin for women's suffrage. I will cast my vote. My voice will be heard. When I believe in something, when I care for something, I fight for it, I work for it. And I believe in statehood now!"

"And you try to persuade others to work for it," Isaac said shrewdly. "What exactly do you want of me, Miss Cavalajo?"

The young woman's passion intrigued him. She was ablaze with conviction—her eyes flashing, her skin glowing. Her cap of dark hair circled her head like a gleaming helmet. She would be formidable in combat. Emma's weapons were carved of ice, but Isabel Cavalajo would do battle with fire.

The thought, unbidden, shamed and perplexed him. Why did he compare the young woman who sat opposite him to his wife?

"I belong to a committee charged with organizing just such a delegation to go to Washington to meet with President Taft. It is a private group without political aims. You will know some of the men who will join us. Ralph Cameron, the owner of the Bright Angel Trail, the attorney Lindsay Tate, Mr. Solomon of The Gila Valley Bank, Brother Timothy, who will speak on behalf of the Indians and the clergy." Her voice was proud. It was, he admitted, an impressive and powerful assemblage.

"And I will represent the merchants of the state?"

She nodded.

"And I will speak for the women and for the creative community. We wanted the poet Sharlot Hall to go, but she cannot manage it, so I will take her place. Of course, I must ask you to advance my vacation, but then the catalogue is finished and I have completed most of the drawings for the fall advertisements." The boldness of her request was softened by her blush.

"I was very pleased with your work on the catalogue," he said. "I did make one small change on the legend. What do you think of the slogan 'The Lewin Look'?"

"I like it." Her response was spontaneous and enthusiastic. Emma would have been hesitant, guarded, weighing the words, the intonation, their implication. Again, involuntarily, this comparison between his wife and the woman who sat opposite him had erupted.

"Will you join our group?" she asked. "Will you come to Washington with us?"

"Will the president grant such an unofficial group an appointment?"

"Yes. That has already been arranged." She spoke with the certainty of a political sophisticate.

"Yes. I will come." His own immediate acquiescence surprised him. Still, he remembered his confrontation with Theodore Roosevelt, his debt to Arizona, to the United States, which had given him refuge. And Emma would enjoy the journey east, he rationalized. She had never joined him on his buying trips east to Chicago and New York. She would enjoy seeing the capital, and it would be good for her to escape the desert heat, to walk with him beneath the shade of Washington's cherry trees. And perhaps if they were alone together, they could examine their differences, relax the tensions that stretched their marriage so dangerously taut. There would be little activity in the store, and Abner Wallach and Johnny Redbird could cope. He felt a thrill of excitement. He was stepping into history.

He paid the check, leaving a generous tip for the Chinese waiter.

"I appear to have become your ally as well as your employer, Miss Cavalajo," he said.

She laughed, and the color rose again to her cheeks. He liked her for the boldness of her words, the shyness of her blush, and the gaiety of her laughter. He moved forward to take her arm, nodding at Henry Stern, who gave them a thin-lipped smile as he passed.

Rhomboids of sunlight danced across the pale green carpet and formed glittering bands on the arms of the small white love seats that faced each other on opposite sides of the fireplace. The hearth was neatly piled with logs that would not be lit for several months, but the White House staff had been trained to anticipate every contingency. Mrs. McKinley, some recalled, had occasionally requested a fire in high summer.

William Howard Taft motioned his visitors to their seats and sat down opposite them, his enormous girth encompassing a seat meant for three. He settled himself with the absorbed concern of a worried and fearful man and studied the Arizonans with a narrowed gaze. One pale eyebrow was elliptically raised, and he clasped and unclasped his hands across the rise of his protruding abdomen. It was rumored that a specially built bathtub had been installed in the White House to accommodate the president's corpulent body. His white handlebar mustache concealed the curve of his lips and emphasized the unnatural pallor of his skin. Like many obese men, he perspired freely and easily, and globules of sweat beaded his forehead and dampened his cheeks.

In contrast, his western visitors' complexions were sun-darkened and wind-roughened. They stared at the president uneasily, as though the dim light of the small White House sitting room obscured their vision. They were accustomed to broad expanses of sunlit desert, large, white-walled rooms dominated by slowly revolving ceiling fans. The president noted their discomfort with secret pleasure. He had not wanted this meeting. It had been urged upon him by his advisers. The citizens of the Arizona territory had, after all, given their support to his opponent, William Jennings Bryan, during the election. They could not vote, but they had filled Bryan's campaign coffers and hung his slogan in their own state house. They, too, fought crucifixion on a cross of gold. Taft had not been surprised. Of course, silver miners would advocate a shift of the economy so that silver rather than gold would back the dollar. But they, in turn, should not be surprised that William Howard Taft was not overly sympathetic to their cause.

"You have come a long way, gentlemen," he said, and he nodded courteously to the dark-haired, gamin-faced young woman in the neat black suit who held a pad and pencil in readiness. A secretary, most probably. "And madame," he added.

"I am honored to be part of the delegation, Mr. President," she said smoothly. "Please accept this gift from us." She held out a leatherbound copy of Sharlot Hall's *Cactus and Pine*. The poet, who had come to the territory in a covered wagon, wrote eloquently of the beauty of the landscape, the patriotic fervor of the settlers.

"Thank you." The president's reply was cordial, but he stroked his mustache—a dangerous gesture, his aides knew. The woman was one of those damn suffragettes, no doubt. A Jeannette Rankin follower. One thing was certain—statehood for Arizona meant senators and representatives who would argue for women's suffrage. It was understandable, he supposed. The women of the territory had worked beside their men to carve out a life in the forbidding arid terrain. "It was good of you to undertake such a journey," he added.

"We are used to traveling long distances, Mr. President," the priest said. "Our territory is vast." He spoke in an untutored brogue, lightly tinged by the leisurely cadence of western speech.

The president studied the list of names his secretary had prepared for him. Brother Timothy, the headmaster of the mission school near Prescott. A Catholic. William Howard Taft frowned. He had known Catholics at Yale, and he had worked with missionaries like Brother Timothy during his tenure as governor of the Philippines. He did not dislike them, but he was wary of them. Their passion frightened him. He himself gave priority to the rule of the law. He was impatient with those who argued from an emotional stance when rules of law and practical precedent were at stake. This delegation of Arizonans would try to sway him to the justice of their cause, and he braced himself for the inevitable onslaught of arguments. He would tell them from the outset of his opposition to the principle of referendum and recall. If judges were subject to recall at the will of a popular referendum, there would be anarchy in the land. He saw now that the young woman was not taking notes. She was drawing, and although she held her pad close, he saw his own likeness take form. Her audacity amused and softened him.

"I am aware of the enormous scope of the Arizona territory," he said. "It must be a formidable landscape."

He himself had no desire to visit the land of deserts and mountains about which Theodore Roosevelt had waxed so passionate during the years of their friendship. The president had been born in Cincinnati, and that was as far west as he intended to travel during his lifetime. It was the East that beckoned him—the cool, shadowed law libraries of Yale and Harvard, the stately courtrooms like those he had presided over during his years on the bench. There were days when he did not know why he sat in the Oval Office when he was happiest in oak-paneled judicial chambers.

"We think our territory would be the crowning star in the Union's diadem," Ralph Cameron said. He was the only member of the delegation who was familiar to the president. He owned one of the largest copper mines in the territory as well as the Bright Angel Trail and Indian Springs within the Grand Canyon. He had been elected a delegate to Congress the year that Taft assumed the presidency, but even before then he had made a bargain with Theodore Roosevelt. The mine owner had promised Roosevelt that if Arizona was admitted as a separate state and freed of the stubborn coupling with New Mexico, on which Roosevelt had insisted, he would sell the trail and the water rights to the springs to the Santa Fe Railroad. That would ensure the proper development of the great national preserve. Roosevelt had agreed, and when Taft took office, he had validated Roosevelt's bargain. He was a man who was faithful to his word, and he had no real disagreement with the concept of separate statehood. It was that damn Populist constitution and the arrogance of the Arizonans that riled him.

"We are not at odds, Mr. Cameron," he said. "I, too, believe that Arizona will be a welcome addition to the Union. And it appears that the Congress will approve the constitution which your Assembly submitted."

"And it appears that you will surely veto it." The dark-haired, heavy-lidded man who spoke sat coiled in the green-and-white brocaded chair near the fireplace. Isaac Lewin, the president decided, glancing at his list. The Jewish department store owner. The successful immigrant. A man accustomed to engineering bargains, negotiating sales. His presence encouraged William Howard Taft. Merchandisers knew how to compromise, how to adjust their prices when items were not selling as briskly as anticipated, how to seek other outlets. The president turned to Isaac Lewin and smiled thinly.

"How can you be so sure, Mr. Lewin?"

"You have spoken out often enough against referendum and recall. I cannot see you signing a document that advocates such a program."

The president nodded. "As a former judge myself—and perhaps a future one—I do not endorse the Populist position allowing the people to recall duly elected judges. Such a measure would impugn the independence and the integrity of the judiciary. I understand that you westerners are used to creating your own forum of justice on the frontier, but these United States must be governed by judgments that will withstand the will and the whim of the people." He had made this statement so often that his words were dulled by the automatic rhetoric, and despite himself, he yawned, displaying a neat array of gold inlays. Probably Arizona gold, Isaac thought wryly.

"Do I understand that if we withdraw the provision for the recall of judges, you will sign the decree of statehood?" he asked. He had discerned a way out of the impasse. The situation was not unlike one he had encountered at a branch store where a manager had asked if he could lower the prices on some fabric. "I can't agree to it," Isaac had replied. "But if you do it after I leave, how could I object to it?" The other managers could not object to a decision made without Isaac's imprimatur.

"I will indeed." The president felt vindicated. He had known that Isaac Lewin would know how to negotiate this last difficulty. The provision for recall would be withdrawn, and the president could sign the statehood decree in good conscience. Once Arizona had gained statehood, the same provision could be reinserted. His constitutional scruples would be satisfied, and the Arizonans would have both statehood and the right of recall. They flashed each other glances of agreement now, secret smiles of triumph.

"We hope, too, that you will continue the policy of conservation," Ralph Cameron said.

William Howard Taft frowned. He may have been Teddy Roosevelt's choice for the presidency, but he was not his puppet. His predecessor's involvement in conservation did not interest him. These westerners were in love with their deserts and their mountains, their rock-rimmed canyons, and their dense forest lands. There was perversity in their passion. They wanted to conquer the frontier, to build their cities on plateaus of sand and in the shadows of coal-colored mesas, but they wanted to preserve that same frontier, natural and unspoiled. They reminded him of an irrational Appalachian farmer who had appeared before him during his early years on the bench, seeking a divorce. The man had deflowered his bride and felt aggrieved because she was no longer a virgin.

"I will, as always, heed the dictates of my conscience," he told Ralph Cameron and heaved himself to his feet, leaving a deep declivity on the love seat. He extended his hand to each member of the delegation, and they touched the roll of fat that padded his palm. The meeting for which they had traversed the country, crossing rivers and mountains on the steel arteries of rail that last linked east to west, was over. The president noticed, as Isabel Cavalajo too swiftly closed her notebook, that she had completed her likeness of him. She had overemphasized his jowls, he thought, and made his neck too thick.

The Arizonans were jubilant as they left. Statehood was imminent, assured. A loophole had been found in the presidential resistance. Outside the White House they shook hands with each other, and Ralph Cameron lifted Isabel into the air and twirled her triumphantly around.

"We won. All we have to do is withdraw that clause and then reinsert it when we have statehood. It would have saved us a journey if we had known," the mine owner said.

"You never know how a customer will react until you're facing him across a counter," Isaac replied.

"I'm not sorry that we came," Brother Timothy said. "It was important, I think." He did not add that he had not left the territory for more than a decade and would not have left it without good reason. His sense of duty to the Indian children was overwhelming. Yet it was important that he meet with other members of his church, exchange ideas and opinions with his colleagues. He hurried away now to an appointment at Catholic University before Isaac could arrange to meet him for dinner.

"And I have promised to show Miss Cavalajo the National Gallery," Ralph Cameron said. He tucked her hand into his own, and Isaac was oddly hurt that they did not ask him to join them. He watched them cross Pennsylvania Avenue, the avuncular mine owner guiding petite Isabel as though she were a child.

The other members of the delegation had their own plans, and he spent the afternoon alone, walking across the broad boulevards of the capital city, marveling at the simple grace of the Doric-columned buildings where laws were made and justice was served.

Again, he felt the thrill of being an American, of participating in the great adventure of democracy. He had a vested interest in Arizona's transition from territory to state. Statehood would grant Arizona sovereignty within the union and would crown Isaac Lewin with citizenship. He who had left a land where his people were restricted to a pale of settlement, persecuted and disenfranchised, would become a naturalized citizen of the United States. Here his contributions were welcomed; his words had been listened to with respect by the president himself. The president! Pride suffused him. Isabel Cavalajo's eyes had flashed with amber sparks as he spoke. *But Emma had not borne witness to his triumph.*

Loneliness overcame him, and he sat on a bench in Potomac Park and wrote a postcard to her and then to each of the children, taking special pains over his message to Gregory. "Play hard, but do not exert yourself," he wrote. He worried about the boy but did not want to coddle him. Emma would disapprove of whatever he wrote, he knew. He was bitter still that she had not joined him on this journey, that she had instead accepted an invitation to her brother Simon's housewarming in San Francisco.

"They wrote to us about it months ago," she had insisted when he pressed her.

"But surely this is more important."

"Nothing is more important than family."

Was he not family? he had thought bitterly. Would her brothers' desires always take precedence over his own?

"We could not take the children to Washington. The journey would be too much for Gregory. But California is a manageable distance, and it is important that they be with their cousins."

"And that you exchange high-minded thoughts with your sister-in-law," he had added with malicious anger.

She had not replied. She did not want to tell him that she wanted to go to California to consult with a doctor in the pediatrics department of the Stanford University Medical School about Gregory. Isaac worried obsessively about the boy, and she did not want to reveal her own fears to him. Again they had stared at each other in defeat, separated anew by the taut silence of unarticulated disappointment.

A chilly breeze blew up from the river, and Isaac shivered. He was alone in Washington, and his wife sat at her brother's elegant dinner table. It was, he remembered, the very same table that had stood in the Coens' Amsterdam dining room; Simon had traced it with great difficulty through an auction house. Would the Coens ever be done with their past? Isaac wondered. Would they forever pursue the vanished grace and luxuries of their childhoods? Henry Stern would not surrender his hatred, and his half brothers and half sister clung with a like tenacity to an atavistic nostalgia. The poverty of his own past, the finality of his own tragedy, was simpler to cope with, Isaac decided.

He had a solitary dinner in the dining room of his hotel and went to a concert. He loved music, and it was rare that a decent symphony orchestra came to Phoenix. The program included Debussy tone poems and Mahler's Fourth Symphony. The majesty and melancholy of the music and the empty seat beside him increased his sense of solitude. His footsteps echoed across the night-deserted boulevards, the vacant plazas. He bent his head as he passed groups of friends and slowly strolling couples; his aloneness shamed him.

The lobby of the hotel was deserted, and although he paused at the doorway of the oak-paneled saloon parlor, he did not enter. The men who sat at the small tables and along the polished bar did not look at him. The room smelled of liquor and loneliness. He walked slowly upstairs to his room on the second floor. He glanced down at the long red-carpeted hallway with the thought of stopping at Brother Timothy's room and saw Isabel Cavalajo fumbling with her key. He strode toward her.

"Are you having difficulty, Miss Cavalajo?"

"I can't get the key to turn." Her face was flushed and her lips were moist.

He took the key from her. The tumbler needed oiling, but he maneuvered the key into place. Patiently, he worked it into the lock, and at last the tumbler gave and the door swung open.

"Thank you." She smiled at him gratefully. "I feel so foolish. I never stayed at a hotel before, and I didn't know what to do."

"It was nothing. Next time go to the desk and they will send a chambermaid up to help you."

"Yes. I would have done that, but still it was fortunate that you came in."

"I am glad to have been of service to you."

They were actors on a stage, reading from a carefully prepared script, exchanging requisite courtesies. He wanted to tell her that she looked very beautiful, that her simple black dress became her gamin looks and the sheen on her smooth cap of hair rivaled the velvet trim on her skirt and cuffs. He wanted to know where Ralph Cameron had taken her for dinner and if she had ordered raspberries because they exactly matched the tiny curved bow of her lips. Would Mahler make her cry? he wondered, and he tried to imagine her golden eyes veiled by tears. Instead, he stepped away from her.

"Good night, Miss Cavalajo."

"Good night, Mr. Lewin."

He went down the corridor to his room and reached into his pocket for his own key, aware suddenly that he had not heard her own door open and close.

"Mr. Lewin." She stood beside him. She had glided so softly and swiftly down the carpeted hall that he had not heard her steps. "I have some fruit. Perhaps you would like to share it with me."

He hesitated. A small vein throbbed at her throat. There had been a tremor in her voice. Wordlessly, he followed her back to her room and closed the door.

She had bought oranges, and she sliced them with a small pearl-handled knife. Her hand trembled and she cut herself; the blood circled her finger in a narrow ribbon of crimson.

"Oh, how clumsy of me." The color drained from her face.

"Let me see."

He took her finger in his hand and with his large white handkerchief wiped it free of blood. Then he lifted it to his lips and kissed it. The blood flowed again, thick against his tongue. He pressed the finger flesh between his lips, the bone bruising his mouth, his hand steady on her shoulder. She did not move. He released her finger, wrapped it in his handkerchief, and bent to kiss her neck, her cheek, her blue-veined eyelids.

"You are so beautiful," he said.

"Say my name. Isabel."

"Isabel. Isabel. Isabel!" The syllables rose with musical tenderness. They filled his mouth with their beauty, and he knew that they had floated through his mind since the day she first sat opposite him in his Phoenix office. "Isabel!"

He took her in his arms and carried her to the bed. She was so small, so light. He undressed her as he would a child, his fingers strangely deft with the tiny buttons of her dress, the narrow straps of her white batiste camisole. She undid his cufflinks, loosening his string tie, her hands dancing across his neck, light as butterflies. She traced the contours of his body, as though tactilely memorizing the curve of his back, the slope of his shoulders, the small birthmark at the base of his spine.

He turned and settled her beneath him. His lips caressed the golden rise of her breasts; the heels of his hands lifted her shoulders. Her shudders and whispers matched his own. Again, her blood flowed between them as she called his name in joy, in wondering ecstasy, while crimson flowerlets formed on the white muslin sheets.

"What have we done?" he asked that morning as the milky light of dawn washed across them. Her face was turned toward him. Her long dark lashes were damp. She had wept as he claimed her, wept as she submitted to him. *Tears of love,* she had said, and he had licked her cheek, covered her eyes with his hands.

"We have loved each other."

"Isabel, it is not as simple as that."

"But it is. I told you once that when I believed in something I fought for it. I acted upon it. I believe in my love for you, and I am not afraid to act on it. I felt it the first day I met you—before you even knew my name."

"I am a married man," he said. *Emma.* Her name thundered in his mind like a reproof. Emma who fiercely protected herself against him, keeping real and imagined ledgers of profit and loss behind an emotional armory which he could not penetrate. Emma who turned her face from him in the aftermath of passion.

"I know. Of course, I know. I am not asking you to divorce your wife. I do not want marriage. I want only to be with you.''

''You are young—a child. You don't know what you contemplate.''

''But I do. I contemplate our being together, yet each of us having our own lives, our own work. It is not so outrageous—that two people who care for each other should share parts of their lives. We do not have to be bound by legal contract to care for each other. Why should there not be freedom, independence, between a man and a woman—between you and me?''

She sat upright, and he laughed and pulled her down against the pillows, circling her head with his hand, gently stroking her neck.

''You are not on a soap box now. Save such rhetoric for your suffragist friends.''

''Don't mock me.'' She bit his finger, pulled his hair, adorably childish in her protests.

''What shall we do?'' he asked soberly. ''Shall we live a lie?''

''We shall live as we must live. It can be managed without hurting your family.''

''And you—I do not want you to be hurt.''

''How can I be hurt if I have what I want? Your love and my freedom.''

''Phoenix is a small city. People will talk.''

''I have an adobe house in the desert near Tempe. I use it as a studio. There are no near neighbors.'' She spoke very softly, her voice almost swallowed in the curve of his elbow.

In her mind's eye she saw them sitting together at the rough-hewn table on her patio. She would feed him a grape from the pale green cluster that nestled in a blue bowl. Together they would watch a desert hawk flash darkly across the sun-bright sky. She was an artist. She imagined her life patterned in broad canvases. When one was finished, she put it aside and began the next.

''Shall we try at least?'' she asked.

''We shall try,'' he said.

He had been too long alone, deprived of warmth, of spontaneity. He could not deny himself the love she offered, the love he felt. Emma would not know. She would not be hurt. The bargain they had made in Galveston would remain inviolate, their partnership intact. He laughed harshly, and Isabel Cavalajo put her fingers to his lips and triumphantly rested her head on his shoulder.

They told the other Arizonans at breakfast that they would not be returning directly to the territory. They had decided to go to New York. Isaac wanted to visit the large department stores there.

"It would be helpful if Miss Cavalajo studies their window displays and the techniques they employ in newspaper advertising," he said.

"A good idea," Ralph Cameron agreed. "With statehood coming, we want to be right on the mark. We'll show our eastern visitors that we not only keep pace with them but we're a jump ahead."

"There's a lot that we'll teach them," Isabel said. "Arizona will be the first state in the union to grant women the vote." She was radiant this morning, aglow with the confidence of her tandem triumphs.

Isaac accompanied the others to Union Station. As the train whistle sounded, Brother Timothy drew him aside.

"Be careful, Isaac," the priest said. His gray-blue eyes were shadowed with worry. Always he had known that Isaac and Emma Lewin lived on the edge of emotional danger, their lives uneasily balanced between strained silences and compounded misunderstandings. But now his old friend hovered too close to the precipice, and all the dreams that they had shared on that distant train journey into Arizona were endangered.

"Don't worry." Isaac embraced his friend but averted his eyes from the searching stare.

He stopped at a florist's stand and bought a bouquet of amber-colored roses for Isabel. The soft petals were of the exact color and texture of her skin.

The War Years,
1914-1918

EMMA looked up and watched as two white-winged doves plunged with graceful precision onto the huge saguaro cactus that grew in a corner of the garden. Delicately they pecked at the flat cream-colored petals, searching out the fruity pods of the carmine seeds, seeking shards of shade amid the thorn-studded branches.

"They're very beautiful, aren't they?" Isaac said.

She looked up, startled. It was a Sunday and she had expected him to sleep late, but he was dressed for the office, his briefcase in hand.

"You are working today?" She struggled to keep her tone neutral.

"I have a great deal of paperwork," he replied. He did not look at her as he spoke but kept his eyes fixed on the crouching olive tree. "The situation in Europe is going to affect our fall imports, I'm sure."

She smiled. "The world grows smaller. An assassin's bullets in Sarajevo may mean that the wives of American oil barons may not have their couturier gowns for the winter cotillions."

"I want to prepare for every contingency," he said. "I must check the inventory reports. We may have enough reserve stock for a limited period."

"I see." Her voice was dry, but he could not tell whether it implied indifference or disbelief. Her eyes remained fixed on the birds, which took wing suddenly, their white wings scissoring the heat-heavy, molten gold air.

"Will you be all right alone here?" he asked. "Leonie is home." He had passed his daughter in the hallway, and had been newly startled by her adolescent beauty. "Where are the boys?"

241

"They rode out to the desert with Johnny Redbird."

There was no accusation in her voice, but he felt a twinge of guilt. He had little time to spare for his sons now, or for grave-eyed Leonie. Like an obsessed miser, he hoarded his free hours, his spare evenings, the precious odd weekends, and secured them for Isabel, who waited for him in the white-washed adobe house sheltered beneath a towering ponderosa pine.

"They didn't take Gregory?"

"He has a sore throat."

"Again?" Isaac frowned. His youngest son's frequent ill-nesses disturbed him. Often, he wakened in the night and went to stand beside Gregory's bed as though his brief pres-ence might shield the sleeping boy from ominous dangers.

"I still think we should take him to the Johns Hopkins Medical Center in Baltimore," he said.

"He was thoroughly examined when we were in Califor-nia two years ago. You remember—when you went on that statehood mission to Washington."

"Of course, I remember," he said impatiently. His heart beat faster, and he searched her face for a hint of suspicion, but as always, her expression was calm, composed. She sus-pected nothing, and her very trust angered him. Another woman would have asked questions about his frequent ab-sences, the constant journeys to other cities, but Emma re-mained undemanding, accepting of his excuses, his vague explanations. "And your brother's wise doctors insist that nothing can be done for Gregory."

"He'll outgrow the weakness," she replied. "He has a predisposition to illness, a lower resistance." She was not lying. The doctors had said just that, adding that the predis-position was caused by a congenital heart defect that weak-ened Gregory.

"It's a rare form of rheumatic fever that tends to recur. Frankly, I should advise you against becoming pregnant again," the thin, bearded Stanford University pediatrician had said cautiously, sadly. He was newly married and hoped to have a dozen children. "You are fortunate that your other children are healthy."

"Gregory will be healthy too."

The doctor had not replied. He had too often confronted tenacious mothers who denied the truth and wrote their own scenarios. Still, there was a determined fierceness in Emma Lewin's tone. She was, after all, an Arizonan. He supposed that people who had tamed a desert and built cities on shifting sands thought they were capable of anything. If they had changed the face of the earth, surely they could wrest life from death.

"Children do outgrow rheumatic fever," he had conceded. "If his heart valve has not been damaged, he may live a full life."

"He will live a full life."

She believed that still, although sore throats and fevers had haunted Gregory and too frequently his joints had become inflamed and a rash had colored his forearms. She had not shared the doctor's prognosis with Isaac. He had buried a small daughter in a distant land. She would not have him consumed with worry over his last-born son, who sang softly into the night. She knew how Isaac fretted over Gregory. Often she feigned sleep when he made his nocturnal visits to the child's room.

"I still think we should take him to Baltimore," Isaac said worriedly now, looking up at the boy's bedroom window.

"Did you listen to the news this morning?" Deftly, she changed the subject.

"Yes. More and more discussion of the assassination. There's speculation that with all the damn interlocking treaties in Europe, the whole continent could be plunged into war."

"And you think so too?"

"A limited war, I think. And one that will be over quickly. But it won't affect this country except for trade. Wilson is pledged to keep us out of it."

"Ah, yes, Wilson's new freedom. Freedom to live in peace." Bitterness edged her voice. She did not expect ever to live in peace. Dissent and danger trailed her. Mysterious desert winds blew through her house in the darkness of the night, and she could not call to Isaac, her husband, because too often he was not there. Besides, they slept in separate bedrooms now. She had, after all, heeded the warning of the youthful San Francisco doctor and resigned herself to a physical loneliness that matched her emotional solitude. Isaac had not protested. She had been both relieved and pained by his acquiescence. There were other ways, she knew, to prevent pregnancy.

"I'll be back for dinner," Isaac said and bent to kiss her on the cheek.

"Will you? Yes, perhaps you will," she said absently. She watched him drive off. The wheels of his Ford tossed up a cloud of yellow dust that hovered lambently in the heavy July air.

"Mama!" Gregory's voice was plaintive, bewildered. He stood at the front door in his white nightshirt and ran his fingers through his mahogany-colored curls. Fever patches burned at his cheeks, and his blue eyes were strangely glazed.

"I called you. I wanted you to come upstairs and hear the rest of my story. I still haven't thought of an ending, though." He was a fanciful child who wrote tales of lost children and talking birds, of enchanted forests and painted deserts where the sands changed color, drifting from lavender to emerald green. He sang, in the night, of an oasis where pomegranate trees grew in secret groves and jewel-colored fish swam in silvery streams. He was writing a story now about a boy who had wandered from his home in search of the secret of happiness.

"I'll come up soon and listen to it," she said gently and walked him into the house, her arm about his shoulders.

Leonie, carrying a white straw hat of the same eggshell shade as her wide-collared dress, stood in the front hall. She smiled at her mother and looked worriedly at her youngest brother.

"Are you going to the movies, Leonie?" Emma asked.

"Yes. Unless Gregory wants me to stay home and read to him."

"No. I want you to see the new picture and tell me the story," Gregory said. How pretty Leonie was with her long dark hair twisted into a single shimmering braid. "It's Charlie Chaplin today, isn't it?"

Leonie nodded.

"Tillie's Punctured Romance. With Marie Dressler. I'll come home early and tell you about it."

"And I'll read you the rest of my story."

Leonie bent and kissed him. "I won't be late," she said

"You're going alone, Leonie?" Emma asked.

Leonie hesitated for a moment and then shrugged.

"A lot of kids from school will be there," she said. She did not look at her mother, and her hands shook as she knotted the dime for the movie ticket into a corner of her handkerchief.

The door slammed behind her, and slowly Emma and Gregory walked up the stairs, the boy's dry, small hand clasped in her own. Isaac had neglected to turn the radio off, and a soft-voiced newscaster assured his listeners that Prime Minister Lloyd George was confident that peace would be preserved despite the sad events of the weeks that had followed the assassination at Sarajevo.

On the patio of the whitewashed adobe house near Tempe, Isabel Cavalajo clung to Isaac and wept. In practiced pose he held her close and softly, rhythmically, incanted his reassurances.

"Will there be a war, Isaac? I'm so frightened. How can men fight and kill each other?"

"There won't be a war, my darling."

He had grown used to her fears and her passions. Isabel soared on waves of joy and plummeted into swirling rapids of terror and despair. She lived with the daring of a child, convinced of her own immortality, her own right to seize what she perceived to be her own, to live by the rules of her beliefs, the courage of her convictions. She was at once courageous and fearful. Isaac smiled always when he remembered that she had been daringly articulate when she confronted the president of the United States but had hesitated to ask a hotel desk clerk to help her with her room key. Still, that fortunate temerity had changed their lives.

She had, true to her promise, made few demands on him. She had her own work at the Emporium, planning catalogue designs and window displays, and her political activity had not abated with statehood. Just as she had predicted, Arizona had been the first state to grant women the vote, but she had turned her energies to the national women's suffrage movement. Always, the oak table in the adobe house was peppered with notices for rallies and meetings, appeals for funds, invitations to conferences.

Often, an unfinished painting stood on her easel, and she carried her sketch pad everywhere. She had a full life, she assured Isaac, yet always she was available when he could manage an evening or an afternoon at the adobe house. She loved to cook for him, and they ate while watching the sun die its slow and brilliant death, scooping up cubes of spiced meat with the golden tacos that she baked herself in the primitive earthenware oven. The ponderosa pine cooled the small house, and the night winds rustled the feathery branches and stirred the ceramic wind chimes that Johnny Redbird had fashioned for her. Isaac kept a few books on her shelves, volumes of history and philosophy, Hebrew texts bound in leather gritty with the sand that blew in through the open windows. Occasionally, he read as she slept, turning now and again to study her face, as though memorizing the curve of her cheek, the dark arch of her eyebrow. In the silence of the night, he heard the musical lilt of her laughter, the haunting wistfulness of her sigh.

Her fingers dug into his flesh now, and her breath was a soft and tender wind against his body. She was his frightened darling, his daring lover, the gamin princess he would hold in his arms through the long golden afternoon. He would comfort her with love and lie beside her until darkness subdued the desert heat. How lovely she was in the loose sky-colored robe of Navajo weave, a blue cactus flower in her hair. He lifted her in his arms, his fragile, secret love, and carried her into the house.

"And if there is a war, I will protect you," he whispered later as they lay side by side. She did not hear him. His hand cupped her head and she slept, exhausted by her fear and by their love.

"Something must be done," he thought. "We cannot go on like this." It was a thought that he had had many times during the two years that had passed since that first night in

Washington, but he had done nothing, nor could he decide what it was that he must do.

Leonie blinked against the impact of the sun's brilliance after the soothing hours of darkness in the movie theater. As always, after a matinee showing at the Phoenix Palace, she felt disoriented, unwilling to divorce herself from the celluloid dream world of the screen and to confront the reality of the busy city street. Classmates, walking in groups, passed her, and she smiled at them and waved as they window-shopped along Washington Street or went to Anderson's Drugstore to sip foaming strawberry phosphates at the long marble-countered soda fountain.

"Do you want to come with us for a soda, Leonie?" Joseph and Reuben Wallach stood before her. The twins were newly graduated from knickers to long pants, and they noisily jingled the coins in their pockets. They had enough money to buy ice-cream floats for Rachel, their sister, and for Leonie, and they had promised their mother that they would include the girls. It was not that they did not like Leonie, they had assured Natalya, but she acted so stuck-up—just because she was a couple of grades ahead of them in school or maybe because her father was the boss. Their own father did most of the work at Lewin's Emporium—everyone knew that. Isaac Lewin spent so much time on the phone or off on buying trips that he was seldom seen on the floors of the Emporium. It was Abner Wallach who soothed the feelings of irate customers, checked the stockroom, and even drove off to the branch stores when problems had to be solved.

"Leonie doesn't think that way," Natalya had assured her sons. "She's just shy."

"We'll ask her, but she won't come. She never does," Reuben had said.

He had been right. Leonie politely refused his invitation. Gregory was ill, and her mother expected her home. But she walked in the wrong direction, they noticed, turning the corner of Washington Street. They lost sight of her and shrugged. It was too hot to stand on the sidewalk and stare after Leonie Lewin.

Leonie walked purposefully to a men's haberdashery store

and stationed herself in the doorway. Covertly, she studied her reflection in the plate-glass window. The straw hat did look nice with the white linen dress. Emma, with her impeccable sense of style, had selected it, and she had also chosen Leonie's white high-buttoned pumps.

"You look so grown-up," her father had said that morning, looking at her with a bemused smile, and she had blushed because she knew that despite the looseness of the dress, her breasts were clearly outlined.

She was only fourteen, yet she was aware that the eyes of men followed her as she walked down the street and that the saleswomen at the Emporium were startled by her full figure when she stood in her chemise to buy new outfits for school. It did not help, she knew, that she herself felt older than her classmates and at a remove from her younger brothers. Always, she had preferred the company and conversation of adults. When there were guests and the children were sent outside to play, she lingered at the table, and her parents accepted her presence as a matter of course. When the family visited their relatives in California and her brothers cavorted with their cousins, Leonie trailed after her aunt and uncles and her mother. She listened to their stories of their Amsterdam childhoods, their family holidays in Germany and France, their memories of their parents, Jacob and Leonie Coen. "We were happy then. Before," Uncle Emil would say sadly. *Before what?* Leonie wondered, but she dared not ask, although once she had wondered aloud why dashing Uncle Emil was not married, and Uncle Simon and her mother had exchanged sharp glances. That, too, she guessed, had something to do with the mysterious *before*.

Leonie's classmates rode their horses into the desert in groups, but Leonie preferred to ride alone or to join her mother on Emma's weekly quests for desert flowers for the Sabbath table. Sometimes she accompanied her mother on visits to the sanitariums that housed the *lungers*, the tubercular Jews who came to regain their health in Arizona's pure dry air. Emma belonged to a committee of Jewish women in Phoenix who brought delicacies to the sickly men and women and the pale, large-eyed children. They spread braided Sabbath loaves, delicate sponge cakes, and gefilte fish, so light that the invalids could digest them without difficulty, on the cloth-covered plank tables. Leonie helped and listened to the stories of towns in Europe left behind, of the crowded tenements of the Lower East Side of New York, the busy streets.

"Here is America. Here is really the *neie velt*—the new world," a woman told her, pointing westward to the broad expanse of desert and mountain. "Here is where a Jew can really become an American."

Leonie went only to those parties and dansants that her mother would not allow her to avoid. Taller than her classmates, pensive since childhood, she stood against the wall at the bar mitzvah parties and Hanukkah and Passover gatherings that were the focus of Jewish communal life in Phoenix. She went to the Halloween and Thanksgiving parties of her non-Jewish classmates and prayed that no one would approach her and invade the dream world she preferred. Once she had heard her mother and Natalya speaking softly about her as they sat in the loggia embroidering the trousseau of a recovered *lunger,* a Jewish girl who would soon marry a Colorado miner.

"You must not be concerned about Leonie," Natalya had said. "There are children who need a sense of privacy, of solitude. You yourself should understand that, Emma."

Emma had laughed bitterly.

"My solitude is not of my own choosing, Natalya. Isaac is so preoccupied that we drift further and further apart. I do understand Leonie, but I worry that she must be lonely, that she must feel the need for a friend, a confidante. I, after all, have you."

Leonie had imagined her mother's pale hand covering Natalya's wrist, her fingers fanning out in friendship. She was sorry that her mother was increasingly alone. Her father was so often away. Even when he was in Phoenix, he sometimes did not come home for dinner or to sleep, and occasionally over the past two years he had even missed a Sabbath dinner. She had wished then that she could reassure her mother and explain that she was not lonely, she was not melancholy. She, too, had a friend with whom she could talk about almost anything—a friend who shared the secrets of her heart, the quiet revelations of thought and feeling. But her mother would not approve of her friendship with Jesse Stern, no more than Jesse's father would approve of his son's relationship with the daughter of Isaac and Emma Lewin.

They had agreed from the outset, she and Jesse, that their friendship would be a secret, and they had become skillful conspirators. They contrived to meet in unlikely places—in a sweetshop in the Mexican section of the city, in the market on Grand Street where they bought peeled cactus fruit from smiling black women, beneath the cottonwood trees in the Encanto and Palmcroft districts. They had discovered a cave on the Tempe road and turned it into a secret hideaway.

Their complicity added a sweet dimension to their togetherness. Each meeting was a small triumph, a daring adventure. They counted themselves fortunate that they had found each other, although, of course, they had known each other from earliest childhood. Jesse was two years older than she, but they had both attended Natalya's Bible classes and they had seen each other when they attended the religious services that were still held above Melczer's Liquor Store, although there were plans now for the building of a real synagogue. Their families sat at opposite sides of the room, barely nodding if they passed one another.

The High Holy Days arrived when the desert heat had peaked and invaded the makeshift synagogue with a fierceness that was unmitigated by the homemade excelsior windowbox that the Melczers had installed to cool the air. The fans of the women moved with desperate rapidity, but always, during the Yom Kippur fast, someone would grow faint and sway dangerously as though sustained from falling by the corporeal torpidity of the heat-heavy air.

Once, fearlessly opening her eyes during the high priest's prayer, Leonie had stared across the room and met Jesse's gaze. They had smiled at each other in recognition and swiftly closed their eyes lest they be blinded.

Leonie remembered the stories that Natalya had told them of the priests who had prostrated themselves before the ark of the Law in the desert capital of Judaea. She thought it wonderful that thousands of years later, in the desert capital of Phoenix, the same priestly benedictions were repeated by their descendants. The continuity of her people's tradition as they wandered from desert to desert awed her, and she forgot the suffocating heat and turned back to her prayerbook. Later, when they became friends, Jesse told her that when he had looked through the window during the service, he had imagined that the buildings of Phoenix, aglow in the afternoon sunlight, shared the golden color of Jerusalem, the city that David had built on the sands of Judaea.

They had at last been thrust together in friendship on the February day on which President Taft signed the proclamation declaring Arizona to be the forty-eighth state of the union. The date selected was February 14, exactly fifty years after Abraham Lincoln had first declared Arizona a territory. The coincidence excited the citizens of Phoenix, and the entire city was caught up in a frenzy of celebration. Lewin's Emporium was closed, and Isaac accepted Governor Hunt's invitation to join the procession following him as he walked from Ford's Hotel to the capitol building. Joshua and Samuel would walk beside him, and small Gregory would perch on his shoulder. Emma, in turn, would stand beside Mrs. Hunt with a contingent of other women on the capitol steps.

It was assumed that Leonie would join the Wallach family, but when Natalya knocked at the door, Leonie said she would meet them later. She relished being alone in the large house. She stood before the full-length mirror in her mother's bedroom and brushed her long dark hair, allowing it to fall in luxurious folds about her shoulders. She smiled mysteriously in imitation of Marie Dressler. She pirouetted, bent in a low curtsy, and felt an unfamiliar cramp course through her body. A crimson circlet had formed on her petticoat, and she touched the fresh blood as the whistle at the Maricopa Mines screamed in celebration of Arizona's statehood. Alone, dancing before the oak-framed mirror, she had become a woman. She found the clean strips of flannel Emma used when she menstruated and carefully protected herself. Proud of her secret, yet fearful as well, she put on her white organdy dress and went alone into the city.

The streets teemed with people. Miners and ranchers had packed their families into cars, pickup trucks, and wagons, and swarmed to the city to witness Governor Hunt's official proclamation and William Jennings Bryan's scheduled oration. Men lifted small children onto their shoulders. They whooped wildly as pistols were fired into the air; the mine whistles continued to shriek. Arizona had achieved statehood, but the frontier spirit had not been abandoned.

Tubs of ice were filled with bottles of beer, and enterprising children sold glasses of lemonade on every street corner. The starched blouses of the women wilted, and their hair fell in damp strands about their foreheads, but they smiled happily. Children held paper flags aloft and danced through the streets to the tunes played by fiddlers and accordionists. Mexican girls danced in a circle, holding their bright skirts above their knees and beckoning partners to join them with braceleted arms.

Leonie's heart beat faster. Distracted, she had wandered into an unfamiliar section of the city. A man, holding a bottle of beer in one hand and a smoking pistol in the other, leaned his face toward her. The scent of carbon mingled with sour breath sickened her, and she ran down the street and paused, breathless, in the shadow of a store's canopy. Thunder rocketed through the street, but when she looked up the sky was clear. A passing woman laughed.

"There's no storm. It's the governor's forty-eight-gun salute in honor of our being the forty-eighth state."

Again the street quivered under the impact of the gunfire. The vibration shattered the plate glass of the store window just behind her, and she trembled. Always, loud noises had frightened her. Summer storms had caused her to flee to her parents' bedroom, and even the sound of train and mine whistles unnerved her. She hurried from the store window to the curb, where a horse-drawn carriage stood. Another salute sounded and the horse shied, rearing backward so that its huge iron-shod front hooves hovered just above her head. She screamed but remained motionless, paralyzed with fear.

Suddenly strong, lean arms encircled her and thrust her out of the path of the careening animal. She fell and looked up at the concerned face of Jesse Stern. Their eyes met and he took her hand in his.

They walked that day to the outskirts of the city, far from tumultuous celebrations. Beneath the shade of a cottonwood tree they discovered their penchant for silence, their shared love for poetry. He recited "Annabel Lee" to her. She had not read it before. She felt herself to be that girl in a kingdom by the sea. One day she would have a love that was more than love. The blood of her new womanhood flowed, and a tall, angular-faced boy read poetry to her in the shade of a full-leafed tree.

"What is grass?" In turn she asked Whitman's question in a trembling voice and offered the poet's answer. "It is the handkerchief of the Lord out of green stuff woven." Her mother loved Whitman, she told Jesse Stern, and often read his poetry aloud to her. *Her mother.* Jesse frowned and she understood. Their parents, his father, her mother, were enemies to each other, prisoners of an incomprehensible bitterness spawned in the distant waterlocked land of their birth.

"We shall have to be careful if we are to be friends," Jesse had said then, and she had nodded solemnly. He was her first real friend. She did not want to lose him.

And for two years, they had been careful. They arranged their meetings carefully, seeking out obscure corners of the city. They went to the movies alone on weekends, sat separately in the theater but met afterward on an appointed corner. Occasionally they were unable to keep their clandestine appointments, and Leonie would return home, choking with the words she had not shared, the thoughts and feelings she would have to store away until they saw each other again.

Jesse was late today, and Leonie glanced nervously up and down the street, hoping he would not disappoint her. She wanted him to explain the clips on Movietone News. The camera had focused on a beautiful woman wearing a long white dress and a hat plumed with snowy feathers not unlike those Leonie's mother had fashioned during the early days in Phoenix. A plump dignitary in a bemedaled dress uniform stood beside her. *The Austrian Archduke and his wife at Sarajevo only minutes before their assassination,* the caption read. *This isolated act of violence may plunge all of Europe and perhaps the entire world into war.* There were additional photos of Serbian soldiers and Russian children grinning as they embraced booted infantrymen. The children in the audience had tittered, but Leonie saw one woman cover her face with her hands and a man place his wife's hand protectively in his own. Did war really threaten them? She had looked fearfully about her in the darkened theater. Jesse sat, as he always did, in the fourth row on the aisle. He had stared intently at the screen. He would explain it all to her. He was sixteen now and had a great interest in the news. He thought of becoming a journalist, perhaps even a muckraker, and he subscribed to *The American* and *Munsey's* and occasionally read articles to her that she had difficulty understanding.

He dashed across the street now, his bright hair, bronzed by the afternoon sun, falling into his eyes.

"I'm sorry I'm late," he said. "But I had to run an errand for my mother right after the movie. There isn't much time left before she leaves for Europe. Only a few weeks."

"Will she go anyway—I mean even with the news so bad?" Leonie asked.

Abigail Stern's journey to England to attend the wedding of a niece had been planned for months. Jesse's mother was a gentle, caring woman whose health had always been threateningly fragile. Leonie had read an occasional wistfulness in her smile, a mute apology for the tension that separated the Sterns and the Lewins.

"My father doesn't see any reason for her to change her plans. The war won't be fought in England, and certainly passenger vessels will be safe on the ocean. He thinks that it will be good for her to escape the summer heat," Jesse replied.

Leonie envied Jesse his loving parents, always so concerned for each other. They held hands as they walked down the streets of Phoenix and looked tenderly at each other as they sat side by side at concerts and plays. Her own parents spoke to each other with the strained politeness of associates thrown together by the vagaries of fortune. Her father's lips grazed her mother's cheek in perfunctory greeting, and they no longer shared the same bedroom.

"It's wonderful that he cares so much for her," Leonie said.

"His life was very sad before he met her. He barely knew his father, and his only brother stayed in Germany when he and his mother came to America. His mother died soon after they arrived, and he was alone until he met my mother. I've never met my uncle David or his sons. It's funny to think that I have cousins who speak German.'' He took Leonie's hand and led her from the shelter of the storefront to a curbside bench. The European chapter of his father's life was a mystery to him, shrouded in secrets that his father would not share.

His classmates in Natalya's improvised religious-school class shared his ignorance of life in Europe. The Jews who had made their way westward clung to their Judaism, but they had little nostalgia for the world they had left behind. Their children were Americans, born on a sun-flooded frontier. They had no need for tales of narrow ghetto streets, the chronicling of ancient fears and bitter personal histories. A new life was being forged in Arizona and Colorado, in New Mexico and California. They would not dim its brightness with the shadows of a distant world.

"I didn't know you had cousins in Germany,'' Leonie said. "Just think, Jesse, if there is a war and you become a soldier, you may have to fight your own cousin.''

It was the sort of dramatic situation that intrigued them both. They had, during the spring vacation just past, written out a novel in a copybook—a western *Romeo and Juliet* in which the daughter of an Indian chieftain and the son of an Arizona ranger fell in love. "A Love Forbidden,'' by Leonie Lewin and Jesse Stern, they had entitled it, and they had concealed it in the cave where they often met. Brasada and cholla cactus concealed the mouth of the cave, which they had furnished with woven Hopi mats, worn blankets, and clay candle holders.

"I won't go to war,'' Jesse said gravely. "My father thinks that even the war in Europe will be quickly over. And Wilson will keep our country out of any war. Our generation wants peace, Leonie. We want to build a better world. You remember what Wilson said in his inaugural address.'' He recited the words by heart, his eyes closed, his hand touching hers.

Sadness and an inexplicable fear gripped her. If only they were older, she thought—old enough to hold each other close as they lay side by side in their secret cave, their faces lit by the struggling flames of the small candles—old enough to walk out together in the evenings, to confront their families and confound the old world enmity that separated them.

Jesse's voice swept on. " 'The feelings with which we face this new age of right and opportunity sweep across our heart-strings like some air out of God's own presence where justice and mercy are reconciled and the judge and the brother are one,' " he finished.

Leonie clapped softly. He would be a great man one day, she knew. He dreamed of being a writer, but he might be a senator, a governor. Their dreams surpassed those of their fathers—the merchant and the banker had been obsessed with security and survival. She and Jesse were Americans, Wilson's inheritors, who would devote their lives to the reconciliation of justice and mercy.

Leonie started as the bells of the Trinity Episcopal Cathedral tolled the hour. "It's five o'clock," she gasped. "I must go, Jesse. I promised Gregory that I'd be home early. He's sick again."

He kissed her, as always, on the forehead—a brush of lips that caused her heart to beat with frightening staccato rapidity. What was a real kiss like? she wondered, and closed her eyes, imagining his lips pressed hard against her own.

Jesse Stern watched as she ran down the street. Once, he had seen a gazelle dash across the desert. Leonie ran with that graceful swiftness, her head lifted to the persimmon-colored sun, briefly veiled now by a smoky gossamer cloud.

Gregory's illness lingered through the long, uncertain summer. Bouts of fever and spasms of weakness kept him confined to his bed. A slowly rotating fan and the excelsior windowbox air conditioner fought the thick summer heat. Dutifully, he drank the freshly squeezed orange juice that Emma brought him and swallowed the medicines that Dr. Lashner prescribed. Emma sat beside him and read the newspapers with sinking heart. Isaac had been too optimistic. The war in Europe escalated at a dangerous pace. As in a child's game of dominoes, one by one the great nations of Europe followed each other into war.

Joshua and Samuel, fascinated by international events, spent hours in Gregory's room, trying to amuse him with an improvised board game that played out the nascent war as they perceived it.

"Look, Gregory, it's like chess. The pawn is France, and England is the defending knight," Joshua said. As a child Joshua had played for hours with lead soldiers. When he traveled with Isaac on occasional journeys to branch stores in distant parts of the state, he insisted on visiting the sites of the great battles with the Apaches. A red rock from the Apache Pass stood on his bookshelf, and it intrigued him to think that Cochise himself might have trodden on it. But the Indian wars were long over, and now he turned his attention to the battlefields of Europe.

The war game, the elaborately crayoned board, did not interest Gregory, but he did not want to disappoint his brothers. He smiled wanly.

"Who will win?" he asked.

"The British," Joshua said. "They have the best navy. If I were old enough, I would join the British navy."

"Don't let Brother Timothy hear you say that," Samuel said.

The war had created odd rifts among Arizonans with close ties in Europe. The Lewin boys had listened to Brother Timothy argue angrily against supporting the British. How could the priest support a nation that denied his Irish brethren their rights? They had listened to murmured conversations after Friday evening services, and they knew that Abner Wallach and other Jews who had emigrated from eastern Europe were against the Russians. The memory of the czar's pogroms had trailed them to the American desert. Isaac thought them wrong.

"We are Americans now. We must stand with our country," he chastised both Brother Timothy and Abner.

Emma agreed with him, but Isabel Cavalajo protested with the familiar febrile passion that dominated all her arguments. There were no sides. All wars were inherently wrong. The very concept was barbaric, inhumane. She joined an organization of conscientious objectors and wrote earnest letters to Woodrow Wilson, urging him to condemn all warring nations.

Leonie, entering the room with a tray of lemonade, glared

at her brothers and purposely scattered their wooden playing pieces as she walked to the table.

"Stop talking so stupidly," she said. "War's not a game. People get killed in wars."

"Your brothers are just playing, Leonie," Emma said warningly. She did not want Gregory to be upset by a quarrel among his brothers and sister.

Leonie stormed out of the room. The war in Europe obsessed her because it obsessed Jesse Stern. His cousin in Germany had been conscripted, and his mother had, despite the ominous news, sailed for England. Henry Stern had remained optimistic that the war would soon be over and that, in any case, it would be fought on the Continent and not in England and that his wife, Abigail, would be safe.

"My father lives in a fantasy world," Jesse complained. "I think he truly believes that he is enchanted—that his power and her own goodness can keep my mother from harm."

"Your mother is very kind," Leonie said, remembering her last encounter with Abigail Stern.

She and her mother had met Abigail Stern and Jesse's sister, Barbara, on a narrow street. Emma had hesitated and moved to step aside, but Abigail Stern, a frail woman with a heart-shaped face, had smiled and extended her hand.

"I was sorry to hear that your son is ill, Mrs. Lewin. I hope he is feeling better."

"Dr. Lashner is optimistic," Emma said. "You are going to Europe, I heard. I wish you safe journey. It is very brave of you."

"I don't think of it as brave. Perhaps it is only self-indulgent. I want to see my family and to walk down the streets that were familiar to me in childhood."

"I understand," Emma said.

Like Abigail Stern, she was haunted by memories of the life she had left behind in Europe. She thought of her cousin Greta in England and of how pleasant it would be to walk with her through the meadowlands of Shropshire, far from the searing heat of Arizona. She wanted to drink tea from a cup her mother had held, to sleep beneath a light comforter crocheted by her grandmother. Imprisoned now, in a new and frightening isolation, she felt an overwhelming nostalgia for distant family and friends; she longed for a sense of connection. It had occurred to her one night, as she lay awake in the darkness, that she had striven for independence and had achieved loneliness.

She held a letter that she had planned to mail to Greta that day. Tentatively, she held it out to Abigail Stern.

"I wonder if you would be kind enough to mail this letter for me when you reach England."

"Certainly. You know, Mrs. Lewin, I have always been saddened that we could not reach out to each other in friendship, but my husband had a difficult life. His anger dies hard."

"We can yet try," Emma said. She felt a sudden surge of hope. All things could change. Enemies could become friends; silences and separations could be bridged.

Emma Lewin and Abigail Stern looked warmly at each other, but their daughters averted their eyes, as though embarrassed by secrets that they knew would remain unrevealed to them. Leonie had wondered then if Barbara knew of her special friendship with Jesse.

Thoughts of her next meeting with Jesse teased her now, and she selected a book of poems that they would read together in their cave, as her brothers continued their game in Gregory's room. They would read Thomas Hardy, she decided and softly she read aloud: "We never loved as others loved . . ."

Each week the war games Joshua and Samuel devised became more complex. They added new counters to their board. Russia and England were joined by Turkey and Montenegro. They planned strategies for the Dardanelles and the Masurian Lakes. They played with even greater zest when Gregory's fever broke. Dr. Lashner still visited daily, but the boy's improvement was remarkable. His appetite returned and he gained weight.

"Perhaps we've turned the corner," he told Emma. "Perhaps with maturity his system has acquired new strength. But be careful, go slowly."

"Of course."

She would be careful, she would go slowly; it was her nature. She was, after all, a skilled businesswoman.

Still, she allowed Gregory to join his brothers in the loggia, where he helped them darken the large expanses of blue on their game board.

"The oceans," Joshua explained officiously. "This will be a war of the sea, and Britain will win it because Britain has the best navy."

Isaac watched his sons play their war games and said nothing. The table in the adobe house on the Tempe road was littered with peace petitions to President Wilson, appeals to Arizona congressmen and senators urging them to keep the United States out of the war. Isabel had a new cause, a new passion. He arrived carrying a bottle of wine, but it remained unopened as she read the text for a new pamphlet aloud to him. "We as Americans must be dedicated to the pursuit of peace. We conscientiously object to the waging of war." As she read, he combed her cap of dark hair with his fingers, kissed the curve of her arm, the slope of her neck. Her voice trembled, and he silenced her with kisses. She was his darling schoolgirl, blazing with enthusiasm, seeking approval, endorsement. Yet there were times when her energy wearied him, when the passionate naiveté of her stance irritated him. More than once, halfway to her house, he turned and drove back to Phoenix.

Joshua cut out small boats, and the German warships *Breslau* and *Goeben* daringly escaped through the Dardanelles.

Emma moved the globe from Isaac's wood-paneled den into the living room. She twirled it gently each evening. There was a lingering sadness in her eyes now. The war had stirred up feelings and memories long dormant. Holland had remained neutral, but its neighbors were besieged. The cities and spas where Emma had vacationed with her parents had become battlefields. The dewy meadowlands of her childhood were moistened with blood. Greta wrote her of young cousins who had already died, of others who were being conscripted.

Emma mourned the waste of young lives, the frivolous spending of years of youth and love. She dreamed one night, for the first time in many years, of the Prinsengracht mansion. She stood on the balcony and watched her father and Benjamin Mendoza leave the house together. They walked in opposite directions and were lost in the swirling fog. She awakened and realized, with incandescent clarity, that she herself was wasting her life, her love. She had transferred her father's betrayal, Benjamin Mendoza's abandonment, into a harsh and punishing mandate. Isaac had not betrayed her; he had not abandoned her.

Isaac returned home one autumn evening and told her that the Germans had taken Antwerp. Tears filled her eyes, and she turned away.

"It just happened," he said.

He did not tell her that he had learned of it as he stood in Isabel's studio and watched her pack. She had taken a leave of absence to work with a new pacifist committee in formation in Washington. She had completed the Christmas catalogues for each region before telling Isaac of her plans. There was a Lewin's Emporium in every major western city and town, and the Lewin Look, a blend of high fashion and frontier flair, had swept the country. Johnny Redbird's department, the "Arizona Experience," had proved so successful that Isaac had introduced the "Utah Experience" to the Salt Lake City store, and the newly opened Butte Emporium featured a boutique called "Montana Adventure."

"I have all the proofs done," Isabel had assured him. "It won't be for long."

He had assured her that it was all right, and driving back to Phoenix he had acknowledged to himself an odd sense of relief at her absence. Her enthusiasm wearied him; he was exhausted by her intensity.

He watched Emma now as Gregory read to her from his copybook. The story of the lost boy who wandered the world in search of the secret of happiness had evolved into a novella. Gregory's young hero had crossed the American continent and was heading for the Fiji Islands. "He'll find it," Gregory told his family solemnly, "because he's strong, and if you're strong you can do anything."

"You'd better get strong, then, Grego, so you'll be able to do anything," Joshua said, and he tousled his brother's fiery curls.

"I *am* getting strong," Gregory replied.

"Of course you are." Leonie looked up from her book.

Emma glanced at Leonie's volume of verse. *The Poems of Vachel Lindsay.* It occurred to her that she had been only two years older than Leonie when she had stood beside Benjamin Mendoza on a narrow bridge and listened to him recite Walt Whitman. She had not thought of Benjamin Mendoza for years, and now, twice in one evening, her thoughts turned to him. The distant war unsettled her, evoked buried memories and mingled them with vague and mysterious yearnings.

Isaac set up the chess board, and he and Samuel played in a circlet of lamplight. She noticed that a swathe of silver had carved its way through his thick dark hair. He smiled tenderly as the child triumphantly claimed his rook. Loneliness overcame her. She wanted to lay claim to his tenderness, to the touch of his hand, to the warmth of his body. She had only herself to blame. She had sacrificed love for vigilance, trust for certainty.

They ascended the staircase together that night. He kissed her lightly on the cheek as they stood in the corridor that separated their bedrooms.

"Good night." Her voice was strained.

"Good night." A tendril of hair teased her eyes, and absently, he brushed it away.

He awakened hours later to find his room veiled in silver light. He heard footsteps on the corridor. He opened the door. Emma, wearing a white nightgown, stood at the hall window staring out at the full moon, crested now by a diadem of glittering stars. She was caught in a web woven of the pale, delicate rays that streamed in through the open window. As he watched she lifted her hands, stretched out her arms. She shivered, although the air was dry and warm; luminous tears jeweled her cheeks.

"Emma."

"I'm all right."

"Yes. Of course you are."

Gently, he took her by the hand and led her back to her room. Unprotesting, she followed him, but when he lowered her into her bed, his arms gentle about her body, she lifted her face to his. He kissed her then. The scent of jasmine clung to her skin. Her hands moved across his face, traced the curve of his mustache, the arch of his cheekbone.

"Gregory has your eyes," she said. "It's wonderful that he has your eyes."

Moonlight silvered her hair. He lifted its silken folds, allowing it to fall in lengths between his fingers; he draped her breasts with its moon-splattered coppery thickness.

"He is getting better," she said. "Our Gregory."

Their son's new vigor had banished her fears; the threat of war and death had sharpened her yearning for life and for love. They had wasted sweet years, but it was not too late. The lucent moon, the distant war, had rescued them, had restored them to each other. Joy surged through her. She drew him close, enfolding him in her happiness.

"He will be fine. Wonderful." His words were at once an assertion and a benison.

His hands moved knowingly across her body as desire and gratitude overcame him. He had forgotten the satin smoothness of her skin, the wondrous rise and fall of her body as he lay poised above her. Like a daring swimmer, he plunged at last into the welcoming chasm of her sweet moistness.

Leonie, who tapped on the door in the morning, and opened it when there was no response, was startled to find her parents deeply asleep, entwined in each other's arms. A sheath of Emma's hair flashed, like a bright flame, across Isaac's shoulder.

Emma moved through the weeks that followed swathed in a haze of contentment. Autumnal breezes dispelled the fierce heat, and she opened all the windows of the house, flooding the whitewashed rooms with the bright, dry air and the scents of citrus and oleander. She baked snowy meringues and sweet fruit tarts; the kitchen was fragrant with the aroma of steaming chicken and savory beef stews. She and Leonie rode into the desert and filled their saddlebags with slender wands of ocotillo branches. Again, she planted tulip bulbs in her garden, blanketing them with specially mulched earth. This time they would root, she was sure. She visualized a flower arrangement with white tulip blossoms nestled against purple stalks of ironweed.

Isaac spent each evening at home. As though soothed by the new peace between their parents, Joshua and Samuel abandoned their war games, and the huge oaktag board was thrust into a cupboard. They listened to the gramophone and did not object when Emma asked them to play a recording of Victor Herbert's new operetta, *Sweethearts*, in place of a more popular piece. The family listened as Isaac read aloud President Wilson's calm, considered words. He assured them that the United States would continue to pursue a policy of "watchful waiting." He was confident that the warring nations of Europe would soon see their folly and pursue the paths of peace.

"But no matter what course the war in Europe takes, American boys will not do battle on foreign soil. I am pledged to keeping this country out of war," the president stated in his dry academic style.

Jesse Stern was less optimistic. His mother had prolonged her stay in Europe because she was involved in relief work with evacuees from Belgium. She would sail for the United States in early spring. She wrote of the urgent need for clothing and linens.

"My school wants to send clothing to the refugees from Belgium," Leonie told her father.

Isaac smiled at his daughter, proud of her compassion, her concern. He directed his inventory clerk at the Emporium that surplus stock be made available to Leonie for shipment to England.

She and Jesse packed the crates at night, working with Johnny Redbird in the dimly lit shipping room. They learned all the words to "Keep the Home Fires Burning" and sang softly as they folded garments and blankets, towels, and swaddling clothes. The Indian watched them thoughtfully. He had known Leonie from birth and felt as protective toward her as toward the daughters of his tribe.

"You must be careful, Leonie," Johnny said to her one night. "Your father would be very angry if he knew that you spent so many hours with the son of Henry Stern."

"We're just friends, Johnny. Besides, it's my own affair."

Her voice took on Emma Lewin's proud and haughty tone, assumed when she felt a liberty had been taken, a friendship overreached. Johnny looked at her sadly and touched the necklace of blue beads that he wore for luck.

Leonie and Jesse grew more daring. They spent long afternoons in their cave. He walked her almost the entire way home each evening and kissed her gently on the lips as they stood beneath the citron tree that had become their parting place. On a moonless night, he unplaited her braid and buried his hands in her raven hair, pulling her closer to him.

"If only we weren't so young," he whispered.

Their youth weighted and restrained them. They felt themselves to be winged, but knew they could not yet fly. They were too young. He was a boy still, who missed his gentle mother. He read her letters aloud ("Dear Jesse, it grieves me to see English boys of seventeen, only a year older than you, in uniform . . ."). His German cousins had been conscripted; they might fight those English boys. ("They have no choice," his father said sadly. "They must fight for Germany. They love their country as we love ours.") The absurdity of the war haunted and angered him, but he could speak of it only to Leonie.

And Leonie, his beautiful dark-haired friend, was a girl who ran to greet her father each evening, who played tag still with her younger brothers, although she sat quietly beside him in the dimness of the cave, her breasts heaving as they read poetry aloud. But they were not children when they stood together beneath the citron tree, reluctant to part. They stood at a dividing line, which one day soon they would cross, hands linked, eyes locked.

Isabel Cavalajo's stay in Washington was extended. She mailed her sketches for the Christmas windows. The chain of Lewin's Emporiums would not be lavishly decorated because of the war in Europe, but Isabel envisaged saguaro cacti hung with Christmas ornaments, a Santa on a pack mule, his saddle baskets bulging. Her drawings were clever but rough. "Please understand how busy I am," she wrote Isaac. "I attend one meeting after another. We are determined to let Wilson know that there is an important pacifist movement in this country.''

Isaac imagined her posture as she wrote; the pen would be tightly clutched and her face flushed with the fervor of her conviction. He thought of writing to her, of explaining his reconciliation with Emma, the new course his life had taken. But brave and vibrant Isabel deserved more than that. She had given herself to him openly and without conditions. He would not withdraw from her without explanation. He wanted her to know that he would always be her friend, her benefactor. He owed her the same directness and honesty that she had bestowed on him. He wrote her warm, affectionate letters and sent her a generous check in support of the pacifist cause.

Gregory's recovery continued with astonishing rapidity. Emma's spirits soared. The San Francisco doctor had hinted that he might outgrow the ailment, that the body would compensate for its own weakness. Her brave and valiant child had prevailed.

He was enrolled in school. Natalya's tutoring had kept him on grade level, and he went off proudly each morning, his satchel strapped to his back, his lunch pail dangling.

"Don't play too hard at recess," Emma cautioned him.

"I won't."

He was a good child, careful and obedient. For the first several days he wrote in his copybook as his classmates dashed about the baseball diamond they had improvised in the schoolyard. A palm tree served as home plate, an olive tree and two cactus plants marked the bases. Gregory sat in the shade of the palm and wrote of his lost boy, who was now in Tokyo but had not yet discovered the secret of happiness. He looked up one afternoon and saw that a ball tossed from the outfield soared toward him. Agilely, he reached up and caught it. He was in the game.

He played every day after that. He was light and fast. His skill exhilarated him. He had been so long an invalided outsider that he exulted in his sudden prowess, his newfound strength.

He stayed after school one day and played yet another game, running all the way home because he knew his mother would be worried. He was in a sweat when he reached the house and gulped down one glass of ice water and then another. He ate very little for dinner that night, and the next day he came home directly from school. He was tired, he said irritably. Everyone got tired. Emma placed her hand on his brow. It was cool. Still, she kept him home the next day and watched him warily. He slept a great deal and perspired freely, but there was no sign of fever. Dr. Lashner saw no cause for concern.

"Let's hold off worrying until we see a temperature," he said in his reassuring, laconic tone.

She repeated the doctor's assurances to Isaac when he phoned that afternoon.

"I guess I'm just overcautious," she said.

"Then it will be all right if I come home late. In fact, it may be very late. Please don't wait up for me."

"I understand. He'll be fine. We'll all be fine."

She willed herself not to ask what would keep him away so late. She would not destabilize the new balance of their relationship by weighting it with questions, suspicions. She had promised herself, on that moonlit night when Isaac lay beside her, that she would replace vigilance with trust. Her new happiness bred confidence, certainty. All was well; all would be well.

Of course Isaac had to work late now and again. The volume of sales at the Lewin's Emporiums had increased with stunning rapidity. An expanded American sphere of influence meant expanded markets. In addition to the branch stores in major cities, mail orders poured in from Hawaii and Alaska, Puerto Rico and the Philippines. The Lewin Look spanned the continent. Regional catalogues were published, and Emma admired Isabel Cavalajo's skillful drawings, the sharp pen-and-ink sketches that evoked an ambience of frontier freshness. The sign that had dangled from the crossbeam of the tent store was emblazoned on the parcels that were shipped from Phoenix to every city in the nation. And with the war in Europe, business was better than ever. The mines and factories were working at full capacity to supply the allied forces. The increased workforce had money to spend, and Lewin's Emporium, which had departments geared to every budget, was the place to spend it.

"Emma, I want to tell you something," Isaac said, but she had rung off.

He replaced the receiver and took it up again. He was moved by a sudden, inexplicable impulse to tell Emma about Isabel Cavalajo and the feelings of abandonment and loneliness that had led him to her. He smiled bitterly. He was excusing himself too easily, and besides, that was not a discussion one had on the telephone.

More than once during the past weeks, he had thought of telling Emma about Isabel, but each time he had feared to jeopardize the new peace and closeness between them. He would wait, he told himself, until their relationship was cemented, until their togetherness was impermeable. And then, at the right moment, he would explain how alone he had felt in Washington and how he had been drawn to the fey young woman.

Emma would know that there had been no commitment. She had spoken of her own feelings of aloneness through the years—surely she would understand his sense of abandonment and his search for solace.

But they needed time, and so he said nothing and allowed the web of sharing and security to thicken and grow more intricate with each passing day. Soon, he would tell Emma everything. Tomorrow, perhaps. Or the next day. Soon.

And then, without warning, as she did all things without warning, unbound by convention, independent and whimsical, Isabel returned. She had phoned him that afternoon, her voice breathless with excitement. She had so much to tell him—so much to share with him. Could he arrange to spend the evening at the adobe house? She would make chili and enchiladas, and there was a bottle of sparkling sangria in her cooler. Of course he would come. There was a great deal he wanted to discuss with her. He injected a monitory note in his voice, but she ignored it.

"When will you come?" She spoke in the teasing tone of an insistent, playful child. "Early, please. I want to watch the sunset with you." She loved the hour before darkness when a rainbow of colors bled across the desert sky as the sun did battle with the encroaching night. It occurred to him that all conflicts excited her. The thought was unfair, he knew.

"I'll try to come early," he promised.

Still, he waited until nightfall before he set out for the adobe house. He and Isabel had shared too many sunsets. He wanted to say goodbye to her in the finality of darkness.

The Lewin house was unnaturally quiet that night. Gregory slept through dinner.

"Boys are like that," Natalya Wallach, who had stopped by to leave a freshly baked apple cake, counseled Emma. "They exhaust themselves and then recuperate with sleep. Like bears." She smiled at her twin sons, who wrestled playfully with Joshua and Samuel.

"I suppose you're right," Emma said. She did not remind Natalya that the twins had always been strong and healthy, unlike Gregory.

"Mama." Gregory's voice, thick with fever, drifted down the stairway, and she hurried to him.

He tossed fitfully amid the mangled bedclothes, his face flushed and his pajamas sweat-soaked. She touched his forehead; his flesh burned beneath her fingers.

"It's so hot," he moaned. He moved restlessly, as though to escape the invasive heat, his eyes glassed over by the fever. "It's snowing but still it's hot."

She realized then that he had crossed a dangerous border and spoke to her from the depths of a febrile delirium.

"The doctor!" she shouted. "Get Dr. Lashner."

The front door slammed, and she heard the Wallachs' Ford speed down the street.

She filled the bathtub with tepid water and lowered Gregory into it. He laughed and cried; his voice rattled on, rising to a shrill.

"Come see the snow," he shouted. "The forests are covered with snow."

He had never seen snow, she knew, but his father had spoken to him about Russia, and in his illness he summoned up the wintry landscapes of Isaac's boyhood, the snow-encrusted woodland where Isaac had lived with another wife, another child.

Joshua and Samuel filled basins with alcohol. Leonie dissolved aspirin with sweetened lemon water. They wrapped Gregory in damp sheets and carried him back to bed. They bathed his burning skin with cloths soaked in alcohol and spooned the lemon mixture between his parched lips. He shivered suddenly, violently, and they piled blankets on him.

"Where does the snow go when it melts?" he shouted, his voice so strong and clear that it startled them. "Ah, I see where it goes," he answered himself softly, dreamily. "I'm following it. I'm walking the trail of the melting snow."

He closed his eyes. The shivering stopped and his lips moved soundlessly for a moment.

Leonie turned to the window and stood very still. *If I do not move, he will be all right,* she thought. She had played such magical games since childhood. *If I keep my eyes closed very tightly, when I open them, Daddy will be home. . . . If I run to this corner without turning my head, I will meet Jesse.* "Get well, Gregory," she commanded with silent ferocity. "Get well."

Dr. Lashner rushed into the room. Natalya had found him at home preparing for bed. He had been on the mesa since early morning, delivering a baby to a Hopi woman. The labor had been difficult, and he had remained with her throughout the day, listening to the incantations of the tribe's holy men. The red-skinned infant had been delivered at last, and he had moved swiftly to sever the glistening cord that was entangled about its throat, threatening it with strangulation. He stood at Gregory Lewin's bedside and looked down at the boy. He had saved one life that day. He counted it as an omen. He was a man of science who knew the power of chance. He slipped a thermometer under Gregory's arm, waited, then frowned and sighed as he read it.

"The fever is high—very high," he said. Emma Lewin was a perceptive woman. He would not deceive her.

"What can we do?" She was dry-eyed, in control. The daughter, Leonie, stood at the window. She had not stirred since he entered.

"I'm going to try quinine," he said. "We don't give it to children, but it's the strongest fever depressant we have."

Emma knew then that Gregory was dangerously ill. The

physician was conservative, yet he was resorting at once to a desperate, experimental measure. Quinine was used for yellow fever.

The doctor spooned the medicine into Gregory's mouth. The child grimaced and spat it out. Grimly, the doctor forced his lips open and thrust a second spoonful in. This time Gregory lay still, unresisting. Emma blanched and took her son's hand in her own.

"Gregory," she whispered. "Grego."

Natalya moved across the room and put her arm about Leonie.

"Come. Let's go downstairs," she said, but the girl remained rigid, and Natalya, the teacher, who understood the magical thinking of the young, did not argue.

"Where is Isaac?" Dr. Lashner asked Emma.

"He's working late at the Emporium. I haven't called him. I didn't want to frighten him."

"That was wise of you. There's no reason to call him yet. Let us wait and see what effect the medication has."

Abner Wallach dimmed the lamps in the bedroom and moved the chairs closer to the bed. Emma and Dr. Lashner took up their vigil while Leonie remained motionless at the window. Natalya took the other children down to the living room where Johnny Redbird sat rhythmically fingering his blue beads. Johnny had seen the Lewin house ablaze with lights and had learned of Gregory's illness.

Softly, he murmured a Hopi prayer, repeating it again and again, now in the language of his tribe, now in the language of the white men who had come to live among them in the desert.

"What is life? It is the flash of a firefly in the night. It is the breath of a buffalo in the wintertime. It is the little shadow which runs across the grass and loses itself in the sunset."

Abner Wallach sat at the refectory table and read from his Hebrew prayerbook.

"Lord, what is man that Thou has regard for him? Or the son of man that Thou takest account of him? Man is like a breath, his days are as a fleeting shadow. In the morning he flourishes and grows up like grass; in the evening he is cut down and withers. . . ."

The ancient prayers converged in the room of sorrow and waiting. The wisdom of two disparate desert peoples melded as Jew and Indian repeated the words that had brought solace to their fathers and to their fathers' fathers before them.

In the dimly lit sick room, Emma rose and led Leonie to a chair. The girl did not resist.

"He is better," she said, but she did not look at her brother.

"Sha," Emma said softly. *"Sha."*

"Mama!" Gregory sat up in bed. His eyes were very bright, and a smile played at his lips. "I know. I know the answer."

Dr. Lashner took his wrist, felt his pulse. Gregory ignored him. The doctor was invisible to him; his touch was a ghostly graze.

"What do you know, Gregory?" Emma asked gently. Her hand was on her son's forehead. His skin glowed, blazed.

"I know the secret of happiness. I know what happens to the melted snow."

He sank back against the pillows, his eyes closed, his breathing stertorous.

"You must call Isaac," Dr. Lashner said. "At once."

"Yes."

Wearily, she went to the phone and gave the operator the private number of Isaac's office at the Emporium. She imagined him bent over ledgers and inventory sheets, his brow furrowed as he searched for an elusive sheet of paper. The phone rang again and again. Of course. He was in the outer office at a file cabinet. The receiver whirred in her ear.

"There is no answer, madame," the operator said.

"You're certain you're ringing the correct number?"

"Yes, madame." The operator was infuriatingly calm, patient, and indifferent. Emma asked her to ring the store's number. Isaac might have gone to the stockroom. He might be checking the floors. The floor phones remained connected at night. She heard the insistent ring and imagined the phone sounding through deserted corridors, where mannequins stood vigil over dust-sheeted countertops.

"He must answer," she thought, but the operator's voice, persistent and forbearing, came on the line again.

"Your party does not answer, madame."

She hung up.

"I don't understand," she murmured.

Dr. Lashner took the phone from her.

"Emma, I want to call the hospital. We can't move Gregory, but we can make him more comfortable. I need a nurse to help me."

"Yes. Of course. Anything."

She pressed her lips against Gregory's fevered cheek, but he did not stir. He was imprisoned in a sleep so deep that neither sound nor touch penetrated it.

"A coma. Early stage," Dr. Lashner said on the phone. "I tried quinine. No. I think mercury would be useless." His arsenal of remedies had been sparse, and now it was depleted. Sound traveled across airways, flying machines traversed the heavens, highways were carved into desert ridges, but still doctors did not know how to fight a fever.

Wearily, Emma went downstairs and stood before Abner Wallach and Johnny Redbird.

"Gregory's condition is very grave," she said. "Dr. Lashner said that Isaac must come. But there is no answer at the store or in his office."

The two men looked at each other. Through the haze of grief and despair she saw the glance that passed between them, the glint of sorrowful complicity.

"We'll bring him home, Emma," Abner Wallach said.

Swiftly, they left the house. She stood at the window and watched Abner's car travel south, in the direction of Tempe.

"Emma." Natalya placed her hand on her friend's shoulder, but Emma shook it off and went to sit beside Leonie on the sofa. The girl was crying now and twisting her handkerchief into tiny knots. Emma took her daughter's hands into her own, stroked the fingers, took up the handkerchief, and wiped Leonie's cheeks, but she did not implore her to still her tears.

It was Natalya who opened the door to the nurse and hospital aides and took them up to Gregory's bedroom. It was Joshua and Samuel who filled kettle after kettle with steaming water and carried them upstairs to be placed in the tent of sheets that Dr. Lashner had erected about Gregory's bed.

The air had to be kept warm and moist, he said. Tirelessly, they replaced the hot water. Basins clattered, and they spoke in anxious voices, but Gregory slept on. He was oblivious to the steamy haze that surrounded him, the doctor's anxious touch at his wrist, the thermometer inserted beneath his arm. The ruddiness that had come to his cheeks during the week of his wondrous good health had faded. Even the flush of fever was gone. His skin was alabaster-white, his lips pale as parchment. Perspiration darkened his coppery brows, matted his thick auburn curls.

Emma sat beside him in the tent of counterpane. She held his hand and studied the wreath of freckles at his wrist. When he was an infant she had kissed each freckle, causing him to laugh and kick his spindly infant legs in the air. She kissed the pigmentations now, one by one, and then, with a cool cloth, she wiped the sweat from his brow and pressed a moistened gauze pad to his parched lips.

She sang softly to him, thinking of how he had so often awakened from sleep and sung softly into the night. She sang the songs he loved the best. The Indian love song Johnny Redbird had taught them. A Dutch lullaby. A Hebrew ditty. The wistful lament of the frontiersmen moving west. ''Green grow the lilacs when winter is through—green grow the lilacs all covered with dew. . . .'' Her voice broke and tears dimmed her eyes.

''Mama.'' His voice was dreamy, remote, as though he spoke to her from a great distance.

''I'm here, Grego.'' She bent close to him. His eyes were closed, and he did not stir.

''Where's Papa? I want to tell him the ending. I see the ending. I know the secret.''

''He'll be here, Grego. He'll be here soon.''

''Snow doesn't melt, you know. I have to tell Papa what happens to it. Where is he? He said he'd be here. Don't you remember he said that?''

''I remember. He's coming.'' *I am here, Gregory. I'll always be here.* Isaac had said that more than once to calm the restless child. Where was he, then? Where was he?

''Tell me the secret, Gregory. Tell it to me.''

Emma bent closer to him; her grasp on his wrist grew

tighter. He had to talk to her. Each word that he uttered was a step backward from the soundless threatening darkness. She would not relinquish him to silence. She would not surrender her son who sang softly into the night.

"Tell me the secret!" Her voice was high and piercing, but Gregory had slipped back into that deep and terrible sleep.

Dr. Lashner thrust the canopy of sheets aside and knelt beside the boy. He whipped off his tie and his belt and tore a length of linen into narrow strips. Deftly, he bound them tightly about Gregory's legs and his right arm.

"Rotating tourniquets," he told the nurse tersely. Pressure applied to the extremities contained the rush of blood to the weakened heart. A desperate measure but their only hope. They worked feverishly, tying the makeshift tourniquets into place and moving them from limb to limb, racing against the boy's own body. Welts appeared on Gregory's pale skin, but he remained limp, immobile, imprisoned in a distant, morphetic country.

The doctor lifted the boy and pressed his face against Gregory's. With rhythmic precision, he breathed into the child's mouth, his own breath coming in stertorous gasps. Still, there was no response. Gently, at last, he lowered him back onto the bed. The nurse moved forward and held a mirror to Gregory's mouth. No hint of breath misted its surface. She turned to Emma.

"I'm so sorry," she said.

"No!" Emma's shout echoed through the house.

She bent over her son and beat her fists against his chest, forced open his lips, and tried to fill his lungs with her own life's breath. He could not die! She would not allow him to die.

"Gregory! Gregory!" His name was at once incantation and prayer, an imperial summons that he could not refuse.

"Emma. My God, Emma. Stop." Strong arms encircled her, powerful fingers grappled with her own and loosened her hold on her child's body. A voice husky with sorrow whispered in her ear.

"I'm sorry, my darling. I'm so very sorry."

It was Isaac who stood beside her at last, his face frozen in a mask of grief.

"Where were you?" she asked in a broken voice. "He asked for you, and you were not here. Where were you?"

He did not answer. Instead, he led her away. Silently, they walked past Joshua and Samuel, who stood in the doorway, their hands linked as they wept for the brother they would never touch again, past Leonie cradled in Natalya's outstretched arms, and past Johnny Redbird, who looked away from them because he understood the painful solitude of sorrow and loss, just as he understood the kinship of desert and sky.

Leonie

MUFFLED VOICES behind closed doors. Natalya's gentle, imploring tone. ("Try to understand him, Emma. Try.") Her mother's stifled sob. Her father's grief-broken plea drifting through the open window to the loggia below where she huddled with Joshua and Samuel.

"I want to explain, Emma. I want to tell you why I was not there."

"There is no need to explain. I know where you were." A deadened retort, laced with despair. Emma Lewin had journeyed beyond anger, beyond grief.

The bedroom door closed softly, and the children crept upstairs. Their father stood in the hallway, his shoulders heaving, his mouth open as though he retched with a sorrow that he could not disgorge.

Mirrors shrouded with sheets; the kitchen wreathed in steam, swathed in whispers as the Jewish women of Phoenix boiled eggs, baked circular rolls. The customs of loss were not abandoned on this new frontier.

The horse-drawn hearse carrying the small pine coffin. Emma and Isaac standing side by side but never touching. The Wallach children clutching each other's hands at the grave site as though to shield each other from danger. One small boy in blue serge knickers crying silently, his face buried in a red calico handkerchief. Black-haired Isabel Cavalajo, standing beside Johnny Redbird, at a distance from the family. Jesse Stern at the fringe of the crowd, raising three fingers when he met Leonie's eyes—their secret sign of friendship, his message of comfort.

Her father's intonation of the Kaddish, the words struggling free over his strangled sobs. The crunch of the dry, rose-colored soil on her palm as she dropped a clump of earth

279

onto the coffin, leaning so close that Joshua and Samuel pulled fearfully at her dark skirt. Shovels scraping across the parched earth. The bleached pine of the coffin slowly obscured by the blanket of gravelly earth. Her mother dropping a single orange blossom into the grave, its fragrance mingling with the sour scent of grief and loss.

"God full of mercy . . ." The men intoned the prayer in unison, their heads erect; the women prayed with their heads bent low. Submission and strength. The sky was unnaturally dark. An unseasonable monsoon threatened. A wind stirred the leaves of a crouching Joshua tree where a Sonora dove perched so tentatively, so elegantly. Gregory, always fearful of storms, would be frightened, she thought, and then she remembered that Gregory was dead and safe from fear. She lifted her eyes and saw the bird fly off, its wings scissoring the ash-colored air. This was the collage of scene and sound that Leonie Lewin would remember always when she thought of Gregory's death.

Almost with relief they observed the traditional seven days of mourning. The Lewin's Emporiums throughout the provinces were closed. Sorrow absorbed them. They sat on low stools in stockinged feet, Emma on one side of the room, Isaac on the other. Joshua, Samuel, and Leonie sat between them, instinctively shielding them from anger and from intimacy. But every night of that week Leonie heard her father knock softly on her mother's door.

"Please, Emma. Please."

She heard, too, the shuffle of defeat as he returned to his own room.

She buried her head in her pillow then, her sorrow compounded. The brief and gentle peace between her parents had been irrevocably shattered, and she blamed them bitterly for allowing their anger to interfere with her grief.

Jesse came to pay his respects to the mourners, hesitant at entering the house that had for so long been closed to him and his family. Emma was in her room resting when he came, and Isaac was absorbed in conversation with Brother Timothy and Abner Wallach.

"I'm sorry, Leonie," Jesse said. He glanced around the room as though to memorize its furnishings—the sand-colored chairs, the polished floors, the rugs of intricate Indian design.

"I wrote my mother about Gregory," he said. As always, his voice softened when he spoke of Abigail Stern. She would sail from England in the spring when her project of organizing an orphanage for Belgian refugee children was completed. He and his mother had an unusual closeness. Always, he had shared his ideas and feelings with her. He thought of her as he sat beside Leonie. Beautiful Leonie, wrenched by her loss, her shoulders bent. Her fingers toyed with the edge of her cardigan, ripped by the rabbi at the graveside to indicate that she was a mourner. A piece of her life had been severed as surely as the fabric of her garment. Jesse and Leonie did not speak. As always, they had little need for words but took comfort from each other's proximity. Jesse left before Emma came downstairs, before Isaac returned to his mourning stool.

"Was anyone here?" Emma asked.

"Just a friend from school," Joshua said, staring hard at his sister.

"My friend," Samuel added.

They had entered into a conspiracy then, Leonie and her brothers, against the parents who bewildered and betrayed them.

On the day after they arose from mourning, Isaac Lewin, still unshaven, as though unwilling to abandon his grief, went to a cattle auction at a ranch near Tucson. He bought each of his sons a russet-colored foal, and for Leonie he bought a silver-maned black mare. He was offering them a kind of freedom, they knew. They did not look at Emma when they thanked him. Johnny Redbird selected a hand-tooled saddle for Leonie's mount and threaded the reins with silver bells. Star, Leonie named the mare, because a five-pointed patch of silver fur sparkled between the animal's huge dark eyes.

Each afternoon, during the months that followed, as soon as her classes at Phoenix Union High School were over, Leonie rushed home, changed into jodhpurs and a loose chamois shirt, mounted Star, and rode into the desert. Almost always she rode toward the cave, and almost always Jesse waited for her. They sat beneath a slender aspen and grimly read the newspapers and journals that filled his saddlebags.

The war obsessed them. They thought of the young men, only a few years older than they were, in the trenches that stretched from the Swiss border to the English Channel. Jesse's German cousins and her British and Russian kinsmen had become adversaries, hidden behind barricades of mud in the desperate struggle for control of the western front. The absurdity of the war haunted them. It had its origin in a quagmire of international alliances, and because of the intransigence of ministers, the arrogance of generals, young men were dying. Jesse wrote a series of poems advocating pacifism. He read them aloud to Leonie and sent them to the journal published by Isabel Cavalajo's Arizona League of Conscientious Objectors. He sent copies to his mother in England. Her sailing date was firm now. She would leave in early May.

Jesse counted the days until her arrival, he told Leonie without embarrassment, crossing them off on his school calendar. His father was too absorbed with the intricacies of his business to spend time with his children. It was Abigail Stern who understood his horror at violence, his abhorrence of war.

"What would you do if the United States went to war and you were drafted, Jesse?" Leonie asked one afternoon.

"I can't imagine wearing a uniform—fighting. It's immoral, Leonie." His voice was grave, his eyes troubled. "Wilson is right. We must stay out of it."

"My father isn't so sure," Leonie said.

Isaac was increasingly concerned about the impact of a long war in Europe. American business was suffering. His own shipments from Europe were consistently delayed. And American neutrality had been threatened by both Britain's blockade of neutral countries and by the more devastating effect of Germany's submarine warfare.

"Well, that's one thing on which our fathers can agree," Jesse said bitterly. More than once he had asked Henry Stern about his animosity toward the Lewin family and he had encountered a blockade of silence. "But I don't think anything can condone the use of force, the taking of life." His

voice rang with youthful certainty, and he ran his fingers
nervously through his bright hair. She turned away because,
for the briefest of moments, he looked so like Gregory that
she thought her heart would break.

The Lewin family did not speak of Gregory. A new atmosphere prevailed in the white-columned house on Mac-
Dowell Road. All spontaneity had vanished. The family
moved through their daily life like actors on a stage, fearful
of departing from their cues, of losing control. Their voices
were restrained, their topics of conversation carefully chosen. Isaac worked long hours. The British blockade had intensified inventory problems. He entered into arrangements
with Sangers' Department Store in Dallas, with Neiman-
Marcus and Rich's in Atlanta. "Musical merchandise,"
Stanley Rich said as they juggled and supplemented each
other's supplies. Problems arose in the preparation of the
catalogues that were such an essential part of the business.
Isabel Cavalajo had resigned, as he had known she would.
Her stiff letter of resignation was on his desk when the store
reopened after the mourning period. She intended to teach
art at the university in Tempe and to work more intensely on
her pacifist journal.

"I'll bet you miss her, Dad," Joshua said. "Her drawings
were really good."

Leonie saw the look that flashed between her parents. Emma's hand trembled as she lifted her wineglass. Crimson
drops spattered on the white tablecloth.

"I'll have to ask you to excuse me," she said and rose
abruptly to hurry upstairs.

Joshua and Samuel looked at each other in confusion; their
father's face was dark with misery.

Isaac sat alone in the loggia that night, his hands clasped.
His eyes burned with the tears he could not shed. Emma
would not forgive him. She could not forgive him. She would
not even hear him out. He had broken with Isabel the night
of Gregory's death. He had broken with her despite her tears
and arguments, and then he had held her close to comfort
her.

"Sweet child," he had said. "Dear child. You will find your own life, your own love."

She was in his arms when he heard Abner's car, and he had held her close even as Johnny and Abner rushed toward him. He had realized then, with searing certainty, that his son was dead, that his own love, his own life, was betrayed.

"What is it, Papa?" Leonie stood before him now in the loggia and took his hands in her own. "Is it Gregory?"

"It's Gregory and it's more than Gregory." His voice was weary. "Life happens to us, Leonie. We do not search for sorrow, but somehow it finds us. It changes us. And too often we are too weak to fight against it."

"You're not weak, Papa." Fiercely Leonie encircled him in her arms. He was her strong, tall father. Presidents and governors sought his advice. He had come to America without a penny to his name, and within a dozen years he had built a merchandising empire. "You're strong, Papa."

"Am I? Perhaps," he said. "Perhaps." But disbelief rimmed his words, and he sat on in the darkness even after Leonie returned to the living room, where Joshua and Samuel crouched on the floor, manipulating battlefields and submarines across their cardboard sea.

Emma stood at the window and watched Leonie ride southward into the desert. Her daughter sat erect in the saddle, her long black hair plaited into a single lustrous braid, the silver bells on her reins chiming softly as she broke into a canter. Where did Leonie go? Emma wondered, not for the first time. Her classmates walked through the city, their arms linked about each other's waists, their heads bent close as they exchanged secrets and laughter. But Leonie had never had close friends. Always, she rode off alone and returned alone. It troubled Emma, who listened now to the sound of girls' voices raised in song and watched as Barbara Stern and two friends, laughing and singing, passed the house. One of the girls plucked an oleander blossom and presented it to Barbara, who placed it raffishly behind her ear.

A pretty girl, Barbara, Emma thought. She had inherited Abigail Stern's heart-shaped face and slight build. And a responsible girl, it was said. She had cared for the family during Abigail's absence in England. She had even sent a basket of citrus fruits and apple cake during the period of mourning for Gregory, although she had not come to the house. Probably Henry Stern had forbidden the visit. Emma's lips pursed.

Gregory, her sweet lost Gregory, had been his father's grandson, and yet Henry Stern, *damn him*, had not acknowledged the child's death. This final rejection blocked any path toward reconciliation. Still, she was not surprised. She had grown hardened to the duplicity and betrayal of men. Her father had lived a double life and willed both his families a legacy of anger and hatred. Benjamin Mendoza, the lover of her girlhood, had claimed her innocence and had abandoned her with facile excuses, false rationalizations. And Isaac, her husband, whom she had come to trust at last, had betrayed her when she needed him most. She had sat alone beside their son's deathbed while he held his dark-haired mistress in his arms. The pattern of deceit had been repeated. Just as Jacob Coen had hidden Analiese Deken in a house in Osdorp, so had Isaac Lewin hidden Isabel Cavalajo in an adobe house on the Tempe road.

"Try to understand," Natalya had pleaded, but her friend's words were meaningless to Emma. There came an end to understanding, an end to forgiveness. Perhaps Henry Stern had been right, after all, to establish emotional barriers that could be neither circumvented nor destroyed.

Wearily, Emma turned from the window. An unfinished letter to her brothers was on her desk. They urged her to visit California for an extended stay, perhaps even to consider the purchase of a home in San Francisco. Many Jewish families from Arizona, Colorado, and New Mexico now lived at least half the year in the far western state. The Jews of Phoenix still gathered in storefronts and rented quarters to pray, but San Francisco had a synagogue. Its climate offered an escape from the oppressive desert heat of the Southwest.

The Coen brothers had discerned their sister's sadness, but they dared not explore it. It was Gregory's death, they told each other, and the increasing frequency of Isaac's absences as he struggled to cope with the inventory shortages in the provincial stores. Their sister was lonely.

"San Francisco is lovely in the spring," Simon wrote enticingly. Still, she would decline their invitation, Emma decided. Somehow, she and Isaac would have to organize their shattered lives.

She took up her pen and dipped it in the inkwell, but abruptly she set it down again. A newsboy passed her window shouting a headline. Since the Germans had launched Zeppelin and airplane attacks on the British coast, she had been addicted to the news. Her young cousins lived in a Cornish village and she worried about their safety. Swiftly, she dashed downstairs, flung open the door, and gave the boy two pennies. She read the banner headline that screamed its way across the front page.

"Devastating!" it said. "One hundred and twenty-eight Americans were among the thousands of innocent persons who lost their lives today when a German U-boat sank the British liner *The Lusitania* off the southern coast of Ireland!"

Impatiently then she flipped through the paper ignoring the ponderous descriptions of proposed amendments to the Clayton Anti-Trust act, a review of the new Griffith film *Birth of a Nation,* and the lengthy summary of a speech Charles Evans Hughes had delivered in Cincinnati. Then she read the editorial she had been seeking.

"Can America retain its neutrality after such an act of international brigandry? This is the urgent question which President Wilson must address."

Emma sighed deeply. The news was staggering. What sort of a war was this that was waged against innocent men and women—civilians who boarded a ship as passengers and became military casualties? *The Lusitania.* She repeated the name of the ship aloud. It was strangely familiar. Where had she heard the name of the vessel before? She remembered now, with sinking heart, a conversation she had overheard earlier in the week at a meeting of the Daughters of Zion. A neighbor of the Sterns had received a letter from Abigail telling her she had booked passage on a British liner with a strange name—*The Lusitania.* An ancient name for Portugal, Emma had remembered, and recalled an engraving in the geography primer she had used in Amsterdam. That was why the name had remained fixed in her mind.

Emma closed her eyes. She had not wept since the night of Gregory's death, but now tears coursed down her cheeks. She grieved for the woman who might have been her friend and her sister. She wept for the son and daughter who had lost a mother, even as she herself had lost a son. Her sorrow encompassed parents and children, husbands and wives, separated from each other, their arms extended, their hands never touching.

"It's not fair," she said softly and went again to the window. Joshua and Samuel played softball in the garden, and soon Leonie would come home. A horse trotted down the road, but its rider was a tall youth. It was, after all, too early to expect Leonie back.

Leonie waited for Jesse at their secret cave. She watched the huge white clouds drift across the clear blue sky, forming celestial sculptures that changed shape wondrously from minute to minute. A cloud shaped like a graceful bridge was briefly stirred by a breeze and transformed into an enchanted castle. Three small feathery formations converged and formed a snowy canopy beneath which Sonora doves cavorted as they dived onto the outstretched arms of a towering saguaro cactus. She did not think the skies anywhere in the world could be as beautiful as the cerulean heavens of her desert.

She watched as the clouds were fringed by the dark gold light of the slowly declining sun and streaks of carmine appeared in the east. The heat of the day was broken, and as always the evening cool invaded the desert with startling swiftness. She shivered slightly and took her sweater out of her saddlebag. Star, who had been laconically grazing at a patch of desert grass, tossed her silver mane and looked at her mistress with soulful eyes.

"He'll be here soon," Leonie assured the horse. "Soon."

Surely, Jesse would come. He had passed a note to her in the school corridor telling her he had just completed an essay which he wanted to read to her before sending it to *The American*. An argument for pacifism. It would be a welcome-home gift of a kind for his mother.

The clouds turned the color of smoke, and long shadows

streaked the rose-red sand. An owl hooted in the distance, and the whistle at the Malapais mine heralded the end of the day shift. Leonie went into the cave and lit a candle. She would read a short poem by Vachel Lindsay, and when she had completed the last stanza, he would be there. Her voice echoed as she read aloud, and she closed her eyes. When she opened them, the aperture to the cave was empty. He was not coming after all.

She rode slowly toward Phoenix through the half darkness, allowing Star to pause now and again to nibble an outcropping of manzanita. The bells on the mare's reins chimed softly, liltingly.

"Leonie!"

Jesse's shout reverberated across the desert stillness, and the hooves of his horse sounded in staccato timpani as he raced toward her. Within minutes he was beside her, his long, lean face strangely pale, his blue eyes burning with agate brightness.

"Jesse, what is it? What's happened?"

She reached out to touch him and saw that his hands trembled even as they clutched the reins, and he sat his horse with tense rigidity.

"You didn't hear?"

"Hear what? I've been out here for hours, waiting for you."

"The Lusitania—my mother's ship was torpedoed by the Germans just off the Irish coast. The goddamn Germans. She's dead, Leonie. My mother's dead. She's never coming home." Tears streaked his cheeks, and his shoulders quivered.

"No," she said softly. "No." It was not his words she protested. It was his desperation she would deny. There was a new tone in his voice, hard and unfamiliar. Hate had hardened his intonation, had initiated him into a new manhood.

She went to him then, dismounting and stretching out her hand until he took it and slowly lowered himself to the ground. Her arms went around him, and he buried his face in her dark hair. She felt the hot moisture of his tears blend with her own, and she calmed him as she had calmed Joshua and Samuel after Gregory's death. Her hands stroked the nape of his neck, and her voice was soft and rhythmic as she said again and again, "It will be all right. It will be all right." It would not be all right, they both knew, but they allowed the repetition of the comforting lie to soothe their sorrow as they sank down on the cool sand and surrendered themselves to the new darkness. Heart beating against heart, tears commingling, they comforted each other against the certain knowledge that their childhood was over: reality had penetrated their enchanted kingdom, invaded their secret desert retreat.

There were no more pacifist poems, no more essays of reconciliation. Now the odes that Jesse read to Leonie beneath the aspens were dark with foreboding, his themes ominous with threat. He had believed all wars to be equally wrong, all combatants equally culpable. But his mother's death had betrayed his naiveté, had forged new convictions. The Germans were the enemy—his enemy and his country's—and he would fight them.

He wrote to the Lafayette Espadrille volunteering his services. They advised him that he was too young to volunteer. He obtained a forged birth certificate, and during the summer school recess he journeyed to Canada and tried to enlist in the RCAF. The recruiting officer was alert to falsified documents, and Jesse returned to Phoenix to confront his father's fierce anger.

"How will your getting killed avenge your mother's death?" Henry Stern asked bitterly.

The banker had taken his own course of action. He traveled to Washington regularly to advise on investments that would benefit the newly created United States Shipping Board. He attended meetings of Arizona businessmen involved in the Liberty Loan program. Once he sat beside Isaac Lewin. They nodded to each other stiffly, each observing how loss and grief had aged the other.

Henry Stern tallied columns of figures all day and slept fitfully at night. He was haunted by dreams of Abigail entangled in a net of oily seaweed, struggling toward him through steel-colored waters. Once he dreamed of himself as a boy, pursuing the shadowy figure of Jacob Coen. Often when he awakened his pillow was wet with tears, but when he confronted his son and daughter at the breakfast table he was dry-eyed, thin-lipped.

"Your mother would have wanted you to finish school," he told Jesse.

The boy was only a year away from graduation. He would send him east to school. Applications from Harvard and Princeton were on his desk. He wrote a letter to the RCAF office in Toronto, congratulating the recruiting officer on his vigilance. He wrote to his brother, David, in Germany, telling him of Abigail's death.

The RCAF office did not reply. David's letter was agonized. He sympathized with his brother. "It is tragic to see this country at war," he wrote. Not "*my* country" but "*this* country." Did David think of Germany as his home? Henry Stern wondered. Did he love the pastoral Bavarian landscape as Henry Stern loved the deserts and mountains of Arizona? The United States was his country as surely as if he had been born there. It had given him sanctuary and opportunity, and in return he had laid the cornerstone of his bank on the shifting sands of a nascent city named for a mythical bird. He did not reply to David's letter. War was not an abstraction. Men were responsible for the deeds of their nations.

Jesse graduated from the Phoenix Union High School. He was first in his class, valedictorian and orator. Letters of acceptance had arrived from both Princeton and Harvard. He looked like a young god as he walked across the stage to accept his diploma, and when he removed his mortarboard, his bright hair glowed in the sunlight. According to custom he tossed the academic hat with careful aim, and Henry Stern saw that it was caught by a tall, dark-haired girl, who blushed and lowered her head as she clutched it, pressing the tassel to her cheek. Henry Stern frowned as he recognized Leonie Lewin.

"We must come to a decision," he said to his son that night. "Will you enroll at Harvard or at Princeton?"

"Neither." Jesse's reply was calm, controlled. "I've signed up for an officer's training program. I'm eighteen now. I have the right. When the war is over—then I'll go to Princeton.'' He held his father's gaze, ignored Barbara's gasp of dismay.

"This country is not at war yet," Henry Stern said harshly, but he did not argue with Jesse.

Leonie did. She shouted and beat at his chest until he clutched her wrists and held her prisoner.

"How could *you* enlist? You said war was immoral. You said you couldn't imagine wearing a uniform.''

"That was before.''

He spoke in the cryptic abbreviation of their intimacy. *Before.* Before his mother's death, before his recognition of encroaching evil, of his own dark desire for revenge.

She held out the pacifist poems he had written at the war's beginning, and he read them as though they had been written by a stranger. He would have tossed them away, but Leonie gathered them into a folio and carried them home.

"Besides," he added, "we are not at war. Not yet."

He did not realize, until hours later, that he had quoted his father.

That fall Woodrow Wilson ran for a second term as president, and Henry Stern voted for him. He stood on line behind Isaac Lewin at the polling place. Lewin would also vote for Wilson, he knew. He had overheard Isaac join a political discussion after Sabbath services the previous week. True to his promise, Wilson had kept the country out of the war, yet he was a man of action. He had taken a firm hand with Huerta and Pancho Villa in Mexico, and his policy of watchful waiting was pragmatic, sensible. Henry Stern the banker and Isaac Lewin the businessman were mutually approving. It was ironic, Henry Stern thought, that he and his half sister's husband were so often on the same side.

"You would like each other if you only came to know each other," Isabel Cavalajo had said more than once.

He often saw the daughter of his old Talmudic study partner, who had died that summer. Grief and loneliness had thrust them together, and he and Isabel often dined together and went for long drives on weekend afternoons.

"We will not come to know each other." Always, his reply was terse.

Abigail's death had reinforced his anger against Emma and her brothers. He had held a small memorial service for his wife and placed a plaque of Arizona granite marked with her name beside his mother's gravestone. *Abigail Stern: Beloved wife and mother in Israel.* The inscription on Analiese's gravestone was limited to her name and the date of her death. Even in death she was unprotected, bereft of status because of the Coen family. The irrationality of his hatred had hardened, had assumed a life of its own. It lived within him as a separate, secret being.

Jesse trained at Fort Huachuca on the Mexican border. When he came to Phoenix, he wore his dress uniform. The Sam Browne belt girdled his narrow chest, the brim of his campaign hat was pulled low about his forehead. As always, he and Leonie met secretly. They walked through the Grand Street market and ate tortillas dipped in guacamole in their favorite small Mexican cantina. They bought bananas and cactus fruit from vendors, who often refused to accept money from Jesse. They pointed respectfully at his uniform, took off their sombreros, and crossed themselves, blessing the soldier, blessing their country. Jesse laughed and Leonie smiled, but a heaviness had settled on her heart.

They were no longer school children. Their innocence had been abandoned. He wore a uniform. His skin had been sunstained to the color of amber, and his body was tight, muscular. Walking beside him, she felt her own fragility, her own vulnerability. Sometimes when they were together in their secret cave, she wept.

"Why are you crying?" he asked gently. "I only wear a uniform. I've fought no battles. I've faced no danger." But his fists were clenched even as he spoke. He was ready for battles, ready for danger.

Woodrow Wilson took his second oath of office that March. He spoke with optimism of an elusive peace. He advised the nation not to lose heart and called for "soundings" to be taken. Mankind might well be in sight of that "haven of peace" for which it yearned.

Leonie listened to the inaugural address with her parents.

"Do you believe that, Mother?" she asked.

"Believe?" Emma repeated the word as though it were

foreign to her. "It is a while now since I gave up the habit of believing."

Hurt flashed across Isaac Lewin's face. He slammed down the philosophy book he had been reading and went out to the loggia. Abruptly, Leonie took her suede riding jacket.

"Are you going out?" Emma asked. "Again?" Her question coupled disappointment and accusation.

"Yes." Leonie did not add that she could not bear to remain in the room where her mother and father sat beneath the taut invisible canopy of their silence and their anger. She rode out to the cave and reread the poems that Lieutenant Jesse Stern had written when he lived for peace and cherished hope.

The president's optimism was short-lived. Germany resumed its submarine warfare with new intensity, and the American Southwest reeled against the impact of the Zimmermann telegram. Even Brother Timothy, hostile to Britain because of its policy in Ireland, was outraged.

"Now the Germans have gone too far," he said, and he told Isaac how he had called a special assembly at the Indian School to read aloud the contents of the decoded telegram in which the German foreign minister, Arthur Zimmermann, had instructed his ambassador to Mexico to forge an alliance with that country. Germany would support a Mexican attack on the United States and help it to "reconquer the lost territory of New Mexico, Texas, and Arizona."

"It would be the equivalent of our offering to 'liberate' Alsace and the Sudetenland," Isaac agreed bitterly. The southwestern states belonged to the Union—they were not lost Mexican territories. It was not sufficient for Wilson to sever diplomatic relations with Germany. There would have to be a declaration of war.

He and Brother Timothy swirled brandy in crystal decanters and watched Joshua and Samuel position their troops on the cardboard map. The priest's fingers touched the cross at his neck, and Emma's hand rested briefly on the mezuzah at the doorpost. They would need their faith, they knew, in the weeks and months to come.

* * *

Jesse Stern arrived in Phoenix for a week's leave the first week in April. He met Leonie at the Mexican cantina. They sat at a small wooden table and toyed with their food. The scent of the piñon cooking fire mingled with the fragrance of the orange blossoms on the branches that thrust their white weight through the open window. The proprietor sang softly so as not to obscure the voice of a patron translating El Presidente Wilson's speech from the afternoon papers. Jesse and Leonie, who had not seen a newspaper that day, listened carefully to the Spanish words.

"We are glad now that we see the facts with no veil of false pretenses about them. We fight thus for the ultimate peace of the world and for the liberation of its peoples, the German people included, for the rights of nations great and small and the privilege of men everywhere to choose their way of life. . . . The world must be made safe for democracy!"

Jesse's fingers gripped Leonie's. They were at war. He would fight to make the world safe for democracy, safe for men and women to travel the oceans of the world, safe for the children of Antwerp and Rouen.

"Don't cry," he said, not looking at her, but certain that her eyes, which so strangely matched his own, were bright with tears.

Joshua Lewin's bar mitzvah was celebrated in a subdued fashion. Gregory's death and the war precluded the lavish celebration that Isaac had planned since the day he began to teach his eldest son the traditional chants. There was still no synagogue in Phoenix, but Joshua read the Torah in ringing tones to the congregation assembled on the lawn.

"I lift up my eyes to the mountains, for the mountains give me strength," he sang and looked out toward the undulating hills. His ancestors had known deserts and mountains, searing heat and cloud-sculpted skies. Their landscape was his own. His father stood beside him, soundlessly mouthing each word, and his mother sat with Joshua and Leonie, flanked by his uncles, Emil and Simon.

His favorite gift was a leatherbound journal, his name embossed upon it in gold letters. His uncle Emil gave it to him with a note that Joshua kept always. "We live in interesting times, Joshua. You will want to record your feelings and observations."

Perceptive Emil Coen, who lived a solitary life himself, had recognized his nephew's need for private disclosure, for a repository to record the unarticulated angers and insights that haunted him. It was odd, Emil thought, how his sister Emma had re-created the tensions and dynamics of the Prinsengracht household in her Arizona home. He supposed that his friend Franz Eisenmann, a young psychiatrist who had received his training in Vienna, would not find it so odd.

"When we do not understand our pasts, we are destined to repeat them," Franz had often said. It was a saying that he attributed to the Viennese neurologist Sigmund Freud, who had been his mentor.

It was Franz who had suggested the journal as a gift, and Emil had been gratified by the way Joshua touched the finely lined blank pages and fondled the small gold lock that guaranteed his privacy.

Each evening Joshua filled his new orange Parker fountain pen with bright blue ink and carefully wrote a page of his journal. He wrote of his sister Leonie's somber mood. "She misses Jesse Stern, I guess. They say he has been sent east for training, but no one knows for sure. Leonie jumps at the mail the way a desert jackal springs on a rabbit." He wrote of his mother's spurt of activity. She and Natalya Wallach spent their days at the Phoenix office of the Red Cross. There were first-aid kits to be readied, clothing packages to be shipped, nutrition programs to be organized. A field hospital was established at Fort Yuma. Emma ordered disinfectants, cotton gauze and muslin for bandages, blankets and surgical supplies, with the same efficiency and clipped accuracy with which she had once ordered linen for Abigail Nathan's English country estate, food stores for the Galveston boarding house, and supplies for the tent store.

But the longest entries in Joshua's journals were reserved for his father's activities. Isaac had volunteered for service and had been summarily rejected. Too old. A family man.

"You'll be more valuable on the home front," the recruiting officer said appeasingly.

Lewin's Emporium had become Isaac's battlefield, the arena of his patriotism. The war offered him an opportunity to repay his adopted country for all that it had offered him since the day the immigration office had waved him on in Galveston.

He set up a booth on the main floor of the store for the sale of Liberty Bonds and assigned his prettiest salesgirls to its operation. Any customer who bought a bond received Lewin Liberty scrip toward the purchase of any item of merchandise on display in the store. The plate-glass windows of every Emporium were wreathed in red, white, and blue bunting and peopled with mannequins dressed in the national colors. The papier-mâché figurines held small American flags, and their arms were linked with huge cut-out figures of doughboys carrying their rifles and regimental banners. Satin streamers and posters reminded Lewin's customers of "Meatless Mondays," "Fuelless Tuesdays," "Gasless Wednesdays." When the president called for the establishment of war gardens, reminding the nation that "food will win the war," Lewin's offered free packets of seed and held special sales of gardening equipment.

"Have you bought a trowel for your war garden?" salesgirls were instructed to ask even the most elegant of customers as they wrapped packages in the distinctive Emporium paper, printed with the emblem of the tent store.

The full-page advertisements in the *Arizona Sentinel*, the *Daily Star*, and the *Arizona Republican* proclaimed the "New Lewin Look." Fabric was needed for the manufacture of uniforms, and overnight hemlines were raised, full skirts replaced with straight-cut sheaths, and wide collars gave way to the Peter Pan look. Leather was needed for combat boots, and high-buttoned shoes were replaced with narrowly cut pumps. "Be fashionable and patriotic!" the Lewin's advertisement advised.

Isabel Cavalajo had resumed her duties at the Emporium. She and Isaac worked together with a harmony of understanding peculiar to lovers who have parted friends. She had grown less intense, slower in her movements; flecks of silver danced in her gleaming cap of hair. She had not lost her acumen for predicting fashion trends, and Abner Wallach was pleased that he had taken her advice and increased the inventory of women's business suits and handbags. As the men left for the army, women reported for work, and their clothing needs had to be met.

Business at all the Emporiums skyrocketed. Arizona copper was essential for the production of weapons, the wiring of radio sets, and the manufacture of walkie-talkies that linked the men in the trenches to their command posts. The miners worked double shifts, and they flocked to the stores to spend their inflated checks.

"Don't you want to buy a Liberty Bond?" the salesladies asked routinely.

Isaac had long understood that his store was a focus of entertainment for the city, that shopping was a diversion as well as a necessity. Since the days of the tent store he had courted audiences with refreshments and performances, parades and window displays. Those who came to watch or to take advantage of a free glass of lemonade stayed to buy. The war caused him to double his efforts. He held victory talent contests. Young soldiers sang "Keep the Home Fires Burning" and tossed their campaign hats into the outstretched hands of misty-eyed girls. A teenaged chorus paraded through the store singing "Over There" in rousing tones and distributing paper flags. The Phoenix Glee Club waved British flags and sang "It's a Long, Long Way to Tipperary" and "Britannia Rules the Waves."

When a shipment of French gowns miraculously arrived, Isaac proclaimed Marseillaise Day and handed each patron a tricolored corsage fashioned of taffeta ribbons. The French consul general in San Francisco traveled to Phoenix for the occasion. Sweating profusely, his red Légion d'Honneur ribbon wilting in his lapel, he thanked the Phoenicians for their support and accepted a large cactus plant that symbolized the toughness of the First Arizona Infantry, soon to sail for France.

"I suppose the First Arizona will make the world safe for Mainboche, Chanel and Lily Daché," young Joshua wrote sardonically in his journal. "I wonder if Jesse Stern is in the First," he added. Leonie was more silent than ever now, her mood ruled by the mail.

The war had energized Emma. The war effort sparked her patriotism, engaged her imagination. She had a challenge, a sense of purpose. She moved briskly through the streets of the city, hurrying from a meeting of the Red Cross to a luncheon on behalf of Liberty Bonds. Her ideas generated excitement, enthusiasm. Her voice rang with authority. She knew how to make things happen—how to conceive of a plan and see to its execution.

The Red Cross organized a blood bank, and she volunteered to be a donor. She discovered, to her surprise, that her blood type was rare—B Rh-negative. She was called upon more frequently than other donors, and always she was available when the call from the blood center came.

"It is the needs of the living that must absorb us," Clara Barton had told her all those years ago as they walked the flood-ravaged streets of Galveston, and Emma recalled her words as she watched her blood drip drop by drop into the clear glass container. The stern-eyed nurse had died a decade ago, but her legacy to the living remained.

Emma intensified her efforts as the war progressed and new programs were initiated on the home front. It was her idea to celebrate the inauguration of Daylight Savings Time with a display of fireworks launched from the roof of the Emporium. "Conserve Energy—Win the War!" Lewin's customers were reminded on large posters that stood on every counter. The fireworks display was preceded by a large cocktail party held in Johnny Redbird's Arizona Experience department. Wine was served in specially sculpted ceramic decanters, and Johnny distributed beaded Hopi pins depicting sunbursts of light. The aristocracy of Phoenix, dressed in their best, moved through the store, sipping their drinks and pausing before display counters.

"We're a long way from the water barrel in the tent store and the lemonade in tumblers we served when Teddy Roosevelt visited," Isaac said to Emma. She looked regally beautiful in a blue chemise that matched her eyes, her flame-colored hair twisted into an elegant chignon. The ghost of a smile paled at her lips, and the color rose in her cheeks.

Joshua confided to his journal that night that the war had offered his parents a respite from their anger, a busyness that diverted them from their grief. They had conversation now to fill the void of silence that had yawned between them since Gregory's death. There was no danger in discussions of their wartime projects, Emma's Red Cross involvements, Isaac's enterprises at the store.

Isaac traveled to Washington for meetings of the War Industries Board. The government had moved to establish fixed prices on military and civilian goods, and Isaac was named to a steering committee because of his merchandising experience. He was somehow unsurprised to learn that it was Henry Stern who had suggested his name to the board chairman, Bernard Baruch, a tall South Carolinian Jew.

"Perhaps Stern's attitude to our family is softening," Isaac suggested to Emil Coen, who had come to Arizona on business. The Coen brothers' knowledge of shipping avenues and the availability of chemicals and metals was indispensable to a nation determined to ship troops and matériel abroad as swiftly as possible. Emil and Simon were often in Arizona now, estimating the productivity of the mines, advising on delivery schedules.

"I think not," he said. "He gave me the usual frosty nod when we met with Baruch in Washington last week. Still, they say that he begins to emerge from his grief. There is even talk that he will remarry. He spends a great deal of his time with that talented young woman who used to work for you, Isaac. Isabel Cavalajo—that's her name."

Joshua Lewin, seated opposite his parents during that conversation, recorded in his diary that the color had drained from his father's face and his mother had knocked over a wineglass. Once before, he recalled, Emma had spilled wine on a white cloth at the mention of Isabel Cavalajo's name. This time, however, she did not hurry from the table but calmly lifted her small silver bell and summoned Rosa to spread a linen napkin over the crimson stain.

"Where is Leonie?" Emma asked as Rosa left the room muttering softly in Spanish.

"I think she's waiting for the mailman," Samuel said. "She's always waiting for the mailman." His voice was plaintive. He was stranded in childhood, abandoned by his brother, who made copious entries in his locked leather journal, and his sister, who wrote too many letters to a mysterious military address.

That June, one week after Leonie's graduation from high school, the letter for which she had been waiting arrived. She read it in the loggia, smiling although her eyes were filled with tears. She smiled because Jesse's division was moving northward from its training camp at the Mexican border to Tucson. She wept because it was clear that he would soon leave for France. The black cavalry officers at Fort Huachuca were satisfied with his regiment's training performance. He himself had earned a commendation.

"The day we have been waiting for is not far off," he wrote cautiously. "Soon it will be our turn to strike a blow in this war to end all wars. Please, Leonie, do not think that I have lost the ideal of peace. I still believe in it, but now I realize that peace can only be guaranteed by strength."

"Be strong, Jesse," she whispered. "Be strong." She pressed his letter to her lips and concealed it with his other correspondence beneath the monogrammed handkerchiefs in her bureau drawer. The scent of orange-blossom sachet clung to the thin sheets of military stationery.

"I want to work in the Tucson store this summer," she told Emma that night. "Johnny said he needs help there. The manager of the Arizona Experience was drafted."

"But I thought you would work with me at the Red Cross," Emma said, frowning. "After all, you're to begin university in the fall. We might at least have the summer together."

Her voice was controlled and neutral, but her children heard the secret strain of a plea. ("I think my mother needs us as a buffer between herself and my father," Joshua wrote in his journal that night. "If we were not at home, they would have to talk *to* each other, not *at* each other.")

"I think this is more important," Leonie replied. She did not argue but spoke with the quiet certitude peculiar to introspective young women. "There are very few people Johnny can call upon, and his people need the work the craft shops give them. When the Indian men leave for war, their squaws do not come into the city to work in offices and factories. We must keep the craft industry going to support them."

"We had a memorial service in school today for Matthew

Rivers,'' Samuel contributed in the high-pitched voice that, he thought desperately, would never deepen. He remembered that a year before his bar mitzvah, Joshua's voice had already reached a baritonal depth, but he himself still spoke in the shrill tones of boyhood.

"Poor boy," Isaac said, and they were silent. Matthew Rivers, a Pima youth, was the first Arizonan to be killed in France. Isaac had sent the family a large food basket from the store's delicacy department, carefully filling it himself with the spicy sausage and sweet guava jams that the Pima Indians especially liked.

"But you'd only be in Tucson for two months," Emma persisted.

"Time enough to train someone. I've helped Johnny Redbird so often that I know the Experience shops well," Leonie replied.

"Where will you live?" Emma asked. The question, they knew, implied her defeat.

"In a boarding house."

"You're only seventeen."

"Exactly your age when you left Amsterdam for London, Mother," Leonie replied evenly. Emma's gaze faltered, and she recalled with startling clarity the green bonnet she had worn on the day of her leavetaking. It had matched the sliver of sea grass from the Prinsengracht walkway, which shimmered still on her bureau. She reached across the table and touched Leonie's hand. The lightness of her fingers signified assent and monition.

A week later Leonie joined the crowd at the Tucson railroad station that had assembled to greet the soldiers of the First Arizona Infantry. The marching band of the Indian School played "Over There," and the men marched quickstep to the joyous music and grinned shyly as the red, white, and blue confetti scattered by patriotic Tucsonians rained down on them. She caught sight of Jesse. He smiled at her and raised three fingers in greeting, but by prearranged agreement they did not approach each other. Jesse's father and sister had come to Tucson.

Leonie watched the banker and Jesse embrace and saw Jesse lift Barbara in his arms and twirl her about. Gravely, he shook the hand of the petite dark-haired woman who stood beside Henry Stern. Isabel Cavalajo. The rumors in Phoenix were true, then. Henry Stern was to marry the daughter of the Marano Talmudic student—a legendary figure now among the Jews of Phoenix. How pretty she was, Leonie thought.

Isabel moved with a swift grace, her head always tilted upward. A scrap of white confetti had settled on the sleek cap of her dark hair, and she plucked it off as though it were a vagrant snowflake, and then, with childlike glee, she threaded it through Henry Stern's lapel. The banker smiled as though amused by the delightful antics of a playful and passionate child and lightly patted her head and enfolded her in a protective embrace. They would be happy, Leonie thought with sudden insight. Isabel Cavalajo sought an older man to shelter her from her own passion, and Henry Stern wanted a vulnerable woman who would claim his protection. Leonie hoped that Jesse would not be upset by his father's remarriage.

She sat high in the stands the next day as the First Arizona Infantry marched in dress parade down Main Street. Jesse, a first lieutenant and group leader, led his division, his swagger stick held smartly at his side, his rifle defiantly rigid at his shoulder. Her eyes smarted when she remembered that once he had written a poem that began: ''The sounds of war are mute to men of peace. . . . '' Still, she could not blame him. *Life happens to us,* her father had said. *Life changes us.* It had, after all, changed Jesse, she acknowledged sadly.

Still, she clapped vigorously when the band struck up ''The Star-Spangled Banner'' and the bright flag emblazoned with the burning sun of Arizona was unfurled. Jesse stepped forward to receive it, saluted smartly, and carried it back to his men. They would carry the banner of their desert state into the dark forests of the Argonne. They would follow the blazing satin sun as they descended into the trenches along the Marne. They stood at attention now, their eyes fixed on it, their expressions confident, determined. The sons of miners and ranchers, of shopkeepers and cowherds, stood beside the Indian youths from the Pima and Navajo territory. Once they had fought each other, but now they were united and would fight as one. They marched behind Jesse Stern, the Jewish officer whose father had come to Arizona from Holland. He would lead them back to the war-torn continent of his parents' beginnings. They smiled thinly and ignored the too-rapid beating of their hearts.

Jesse's family returned to Phoenix the next day, and Jesse, his brass buckle polished to the color of his bright hair, came to Leonie's boarding house. She waited for him in a pool of sunlight that infiltrated the shaded porch. Wordlessly, he took her into his arms. He tasted the tears that streaked her cheeks, stroked her long dark hair with trembling fingers. She wore a white dress, and the sun splashed golden across the skirt, caped the bodice with radiant folds.

"You wore a white dress that very first day," he said. "The day of the statehood celebration."

"I remember. We were such children then." Her voice was oddly wistful.

"And are we so old now?" He smiled teasingly, but she pressed her head against his chest and did not answer.

"How long do we have?" Her question came in a whisper.

"We have tomorrow and the day after tomorrow. Then the regiment leaves for the East. A troop ship is waiting."

"Two days." Pain edged the words.

"Two days. All to ourselves. My father had a meeting of the War Industries Board in Washington, and so he couldn't stay. It sounds so disloyal to say it, but we were lucky."

"Yes. Lucky," she repeated, light-hearted suddenly. Two days alone together—free of family, free of the need for secrecy. They had never before, during all the years of their intimacy, had more than two hours.

"It will be a wonderful two days," she promised, and they smiled at each other and moved out of the circlet of sunlight.

The proprietress of the boarding house, a plump, good-natured woman, smiled at them benignly and packed them a picnic basket, encasing it in a blanket. She stood on the porch and watched the handsome couple walk down the street. The soldier wore khaki fatigues, but his high boots were polished and his campaign hat was pulled low to shield his eyes from the sun, its strap cutting into the cleft at his chin. The girl's dark hair was gathered up beneath a large white sun hat, and the skirt of the white dress was patterned with tiny blue cornflowers. They were so young, so vulnerable. The landlady was grateful that her own son was a schoolboy still in knickers, her daughter still in pinafores and pigtails.

Leonie told her that they planned to hike the Canda del Oro. She was not to worry if they did not return by evening. They might stay the night with relatives. The landlady had nodded, although she did not believe them. There were different rules for lovers in time of war.

Talking and singing, their arms linked, Leonie and Jesse hiked from the flat bush country of alkali flats through the slowly changing desert. They inhaled the pungent scent of creosote from the *bajadas* along the Canda del Oro and stopped to eat their lunch beneath a Joshua tree. The low-hanging branches, thick with new-grown foliage, sheltered them from the sun, and they fed each other bits of fried chicken, thinly cut carrot sticks, and blood-red tomato slices, which the landlady had seasoned with salsa and wrapped in thin flakes of tortilla bread. Jesse plucked cactus fruit from a towering plant and practiced the childish skill of peeling the prickly carapace in a single skein. He dangled the peeled skin in the air.

"It will form a letter—the first initial of the person you will love and marry," he reminded her. They had played the childish game in Natalya Wallach's improvised Sunday school classroom in the schoolyard. With mock seriousness now, he spread it on the ground.

"You see—it's an *L*, " he said teasingly. "Let me see—do I know anyone whose name begins with an *L?*"

"Perhaps a Mademoiselle Lisette is waiting for you in France," Leonie replied. "Let me try."

She peeled a second fruit with his army knife, her lips pursed. A drop of the juice fell onto her skirt and formed a pink star-shaped stain amid the pale blue flowers. She studied the long peel and twirled it about.

"A *J*, " she said. "Unless I turn it this way and it becomes *U.*"

Playfully, he wrestled it away from her.

"It stays a *J*," he said. He gripped her arm and his breath was soft at her ear, at her neck.

Tenderly, then, they offered each other the pink fruit, and when they had finished eating they kissed. Their lips were moist and sticky, their tongues heavy with the sweetness of the desert harvest. They fell asleep in the shade of the tree. Her head rested on his shoulder; her fingers were pressed against the cleft of his chin, marked now by the strap of his campaign hat.

It was cooler when they awakened, and they continued their walk. The long stretch of sand surrendered to flowering hillocks, and they walked through a field of golden poppies and another of scarlet anemones. At sunset they paused again, and Leonie picked columbines and fairy ferns beside a sparkling spring that trickled down from the granite ledges of the Santa Catalinas. She curtsied and offered them to him as he trailed his fingers through the icy water.

"A bridal bouquet," he said. "Are you my bride?"

"I have always been your bride," she replied gravely.

White she had worn at their first meeting, the day the blood of her new womanhood first flowed; white she wore now as she sat beside him and listened to the singing of the flowing spring, the gentle whistle of the upland wind.

"Look." He held her close and pointed to a plant, bent low by the weight of a white blossom, its petals curled together in a bulbous knot. As they watched, each petal opened, stretching forth like a finger of moonlight, until together they formed a graceful flowering circlet that filled the newly darkened air with a melancholy fragrance.

"It's the cereus," Leonie said. "The night-blooming cereus." She had inherited her mother's love of flowers and their lore. She had seen pictures of the cereus, which once a year achieved full blossom, stretching open at sunset and closing in upon itself at dawn. It was magical that she and Jesse had chanced upon it, had watched the mystery of its birth. She took it as an omen.

They ate the rest of the food and cupped their hands to drink the clear, cold water. Sated, they talked, speculating on the origin of the enmity between their families. An ancient business quarrel in distant Amsterdam, they thought, but it did not matter.

"They'll accept us. They'll have to," he said.

"And it will make no difference if they don't," she replied. Nothing would separate them, ever.

They stayed the night beside the stream and watched the white blossom of the cereus turn silver as the moonlight canopied them with radiance. His jacket formed their bed, her white dress their counterpane. They blanketed themselves with their bodies, pressing against each other for warmth and love. Laughter came easily to them and remembered fragments of poetry. Their shouts of gladness echoed through the night. His fingers traced the rise of her breast, and he kissed the tiny birthmark that flowered at her waist. Her hands traveled across his body, her fingers kissed his flesh. She bit into the softness of his neck, felt his blood upon her tongue. Then his love exploded within her, and her body was flooded with joy.

"Jesse." She loved the sound of his name. Her fingers were velvet-soft against the taut tendons of his throat.

"You are my bride," he said. "My desert bride."

He plucked up long blades of golden desert grass and tied them into a ring, which he placed upon her middle finger.

"Behold you are consecrated unto me according to the laws of Moses and Israel."

They slept then, covering themselves with the landlady's coarse blanket against the nocturnal chill. When they awakened, heart beating against heart, they saw that the pale light of dawn had already begun its slow sweep across the earth. Their magic flower had closed upon itself, leaving only a redolent fragrance and a single fallen petal, the color of moonlight.

Heat blanketed the Southwest during the summer of 1918, and even veteran Tucsonians swore that they had never known such an unrelenting season. The desert wind blew with furnacelike ferocity, and galvanized tubs were moved into parched backyards and filled with water to cool fretful children. Even when a block of ice was placed in the tub, the water turned lukewarm within the hour. Leonie consulted

with the manager of the Tucson Emporium, and they decided
to increase the number of "swamp" coolers so that Lewin
customers would be guaranteed some respite from the heat
when they shopped. The evaporative coolers with their wa-
ter-soaked pads moderated both the low humidity and the
high temperature, and shoppers lingered in the store, unwilling to face the heat of the streets.

"The heat can be a shopkeeper's ally," her father said
when she spoke to him on the phone. "Sometimes I think
department stores like ours and Goldwater's and Neiman-
Marcus in Dallas have succeeded so well because we gave
our customers a place to come to and get out of the heat."

"Be serious, Papa," she said.

"All right, I'm serious. Are you all right, Leonie? You
sound a little tired."

"I'm not tired," she said. It was sadness he heard in her
voice. Sadness and worry. Jesse was somewhere on the Atlantic Ocean, on a crowded troop ship. Weeks would pass
before she could hope to hear from him.

She served lemonade to the soldiers who came to the Arizona Experience to shop for souvenirs. Their leave pay was
thick in their regimental-issue wallets. They were bound for
France, they told her proudly, and they worried jovially that
the war might be over before they got there.

"We got to teach the Huns a lesson," a young Californian
told her. "Black Jack Pershing sure let them know who was
boss at Château-Thierry."

Leonie did not reply. She had seen the news photos of the
hastily dug graves dotted with American flags on the French
battlefield. The American Third Division had paid dearly for
that victory. A memorial candle burned still in Natalya Wallach's living room for her nephew, who had died near Rheims.

"We left Vilna so that we would survive," Natalya said
bitterly. The fallen lad was her sister's only son.

"We left for more than that," Abner reproved her sternly.
"Better to die fighting for democracy than to be slaughtered
in a pogrom."

Leonie sold the Californian a turquoise necklace for his
mother, a carpet of Navajo weave for his sister, and wished
him well.

"Will you come to a film with me tonight, miss?" he asked her shyly.

"I'm afraid I can't," she said kindly. "I must write to my fiancé in France."

She wrote to Jesse every day, long, ardent letters. She told him what she was reading. A long poem called "Prufrock" by an American named Eliot who lived in England. ("The images are strange, and I'm not sure I understand them— we'll read it together when you get back.") She wrote him about her father's new enterprise. The lunchrooms at the Emporiums were converted into canteens for servicemen. ("My father says he remembers what it was like to be a young man far from home. Joshua, in his sarcastic way, says that the wandering Jew has become a host to the wandering G.I.") She gave him the news of their classmates at Phoenix Union High School, never mentioning the Loomis boy, who was missing in action, or Greg Nelson, who had been killed in an accident during training.

His own letters were brief and cryptic. The Arizona First was based at a training camp, but he could not say where. He was proud of his men. They were ready for action, keyed for adventure. "Write," he implored. She kissed his signature and held each letter against her heart.

She wrote him a very long letter on a day when dark clouds encompassed the azure sky and fiery shafts of lightning rocketed through the jagged mountains around Tucson. Rolls of thunder reverberated ominously, and rain fell with steady, mercurial rapidity. Palm trees swayed against the sharp wind, their fronds snapping and falling into flooded creek beds and arroyos.

Mothers shouted for their children to come indoors, fearful that the flash floods might turn the desert floor into a raging river.

"A monsoon is raging now, my darling," Leonie wrote to Jesse. "Do they have monsoons in France?"

She sealed the letter and brought it down to the mail tray in the vestibule. The landlady and her children stood at the screen door watching the storm.

"At least when it's over, the heat will be bearable," the good-natured woman said. "You'll feel better then, miss."

She had noticed that Leonie was very pale and had little appetite. Often in the morning the girl drank only a cup of lukewarm tea at breakfast, forgoing the ample servings of porridge and eggs.

"Oh, I'm fine," Leonie protested, but even as she spoke a sudden dizziness overwhelmed her, and she clutched at the newel post for support.

"Are you all right?" The older woman rushed toward her, sympathy and recognition glinting in her eyes.

"Yes. It was just the excitement of the storm, I suppose," Leonie said weakly.

She went up to her room and found a calendar. Six weeks had passed since she had last menstruated.

"Of course," she thought drowsily. "Of course." She pressed her hands against her abdomen, strangely content with her secret.

She received only two letters from Jesse during August. Breathlessly, she read the newspapers, devouring and interpreting every scrap of war news. The allies had launched the Aisner-Marne counteroffensive. French, British, and Italian troops massed in strength to reduce the German salients of Marne, Amiens, and Saint-Mihiel. They were joined by eight American divisions. The Arizona First Infantry was deployed at Saint-Mihiel. Leonie listened to the hourly news broadcasts and bought a map of France, which she hid in her drawer after circling the barely discernible town of Saint-Mihiel. She placed the map at the bottom of her suitcase when she packed for her return to Phoenix at summer's end.

"You will always have a home here," her Tucson landlady said, hugging her. "No matter what."

"I know."

It comforted Leonie that the good-hearted woman shared her secret. They were bound together in sororial complicity.

"I'll write to you," she promised.

She would invite her landlady to the wedding. She and Jesse would be married beneath the orange tree in the Lewins' garden. Their fathers would shake hands before the ceremony. Their acknowledged love would nullify their families' grievances. Their marriage canopy would be woven of the boughs of the citron tree, and she would carry a bridal bouquet of white tulips—the flower of her mother's yearnings.

In Phoenix, she went with Joshua each day to the office of the *Arizona Gazette,* which posted the names of American casualties. Her throat tightened and she clutched her brother's arm as they scanned the list together. Always, afterward, she felt faint with relief. Her fears were allayed for another day. Joshua steadied her but she said nothing.

Walking slowly home one afternoon, they met Barbara Stern.

"Leonie." Jesse's sister extended her hand and smiled warmly. "I was just coming to see you. We've had a letter from the Red Cross. Jesse's shoulder was grazed by shrapnel at Saint-Mihiel. It's not at all serious but enough to take him out of action."

"Oh, Barbara." A strange giddiness took hold of her, and she embraced the slender girl—her lover's sister, aunt to the child that grew within her. Their cheeks touched and their tears mingled. Jesse was safe. He would remain safe. The future was theirs. The war would soon be over, and he would be home. She imagined him striding up the street, his lithe, muscular body girdled by his Sam Browne belt, his campaign hat barely covering his thick bright hair.

"Did you know that my father and Isabel Cavalajo will be married next week?" Barbara added. "I think Jesse will be pleased." Barbara had inherited her mother's sweet generosity, her gentle, lilting voice. Her forehead was high and smooth, as Abigail Stern's had been, and she wore her soft brown hair in a sweeping pageboy reminiscent of her mother's coiffure. How tenacious were these family characteristics, the heritage of form and feature, Leonie thought. Her own child would be similarly bonded to her own family and to Jesse's.

Joshua and Barbara shook hands solemnly. They were silent accomplices, secret sharers.

Leonie chatted excitedly as they walked home. Her courses at the university at Tempe would begin the next day.

Joshua wrote in his journal that night, his pen moving slowly across the paper, his brow furrowed. "Leonie is her old self again—or perhaps this is a new Leonie. I wonder. . . ."

A silken cool laced the air during the early days of autumn, as though to compensate for the brutal heat of the summer just past. Leonie walked up the path and paused to admire a hummingbird precariously perched on the silver-leafed branch of an olive tree. Her mother and Natalya Wallach sat in the loggia. They were working on their list of Red Cross supplies, she knew. The wounded were being sent home from the western front, and the beneficent air of Arizona made it a preferred location for recuperation facilities. The two women spoke softly, intimately, as they worked. Perhaps now was the moment to confide in them—to share her secret with her mother and with Natalya, who was so caring and so wise. She felt light-hearted suddenly and hurried toward them as the hummingbird soared skyward and disappeared from view.

Emma smiled welcomingly at her daughter, and Natalya lifted her face to be kissed, but there was no break in the exchange between the two women.

"It's so very sad," Natalya said. "He was the most promising boy I ever taught."

"Who? And what's so sad?" Leonie dropped her book bag and settled back in a wicker chair, surrendering to the heat and to the lassitude that overcame her with increasing frequency during the late afternoon.

"Ah. You've been at the university all day. You haven't heard about Jesse Stern," Emma replied.

A weight rolled across Leonie's heart. Her hands and feet turned ice cold, yet sweat stained her white middy blouse and beaded her forehead.

"What about Jesse Stern?" She asked the question in a voice she did not recognize as her own. Her lover's name was thick on her tongue.

"He's dead," Natalya said wearily. "He died in an army hospital in Amiens."

"No! You heard wrong." Leonie's reply was shrill, riddled with protest and disbelief. "He's fine. He was wounded, but it was just a bullet graze on his shoulder. He's fine, fine!"

"He didn't die of the wound, Leonie," Natalya said. "He died of influenza. An epidemic swept through the hospital there."

"It can't be." She spoke in a whisper now, and her face was frozen into a mask of agony that frightened the older women. Emma's pen clattered to the slate floor, and she looked fearfully at her daughter. Leonie trembled, and her eyes were glazed. She shook her head wildly from side to side. "No," she repeated. "It was not Jesse. No. No."

Emma went to her daughter, her arms outstretched, but Leonie recoiled.

"Don't touch me. No one must touch me." She hugged her abdomen. Her body contained his secret, his treasure, all that remained of his life. "Oh, Jesse, my Jesse." She sank to her knees, tears spilling down her cheeks.

"Leonie—I didn't know. I never knew." Emma knelt beside her, her own eyes moist, her heart twisted.

"We couldn't tell you. How could we tell you? There was too much anger between you and his father. We were afraid." Anger riddled her own voice now. "But now you know— and soon everyone will have to know." Her shoulders shook, and she swayed from side to side.

"Leonie, what do you mean?" Natalya struggled for calm although tears seared her eyes.

"I'm saying that I'm going to have Jesse's baby. At least I'll have that. At least a part of him will live. Oh, Jesse, Jesse." Sobs welled up, breaking free from the dark canyon of her grief and emerging with wild and alien resonance.

"Leonie, you must listen to me." Emma's fingers gripped her daughter's shoulders, willing her to calm, to submission, but her voice was steady, almost enervated.

"You say there is anger between Jesse's father and our family. It is more than anger. Henry Stern hates us—he hates me and my brothers."

"Why?" Leonie's question was dispirited, almost indifferent. Jesse was dead. Nothing else mattered. Not mysterious quarrels that fueled and perpetuated foolish anger. He was dead. Her bright-haired darling. The sweet friend of her childhood. Her gentle lover. He was dead. Still, he had not abandoned her. His child would live. She settled her clasped hands against her abdomen. She was tired, so tired.

"He hates us because he is our half brother, the son of Jacob Coen, my father. And in some twisted and terrible way, he blames us for the sadness of his life, the tragedy of his mother's life," Emma said, struggling yet again to create reason out of the irrational. "Do you understand what that means, Leonie? You and Jesse had the same grandfather."

Leonie stared at her, wide-eyed. "We were cousins, then." She and Jesse had been linked by blood as well as love. Their chimerical closeness had been no accident.

"You were cousins. I should have guessed," Natalya spoke softly, regret wreathing her words. "You understand what that means, Leonie. It is dangerous for first cousins to marry, to have children." She was the patient pedagogue now. "So many things can go wrong. And you're so very young, Leonie. How far along are you?"

Leonie stared at her, eyes brimming, cheeks burning.

"When did you have your last menstrual cycle?" Natalya persisted.

"Late in June." The week before her arrival in Tucson. Her breasts had been tender still when the night-blooming cereus had exploded into luminous blossom. It would not bloom for another year, but she knew now where to find it. She would take their baby to see it. The infant's cheeks would be soft and pale as the moonlit petals—as soft and pale as the tender skin of Jesse's forearms brushed by her lips at the moment of sleep and again at the moment of wakening.

"Two months. It's still early enough," Emma said. "Simon's wife spoke of a doctor in San Francisco—he helped a cousin of Matilda Schiff's. We could leave at once—tomorrow."

"What do you mean?" Leonie cried. She stared at them and drew back. Her grief was a veil behind which Emma and Natalya moved like shivering shadows. Their voices wafted toward her in whispers, husky with a threat and intent she could not comprehend.

"Surely you understand that you cannot have this child," Emma said gently. "It would be dangerous for you, for the baby. You have your whole life ahead of you, Leonie. You'll fall in love again—there will be other children.''

"No! No!" Leonie shrieked with defiance, shouted with sorrow. She held her hands out in a shield, as though to defend herself against the two women who all her life had protected her. Betrayals had compounded that afternoon, too many revelations had thrust themselves upon her. Like a child sorting out pieces of a complex jigsaw puzzle, she struggled to separate out the terrible new truths of her life and of her loss. Emma moved toward her, but with lightning swiftness Leonie ran from the loggia to the stable. Minutes later they heard the staccato clatter of Star's hoofbeats, and they stared at each other in despair and defeat.

"She's a child," Emma said brokenly. "A child."

"Let her be," Natalya said softly as the chime of the bells on Star's reins faded and they saw Leonie gallop through the gate, her long dark hair loose, her riding crop beating at the air. "She must have some time alone, Emma. Give her an hour. Two hours."

"I know." She remembered herself as a young girl seeking solitude along the canals of Amsterdam after Benjamin Mendoza's betrayal. "How could I have been so blind, Natalya?"

"They were very careful."

"Did you ever suspect?"

"I didn't suspect. But somehow I am not surprised," Natalya acknowledged. Once, on a hot spring evening, she had seen Leonie and Jesse walk beneath the aspens on Embarcadero. Twice she had glimpsed them strolling through the Mexican market, talking and laughing.

"If only I had not been so involved in my own problems," Emma said bitterly. Isaac had betrayed her, and together they had betrayed their daughter.

"It was not your fault, Emma," Natalya replied, but she knew that her friend did not believe her.

Together, they waited in the loggia through the afternoon, speaking softly, glancing now and again at their watches. Soon, any moment now, Leonie would be home, exhausted by her grief, ready to listen, to accept their comfort, their advice.

The school bell tolled the end of classes, and Joshua and Samuel arrived home with the Wallach children. They went at once to add new positions to their war map.

"I'll bet there's an armistice by October," Samuel said.

"No. Not before December. There's still Flanders to be settled. And Aleppo and Homs." Joshua swiftly placed pins on the map.

The children stayed indoors, glancing now and again at their mothers, who sat so strangely still in the loggia, their eyes turned southward. Now and again Natalya would rise, pace briefly, and then peer into the distance, but Emma sat immobile, and her sons did not approach her.

At last Natalya phoned the Emporium, and within minutes Isaac, Abner, and Johnny Redbird arrived at the house. They went at once to the loggia, and Joshua watched them from the window. He saw his father blanch and slam his fist down on the table, scattering lists and ledgers. His voice, harsh with anger and disbelief, thundered through the open windows.

"No. It cannot be. How could it have happened? Our Leonie, our darling girl." Leonie was his jewel, his cherished princess, the American daughter whose birth had soothed him against the death of the child killed in Russia. "And how could you have let her go off?" He pointed an accusing finger at Emma. Color flooded her cheeks, and her fingers trembled.

"She needed time alone, Isaac," she said and turned from him. Always, she and Isaac would be caught on an endlessly whirring carousel of guilt and blame, yearning and distrust.

Joshua turned from the window. They were talking about Leonie, he knew. He had heard about Jesse Stern's death that afternoon and had willed himself not to think about it, not to think about what it would do to Leonie.

The slow, lingering sunset of autumn began. Golden filigree trimmed the edges of the huge white clouds and arches of mauve and violet were etched against the cerulean skies. Slowly, the persimmon-colored sun began its descent toward the mountain peaks. Joshua shielded his eyes against its brilliance and went to stand beside his parents.

"We must find her now," he said.

They could wait no longer. The encroaching darkness was their enemy. They knew too well the stories of children who had disappeared into the desert night, lovers swallowed by the darkness, men and women whose horses had returned riderless at dawn.

Abner Wallach and Isaac Lewin rode north to Squaw Peak and the Camelback Mountains. Joshua and Samuel rode east to Four Peaks, where the mountains melted into dry desert yellow. They stopped to ask a Hopi maiden if she had seen a black-haired *gringa* ride by. She shrugged her shoulders and lifted her eyes skyward where a hawk circled with ominous slowness. They understood that even if she had seen Leonie, she would not tell them. The Indian code of honor protected fugitives, and that was how she perceived the girl they sought.

They galloped to the lookout point on South Mountain and trained their binoculars on the landscape below, the rolling expanse of desert laced with arroyos and dry creek beds. How easy it was for a horse to lose its footing in the darkness and plunge into a concealed enclave. They rode on, past the giant saguaro cacti; nightbirds perched on the huge thorny arms of the plants, and their sweet nocturnal singing seemed a mocking threnody to the brothers.

It was Johnny Redbird who rode southward with Emma. He knew the terrain, the secret caves and the red rock formations that rose so intricately and gracefully from the desert floor. He understood the desert silence and knew how to listen for the slightest sound, the flutter of a night hawk's wings, the gentle thud of a cactus fruit falling onto the soft sand. It was he who heard the gentle chime of bells just off the Tempe roadway.

"Listen," he said. The sound was barely discernible, but they sat very still, straining to catch the slightest reverberation.

"There," Johnny whispered and veered his mount slightly eastward. Now the bells sounded with perceptible clarity, and they followed the faint tintinnabulation at a slow trot until a horse's mournful whinny quivered in the air. Star stood silhouetted against the dark sky; she was riderless, and the bells on her reins jangled softly as she pawed at the earth.

"What happened? Where is she? Leonie!" Emma had thought to shout her daughter's name, but her voice emerged in a whisper.

Johnny dismounted and slowly approached the horse.

"Easy, friend. Easy, Star." He took the reins in his hand and motioned Emma to follow him. Star moved slowly forward, leading them to a hidden path carved into the desert bracken. A cave loomed ahead of them, and in the dark cavity of its embrasure, Leonie lay, her eyes closed, her pale blue skirt streaked with crimson ribs of blood. Her skin was camellian white, and her eyes were closed, the thick, tear-matted lashes sweeping across her cheeks. She did not stir, even as they drew nearer and Star whinnied softly.

"Not Leonie," Emma whispered. "Never Leonie." There had been too many deaths. She could not, she would not, submit to another. She pulled her shawl tight about her, as though it might subdue the shudders that ripped through her body.

Johnny Redbird knelt beside Leonie, his head pressed against her chest, his fingers at her wrist. The girl moaned and a tear escaped her lashes and drifted down her cheek. He smiled thinly. The dead did not weep.

"She's all right," he said, and Emma leaned back, faint with relief.

"What happened, Leonie?" he asked gently as her eyes fluttered open.

"I fell." She spoke as though each word were summoned from a distant part of her being. "A jackal on the path frightened Star, broke her gallop. She threw me. She didn't mean to. Of course she didn't mean to." Pain and fatigue thickened her voice.

"Of course she didn't. Star is a good horse. And you are a good girl." He spoke to her as he spoke to his own daughter, beautiful Lonely Star, who pursued solitude as other children pursue friendship.

Leonie moaned softly.

"What is it, darling?" Emma knelt beside her daughter.

"I hurt, Mama. Here. Here." Her hands were on her abdomen, her fingers linked in an instinctive protective gesture. Her eyes closed.

"She's fainted," Johnny said. "We must get her home."

Gently, he propped the unconscious girl in front of him on his saddle, using Emma's blue shawl to secure her to his own body. Slowly, they rode northward to Phoenix.

She had lost the baby. Dr. Lashner's voice was subdued. Still, she was a healthy young woman. She would have other children. He averted his eyes as he spoke to them, aware that Emma and Isaac sat at opposite ends of the long couch.

"What worries me is her lassitude, her strange lack of mobility. I would have anticipated a normal depression—considering." He hesitated over the word. *Considering.* Considering the enormity of her losses—her lover, her unborn child, her innocence—all vanished within the space of a few hours. The doctor turned to the window. He did not want to see the pain that flashed across the parents' faces.

They could not forgive themselves, he knew, for their inability to protect their daughter. Absorbed in their own anger, their own sorrow after Gregory's death, they had not perceived the realities of Leonie's life. ("I should have known. I should have guessed," Emma had said again and again to Natalya. "How could we not have known about her friendship with Jesse through all those years?" Isaac had asked Brother Timothy.)

The doctor touched his bag. He could offer them potions—stimulants and relaxants. But he had no words to ease their regrets, no panacea for the pain of remorse.

"She claims that she has difficulty walking," he continued. "Yet I can find no medical basis for such discomfort as she describes." The technical language of his profession reassured him, and he retreated into a description of the neurological examination he had administered.

"What is your advice?" Isaac asked impatiently.

"My colleagues have found that a change of scene often works wonders in such cases," he replied carefully. "A new landscape. A new environment where she will not be reminded of previous associations. I think it would be advisable for Leonie to leave Phoenix temporarily—at least until she has recuperated, both physically and emotionally."

Emma and Isaac glanced at each other but made no response. Isaac rose from the couch.

"I must get to the Emporium," he said tersely. "Let us discuss it this evening, Emma."

She nodded. Gestures replaced words between them.

He was late in returning that night, but she waited up for him.

"I've decided," she said in the calm and distant tone he knew so well. "Leonie and I will go to California. To San Francisco. It will be best for her."

"Will it?" he asked bitterly, startled at the weariness that descended upon him. "And what of your projects here?"

"I can work with the Red Cross there. The war will be over soon, and there will be a need for recuperation facilities. Besides, it will give us—you and me—time to sort out our feelings." Her tone was cool, but her turquoise eyes glittered with agate brilliance.

"I know my feelings, Emma. I have always known them. From that very first day in Galveston." He closed his eyes and saw her again as he had first seen her, lighting the Sabbath candles, the flames as brilliant as her thick and silken hair. He opened them and saw her in the beauty of her womanhood, the color mounting in her high curved cheeks, her hair coiled into a loose, copper-colored knot in which tendrils of silver glinted.

She did not reply but looked out the window. A nocturnal wind caused the branches of the orange tree to tremble and scrape against the loggia screen. She had planted her tulip bulbs beside the tree, and although their shoots had thrust their way through the earth, no blossoms had formed.

"When will you leave?" Resignation rimmed the question.

"Within a few weeks. I will write to my brothers. You and the boys will come to California for the holidays—Rosh ha-Shanah, Hanukkah."

They were to become two families, then—Emma and Leonie on the coast, he and his sons in the desert city.

"You have it all planned out," he said bitterly.

"Do you think so?" Her voice was faint.

She clutched the back of her chair and willed him to do

battle with her. His sadness pierced her heart. She wondered at his silence and waited breathlessly for his protest. She braced herself in anticipation of his anger. He would insist on coming to California with them. Swiftly, he would cross the room, place a strong hand on her shoulder. He would whirl her about, his fingers cutting into her flesh. But he sat motionless on the divan. His own sorrow paralyzed him. He was powerless to argue with her; he had abrogated that right the night of Gregory's death. He could weigh neither the rightness nor the wrongness of her decision. He knew only that their lives would never be the same, that a new border had been crossed.

Emma remained at the window, her burning cheek pressed against the beveled pane. And because she did not turn, she did not see the tears that glittered with liquid brilliance in Isaac's dark eyes, so lightly flecked with sparklets of gold.

California,
1920

NEATLY SPACED LANTERNS dangled from the fretted wrought-iron cornices and cast their soft light across the intricately patterned slate floor of Simon Coen's terrace. The strains of a Strauss waltz mingled with the laughter and talk of the Coens' guests. Chinese waiters circled the room with trays of champagne cocktails. Simon had stocked his wine cellar well, and prohibition had no effect on his formal dinner parties. A Mexican maid moved quietly across the terrace, collecting the glasses left on the small tables that Thea Coen had thought to set up outside at the last moment. The view of the San Francisco Bay from the Coens' Pacific Heights estate was famous, and couples drifted outside and stared down at the lights that spangled the undulating hills of the city.

It was late spring, but the women shivered against the moist breath of the sea breeze, and their escorts gently tied the scarves and stoles that covered their shoulders. They inhaled the citrus-scented air and speculated as to whether the high-masted sailing ship gliding into the dimly lit port below carried copra from the South Seas, tea from China, or mahogany from the Philippines. Their host could surely tell them, and they were oddly pleased to be the guests of a man who controlled the intricacies of commerce, the mysteries of international transfer and trade. Here, on his terrace, drinking his wine, they themselves were brushed by his power. The laughter of women trilled with pleasure, and the voices of the men were deep and confident, insulated by wealth, cultivated by position. They smiled as they returned to the warmth and brightness of the house and nodded politely to the tall, auburn-haired woman who leaned against the balustrade, an empty glass in her hand.

Emma drew her pale blue stole closer and fingered the turquoise pendant at her throat. Two years had passed since she and Leonie had arrived in San Francisco and moved into the house on Lombard Street that her brothers had rented for them. Within weeks of her arrival she had opened a small boutique on Stockton Street. "The Lewin Link," she called it, and emphasized that it offered the same merchandise available in the accessories department of the Emporium but catered to customers who wanted a more intimate ambience. The wealthy matrons of San Francisco craved the deference of salesclerks who knew their names and seated them in tufted velvet chairs for the selection of their scarves and pins. (In Phoenix, Isaac read the description of her enterprise with a bitter smile of approval, and arranged for a similar shop. As always, Emma had her finger on the pulse of the market.)

With equal swiftness she had been caught up in the social whirl of San Francisco. She was familiar now with the round of parties and dances, the concerts and receptions that absorbed her brothers and sister-in-law. The Coens were an integral part of the gilded circle of San Francisco Jewry, and Leonie and Emma had been welcomed and accepted. They had spent the requisite weekends at the San Rafael estates of the Seligmans and the Slosses. Emma had watched tennis players in immaculate whites move gracefully across the red clay courts at the Gerstle summer palace. Leonie, who sat beside her, had been invited to play, but always she pointed apologetically to her cane, and soon she declined all invitations, preferring to remain at the Lombard Street house. Emma went alone to the Lilienthal picnic and ate a gourmet lunch beneath towering evergreens. The fragrant green needles dropped softly onto the white linen cloths that covered the wooden tables. She tried not to think about Leonie, who complained still about the mysterious pains that gripped her legs, although the most eminent physicians in the city could offer no medical explanation.

She needs time, Emma had told herself fiercely. She listened carefully to her brother Emil's psychiatrist friend Franz Eisenmann, who irritated a hostess at a dinner party by speaking too long and too seriously about his work. Sorrow and loss, the bearded doctor had explained, were not unlike gaping wounds that radiated pain until they closed and healed. Strangely, his words had comforted Emma, offered her hope.

"Leonie grows stronger," she wrote to Natalya Wallach, whose weekly letters kept her informed of events in Phoenix. Isaac and the boys were well, but they spoke often of her and Leonie, and Samuel especially seemed depressed each Friday evening when he watched Natalya light and bless the Sabbath candles. Isabel Cavalajo Stern had suffered a miscarriage that winter, but she was pregnant again. Johnny Redbird's daughter had married, and Isaac had accompanied the Wallachs to the mesa for the nuptial feast and dances.

"We urged him to go," Natalya had written. "But perhaps we were wrong to do so. He seemed so sad and lonely. He and the boys miss you very much, Emma—you and Leonie. Perhaps you will think of returning to Phoenix soon."

Emma had read and reread her friend's letter. Natalya had written with her usual tact and caution, and yet she could not mask her concern. Emma imagined Isaac standing at the edge of a circle of spectators as the Indians whirled through their joyous dances. He would look up at the starlit skies, she knew, and she remembered suddenly how on their journey west to Phoenix they had looked skyward at the first hint of darkness, searching together for the evening star. She did not doubt Natalya's words. Isaac's loneliness matched her own.

Despite the gaiety of San Francisco society, the frenetic pace of life in the Bay City, solitude clung to her, weighted her steps, stirred her to wistful reverie. Often she awakened in the night and felt herself a woman bereft in her empty bed. She acknowledged then, in the desolate darkness, that she missed her husband's presence—the oddly light touch of his hand, the thoughtful cadence of his voice, the intensity of his gaze. And yet she could not return to his home—at least, she thought bitterly, until he understood why she had left and until Leonie was well again. She did not want loneliness to be her tether. She waited now, as years before she had waited in London, for something to happen that would shape her decision, forge her understanding. Then she had been alone. Now she had her family to consider. Leonie. Joshua. Samuel. And Isaac. Always Isaac.

She swayed now to the music that drifted out to the terrace.

A Viennese waltz. She had danced with Isaac to that same music on the Galveston green the night of the Juneteenth celebration. He had dizzied her then with his grace and strength as they whirled to the blended strains of the fiddler and the accordionist while poor little Miriam watched from a bench. There had been magic between them that night, she remembered, but even then she had feared and fought its spell. And yet she had felt a nascent happiness as they had walked back to the boarding house together, Isaac carrying Miriam, the air soft and scented with the fragrance of the newly blossomed oleander.

Odd that she should think of Miriam now. She had not seen or heard about the Weinglasses for many years, yet only a few days earlier a well-dressed woman had rushed up to her as she stood at the glove counter of I. Magnin and embraced her.

"Emma, is it really you?" The voice and accent had been unmistakable. Basha Weinglass, the exhausted immigrant woman who had peeled potatoes in Emma's Galveston kitchen and dreamed of a cure for her crippled child, had been transformed into a prosperous California matron. She and Avrum owned a small cannery near Monterey, and the citrus marmalades she had learned to prepare in Emma's kitchen were now manufactured in the family's small factory. "California Gold," she called her preserves, and she promised to send a case to Emma.

"Others searched for gold beneath the ground," she said. "We lifted our eyes and found it in the trees."

She and Avrum had two daughters, strong, healthy girls, but still, she confessed, fingering a pair of soft kid gloves, she often dreamed of Miriam. A sudden Monterey storm reminded her still of the terrible rain that had brought death to Galveston. She trembled at the sound of thunder, and each summer she cautioned her daughters against swimming in the creek and growing too tired; polio haunted the lives of children, but her daughters laughed when she asked them to wear an amulet of garlic about their necks. They were American girls, impatient with the superstition of the old country. Basha smiled, at once proud and fearful.

"We always remember, Avrum and I, how good you and

Isaac were to our Miriam. We were so glad when we saw the advertisements for the Emporium. It is good to know that you have found a life together. You must come to see us."

"We will," Emma promised. She did not tell her old friend that Isaac and her sons visited San Francisco only twice a year—during Passover week and the celebration of the Jewish new year, Rosh ha-Shanah. Isaac was ill at ease in San Francisco. He disliked the austere, formal services at Temple Emanuel where a choir sang and the rabbi wore an academic gown and spoke in sonorous tones, his podium at a remove from the elegantly crafted pews of his congregation. He disapproved of the Christmas trees that were routinely placed in the living rooms of Jewish homes.

"It's not a religious custom," Thea Coen, Simon's wife, patiently explained. "Christmas is an American holiday." She could not understand how Isaac could question her Jewish commitment. She sat on the board of every Jewish charity and contributed generously to every Jewish cause.

"Your sister-in-law confuses her checkbook and her prayerbook," Isaac had said sourly. "She thinks her children will remain Jewish because she wrote a check to the Eureka Benevolent Society."

Thea had given a small family dinner during his last visit from Phoenix, and afterward he and Emma had sat outside on this terrace and looked down at the lights of the bay. The night was cool and she had worn a dress of light white wool. When a sudden breeze blew, he draped his jacket over her shoulders, his hand resting briefly on her neck. She did not stir but lifted her eyes to study the sky. Gossamer clouds drifted across the new darkness and danced westward toward the sliver of silver, the waning autumnal moon.

"Do you remember how we sat on the porch of the boarding house in Galveston and watched the night skies?" he asked.

"I remember." She reached up and took his hand. His fingers closed against her own.

"Emma, come home. Come back to Phoenix."

She stiffened, closed her eyes. The lonely strains of the opening movement of the Mendelssohn violin concerto wafted out to the terrace. Simon's eldest daughter played with a rare sensitivity that surprised them all. They had never been a musical family.

"What do you do in the evenings at home, Isaac?" she asked.

"I work. I read. I try to help the boys with their homework. And when the house grows too quiet and the hours grow too long, I ride into the desert."

"Alone?"

He loosed her hand then and strode over to the balustrade.

"Alone, Emma," he said harshly, not facing her. "There is no other woman. I have learned not to surrender to loneliness."

She stood and moved toward him. Lightly, she touched his arm. He wheeled about and drew her to him, his embrace crushing and frenzied, his lips bruising against hers.

"I need you," he said, his voice trembling. Now his arms encased her shoulders and he lifted her hair, buried his face in its fiery folds. "Come home, Emma. Come home." Plea and demand commingled. She stood very still. The slightest movement might betray her yearning.

"When Leonie is stronger," she said at last. *And when I am stronger,* she thought to add, but remained silent. He released her then and they stood together, leaning across the fretted iron railing as the clouds cleared and revealed the glinting stars.

He had left for Phoenix the next day, and his leavetaking had melded hope and sadness. They approached a time of decision.

What was he doing now? she wondered, and imagined him reading alone in the loggia or perhaps riding out to the desert. He would not have enjoyed this party. Of that she was certain. Isaac was impatient with the social life of Pacific Heights and Nob Hill, the glittering parties of Van Ness Avenue. Her sons were happier riding into the desert on their horses than they were playing tennis with their cousins at San Rafael and Atherton. They grew so rapidly now. Joshua was as tall as Isaac, and Samuel was plunged into a moody, brooding adolescence. Sometimes she feared that they would become strangers to her. She shivered at the thought.

"Isn't it too cool for you out here, Emma?"

Franz Eisenmann stood beside her. Absorbed in troubled reverie, she had not heard him walk across the terrace. He pulled at the starched white collar of his dress shirt and stroked his chin absently.

"You miss your beard," she said, smiling.

"Yes, I suppose I do," he admitted. "Still, I am not sorry that I shaved it off. It occurred to me that I had been hiding behind it. You see, Emma, I am as merciless with myself as I am with my patients."

She studied the young man's face gravely. The absence of the beard made her more aware of the sensual fullness of his lips, the soft curve of his chin. She perceived an almost boyish vulnerability she had not noticed before.

"Perhaps you are right," she said. "One day you will have to tell me how you reached such a conclusion."

"That is a professional secret," he replied. "Surgeons do not reveal their mysteries. Why should psychiatrists?"

"The secrets of surgeons do not interest me as much as those of psychiatrists," she said, and now all teasing laughter left her voice. She turned to him and he saw that her face was strained and pale. Her fingers moved restlessly, from the turquoise pendant at her neck to a vagrant curl that had escaped the severity of her chignon. "My brother Emil tells me that you have the power to cure the sickness of the soul."

"Emil flatters me," he said bitterly. He had arrived late at the Coens' party because he had been delayed in Palo Alto. He had been called to the mortuary to sign the death certificate of a Stanford University medical student who had killed himself by ingesting cyanide. The young man had visited Franz in a state of depression only the week before, yet none of Franz's reassurances had reassured him. The scent of bitter almond had clung to the youth's lifeless lips, and his open staring eyes were glazed still with the terror that Franz had been unable to penetrate.

"Still, you have had success?" Emma's question was urgent. Franz wished that he had brought a drink out to the terrace with him. He had anticipated, even craved, her question, for months as his friendship with the family intensified; it was his own answer that he could not predict.

"Some limited success," he said cautiously at last. "Psychoanalysis is a very new study, Emma. We who practice it are like wanderers in the dark, searching for a hint of light.''

"You disappoint me," she said, and her voice was very low. "You must know how worried I am about Leonie."

"Yes. She is not here this evening?"

"No. She said that her legs were too painful. I see her slipping away, withdrawing more and more. Will you help her, Franz? Will you try?" Her voice was very low. She was a woman who was unaccustomed to asking for favors, yet he discerned the plea implicit in her request. She had, he knew, consulted neurologists and diagnosticians, adhered to a diet designed by a nutritionist at Stanford, an exercise therapy program developed by a physical therapist at Berkeley. He was her last hope.

"It is not usual in my field to accept one's friend as a patient," he said.

"Then you must treat her as your friend," Emma replied. "Leonie herself would not seek out a doctor, but she likes you. She will speak with you. Will you come to see her tomorrow?"

He hesitated then, but she stared hard at him, her eyes beryl bright, willing his consent.

"I will," he promised.

Emma smiled then and linked her arm through his. Her brother's friend would help her; his soft voice would coax Leonie out of the shadows of her reveries and soothe the pain that imprisoned her in a vanished past.

"Thank you. And now I think we are being summoned into dinner, and you may be sure that it will be a splendid meal. Simon applies my husband's merchandising rules to his philanthropic evenings. Customers who are not too hot and not too thirsty reach more easily for their checkbooks. And Simon and Thea know that good food and good drink mean generous contributions to the Huntington Park Jewish Orphans Home," she said lightly. Her mood had lifted, and she felt an unfamiliar gaiety, a sudden surge of optimism.

Franz smiled. "Ah, yes. Tonight we are here on behalf of Jewish orphans. It grows difficult for me to remember for which cause I so dutifully drink Lafitte Rothschild and eat filet mignon. Two weeks ago I went to a dance on Nob Hill which I thought was in support of the Hebrew Consumptive Relief Association and discovered that I was inviting partners to waltz to benefit the Kaspare Cohn Hospital,'' he said wryly.

Emma nodded in mock sympathy. "Yes. I confused my invitations to the Fleishaker benefit with the San Francisco Symphony, and the Rosenwald tea with the Pacific Musical Society. Really, life was much simpler in Phoenix.''

''I cannot say as much for Vienna,'' Franz said, and he stared down at the flickering bay lights.

His native city had assumed a dreamlike quality for him, and often now he had difficulty recalling the winding street where his parents' dark stone mansion stood. His own room had been isolated from his parents' suite by a long, dimly lit corridor, and his childhood had been grimly surpervised by a *Kinderfräulein* who had taken the children to see their parents before dinner each evening. His mother's lips then had been dry against his brow, his father's fingers bone-crushing against his own.

Franz's father was a grain broker who dutifully sent a percentage of his income, over and above his annual taxes, to a fund maintained by the emperor's viceroy for charitable distribution. He sent a smaller amount to the Jewish Communal Council with the understanding that it be used to settle the Jews from Galicia, Hungary, and Bukovina at a distance from the city limits of Vienna. History and instinct had taught him that Jews must not become too numerous or too noticeable. Twice a year, on Rosh ha-Shanah and on Yom Kippur, he went to the City Temple on Seittenstettengasse. It was important, he instructed his children, that the Jews be observed to be faithful to their tradition.

He wrote a check each year to the Viennese Zionist Union. He himself had no desire to emigrate to a Jewish homeland, but he did not object if other Jews aspired to such a dream, as long as they were quiet and circumspect in their aspirations. He was a cautious and tolerant man, and he relied heavily on the caution and tolerance of others. But never did he overestimate their capacity for such caution, such tolerance.

He had wanted Franz to join him in the grain business, but

he did not object when his youngest son chose to study medicine and decided to specialize in neurology. Still, he was uneasy when Franz spoke of the work of another Viennese physician, Professor Sigmund Freud. The grain merchant knew little about medicine, but he had heard Freud discussed disparagingly by a Gentile business acquaintance who had taken his son to him for the treatment of a nervous disorder that resulted in a persistent nausea. The doctor had refused to administer pills and potions but had wanted the child to talk about his illness. What did the boy think about before he became nauseated? What dreams did he have before an attack of vomiting? The boy's father had been indignant. The Jewish doctor was in need of a doctor himself, to expect people to pay for a cure that consisted of talk, not of therapeutic medicine.

The Jewish doctor. The words had a minatory effect on the grain broker, stirring up ancient fears. Franz went to Sigmund Freud's lectures, consulted with him. It was possible that such an affiliation could place the family in jeopardy. A week later he read in the *Wiener Neue Freie Presse* that Freud had been denied an appointment at the university, that his theories were disparaged.

The grain broker summoned Franz and ordered him to dissociate himself from Freud. The father and son, who had always spoken politely to each other, who had slept in different wings of the large house, quarreled briefly and bitterly. Franz would not abandon his study of psychoanalysis. His father might understand wheat or barley, but he had no comprehension of psychiatry or neurology. The father then would abandon his son. He might not understand psychiatry or neurology, but he understood the currents of anti-Semitism. It did not befit Jews to attract unfavorable attention or controversy to themselves. Franz countered that Vienna was not ready for Freud's revolutionary theory of psychoanalysis; it was draped in the dark shadows of its arcane traditions, its time-nourished prejudices.

"If our world is not good enough for you, then find a new world," the father had thundered.

A new world. The New World. America beyond the sea. Romantic Franz had long been intrigued by tales of America and by its literature. He had read Bret Harte and Mark Twain and had just completed Robert Louis Stevenson's *Silverado Essays*. Stevenson wrote of the American state of California where adventurous men dredged gold from rushing Sierra streams, and scraped at veins of silver encrusted in the sinews of mountains. Such men stood upon bluffs that towered above the Pacific Ocean and built cities in gentle valleys with melodious Spanish names. There were Jews among them who did not share his father's fear of the Gentile's notice and derision. They had come to the great American West as pioneers, at one with other pioneers, to forge new lives in a new land. Men who dared to confront a new frontier would not be frightened of a science that dared to cross the mysterious borders of the mind and plunge into the depths of long-buried memories.

He spoke to Freud of going to America. His mentor nodded thoughtfully.

"I think that psychoanalysis will have an excellent future in America. It is an adventurous science for an adventurous people."

Franz booked passage. He sailed into the Golden Gate the day that Emperor Franz Joseph died, and because, like many men of science, he had an almost mystical belief in symbolism, he took that as a sign. An old, decaying order had passed, and a new world was in the birthing.

He had a modest consulting room on Telegraph Hill and served on the staff of the university medical school. He had met Emil Coen at a B'nai B'rith meeting and the two introspective, intellectual men had become friends. Franz had been a guest at the dinner party that Emil gave to welcome Emma and Leonie to San Francisco. He and Emma had established an immediate rapport.

He recognized the solemnity of her gaze, the low, almost melancholic tenor of her voice, yet he sensed her strength; he intuited that joy lay coiled within her, ready to spring free at the magic touch of a secret lever. She was a survivor. Even her melancholy, so carefully controlled, served as a protective shield. He was concerned about Emma, but he did not fear for her.

But Leonie had at once troubled and intrigued him. Her

deep-set eyes were shadowed with the grief of irrevocable loss, and it seemed to him that when he held her fingers to his lips, he felt pain course through her lucent flesh. She leaned heavily upon a wooden cane, and her voice was the whisper of a shy and frightened schoolgirl. She seldom came to social functions, but when he visited the Lombard Street house, she sat beside him, always wearing the demure, wide-sashed dresses she favored, her hands clasped on her lap. He had thought a great deal about Leonie and had even written a letter describing her to Sigmund Freud in Vienna. Tomorrow, then, he could begin to help her.

"Shall we go in?" he asked Emma, and together they walked through the French doors to their separate tables.

The Coens' dining room was brilliantly lit. The long table was covered with a white damask cloth, and crystal bowls filled with California fuchsia were ranged across its center. Franz found his placecard first. He was seated between two of Levi Strauss's nieces, the pink-cheeked Stern sisters, whose cheeks grew even pinker when he smiled at them. Emma's own place was at the other end of the table, between Jessica Peixotto and a tall, silver-haired man whom she did not recognize. Jessica, a university professor whose family had come from Holland, smiled affectionately at Emma, and her companion rose and pulled her chair out.

"Good evening, Mrs. Lewin," he said, and she looked at him curiously as she took her seat. "You don't remember me, do you? Of course, I should be surprised and flattered if you did. We only met once, and that was a very long time ago."

He spoke with a clipped British accent. His features were angular, giving his face a hawklike cast. He looked vaguely familiar, and she searched her memory. Surely she met him during her years in England. There had always been visitors at her Anspacher cousins', handsome, well-spoken young men with brilliant futures, whom she knew had been invited expressly to meet her and to whom she was polite and indifferent. She was recovering then from her parents' deaths, from Benjamin Mendoza's betrayal, and her life was in abeyance. She had waited then, in London, as it seemed she waited now, in San Francisco, for something to happen, to speed her recovery, her decision.

"I assume it was in London, but I'm afraid I can't recall when or where," she said apologetically. She noticed now that his widely set eyes were obsidian gray in color and fringed by short, straight dark lashes. She thought it strangely comical that his lashes had not silvered with the silken luster of his hair.

"We met twenty years ago at a dinner party at the Rothschilds'. Of course you would not recall me when the other guests formed such a distinguished assemblage. Jacob Schiff and Israel Zangwill were there, I recall, and my own mentor, Sir Ernst Cassel."

She stared hard at him and remembered suddenly, with startling clarity, that he had sat across the table from her and that his thick hair, black as night then, had fallen across his forehead as he bent his head to speak with Theresa Schiff.

"You are Philip Sasson," she said and recalled that her cousin Greta had spoken highly of the Sephardic Jew who had apprenticed himself to Sir Ernst and had become an international expert on transportation systems. His name had often appeared in the clippings from The Anglo Jewish press that Greta enclosed in her letters. He had married a childhood sweetheart, she recalled, and during the war he had been named to a royal commission on troop transports. There had been speculation about a knighthood, a cabinet appointment.

"Ah, you do remember." He was pleased, and he flashed her a smile of almost boyish vanity.

"I do. Perhaps because I remember that dinner party so well. In a way, it changed the course of my life."

"I find that difficult to believe." He looked at her gravely, appraisingly. "I would guess that you are a woman who has always charted her own course."

"All right," she conceded. "Let us say then that the conversation at that dinner party gave me some navigational insights. It was that night that I decided to migrate to the American West."

"A decision you don't regret, I assume?"

She hesitated for the briefest of moments and felt his gaze upon her, at once doubting and strangely insolent.

"No, I don't regret it," she said and turned to Jessica Peixotto, who was speaking quietly to Isidor Magnin about the economic development of the West. The department store magnate listened respectfully. Jessica, after all, had just been named a full professor of economics at the University of California at Berkeley, the first woman to achieve that rank. He spoke a few words of Dutch, and Emma and Jessica laughed.

"Do you think it is by chance that your sister-in-law seats Dutch compatriots together at her dinner parties?" Jessica whispered to Emma as Isidor Magnin turned his attention to Philip Sasson. He wondered what the English transportation expert thought about the possibility of these new large airplanes actually becoming conveyors of merchandise.

"Hardly," Emma replied. "But I am glad she did."

She smiled at Jessica, and turned to greet Thea, who circled her table now, elegant in her black velvet gown and the long pearls Simon had given her at the birth of their son Jacob. Thea glowed with the pride of the successful hostess. Still she glanced anxiously at the table, checking the crystal and the silver, concerned that the gold-trimmed china might be just a bit ostentatious.

"Is everything all right?" she asked Emma.

"Perfect," Emma replied.

Her sister-in-law needed reassurance, she knew. Thea's father had been a tailor in New York, an immigrant from Posen, struggling over a cutting table in a basement factory when an advertisement in the Yiddish newspaper caught his eye. The California Emigration Society offered passage in a clipper ship for one hundred dollars per adult. Fortunes awaited the traveler at journey's end. The tailor had managed to save a few hundred dollars, but he saw no fortune awaiting him on the crowded streets of the Lower East Side. He booked passage. He had endured one ocean voyage, and he would survive another. During the long voyage to the Panamanian port of Chagres, he dreamed of gold. Often there was a metallic taste in his mouth when he awakened. He had dreamed of biting down on the glittering metal, rolling it about on his tongue. Chagres was a cesspool, he told his children years later. In Chagres he ceased to dream of gold and fantasized instead about a clean sheet and drinking water that was not rimmed with green slime. In Chagres the Jewish emigrants searched each other out. They needed a minyan, a prayer quorum, to bury a shoemaker from Vilna who had died of malaria in a reed hut. The Indians stared at the Jews, who donned strangely fringed serapes to pray and inclined their covered heads to the east.

Solomon Levy, Thea's father, traveled by canoe, foot and mule across the isthmus. Mosquitoes darkened the air, and crudely marked graves lined the rutted trail that the Spaniards had built to transport the gold of Peru to the Atlantic and then to Europe. At last he reached the town of Panama and the sailing ship that carried him to harbor in San Francisco. He had waded ashore, weaving his way through the hulls of sailing ships sinking into the beachhead.

Weak with malaria, he acknowledged that he could not undertake the arduous life of a prospector. He no longer dreamed of gold but hoisted a tent and opened a store, using his own possessions as his only stock. The tent store had become one of San Francisco's leading haberdasheries, part of the mythology of early San Francisco. Her family's early poverty frightened and embarrassed Thea. Even now she could not confront it. Often she spoke of her father's experience in lofty terms—it was an early California venture in quality men's fashion, she would say in a tight, small voice. She spoke of her father's first store now as the Chinese waiters served the salad.

"It was primitive, of course, but then Daddy was a pioneer. They were all pioneers then—the Zechendorfs and the Guggenheims, the Sanfords, the Hopkinses, the Huntingtons."

Deftly, she blended the names of the founding Gentile families with those of the Jewish argonauts. They had, after all, built the city together. Together they had fought its fires, endured the devastation of its earthquake and united to rebuild, Jew and Gentile in joint effort.

"But don't you find that that sense of ecumenical camaraderie has somewhat diminished?" Philip Sasson asked, his voice raised so that it traveled the length of the long table.

The guests, arrested by his accent as well as the audacity of his question, turned to him, their salad forks poised. Emma felt a stirring of irritation. He was baiting them, of course, with typical English sangfroid.

"I do not think so," Simon Coen said. "I serve on the Stanford University Board of Governors with Mr. Hearst and Mr. Hopkins. Jews are on the board of the San Francisco Symphony, the art museum. There has never been any question of our acceptance."

"Of course that business with the Bohemian Club was unfortunate for you," Philip Sasson persisted.

An embarrassed silence fell across the table, too swiftly followed by sudden chatter, rapid changes of topic, and the clatter of silverware. Young Walter Zeckendorf spilled his water and smiled apologetically at the Chinese waiter who hurried to spread a dry linen square across the offending spot. The Jews of San Francisco did not like to be reminded that the Bohemian Club, which had been organized by intellectuals and artists, including many Jews, had adopted an unwritten policy that systematically excluded Jews. They preferred not to discuss the Burlingame Country Club and the Pacific Union, where they knew they were unwelcome. They had, of course, organized their own clubs, the Beresford and the Concordia, the Alta and the Argonaut; there was the Philomath Society for the women and the B'nai B'rith, which offered intellectual forums. Still, their exclusion from the clubs pained them. It was a grim reminder that the encroaching shadow of anti-Semitism, which had caused many of them to leave Europe, had tenaciously followed them to the beautiful new city they had built in sun-bounded California.

"Of course," Emil, who sat opposite Emma, said softly, "one can't compare being excluded from the Bohemian Club's annual picnic on Russian Hill to a pogrom in Kishinev."

She nodded. "Of course not. The English simply do not understand America. By the way, how does Simon know Philip Sasson?"

"We are working together on some new shipping routes—possible trade exchanges with Australia," Emil replied. "The war in Europe taught us that we must explore new commercial routes. We don't want to be caught in another Atlantic blockade. And Philip Sasson has new ideas, new insights. A fascinating personality."

"And so handsome," Jessica Peixotto said. Like many academic women, she had a special awareness of attractiveness and sensuality.

"Jessica," Emma said reprovingly and turned back to Emil. "Surely, there won't be another world war, Emil." The suggestion was preposterous. They had seen the devastation and terror of modern warfare, and they were just beginning to recover from the war that had been fought to end all wars.

"We hope not," Emil said gravely. "But we must be prepared."

Emma tried not to think of her brother's words as the guests adjourned to the living room after dinner for the lantern slide show. Dutifully they marveled at the beauty of the wide-eyed orphans and the care given them at the orphanage. The municipal authorities would never have the burden of caring for Jewish orphans or Jewish destitute. The men pressed checks into Simon's hand as they left, and the women spoke softly to each other about other benefits.

Philanthropy united the Jews of San Francisco. Ancient teachings, osmotically absorbed, latent memories that perhaps haunted cryptic dreams, impelled their generosity, engaged their commitment. They ignored the dietary laws, seldom visited the synagogue, adorned their homes with Christmas decorations and gathered for Easter dinners, yet they were vigorous on behalf of Jewish causes. They were a congregation of the privileged, and they assumed the obligations of that privilege.

Emma nodded to departing guests. Young Mrs. Belasco, whose husband had connections with the theater, was organizing a dramatic evening to benefit the Ladies United Hebrew Benevolent Society. Mrs. Sloss had offered the specially designed small theater on her San Rafael estate. Could Emma's "Lewin Link" contribute a raffle prize and could her lovely daughter be persuaded to be on the committee? They all looked forward to seeing more of Leonie. Such a delicately beautiful girl. Was she feeling better?

"Yes," Emma said, flustered. "We hope so, and we will try to come."

Philip Sasson prepared to take his leave and stood behind her, twirling his hat. His proximity made her oddly uncomfortable, and she scanned the room in search of Simon and Thea. She was weary suddenly and anxious to return to Leonie. But the Englishman stepped up to her.

"May I also claim a favor?" he asked. "I wonder if you might share your knowledge of San Francisco with me? Your brothers promised to tour with me tomorrow, but they are overwhelmed by a sudden press of business. Could you spare me a few hours in the afternoon?"

She looked up at him, angered by the presumption of his invitation, by his arrogance in proffering it in public. She was prepared to refuse him, politely, coldly, but Thea came up just then, pink-cheeked and exuberant at the success of her party. Simon had whispered to her that they had raised more than ten thousand dollars.

"What a good idea. How clever of you to think of it, Mr. Sasson, and I do want to thank you for your generous contribution. Emma, Simon would be so relieved to know that our guest is in good hands. I had planned to escort him myself, but then I remembered that I had to see to the opening of the house in Atherton. And perhaps Leonie could join you. It would do her a world of good."

"No, Leonie has an appointment tomorrow," Emma said, and she smiled at Franz Eisenmann, who waited patiently to say goodbye to Simon and Thea. He nodded and again lifted his hand to his chin as though to stroke the vanished beard.

"I will be glad to accompany you, Mr. Sasson."

"I look forward to it, Mrs. Lewin."

She wondered if she imagined the teasing edge in his voice, the flintlike glitter of his gray-eyed gaze.

"But why does Franz want to see me alone, Mama?" Leonie asked. As always, she wore a simple white dress, and her black hair was braided like a schoolgirl's in a single thick plait that trailed to her waist.

She leaned back in the paisley chaise longue that Emma had placed at the bay window of the Lombard Street house, and studied the beds of geranium plants, the bright-blossomed heliotropes so carefully cultivated by their pigtailed Chinese gardener. She felt better lying in the chaise, she said, and she spent most of her time sitting at the window reading the books of poetry she had brought with her from Phoenix. Some of the books, Emma knew, were from Jesse Stern's library. Barbara had brought them to Leonie before they left Phoenix.

"My brother would have wanted you to have them," the girl had said softly, and Emma had wondered if Henry Stern knew of his daughter's errand.

"Franz wants to talk with you. He is a wise man, Leonie. He understands a great deal," Emma said. Her words were awkward, she knew, clumsied by all that she could not say. "Besides, he is a friend," she added.

Leonie opened her book. Edgar Allan Poe. "Annabel Lee." The first poem Jesse had read to her. Her lips moved soundlessly.

"You'll see him, then?" Emma persisted.

"I'll see him." Her voice was flat. Always, she had been the good girl, the quiescent child, doing as her parents wished. She had served as a buffer against their unarticulated angers, their constrained silences, all the while living her own secret life. Now it no longer mattered. She would agree because there was no point in disagreeing. Besides, she liked Franz Eisenmann. His voice was always gentle, and he knew how to sit very still and listen closely when others spoke. He often walked alone, he had told her, and that summer he had camped alone at Lake Temescal, in the hills behind Oakland. Jesse, too, had known how to listen and had understood the mysterious sweetness of solitude.

Emma answered the door herself when Franz rang.

"She'll see you," she said, taking his hat and the light fawn coat that he wore against the chill of early spring.

"I'm glad. But Emma, I hold out no promises. We can only try."

"That is all I ask."

"I know."

He followed her then to the front room. Leonie looked up. "Good afternoon, Franz," she said dutifully, politely.

"Good afternoon, Leonie." He pulled a chair up beside her so that the light streaming through the window encased them both in a cornucopia of radiance.

Emma left the door slightly ajar. She would wait for Philip Sasson on the porch. As she adjusted her wide-brimmed hat, she heard Franz's voice, gentle, probing.

"Will you tell me something, Leonie? Why do you so often dress in white? When I think of white I think of the first snows of winter as they covered the streets of Vienna, or perhaps the foam that crests the waves of the ocean, or perhaps the small bouquets of babies'-breath that my sisters put in their baskets when we went on our woodland walks. What do you think of when you think of white, Leonie?"

Leonie's voice rose and fell in the singsong lilt of a somnolent child. "Sand is white," she said, "and wedding gowns are white. Clouds, primroses, and the desert flower—the cereus that blooms at night . . ."

Emma left the house and stood trembling on the porch. Yet she forced herself to smile as Philip Sasson's chauffeured car pulled up. Sternly, she willed herself to calm. She was seeing the tall Englishman as a favor to her brothers. She would spend two hours with him and then plead other engagements, an appointment with a buyer at "The Lewin Link."

Philip Sasson's air of superiority irritated her. His questions were too piercing, his gaze too penetrating. She would give him a dutiful tour of the city's landmarks, guide him through the cavernous, formal sanctuary at Temple Emanuel, perhaps take him up to the Coit Tower on Telegraph Hill, and then leave him, her duty done. She had not seen him for two decades. She would, in all probability, never see him again.

Philip Sasson plucked a sprig of heliotrope as he approached and held it out to her.

"The day is so beautiful," he said. "Would you mind if we walked?"

She hesitated, and before she could reply he waved his soft gray fedora and the chauffeur drove away. He did not require words to issue orders. He expected his slightest gesture to be understood and obeyed. Clearly, from childhood on, he had felt a sense of entitlement. Elegant clothing, luxurious home, obedient servants, and acquiescent women were implicit in his birthright. Still, she thought, birthrights were often violate, as her own had been.

Wordlessly, she fell into step beside him and they walked north through the bright sunlight, up sloping hillsides, to Fisherman's Wharf. She grew breathless, and once, as they negotiated a steep curve, he placed his hand on her waist to help her up the incline. Her face grew hot at the tensile strength of his fingers, and she hurried ahead as they reached the hill's peak.

They paused at the foot of Taylor Street and watched the brightly painted boats of the crab fishermen bob up and down in the clear bay waters. A high-masted trawler from the sardine fleet was moored amid the square-sailed junks of the Chinese shrimp fishermen. Topaz-skinned Mexicans in bright serapes held their baskets out to the blue-gowned, pigtailed fishermen and carefully counted out their coins in payment.

Gulls swooped down to the lagoon and perched on the bows of the colorful Italian fishing boats, rigged with the triangular lantern sails that reminded her of the Gulf of Genoa and the Bay of Naples, her father's favorite summer retreats.

As though plucking the words from her mind, Philip Sasson spoke.

"They make me think of our family holidays near Naples. We often went to Italy in the summer when I was a child."

"My father was partial to Genoa," Emma said wistfully, spirited briefly back to the distant summers the Coen family of Amsterdam had spent on the Italian shore. What had Analiese Deken told her sons to explain Jacob Coen's long absences? she wondered suddenly. And what did Joshua and Samuel understand of her own long absence from Phoenix? She and Isaac had explained their separation to their sons, choosing their words carefully. It was for Leonie's sake, they had told the boys, their eyes meeting as they spoke, their gaze acknowledging the truths they dared not speak. The thought, unbidden but invasive, saddened her now.

But Philip Sasson continued to speak of Italy, of the

beaches he loved, of the synagogue of gold he had visited once in Florence. She had been there too, and interrupted with memories of her own. His words resurrected her childhood, and they laughed as they strolled along the wharf and recalled the formal breakfasts in the gardens of elegant hotels, the remonstrances of parents and governesses.

"I remember the waiters who had to wear starched collars and morning coats on the hottest days. The poor boys from Palermo looked like bridegrooms in those oversized dress suits. And my brothers and I wore sailor suits with starched collars that scratched our necks. How we envied the barefoot beggar boys."

"And I remember how my hair was twisted into tight curls each morning by Fräulein," she said.

"Was your hair as beautiful then as it is now?" he asked. Deftly he removed her wide-brimmed hat and lightly touched her soft bright hair. She blushed and took the hat from him, yet she did not replace it but dangled it carelessly as they walked on.

They passed old men who sat cross-legged on the docks and smoked intricately carved pipes as they mended huge sea-scarred nets with long wooden needles. Fishermen, tanned by the sun and the wind, called loudly to each other as they strode down the wharf carrying their ironware to the blacksmith's shop, their battered tackle to the mender's shanty.

"How simple their lives seem," Philip Sasson said. "I envy them."

"Do you?" she said. "I think you make a mistake. They have their griefs and disappointments, their anguish and their sorrows, just as we do."

"Anguish. Sorrow. Grief. Disappointment," he repeated musingly. "Strong words, Emma Coen Lewin, to be used by a beautiful woman on such a beautiful day in this city of the gods." He turned and looked at her. "Your life has not been easy, has it?" All brittle irony had vanished from his voice. He spoke not with curiosity but with concern and, she recognized, with a small amount of daring.

"No, it has not been easy," she acknowledged. "Do you want to hear about my life, Philip Sasson?"

He nodded.

"Then you must tell me about yours." Her tone was solemn. It would be a fair trade, a safe exchange. They were casual acquaintances, thrust together in a strange city and oddly united by a common background. Their most intimate revelations placed them in no danger. She felt instinctively that all she could not tell her brothers she could tell this man, who would soon disappear from her life. She had not seen him for two decades. She would, perhaps, never see him again. She recognized, with a flash of insight, that her original dislike had been fear of intimacy, and with that recognition the fear dissolved, and she smiled at him.

They sat then at one of the small wharfside tables set out by the cafés; its wooden surface was scrubbed clean and bleached by the salt air and the wind. They ordered bowls of chowder and watched the cook ladle it out of the huge iron cauldron that simmered over an open boxwood fire. The steaming soup was served with thick slices of fresh-baked bread, and the elderly Chinese waiter smiled with shy complicity as he placed a large blue bowl of California peaches on the table. The fruit was newly washed, and droplets of water clung to the fine pink fuzz and shimmered on the rough green leaves.

"He thinks we are lovers," Philip Sasson said. "He does not know that you have a husband in Phoenix, Arizona, and that I have a wife in London, England."

"Tell me about your wife in London, England," she said.

"Eleanor." He said her name in a dull, flat tone and lit a cheroot, which he puffed at rhythmically as he spoke.

He had known Eleanor from earliest childhood. They had attended dancing classes together and always they had sat side by side at parties and recitals and during intervals at the West London Synagogue on Upper Berkeley Street. Always the same things had amused them; they had laughed softly at other children's vagaries, the dancing teacher's pretensions, the rabbi's sonorous Sephardic accents. They were both only children, but Philip's brother had died in early adolescence, and he felt himself doubly responsible for his parents' happiness. Their families were close friends, and often they dined together on Friday evenings. Together their

mothers uttered the benedictions over the Sabbath candles
and smiled at the boy and girl who looked up at them. They
even looked alike—both gray-eyed and raven-haired, fine-
featured and pale-complected.

They grew into adulthood, never speaking of love and
marriage but always assuming that they belonged together.
Eleanor and Philip. Their names were coupled before they
had ever kissed. He went to Oxford, and she came often to
visit him, sometimes accompanied by her parents, sometimes by his. Shortly after he took his degree, his mother
called him into her dressing room. Her jewel box was open,
and she lifted a ruby pendant to the light and showed him
how the crimson prisms could be angled to capture the rays
of the sun. She placed it on the heavy gold chain his grandmother had brought to London from Portugal.

"Give this to Eleanor," his mother said, and so he did
and they became engaged. He had kissed her as he clasped
the chain and straightened the pendant at her neck, and he
remembered afterward the bowlike curve of her lips as he
bent his head. He had not thought it strange then that she
smiled as he kissed her. They were married as everyone had
always assumed they would be, and he was pleased because
he had made his parents happy and had made Eleanor happy.
His own happiness he assumed without question. He had
accepted his marriage as he had accepted his position with
Sir Ernst Cassel. There were things in life that one was meant
to do.

"In that," he told Emma as he bit into a peach, "I was
quintessentially English and obediently Jewish."

The marriage was not unhappy. He did not think it strange
that Eleanor was passive during their lovemaking, her body
dry and cool against his touch and thrust. Two daughters
were born and then a son. After the birth of their son she
slept in another room. She had begun to suffer from mi-
graines, she said, and Philip Sasson, who was absorbed in his
work and delighted with his handsome children, did not press
her.

He bought a country home in Scotland, and Eleanor spent
summers and holidays there with the children, accompanied
by Mlle. Jeannette, the slender French governess, who wore

her golden hair in a tight bun. He joined them for his own two-week holiday in August and phoned them dutifully each Friday just before the Sabbath.

But one July he traveled to Keswick on urgent railway business, which was swiftly concluded, and he realized that his son's sixth birthday would be celebrated the next day. Impulsively, he decided to journey north and surprise the child with the beautifully crafted wooden train set he had discovered in a Windermere shop. He did not phone but drove on through the night and arrived at his home just before dawn broke.

He let himself in with his key and, giddy with pleasure, he wandered through the beautiful, well-ordered house. He opened the door of his daughters' room and looked down at their peaceful, sleeping faces. In his son's room, he knelt beside the child and took his dangling hand into his own. Young Robert's skin was nut-brown, and his sleep-moistened black lashes were as straight as Philip's own.

Philip Sasson was suffused with joy. He had been triply blessed by these three beautiful children. He had been rewarded because he had been a good son and a good husband and because he had done what was expected of him. The boy's fingers tightened about his own, and gently he released them and went to his wife's room. Tonight he would disregard her excuses and claim her as he had not claimed her before.

The nocturnal journey through the mist-veiled highlands had fired his passion; the sight of his sleeping children had stirred his love. *Eleanor.* His friend. His love. He opened her door. The curtains had not been drawn, and the waning moonlight brushed the room with a delicate radiance. Eleanor lay naked on the large bed, her arms cradling the slender body of Mlle. Jeannette, whose golden hair, released from its tight bun, cascaded across the pillow. His mother's ruby nestled in the cleft of the governess's neck, and strands of golden hair were caught in the heavy chain that had belonged to his grandmother.

He stood immobile. A lark sang with piercing clarity. Eleanor stirred, opened her eyes, and met his frozen gaze. Her lips curved upward in the familiar bowlike curve, which at last he understood. He left then and drove until fatigue overtook him and he pulled over to the side of the road. He wept as he watched the pale highland sun emerge over a hillside strewn with heather; his shoulders heaved and his stomach writhed. Nausea overcame him, but he could only retch because he had eaten nothing since high tea the previous day.

When he came to Scotland for his August holiday, Mlle. Jeannette was gone. She had left suddenly, the children said. Her father had been ill, or perhaps it had been her mother. Eleanor calmly poured the tea as they spoke of her.

"I will expect you to be discreet," he had said coldly to her that first night. He had decided, after much thought, that he could not think of leaving her, of losing his home, his beautiful children, his well-ordered, well-tempered life.

From that night on, he and Eleanor had shared a home but had lived separate and secret lives. He asked no questions about her holidays in Scandinavia, her weekends in Shropshire and the Lake country. And she did not ask him about the nights he spent at a flat in the Marylebone Road or the sweet-voiced Irish secretary who often accompanied him on his business journeys. She understood, he supposed, that lonely men must make their own accommodations, and besides, it was of no concern to her.

"We learned to observe each other's privacy," he told Emma drily. "We sit beside each other at the dinner table, at our children's piano recitals and at their commencements. We go to concerts together and to dinner parties. 'Eleanor and Philip.' Still our names are coupled, and still we laugh at the same things, like the same books, the same plays. But I have learned to challenge appearances, to ask questions."

Emma understood. His acerbity, then, was vigilance, his sardonic manner was a protective carapace. He had been deeply wounded, and he protected himself with practiced skill. Did she not do as much?

"And now you know my story," he said. "You must tell me yours. Bargains must be kept after all."

"Who knows that better than I do?" she asked, and the bitterness in her own voice surprised her.

She told him then of her father's double life and of the

terrible sense of loss and betrayal it had inflicted on his children.

"Emil has never married. He never spoke of it, but I think he lost his ability to trust. Simon married a woman who would not have the imagination to betray him. Henry Stern, my half brother, is so consumed by an irrational hatred for my family that he cannot believe that we too suffered, that we were victims, not accomplices," she said sadly. "And of course, I have never seen David, although I know that he is a doctor and lives in Berlin."

"And you, Emma? How were you affected?"

"I could not comprehend my mother's weakness, her vulnerability. She chose death rather than confront life. Because she had shared nothing with my father, in the end she had nothing. I almost followed her pattern." She closed her eyes and thought of Benjamin Mendoza. He had died that year. A friend had sent her the obituary, which appeared in an Antwerp paper, and she had been surprised to find that she grieved for him, that she wept to see that his dark hair had faded to the color of ashes.

"But you did not live as your mother did," he observed mildly.

"I willed myself to live differently, to retain control of my own life. My marriage would be a partnership, I thought. A sharing." Her voice trailed off as she remembered the rising floodwaters that had turned the streets of Galveston into treacherous rivers, Isaac's arms holding her close in the bower of fur pelts, her words rising and falling. A sharing in all things, she had said, not realizing that such a sharing could not be mandated, that the togetherness she demanded would drive them apart.

"And was it?" he asked.

"In some ways." She described the early years in Phoenix, the arduousness of their initial struggle, the slow, carefully gained success of the Emporiums. Her voice broke when she told him of Gregory and the night of his death.

"I understand now how deeply lonely Isaac was, but I do not know what to do with that understanding. Can something that was broken be made whole?"

"I don't know," he said gravely. "God knows I have tried.

As you are trying. In that we are alike, Emma. Beautiful Emma.''

He reached across the table and stroked her cheek. They sat quietly then as the Chinese waiter removed their dishes. The fine mist of approaching evening floated up from the sea.

They followed the Embarcadero back to Lombard Street, swathed in the comfort of their new intimacy. A fog siren thundered a warning, and a circling gull shrilled its protest. The blasting whistle of a departing steamer sounded, and they leaned for a moment against the harbor rail and watched the lights of the ship disappear into the vaporous darkness.

Again, his hand rested on her hair. She lowered her head and moved away, a mute and gentle gesture of withdrawal. Obediently he too edged away, but he continued to stare at her, his gaze probing, insistent.

"But we can be friends?" he asked.

"We are friends," she replied. "Friends and more than friends."

Hand in hand, then, they walked through the swirling fog toward the lights of the city below.

Spring drifted into summer. It was the hottest summer they had experienced since their arrival in Phoenix, Isaac wrote Emma. He had increased the number of boxlike coolers in the windows of the Emporium, and he and Abner had jointly bought aspen forests in the north of the state to ensure a steady supply of excelsior. The wood shavings were moistened, and the evaporated air was drawn into the store's interior by whirring electric fans.

"I am glad that you are escaping this heat," he added, bearing down so heavily on his pen that the words were almost blotted out. He was not glad. Loneliness gripped him in an unrelenting vise, and he sought release from it by working long hours, traveling to the Emporiums in other cities, sometimes accompanied by Joshua and Samuel, more often alone. The boys had their own friends, their own lives. Joshua spoke of applying to eastern universities.

"I want to expand my horizons," he said, but Isaac knew

that he wanted to escape a home deserted by his mother, haunted by sadness.

He went with his sons to the inauguration ceremony of Temple Beth Israel, the first synagogue in the Gila Valley. Henry Stern sat on the dais, but Isaac saw Isabel standing in the rear, an infant cradled in her arms. He made his way toward the petite dark-haired woman, who gently fanned her child against the blistering heat. He was glad that she had found happiness, that she was a mother. There had been no bitterness between them; a sweet affection had survived their passion.

"Isabel, I heard about the baby. I wanted to wish you all happiness."

"Thank you, Isaac."

She held the child up, and he reached for the tiny fingers, but his eyes blurred as he saw the infant's face. The turquoise-blue eyes were fringed with thick copper lashes, and the small blue sunhat had slipped back to reveal a cluster of curls, moistened to a rich mahogany color. Gregory had looked like that as an infant. Isabel's child might have been his dead son's twin. Perhaps he, too, would grow into a sweet singing boy and invent intricate tales to explain the mystery of melting snow.

"He has his father's eyes," Isabel said softly.

"Of course," he said. There was no mystery, no caprice, to the child's coloring. Like poor Gregory, like Emma herself and Henry Stern, he had inherited Jacob Coen's blue eyes and the hair that would turn a burnished bronze beneath the desert sun.

"What is his name?" he asked.

"Jesse," she said. She spoke very softly and lifted the child to her shoulder as though to protect him from the sadness in Isaac's gaze.

"I wish your Jesse good health, long life, the privilege of good deeds." He offered the traditional benediction in a grave and gentle voice, but he left the ceremonies before the speeches were concluded, before the mezuzah was ceremoniously affixed to the first permanent house of worship built by Jews in the desert city.

That night, he sat alone in the loggia, stared up at the stars through the slatted *viga* roof, and wrote Emma a long letter, which he neither mailed nor destroyed. He wrote of all that she had meant to him since his first glimpse of her as she blessed the Sabbath candles that distant Friday evening in Galveston. "I loved you then. I love you still. And I will love you always. Our life has gone off course, but let us find our way again. Emma. My life. My bride. My love." He placed it between the pages of a volume of Maimonides and wondered if he would ever give it to her. He took small comfort, before he fell asleep that night, remembering that in her last letter she had written optimistically of the effect Franz Eisenmann's visits were having on Leonie. "She grows stronger and seldom uses the cane now. She even speaks of coming to the boutique to help me. Perhaps she will come full circle now, back to us." He dreamed then that he and Emma walked through the desert, hand in hand with Leonie and their sons. They reached the shadow of a mesa where a small bright-haired boy awaited them, his outstretched hands filled with clumps of turquoise that matched his eyes. He dropped them, and they fell soundlessly onto the sand as he joined the family in a slow and graceful circle dance.

Isaac awakened later than usual the next day, suffused with a mysterious calm. In his dream he had held the child's hand, and his touch had been as soft as that of tiny Jesse Stern's finger curled about his own.

Simon Coen's family left for their Atherton home late in June. Leonie had politely declined their invitation. She would come on weekends she promised, and often she did drive out with her mother and Philip Sasson. The tall, hawk-faced Englishman was a frequent visitor to the house on Lombard Street. He was lonely, Emma said. So many San Franciscans had left the city. It was only courteous that they invite him to dinner, that she accompany him to concerts and galleries. He was so helpful to Emil and Simon, so knowledgeable about music and art. Leonie listened as her mother and Philip discussed the museums they had loved in Europe. They both preferred the Musée Rodin to the Louvre, the gardens of the Pitti Palace to the long corridors of the Uffizi. Philip Sasson had touched a concealed spring, and a part of her mother's past had been revealed. The Englishman made Leonie feel vaguely uncomfortable.

"Why?" Franz asked when she mentioned it to him.

She shrugged and smiled at him. He looked so handsome in his white duck trousers and dark blue blazer. It amused her that his straw hat was never properly balanced on his thick dark curls.

"I don't know. Perhaps I think about him too much because I get so bored waiting for you," she said and fingered the sash of her pale blue dimity dress.

"Of course you get bored," he replied. "You must find other things to do."

She began then to join Emma at the boutique on Stockton Street, taking on simple tasks. There was time to think as she checked the inventory or routinely folded the soft woven Indian shawls that had become so popular suddenly with San Francisco matrons. Dreamily, she recalled her conversations with Franz, reviewing her questions, her answers. His voice was so gentle, his queries so carefully phrased, his silence, as he waited for her reply, so patient. Always, he sat very still, as though his slightest movement might disturb her thoughts, distort her memories.

She lifted a richly patterned scarf that Emma had especially ordered for one of Levi Strauss's pink-cheeked nieces, newly engaged and assembling a trousseau. It was of Pima weave, and she remembered how once Johnny Redbird had taken her to the mesa and she had spent a long afternoon watching an old woman weave a stole, using two wools of different texture, one as bright as the Arizona sky and the other as black as a raven's wing. The weaver had hummed as she worked the skeins through warp and weft, pausing now and again, her eyes closed, before selecting the next strand. Slowly, a pattern emerged. A black bird soared across the bright blue sky. The disparate yarns, so soft and formless, assumed a choate pattern, a purposeful form.

It seemed to Leonie that Franz's questions were not unlike those separate strands of wool. He, too, searched out a pattern, and now and again, when she looked at him as they spoke, she saw that a smile played at his lips as though, like the weaver, he had at last discerned a workable shape, a usable image. And just as she had so swiftly perceived the old woman's intent even before the bird's wings were apparent, so she perceived the intent of Franz's questions and her own answers. Memory and association, vagrant thought and sudden insight, were deftly interwoven, and the pattern of her past emerged. She recognized that her sorrow was not without its own intricate and mysterious design. Her sadness did not abate, but, strangely, it no longer frightened her. She used the cane very seldom now, and the pains in her legs were less severe.

"Read me a poem," Franz said one afternoon.

She hesitated, and then with trembling voice, she recited from memory the opening verse of "Annabel Lee."

"Why does that poem make you so sad?" he asked.

"It was the first poem Jesse taught me," she replied, and she closed her eyes. "I was a schoolgirl then. My white dress had a sailor collar. And I wore white stockings. My first silk stockings."

"But that was many years ago. You are no longer a schoolgirl, Leonie," he said in a firmer tone than he had ever used before.

He touched her braid so neatly tied with white ribbon. He fingered the childish lace frill at her wrist.

"You wear a costume, Leonie. A schoolgirl's dress and ribbons. You speak in the soft voice of a child. You tell me that your legs cause you pain so that you cannot cross the threshold of childhood into a world where men and women live. Why, Leonie? Is it so terrible in that world?"

"Yes!" she screamed and rose from the chaise. "It is a world full of secrets, full of danger and pain."

She clutched her abdomen and writhed as he had seen women do while in the throes of childbirth. Her face was distorted, and flecks of foam gathered at the corners of her mouth. It had been cold on the desert the night she lost her baby, the night the blood had flowed, staining and wounding her legs, and she shivered now and tossed her head wildly from side to side. He feared that she might fall, and he moved toward her, but she ran past him and up the stairs. The acidity of truth dissolved the pain in her legs; her flight was swift and desperate. A door slammed and he heard her cry out.

His palms were moist, and sweat beaded his forehead. Still, he did not go up to her but remained downstairs until Emma arrived home.

He waited as she said goodbye to Philip Sasson. Their voices were soft, breathless with the intimacy of a man and a woman who have been friends for many years and have few secrets from each other. There was talk about them in San Francisco, Franz knew. There were those who thought that they were lovers, and Emil had spoken to Franz about it with sardonic wariness.

"Perhaps I should warn my sister that the cardinal laws of San Francisco Jewry must not be violated. Thou shalt not change thy name. Thou shalt not intermarry. Thou shalt not engage in extramarital affairs. The eating of pork, the desecration of the Sabbath, and the hanging of Christmas wreaths are, of course, permitted."

"I don't think Emma needs such a warning," Franz had replied.

Still, he noticed as she entered that her eyes were bright, her color high, although she paled when she saw him and read the worry in his eyes.

"Do not be frightened if Leonie is very upset tonight," he cautioned her, although he himself was light-headed with fear.

"Franz, what is happening?"

He shrugged.

"We make progress. Great progress. But it is very painful. Still, we must be patient."

"I trust you," Emma said gravely. "You are concerned for Leonie, I know."

"Yes."

He did not tell her that he was concerned for all his patients, for all the sad men and women, the melancholic children, who drifted into his consulting room with their fragile memories, their half-remembered dreams, seeking surcease from pain and bewilderment through his mysterious talking cure. He suffered with them, for them. Transference works both ways, Sigmund Freud had warned him—patient to doctor and doctor to patient. But it was not transference that he experienced when he sat beside Leonie Lewin. It was love.

He had known it from the first, almost from the moment he first took her hand in his and brushed it with his lips in Emil Coen's living room.

Leonie would not see him again that week, nor did she go to the boutique. She was deeply depressed, Emma said, her voice riddled with worry. She barely left her room. Still, she walked briskly now, and for the first time in two years, she wore her dark hair unplaited. Franz breathed deeply. Always, as an analyst, he warred with resistent patients who clung tenaciously to the safe haven of their evasions, the security of their disguises. Too often he lost. He could not afford a defeat in his struggle with Leonie.

He sent her a bouquet of red roses, and his fingers trembled as he penned the card.

"We know that white is the color of desert sands and winter snows. May I come to see you tomorrow? Will you tell me the secrets of the color red?"

She waited for him the next day, beside the bay window, holding a single red rose in her hand. She wore a blue dress, and her black hair draped her shoulders in silken sheaths. She did not speak in the wispy tones of an introverted schoolgirl but in the clear, rich tones of young womanhood. She had crossed a border, he knew, and now at last had reached an emotional clearing and could confront the source of her sorrow.

Again, they sat in a circlet of sunlight and she spoke of her love for Jesse, of the sweetness of their talk and the companionable ease of their silences. With Jesse, she had escaped the tensions of her home where her parents spoke to each other with the careful courtesy of strangers and slept in separate bedrooms. Always, she told him, from her earliest childhood, she had felt the cool constraint between her parents.

"Always?" Franz asked in surprise.

He had judged Emma to be a passionate woman, seared by her own pain yet possessed of a deep and sympathetic warmth, a natural sensuality. She entered a room with the poise and confidence of a woman who has been admired since girlhood, and she moved with the subtle grace peculiar to women who neither doubt nor ponder their beauty.

He had met Isaac Lewin when the Phoenix merchant visited San Francisco, and he had been impressed by Isaac's warmth, the depth of his intellectual curiosity, his vibrancy. He was a man who had relied throughout his life on his own physical and intellectual strength, on the force of his will. Franz had watched him stare at Emma as she moved toward them at one of Simon Coen's large parties.

"How beautiful she is," Isaac had said softly, and Franz had understood that Isaac Lewin was a man who loved his wife with a rare passion that had not been diminished by the complacency of marriage. He missed his wife and daughter, he had told Franz, but their family doctor had felt that Leonie would recover her strength more quickly in San Francisco. Franz had not doubted Isaac then, and he did not doubt him now, but neither did he doubt Leonie's perception of her parents' marriage.

"Each family lives many lives," Sigmund Freud had told him. Isaac perceived one life, his daughter another, and neither knew or guessed the other's secrets.

"Always," Leonie said firmly. "Except for a few weeks, just before Gregory died."

Still, she could not speak of her lost brother without weeping, and she turned her face away, but Franz leaned toward her, cupped her chin in his hand, and gently wiped her tears. It was a good sign, he told himself, that the cleansing tears fell so easily.

"My Indian friend, Johnny Redbird, told me once that there are holy men among his people—shamans—who can bring back wandering souls by inducing a trance. I think, Franz Eisenmann, that you are my own shaman," she said when at last her tears had ceased.

They sat together then in silence as the light faded and the fog-edged evening drifted in across the dark blue waters of the bay.

He met Emma for lunch the next day. It would be easier for him to help Leonie if he understood her parents, he explained carefully. Leonie had spoken of an uneasiness in her home, of the unnerving tension between her parents that had distressed her.

"I didn't know she felt it," Emma said. "I thought we had concealed it so carefully." Did Philip Sasson's children feel the anger between their parents? she wondered. Had all their efforts at concealment, at creating a civilized veneer, been in vain?

"Children sense an atmosphere," Franz continued in a controlled professional tone. "Such sensations are absorbed in a part of the mind that we call the unconscious and fester there. Think of it, perhaps, as a hidden psychological virus that slowly develops and takes over the mind just as a physical virus takes over the body. Some people are able to cope and develop their own immune system, their own refuges and defenses. But sometimes such refuges are temporary and ill-conceived. Leonie found such a refuge with Jesse, and when he died and she lost his child, she felt abandoned yet again."

"Again?" Emma asked.

"A child who grows up in a home where love between the parents is withheld feels abandoned," he explained patiently.

"Surely I can understand that," she said bitterly.

She told him then of her own life, and as she spoke it seemed to her that her heart unclenched and that she surrendered a sorrow she had carried too blindly for too long. She spoke to Franz not as she had spoken to Philip Sasson. That had been an intimate exchange, an emotional trade of a kind, a revelation that did not require understanding. Now she spoke with a sense of urgency, a plea for understanding. Her words flowed with a febrile swiftness so that often he had to interrupt her with his gentle probing questions, his cautious insights.

"Do you love your husband?" he asked.

She smiled sadly. "If I did not love him, perhaps our lives together would have been easier."

They spoke again later that week and then the next.

"It's strange," Emma said, "I asked you to help Leonie, but you have helped me as well."

"Only because you were strong enough to be helped," he told her. He did not ask why she had never, during their long and deeply intimate conversations, mentioned Philip Sasson.

* * *

Leonie grew stronger. She worked longer hours at the Lewin Link, charming the patrons with her intuitive instinct for fashion. She and Franz took long walks down Fisherman's Wharf and the Embarcadero. She bought richly hued dresses with wide skirts and loose tunics. She opened invitations with enthusiasm, and when Franz invited her to a concert at Temple Emanuel, she accepted with alacrity.

"It's only a boy violinist," he warned her, but her enthusiasm was undiminished, and she dressed carefully that evening.

The huge ballroom of the temple was decorated with urns of fresh flowers, tall gladioli, brilliant delphiniums, and luxurious sprays of pale mountain laurel. Green velvet highback chairs were arranged in serried rows, and, as always, the Jews of San Francisco chose their places with calculated design—the Lilienthals, the Gerstles, and the Haases in the front row, the Magnin clan claiming the center rows, with the Fleishhakers and the Zeckendorfs seated behind them. By tacit agreement, the Jews of eastern European origin took up seats in the rear. They, too, were elegantly dressed and bejeweled, but the women fingered their necklaces and twirled their rings as though fearful that the glittering symbols of their success would mysteriously vanish.

The aristocratic German and Sephardic Jews of Temple Emanuel and the more observant eastern European Jews of Temples Shaarit Yisrael and Ohavei Shalom formed an uneasy alliance to support worthy Jewish causes. Where would her father sit if he were present tonight? Leonie wondered vaguely as she observed the invisible demarcation lines between the various Jewish communities.

Emil Coen slipped into a seat beside Franz and kissed his niece on the cheek.

"I like your haircut," he said, and Franz frowned.

She had cut her hair in a flapper bob, and a cherry-red headband that matched her loose chemise dress was pulled across her forehead. The haircut had surprised Franz. He had loved the samite sheen of her long dark hair. She smiled at his disapproval.

"But I only did as you said and crossed the threshold of childhood," she had said teasingly.

He felt an oddly familiar sadness, not unlike the melancholy he had experienced as a child when he had nursed a bird with a broken wing back to health and watched it fly away when it was healed.

"You do look beautiful," he whispered to Leonie as the dark-haired child violinist appeared at the front of the ballroom, led by Cantor Reuben Rinder.

"Ladies and gentlemen," the cantor said. "It is my great pleasure to introduce a rare talent, my young musical colleague, Israel Kaplan."

The beautiful, dark-eyed child stared out at the audience and smiled. He was eight years old, and his innocence and naiveté protected him from shyness and uncertainty.

"Play as you do for your own family," Cantor Rinder had advised him. "This audience will feel themselves part of your family."

His parents and his sisters always listened attentively when he played and embraced him when he was done. This larger family, who had donned their most elegant garments, their most brilliant jewels, to hear him play in this brightly lit room, would not withhold their applause and affection from him. He tucked his violin under his chin and slid the bow across the gleaming strings. Effortlessly, he played Mendelssohn's Violin Concerto. He was so absorbed in the music that he did not hear the women gasp for breath or see the men lean forward as they listened. The haunting music pierced their hearts. They closed their eyes and smiled dreamily, but when the last movement was completed they sprang to their feet and clapped with fierce pride, with wild joy.

The child's name was Israel Kaplan, and they repeated it to each other, secretly glad that it revealed him at once to be a Jewish child. It was the child's dark Semitic look, his name, that proclaimed his faith to be their own, that caused their eyes to fill with tears, their hearts to pound. The women turned to each other, their hands trembling, their cheeks flushed. Each one of them might have birthed the graceful child, whose dark hair fell into his eyes as he played. He *was* their son, child to them all. Communally, they adopted him, acknowledged him as yet another blessing granted them in this beneficent frontier state where golden fruit gleamed on dark-leafed trees and golden dust was hidden beneath swirling waters.

"Our child prodigy has arrived at an apt time," Emil said to Franz. "Now that San Francisco Jewry has endowed libraries, hospitals, and orphanages, we can endow our own musical genius."

"You are too cynical, Emil," Franz replied. "Philip Sasson's sarcasm has had a bad influence on you." He felt uneasy with the tall, hawk-faced Englishman; too often his comments were caustic, and always there was a cruel, defensive edge to his humor. During their infrequent meetings at the Lombard Street house, Franz had often sensed a danger he could not articulate.

"By the way," he added, "I met him at the Wells Fargo office today. He told me that he was closing his account. I gather he is leaving San Francisco."

"Yes. His work here is accomplished. He leaves next week. And just as well." He stared moodily across the room to the corner where Emma stood with the tall Englishman. He leaned forward and whispered into her ear, and she laughed with a swift spontaneity and linked her arm in his. He glanced at Leonie, but she had not noticed her mother. She was speaking eagerly to Jessica Peixotto about the possibility of enrolling at the university in the fall.

"Do you really want to go to the university?" Franz asked that night as they stood on the porch of the Lombard Street house. A vagrant dark curl had escaped the headband that slashed its way across her high forehead, and he gently tucked it in.

"That was what I planned to do before Jesse died," she said, and her voice did not waver. She had come full circle then and could confront the pain of the past and plan for the future.

"I will not be coming to see you each afternoon now, Leonie," he said.

Her face paled, and she bit her lips.

"Why not?" Her voice reverted to the schoolgirl whisper.

"You are well now, Leonie. I do not want to be your doctor. I want to be your friend."

"Friends spend time together," she retorted.

"And we will spend time together," he promised. "Be ready early Sunday morning. I will take you on a mystery picnic."

She smiled. "I think I will like being your friend," she said and held her hand out to him.

He pressed it to his lips. "Until Sunday then."

"Good night, Franz, my friend."

"Good night, Leonie." The door closed behind her, and he looked up as a chalk-white gull flew in solitary grace through the darkness. "Leonie, my love," he added in a whisper, and he worried, as he drove home to Telegraph Hill, that he had moved too swiftly, but he knew that he could bear to wait no longer.

Franz awakened at dawn on Sunday and stared out at the fog that enfolded the city in a gossamer-silver mist. A grim foreboding seized him, slowing his steps. His movements were clumsy. He selected a dark blue cravat and discarded it in favor of a bright red bow tie. The coffee that he brewed himself was bitter and scalded his tongue. Angrily, he stared at himself in the mirror and frowned at the strands of silver that threaded their way through his dark hair.

He had made a mistake, he told himself. He could not compete with the ghost of Leonie's bright-haired lover. Jesse Stern had represented the new world, a brave and daring son of the American desert. He had galloped across the sands, fired by poetry, brimming with ambition. If the world was out of joint, surely he had the power to set it right. With all the certainty of youth, he had dreamed of peace. With all the passion of that dream betrayed, he had gone to war. And Leonie had been accomplice to his hope, companion to his dream. Franz could not offer her comparable innocence, comparable optimism. Jesse had offered her refuge. Franz had exposed her to confrontation. With Jesse she had read Whitman and Poe, Emerson and Thoreau. Franz's poets were Rilke and Schiller, Heine and Lessing.

His depression increased as he drove to the house on Lombard Street. He was, after all, ten years her senior. She perceived him as an older friend, a sympathetic healer. He could not hope for more.

She waited for him on the porch, dressed for the promised picnic in a brightly woven Mexican skirt and a white peasant blouse crafted of a cotton so fine that he could see the rose-gold skin of her shoulders, the blue-veined rise of her breasts. Emma and Philip Sasson sat beside her on the glider.

The Englishman, as always, was impeccably dressed in a dove-gray suit, a snowy shirt, and a silken maroon cravat.

"I am glad to see you, Franz," he said. "It gives me the opportunity to say goodbye. I leave for New York tomorrow, and I sail for England in a month's time."

"A good journey, then," Franz said and glanced at Emma.

She wore the long-jacketed navy blue walking suit, offset by the bright plaid ascot, which typified the Lewin Look that season.

"We are going to do a final tour of the city," she said. "Philip has never seen the Presidio or had a meal in Chinatown." The gaiety in her voice was strained, and she plucked nervously at her white gloves.

The two men shook hands and stared gravely at each other, their gaze confirming a mutual respect and an odd regret that they had not become friends, that there had been no trust between them.

They drove west through the city. Franz followed Geary Street on its straight flat course toward the ocean. The strong summer sun had burned its way through the mist, and the lazily drifting clouds were threaded with gold. Already they heard the crescendo of dashing waves, the muted shrills of the low-flying gulls.

"I know where we are going," Leonie said teasingly. "My uncle Emil took me there when we first visited San Francisco. Your surprise is no surprise, my shaman."

"Where are we going, then?"

"To the Sutro Baths, where all good uncles take their obedient nieces."

Her laughing words were like pellets against his heart, confirming his morning fears. He was her shaman, her "good uncle." He had cured her, rescued her from the childish world into which she had withdrawn, and in the process, he had lost her. He pressed down on the accelerator and was silent until they reached Point Lobos Avenue.

There, they walked through the fairyland that restless Adolf Sutro had built at the ocean's edge. They lingered along the wide-tiered glass-enclosed pavilion bordered by palm trees and tropical plants. They climbed the great staircase and looked down at the bonsai gardens, the intricate rock sculptures. Franz led her to the sloping beach in the lee of Point Lobos and showed her the basin scooped out of solid rock that captured the ocean waves as they crested and diverted the water to a settling tank, and from there to the six pools that had made the baths famous throughout the West.

"I often wonder about men like Sutro," Franz said pensively. "What impelled a Jewish tobacconist from Aix-la-Chapelle to pack up and come to California? What gave him the sheer chutzpah to fight to build that tunnel at the Comstock Lode? He was a merchant, after all, not an engineer, and yet he succeeded. Just as he succeeded in building these baths and in becoming mayor of San Francisco. In Russia, Jews couldn't live outside the pale of settlement, and in San Francisco a Jew presided over City Hall."

It was not only Adolf Sutro who engaged Franz's imagination. He was gripped by a curiosity that he alternately ascribed to professional interest in the creative personality and to sheer Jewish introspection, which caused him to wonder about the unprecedented success of the Jews of San Francisco. An economist with whom he had gotten pleasantly drunk at the University Club had told Franz that during the course of his research for a paper on the economic development of San Francisco, he had discovered that as early as 1855 twenty Jewish families paid taxes on two million dollars' worth of assessed property.

"How do the clever bastards manage it?" the economist had asked, and then, perhaps remembering that Franz was Jewish, he had ordered yet another round of drinks. "Not that I have anything but admiration for them," he had added, lifting his brandy snifter, "but how the hell did they do it?"

Franz wondered himself. It seemed to him that Jews had penetrated every area of the city's economic life. The Friedlanders were active in the grain market, the Jacobis and Lachsmans owned wineries, the Jastros managed cattle ranches. The Seligmans and the Hellermans of Wells Fargo had faced the economic adversities of fire and earthquake and increased their investment assets. Daniel Meyer's underwater irrigation investment had invigorated the economy of the city. Workers flocked to the Zellerbach and Fleishaker paper mills, to the factories where Levi Strauss formed the tough canvas of Nîmes into work pants, to the canneries where the Sussmans and Wormsers preserved the lush produce of the state under the S&W label. Emil and Simon Coen looked down at the port from their glass-walled offices on the Embarcadero and plotted the routes of huge freighters, and women throughout the country studied fashion magazines and followed the Lewin Look.

Franz had sat beside Guggenheim heirs at dinner parties and had explained the need for a resident psychiatric hospital to a pleasantly vague Alice Haas at a luncheon party on Van Ness Avenue. He spoke to the women of the Philomath Society on "The New Science of Psychoanalysis" in the Gerstles' living room and marveled because an original Rousseau hung on the wall.

It had occurred to him that the Jews of the gilded circle of San Francisco had succeeded because they could not afford to fail. Past struggles had energized them for future successes. Here, in this ocean-edged city, at America's last frontier, all the energy that had been constrained for generations was released. In Europe they had often been forbidden to buy land. In California vast acreage was available, and they acquired it, exulting over the acquisition of swampland and expanses of arid desert. They seized the opportunity to own the houses in which they lived, the fields on which they grew their crops, the vineyards and citrus orchards where their fruits swelled in the sun.

In Europe they had grown accustomed to struggle and persevere for mere survival. Now that struggle, that inbred perseverance, exploded into success. They had been schooled to accept responsibility for each other. Jew helped and sheltered Jew, kinsman trusted kinsman. It had been natural then, in this far western city, at a remove from a center of Jewish authority, for Jews to turn to each other, for cousins to lend each other money and arrange extensions of credit. They had learned to invest their limited savings and to turn adversity to advantage.

They had come to San Francisco determined to remain there. They were not seduced by fool's gold or disappointed because mica rather than silver veined the mountain crevices. They relied not on nature's gifts but on their own ingenuity and tenacity. And when success came, they reveled in it. Adolf Sutro had built this fairyland where shimmering lights banished the shadows of his early struggles. The merchant princes and investment bankers, families like the Coens, the Lilienthals, and the Magnins, built their summer palaces in San Raphael and Atherton and picnicked beneath the trees of their own forests on tables spread with snow-white cloths. Twice a year the enchanted families prayed in the polished pews of Temple Emanuel that they might live happily ever after.

Leonie picked up a pebble and dropped it from the promontory on which they stood to the crenelated ocean wall below.

"I once asked my father why he chose the West," she said. "He knew no one in Texas or Arizona. It would have been easier for him to go to Boston or New York, where families from his town in Russia had settled."

"And what did he say?" Franz asked, noting that her voice softened when she spoke of Isaac Lewin.

"He said that he had come to America to begin his life over, and in the West it was possible to do just that. His religion was irrelevant. Only his skills mattered. He chose Phoenix because it was a new city. It had no history, no restrictions. In Phoenix no one asked if Isaac Lewin was Jewish. They cared only about what he could contribute to Phoenix, to Arizona," Leonie replied. "Still, he was always conscious of being a Jew in Arizona. He still says that he is glad he came to Phoenix before the Roosevelt Dam was built so that people would know Jews had endured the early years, when water was scarce in the valley. I think perhaps that is why his first tent store is still the motif for all the Emporium wrappings and advertisements."

"Like Levi Strauss's horse-and-cowboy trademark," Franz said. "A constant reminder of origin, of history. We are a stiff-necked people, tenacious in our allegiances, our memories."

She discerned the bitterness in his voice and looked at him curiously.

"Why did you come to California, Franz? Why did you leave Vienna?" she asked, and he realized that it was the first time she had asked him about his own past, his own choices. She had taken a giant step forward then and had emerged from the miasma of self-involvement. He answered her carefully, weighing and measuring his words.

"I don't think my reasons are too different from your father's, Leonie. Psychoanalysis is in its pioneering stage, and I wanted to practice it in a pioneering city where suspicions and prejudice had not taken root. And like your father, I too was bewitched by the dream of vast, unsettled frontiers where all men were equal and all were accepted on equal terms." He closed his eyes against the memory of his father's angry epithet. "Find a new world," the aging grain merchant had thundered, and he, the obedient son, had taken the old man at his word.

"And have you been disappointed?" she asked gently.

"No—at least not entirely," he replied. "When I speak of my talking cure at the medical school, there is no mockery. This is the state of miracles. Men who panned for their fortunes in rushing waters, who built a city out of a hamlet of tents, do not laugh at the dreams of others. Californians live on nature's cusp, where all things are possible. And it is true that Jews are a part of the pioneer vanguard, welcomed for our energies and our ideas. But we dare not deceive ourselves, Leonie. Already, we reconstruct the ghettos we left behind in Europe, only now we do not build houses on curving streets and narrow alleys. Instead we construct mansions on Nob Hill and Pacific Heights and plant geraniums and heliotropes in our gardens. Jews live among Jews, socialize with Jews, and hope that their children will marry each other. *Plus ça change, plus c'est la même chose.* The more things change, the more they remain the same. Still, I am neither deceived nor disappointed." He lifted his arms as though to embrace the carousing waves of the Pacific, the ivory-sanded beach, the apricot-colored sun. "I cannot imagine living anywhere else."

Leonie lifted her face to the sun's warmth and closed her eyes against its brightness. The ocean spray flecked her dark hair, her long lashes. He thought that she had never looked more beautiful.

They ate lunch at the Cliff House, the gingerbread palace of a restaurant that Adolf Sutro had built so that he could watch the sea lions cavort on Seal Rocks, across the water, as he ate.

"I feel like a spoiled child, shaman," Leonie said when Franz urged her to order the strawberry shortcake for which the restaurant was famous.

"Do you?" His tone was short, and he did not look up to meet the laughter in her eyes. He would spoil her, but not as a child. He would bewitch her, but not as a shaman. His ice cream had a bitter taste, and he averted his head as he ate so that he would not see how the sun cast its glow across her face.

After lunch they walked across the esplanades. She laughed at the playful antics of the sea lion pups as they roared and barked, but he remained silent.

"Did you know," she asked, "that the Gabrielano Indians believe that porpoises guard the world and swim around it to keep the earth from coming to cosmic harm?"

"A foolish fantasy," he said with impatient bitterness. He was impatient today with all fantasies, with all false hopes.

"Franz, is something wrong?"

"No."

It was now, at this languid après-midi hour, when the rocks of the esplanades were splayed with sunlight, that he had thought to declare himself when he had planned the day, but now he would not. He could not risk her startled reaction, her kind rejection. She could not marry her shaman, the avuncular friend who had spoiled her, the persistent doctor who had wrestled her secrets from her. He had lost the power to ask her what she was thinking, what she was feeling. He had severed the emotional leash that bound her to him and surrendered her to freedom.

They stood side by side, trapped in a melancholy net of silence, and watched two gulls plunge in tandem swoop into the ocean. Suddenly the cliff on which they stood trembled, and the vibration thrust her into his arms. All around them the earth rumbled and quivered. A rock was catapulted from the promenade and thundered down to the ocean wall. The sea lions screamed, and the shrill of their fear was piercing, humanoid. Fronds tumbled from the high palms, and birds winged their way wildly, desperately, through the air. The solitary walkers on the beach flung themselves onto the sand and hugged the heaving earth.

"Franz, I'm so frightened." Leonie clung to him, her breath moist against his neck, her body trembling.

"Shh. It's over. You see. All is as it was. It's over." Now the ground was still beneath their feet and the air was filled with a breathless calm. "It was just a tremor. Not an earthquake but a severe tremor." He had experienced such tremors before and understood the terror they incurred.

"It was horrible." She clung to him still.

"No need to be frightened. I'll take care of you. You know that."

She relaxed then, but she did not move away. Still locked in his embrace, she looked up at him, her blue eyes almost violet-colored, a shy smile wreathing her lips.

"Always, Franz?" Her voice was serious, searching.

"Always. Always and forever."

And now it seemed to him that again the earth trembled, but it was only his heart that beat with timpanic rapidity as his lips met hers in pledge and affirmation.

Emma Lewin and Philip Sasson did not spend the day touring San Francisco. They decided instead to drive south to Monterey and visit the Weinglasses. Philip felt the need to leave the city. He had, he claimed, been trapped for too long in the offices and conference rooms of Montgomery Street and the Embarcadero, and he knew that when he returned to London, he would again hold lonely court behind the huge desk in his oak-paneled office on Threadneedle Street.

"London offices were constructed to block sunlight," he said with characteristic cynicism as they drove southward along the coast. "Our architects, in their wisdom, invariably specify narrow casement windows, and the decorators, in turn, have a penchant for thick and hideous drapery, usually bile green in color. I must store up a reserve of California sunlight to see me through the dark days ahead."

"But it will be high summer when you return. Surely, you'll go to Scotland," Emma said and immediately regretted her words. Philip had not spoken of his wife and children since that very first afternoon. Nor, she acknowledged, had she spoken of Isaac. They had, from the start, delineated their emotional boundaries and moved cautiously and circumspectly about them. Always, they had known that he would leave San Francisco when his business was completed. Their friendship was rooted in the present and sustained by an unarticulated acknowledgment of its brevity.

"Perhaps," he answered shortly. "The air will be bright in the highlands, I expect, but hardly warm." He looked hard at her, and she turned away. Tomorrow, at this hour, he would be gone, and once again she would return from the boutique to confront loneliness and solitude.

During the weeks since their first meeting at Simon's dinner party, she and Philip had spent long hours together. They had ridden the cable cars up and down the city's hills, smiling at each other in mischievous complicity. They had taken a ferry to Belvedere Island and leaned against the deck rail during the short journey, their faces turned upward to catch the scent and touch of the salt spray. Short journeys intrigued them, and, like small children, they relished the magic of movement, the excitement of being mysteriously transported from one landscape to another, from valley to mountain, from an urban mainland to a rural inlet. They had been born in small countries, and they acknowledged their shared bemusement at California's vastness.

They stood on a Berkeley hillside one afternoon and watched a flotilla of sailboats move through the bay, gliding smoothly across waves lightly capped with froth.

"They look like the fairy craft our governesses told us about, the sailing ships that carried good children to the shores of sweet and gentle dreams," she said.

He nodded, remembering the good-night tales of his own

childhood. It was that silent rapport, that instant recognition of meaning and memory, that had drawn them together throughout the spring and summer. Together, they went to concerts and walked the corridors of museums and galleries. She might lean forward or perhaps incline her head, and he at once understood her reaction to a musical composition, a painting, or an Indian sculpture.

And he, in turn, might stir restlessly in his seat at a concert, walk too swiftly past a painting exhibit, and immediately she comprehended his restlessness.

"Yes, let us leave," she said, as though replying to a suggestion he had made.

They visited the Palace of Fine Arts and smiled at the ornate architecture, the imposing domes and columns, the barque and swans afloat on the quiet lake.

"Californians yearn for a past that was never theirs," Philip Sasson observed.

"They race to create their own history," Emma agreed.

Throughout the city and its environs, feverish construction was in progress. Boulders were blasted in the rocky wasteland to the south, and shafts and conduits reached subsurface water. Parapets were carved into hills of rock to protect waterfilled reservoirs. Barren expanses were seeded, and already, thick foliage had taken root and stretches of countryside were dark with eucalyptus.

It amused Emma and Philip to hear San Franciscans refer to their city as the Paris of the United States. They had both visited the French capital often as children, and often they spoke of their shared wonder at *l'heure bleue*, when the city of light was awash with a mysterious incandescence. Their memories merged and matched and they spoke of people and places that she had thought woven into obscurity in the complex fabric of her past. Never had she been able to speak to Isaac of her childhood. It had been so foreign to his own.

Her Europe had been the cosmopolitan world of sophisticated Sephardim where children were raised by governesses, and Isaac's Europe had been a small hamlet on the forest's edge where mothers sang to their children in gentle Yiddish. Her world had been one of wealth and grace, while Isaac's had been one of poverty and fearful vulnerability. She had studied French and learned to love art and music. He had studied Talmud and Jewish philosophy. Always, the disparities of their backgrounds had haunted the marriage; small irritations had festered, minor differences had compounded. She had realized, through Franz Eisenmann's probing questions, that she and Isaac had exchanged politeness for intimacy, vigilance for trust. Always they had been fearful of trespassing on each other's pasts. Even the love they felt for each other constituted a threat, invited a vulnerability that frightened her.

But her past and that of Philip Sasson melded, and a compelling emotional chemistry drew them together. Their intimacy had been assumed from the outset after that first afternoon on Fisherman's Wharf; they had not questioned it, although it had inspired a studied restraint.

They sat side by side at concerts, their hands clasped on their laps, yet she was aware of his every indrawn breath; she quivered at the touch of his fingers against her neck as he helped her on with her cape. Always they drew apart with a smile at an accidental touch—his elbow against hers as they leaned against he rail of the ferry, her hand grazing his as she reached across the dinner table for a salt cellar, a carafe of wine. At each parting he lifted her hand to his lips. He was a European gentleman, politely taking leave of a kinswoman. Yet always he held her hand just a fraction of a moment too long, and always she drew it back with a faint sinking of her heart, at once relieved and disappointed.

Often during those long weeks, as the evenings surrendered their fog-bound chill, she awakened from a dream in which she stood alone on a pier, staring with profound sadness at a slowly vanishing sailing ship. Desperately, she waved at a solitary traveler, a man who stretched his arms out toward her, his shouts muted by the rushing waves. Once, she had thought of telling Franz Eisenmann of her dream, but she had remained silent. He would want to know the identity of the man, and she could not tell him and feared her own conjecture. Sometimes she thought it was Isaac and sometimes Benjamin Mendoza. Once, she awakened in a cold sweat, certain that it was Philip Sasson.

She was glad now that they had decided to drive to Monterey. The journey southward had soothed her, and she looked forward to seeing her old friends.

Basha and Avrum Weinglass waited for them on the wide porch of their mission-style home. Emma had phoned to tell them she would be arriving with a friend, but she discerned their uneasiness when they saw Philip. Hastily, she introduced them.

"Basha and Avrum are my dear friends from Galveston days," she said. "Philip Sasson is a visitor from England. He has been advising my brothers and leaves for New York tomorrow."

Basha smiled and flashed a glance of relief at her husband.

"So many years have passed, Emma. We have become Abe and Bess. Easier names for the customers to manage, and the clerks in the bank don't have to ask always how to spell, how to pronounce. But the truth is, I don't feel like a Bess. In my heart, I'm still a Basha."

"And in my heart you're still a Basha," her husband said. He kissed her cheek and smiled proudly at his guests.

"Something to eat? Something to drink? Come, come inside."

He was proud of his home, he rejoiced in the thick carpets and golden oak furnishings, the heavy cut-glass vases always filled with fuchsia from his own carefully tended garden and the desert poppies his daughters favored. He had been poor for so long, always a boarder in other people's homes, a worker in other men's enterprises, that his own prosperity still astonished him. Each acquisition was a new miracle, a new affirmation of his success. His California-born daughters, who bought their clothes at I. Magnin, their accessories at the Lewin Link, laughed at the gifts he offered them, at the huge credenzas and breakfronts he bought for the salon and the dining room.

"Daddy wants to fill the house with heavy things because he's afraid it will blow away," his older daughter once said with affectionate laughter.

He did not tell her that she had touched a grain of truth. He did want to weight his house down, to anchor it securely against flood and earthquake, against poverty and adversity. He had instructed the contractors to build the doors of his home with a double thickness. He had changed his name, but he had not vanquished his fears.

He had insisted that the table be set with their finest china and the sterling silver flatware he had bought on his last trip to San Francisco. Once his wife had washed dishes and peeled potatoes in Emma's Galveston kitchen, and now Emma, at last, was a guest at their table. Her presence endorsed his success, negated the shame he had felt during those early years in Texas when he had been unable to afford medical treatment for his daughter, lodging for his family.

Over coffee and cake, they spoke of their friends in Galveston. Rabbi Cohen was still at B'nai Israel. There had been an article in a recent issue of *The Gleaner* about his campaign for prison reform.

"A good man," Abe Weinglass said. "I remember how beautifully he spoke at your wedding. It was a sad time for us, but for a few hours he made us happy." The Weinglasses had risen from their mourning stools to witness Emma's marriage to Isaac. The putrescence of decaying bodies had mingled with the scent of oleanders. When Isaac broke the glass, they had shouted, *"L'chaim,"* and shivered at the stench of death.

Philip Sasson stared across the table and saw the color rise in Emma's cheeks. He wondered suddenly why, on this, their last day together, she had chosen to visit these old friends whose history was so closely linked with that of her husband.

They spoke of other friends and acquaintances. The Freundlichs had moved to Portland and had a dry-goods store there. Emma told them of the Wallachs' success in Phoenix.

"Whatever happened to Hyman Greenstein?" she asked, remembering the young Rumanian socialist who had yearned for a utopian society in the American West and had trailed after her reading excerpts from the *Arbeiter Tseitung*, the poems of Morris Winchevsky and David Edelstadt.

Abe Weinglass smiled. "Hyman Greenstein is now Harry Green. He went to New Mexico and married a pretty Chicano girl—some say she converted and some say she didn't. He opened a shoe store and then a small shoe factory that became a large shoe factory. He bought a small house and then a bigger house and then a mansion. The Mexican girl became a Castilian lady when they moved into the mansion, and he canceled his subscription to the socialist newspaper and instead he gets the *Wall Street Journal*. Somewhere I read that now his workers want to organize and he fights the union. *Nu?* What can you do? This is America, where an Avrum becomes an Abe, a Basha is all of a sudden a Bess, and a socialist becomes a millionaire.''

They laughed then at the strange tricks life had played on them. The Weinglasses had come to California dreaming of gold but had found their fortunes in the sweet fruits that grew on their trees. The Lewins, in turn, had transformed a trunk-load of evening gowns, damaged by the floodwaters, and a wagonload of ostrich feathers into the first of their Emporiums.

Abe took Philip to see his orchards and the new mechanized sorting equipment he had just purchased.

''The first in Monterey,'' Basha said proudly as she and Emma sat on the porch and watched the two men drive off in the small tractor.

''You're a lucky woman,'' Emma said. ''In spite of everything.'' They would not, they could not, forget poor drowned Miriam, the years of struggle, the long journey toward the sunlight and prosperity of their middle years.

''And fortune has been with you too, Emma,'' Basha said. ''You found a man who loved you deeply, and together you have built a good life, a fine family.''

The two women had shown each other photographs of their children, and Emma had exclaimed at the beauty of the elegantly dressed Weinglass girls, full-cheeked and narrow-eyed like their mother, with their father's fair hair and large-boned build. She had been relieved that they did not resemble Miriam. It would be difficult to be reminded daily of the child lost to death. Always her heart stopped when she glimpsed a boy who reminded her of Gregory, and always she was relieved to see that the resemblance was, after all, superficial.

''Yes, Isaac and I have been successful in some ways,'' she said carefully.

''I'll never forget how Isaac came tearing into the house looking for you,'' Basha reflected. ''He stood on the porch and shouted your name over the noise of the storm, as though he warned God Himself to protect you. Avrum still speaks of the morning of your wedding day. He went to the synagogue to say Kaddish for our Miriam, and Isaac was there, and Avrum saw that he cried as he prayed. Avrum begged him not to be sad and reminded him that it was a mitzvah for a groom to rejoice on his wedding day. Isaac explained that he wept not from sadness but from joy. He had never thought to find love and happiness again, and then at last he had found you. 'The tears stood in his eyes like diamonds,' Avrum said. My Avrum, my Abie.'' She laughed. ''He thinks himself a poet. The only writers he reads are the Yiddish romances he has sent from New York. Still, it's not a bad image—tears like diamonds. Especially with Isaac's eyes, so dark and deep. You'll bring him to see us, Emma, when he comes to California?'' She looked at her friend and was surprised to see that Emma's hands were trembling and her face, drained of color, had taken on a camellian pallor.

''Is everything all right?'' she asked anxiously.

''Yes. Of course,'' Emma said. She stared westward to where Philip Sasson stood with Abe Weinglass amid the darkleafed trees. She watched as he stretched and, with elegant grace, plucked one peach and then another from the thickly laden branches.

''He's a married man, your friend?'' Basha asked.

''Yes, he's married,'' Emma replied, and Basha smiled.

''Soon your Isaac will come,'' she said.

''Yes. Soon Isaac will come.''

Emma closed her eyes and saw again the narrow pews of the Galveston synagogue. She imagined Isaac praying there on the morning of their wedding day, weeping as his lips moved soundlessly. ''Tears like diamonds,'' Avrum Weinglass had said. Yet she and Isaac had been man and wife for two decades now, and she had never seen him weep—not even at Gregory's funeral, when they had stood side by side but mourned alone, at once bereaved and betrayed.

Emma and Philip Sasson drove back to San Francisco along the coastal road, pausing en route to rest in a glen shaded by tall conifers beyond which stunted pepper trees grew in a dense thicket. Emma stretched out on the dry, sweet grass and nibbled at a cluster of the yellow mustard that grew wild in the meadow. She loved the taste of the bitter blossom. A lemon-colored petal adhered to the corner of her mouth, and Philip Sasson brushed it off with an outstretched finger and then pressed it to his lips. The day was warm, and she removed her dark jacket. Leonie had been wise to wear a light summer outfit, she reflected, and she smiled as she thought about her daughter. Franz had worked miracles. Leonie was reborn; like a butterfly emerging joyously from a chrysalis, she winged her way through her new life claiming the joy and excitement of her young womanhood. And Franz watched her flutter and soar, waiting for the moment when at last she would come to rest. Gentle, patient Franz, with whom Emma herself had shared so many secrets and from whom she had withheld so many others.

"What are you thinking about?" Philip asked, leaning against a huge ancient Monterey pine.

"Just that I'm thirsty," she said, the lie falling with practiced ease. She had, through the years, grown skilled at concealing her feelings, her thoughts.

"Then you must quench your thirst with California gold," he replied and reached into his pocket for the two perfect peaches he had plucked from the laden trees. She bit down. The rose-colored fruit tasted of sunlight and sweetness. Its thick juice spurted forth and stained her lips and chin. Philip Sasson took out his large white handkerchief, the fine linen embroidered with his initials, and wiped her upturned face as though she were a small girl whose delicate skin might be bruised by too harsh a touch. She closed her eyes. How good it was to be cared for so tenderly, to be offered peaches in the shade and sweet silence in a flowering meadow.

"Emma."

She heard the plea in his voice and stood abruptly.

"We must get back," she said, frightened now, because the touch of his hand, the sound of his voice, had called forth urgent stirrings and her body was awash with the silken moisture of her own yearning.

Trembling, she brushed the flecks of grass from her skirt with his handkerchief. Her hair was heavy against her neck, and she swept it up and twisted it into a coiled topknot, pinning it firmly into place.

He watched her, his mouth a taut, tight line, his eyes narrow. The sun beat down on them, and he shielded his eyes and looked up at it. It was honey-colored and almost exactly matched her hair.

They continued along the coastal road and listened to the rush of the sea, muted by the wind that rushed through the leaves of sequoia trees that lined their route. As always, they spoke little, but a new tension limned their silence, broken only when they marveled at the flock of gold-breasted orioles that soared past them on their flight northward to their nesting place amid the mountain yucca.

"We haven't had any lunch," he said when they arrived at the St. Francis Hotel, although they both knew that the lunch hour was long past and the white-jacketed waiters were already laying the tables for tea.

"I am hungry," she said. The ride had calmed her. She was once more in control, her voice cool. She lifted her hand to her hair. The topknot had held and formed a soft and graceful crown.

They had sandwiches and coffee in the almost deserted hotel dining room, served by an elderly waiter who hovered over them and hurried to bring extra cream for their coffee, curls of butter for the scones that the St. Francis baker produced especially for Philip Sasson.

He was their spoiled gentleman, and they yearned for his compliments, his favor. Did he always get what he wanted, Emma wondered, this elegant and bitter man, this friend and confidant whom she might never see again? No, not always. She remembered his marriage and scolded herself for feeling angry at him when, after all, she was only angry at herself, at her own weakness.

"It occurs to me," he said, "that you have never seen a photograph of my children."

"I should like to see one," she said.

"They are a handsome trio—Miranda, Melanie, and Robert." A smile played at his lips and warmth stole into his voice as he mouthed their names. They were the touchstone of his life. He had sacrificed all claim to love, to any married happiness, to them. Had he divorced Eleanor, their lives would have been destroyed by the rumored whispers that defied any stilling.

"I have a framed photograph in my suite," he said. "Shall I bring it down?"

"How foolish." She smiled. "I will go up with you to look at it."

His suite was comfortable, furnished in the ornate and lavish style of the great Mediterranean hotels. His newspaper was neatly folded on a low table before the green plush sofa, and low-backed gold chairs flanked a fireplace where no flames would ever blaze. The portrait of his children stood on the mantel, and she lifted it and studied the grave faces. All three children had inherited his short-lashed, deep-set gray eyes, but only the boy's face was angular, with hawklike features and a long, sharp chin like Philip's own. The girls' chubby visages were dreamy with innocence, and Emma thought that Philip Sasson was a courageous and generous man to safeguard his children's sweet naiveté.

"They're lovely," she said and turned to hold the picture to the light. Suddenly the floor beneath her feet quaked and the glass in the wide-paned windows trembled and rattled. She lost her balance and pitched forward onto the green couch, still clutching the picture so that the gold frame cut into her chest.

"What is it?" she gasped.

"A tremor. It's almost over, I think." But again the floor trembled, and she rose in fear and stepped into the shelter of his outstretched arms. A window shattered and shards of glass sparkled at their feet.

"Emma."

He lowered his face toward hers and his lips brushed her own, light at first and then with a desperate tenacity. Now the earth's trembling had ceased, and in the new and eerie stillness, he led her into the adjoining bedroom. Gently, he removed her jacket, undid the buttons of her white blouse, the narrow blue satin ribbons of her camisole. She made no protest. Loneliness and desire, danger and fear, had mingled and subdued her. She had been too long alone. The earth itself had trembled and coaxed her into submission. She stood naked before him.

"Turn around," he said softly.

She pivoted on her heels, an obedient and vanquished ballerina. She was his to command. As she turned, she caught sight of herself in the mirror, saw her long pale body, the fiery brush of her womanhood, the taut, rose-tipped nipples of her firm and swelling breasts.

"How beautiful you are." His voice was silken with desire. He pulled down the spread of the large bed. "I'll be right back," he said and disappeared into the adjoining dressing room.

She lifted her hands to her hair, yet she did not remove a single pin. Again she studied herself in the mirror and saw, with surprise, that tears stood in her eyes. She wept, just as Isaac had wept on the morning of their wedding day. *Tears like diamonds,* Basha had said. "Isaac." She whispered his name into her own reflection, into the still aftermath of that distant day. Still, she did not loosen her hair but tucked a vagrant tendril into the loose coronet. Then, slowly, she began to dress. When Philip emerged from the dressing room she was buttoning her blouse, fumbling with the tiny pearl fasteners.

"Philip, please forgive me, but I cannot." It was loneliness, not love that had drawn them together. The earth tremor (so common in California, she now remembered) had punctuated their mortality and thrust them together in desperation.

He did not reply but watched her, his chin cradled in his hand, as she finished dressing. She stood before him at last, willing him to forgiveness, to friendship.

"I will miss you," she said.

"I do not doubt it." His voice was bitter, but she saw the sadness that shadowed his gray eyes.

Still, he lifted her hand to his lips, and briefly he rested his palm on the copper ring of her upswept hair.

She dreamed that night that she stood on a platform and stared after a departing train. A desperate sadness overwhelmed her, but suddenly a whistle hooted and the train ground to a halt. A figure, all but concealed by the fog, walked the length of the tracks, boldly, purposefully. A beam of light, laser-thin, illuminated his face. She hurried forward, her hair caping her shoulders, and fell into her husband's outstretched arms.

"Isaac."

His name meant laughter, she knew, and she laughed in her sleep, was laughing still when she awakened and uttered it aloud, again and yet again.

Leonie Lewin and Franz Eisenmann were married that fall in the flower-filled garden of Simon and Thea Coen's Atherton estate. The guests sat beneath purple-barked redwood trees; the delicate feathery foliage shaded them against the sun, which burned with an intense radiance that day. The children surreptitiously plucked huckleberries from the flowering bushes, and always Joshua would remember that he tasted currants for the first time on his sister's wedding day. He plucked them one by one and savored their sweetness as the cantor intoned the marriage hymns.

The wedding canopy stood beneath a lush green arbor. Emma had fashioned it herself of mariposa tulips, tiger and leopard lilies, and the pale primroses that grew in profusion in her brother's garden, weaving the long-stalked flowers into an intricate pattern.

Emil watched her. "Mother loved to work with flowers," he said.

"Yes. I remember." Often Leonie Coen, their mother, had crafted the floral altar displays for the Portuguese Synagogue, singing softly as she worked. The craft was a delicate legacy, a gift of a kind from Leonie Coen, buried in Amsterdam's Ouderkirk cemetery, to her granddaughter and namesake, the bride who would be married in a California garden.

Emma's voice was gentle. She thought of her mother now with compassion rather than bitterness. An emotional symmetry had been reached, a peaceful equinox in the seasons of her life. She wondered wistfully, as she threaded a yellow leopard lily through a net of white primrose, if the mariposa tulips would bloom in her Phoenix garden.

Leonie's wedding dress was of Emma's own design. The

high-necked winter-white satin was sculpted to her slender form, and the long, sweeping train was appliquéd with rosettes of delicate lace that matched the jabot at her throat, the frilled cuffs at her wrists. Snow-white ostrich feathers sent express from the millinery department of the Phoenix Emporium formed her Juliet bridal cap, and Emma smiled as she placed it on her daughter's dark curls, remembering the hats of ostrich feathers she had fashioned that first year in Arizona. She had been pregnant with Leonie then, always weary; often her fingers had been bloodied by the spikes of the feathers. She felt Isaac's eyes upon her and wondered whether he, too, thought of those early days, of the ambitious dreams and desperate fears that had haunted them as they slept beneath the canvas of that first tent store.

Isaac watched his wife and daughter. Briefly, he closed his eyes against their beauty. Leonie was a radiant bride, and Emma was regal in a taffeta gown of turquoise blue that exactly matched her eyes and the pendant at her throat. He had sensed a change in Emma since his arrival a few days earlier. There was a new softness in her tone, a gentleness in her manner. As always, after the months of separation, they were shy and uneasy with each other, yet he felt a relaxation of tension. Still, caught up as they were in the swirl of prenuptial festivities, the rehearsal dinner at the Lombard Street house, and the bachelor party at the Black Cat, there had been no time for them to talk.

Even Emma's hair was different, he observed. She wore it swept up and coiled into a smooth, soft crown. A swathe of silver frosted the honey-colored tendrils, and she passed her hand across it as she plunged the long pins into place.

"You look very beautiful, Emma," he said.

She turned to him, straightened his striped satin cravat, smoothed the collar of his snow-white dress shirt. He stood very still, as startled by the intimacy of the gesture as by the touch of her fingers, light as butterfly wings at his neck.

They listened to the strains of the violin played by young Israel Kaplan, who stood beneath a cypress tree. The child violinist had, as Emil Coen had predicted, become the cherished protégé of San Francisco Jewry. Funds had been raised for his musical education, and he played at fashionable weddings, in private salons, and in concert at the synagogues and conservatories.

The bridesmaids approached first, flushed and pretty in their wine-colored, high-necked dresses, carrying nosegays of primroses and fuchsia. Rachel Wallach and Barbara Stern walked shyly and gravely down the gravel path that served as an aisle. Barbara held her head high, proud that Leonie had asked her to be a bridesmaid and proud, too, that she had fought her father and accepted the invitation. The Sterns had spent the summer in San Francisco, and Leonie and Barbara had met at a tennis party at the Lilienthals' San Rafael estate. It had seemed natural to Leonie to ask Jesse's sister to be her bridesmaid. Emma had frowned but raised no objection. She had a secret fondness for her half brother's gentle daughter. Always Barbara had been kind to Leonie. The girl could not be blamed for her father's bitter anger against the Lewins and the Coens, an anger compounded through the passing years as the lives of the two families chafed against each other. Would that anger ever end? Emma wondered as Barbara and Rachel reached the arbor. Still, it had been right of Leonie to invite her. It was a tribute, of a kind, to Jesse, an acknowledgment of his loss and of their love. Emma smiled and kissed her daughter on the cheek.

The guests leaned forward as Israel Kaplan played the bridal march. Franz Eisenmann trembled as he watched Leonie move toward him. She walked between Emma and Isaac, one white-gloved hand resting on her father's arm, the other nestled in her mother's gentle grasp. She smiled as Cantor Rinder intoned the marriage prayers and went to stand at her groom's side beneath the marriage canopy woven of flowers and fern. "With this ring thou art consecrated unto me according to the laws of Moses and of Israel." Franz sang the ancient vow in his deep tenor, and she trembled, but the ring that he slipped on her outstretched finger was not woven of desert grass but crafted of white gold. He had taken careful measurement; it fit firmly and seemed possessed of radiant heat of its own. The wine cup was passed from his lips to hers, and she drank deeply, joyously. And then his foot smashed the white-wrapped glass, and the Atherton garden resounded with cries of *"Mazal tov!"* "Good luck!'' *"Felicidad!"* Johnny Redbird, seated beside Brother Timothy, with whom he had traveled from Arizona, lifted his eyes and smiled to see a falcon soar skyward. The holy men of his people, the wise-hearted shamans of the mesa, said it was a good sign to see a single bird fly by after a marriage ceremony: It meant that two souls had been forged into one, two lives had been entwined forever.

Leonie and Franz dashed down the gravel-studded aisle, laughing as the guests pelted them with flower petals and trailed after them on their joyous race to the reception beside the swimming pool. The blue-green lagoon was surrounded by white-clothed tables laden with the delicacies of a champagne lunch.

Emma and Isaac stood alone beneath the fragrant marriage canopy. He took her hand in his and slowly turned the gold ring he had slipped on her finger so many years ago.

"Thou *art* consecrated unto me," he said, and his eyes glinted with a dangerous brilliance. *Tears like diamonds,* she thought and touched his cheek. The tear, warm and commingling joy and sorrow, fell upon her finger. He inclined his face toward hers and kissed her gently.

"I love you, Isaac." The words, so long withheld, fell softly. He did not ask why she spoke them now. It did not matter.

"And I have loved you always."

Sunlight blazed through the canopy of woven flowers and slatted her hair with bands of gleaming copper, brushed his skin with gold. They looked at each other, content in their silence. They needed no other words, neither explanations nor pledges.

A single tulip fluttered loose and drifted to their feet. Isaac picked it up, threaded it through her hair, and again he kissed her, holding her so close now that their hearts beat hard upon each other. They wept, and their freshly flowing tears mingled; their faces were awash with their shared joy, their bittersweet regret. They stood together beneath a marriage canopy, and yet again she was his bride. But now, at last, they had banished the swirling shadows of their separate pasts and affirmed their future. Their ghosts were laid to rest, and their daughter's wedding day marked their own sweet union and reunion. Gently, they brushed away each other's tears, and, hand in hand, they went to embrace their children, to toast their daughter's happiness and their own,

A canvas had been spread across the tennis court, and a blue-and-green striped awning had been stretched above it to protect the dancers from the noonday sun. Leonie and Franz danced the stately marriage waltz. Joshua invited Barbara Stern to dance, and Emil and Simon watched them glide across the canvas dance floor.

"Our father's grandchildren," Emil said sadly. "How foolish all this concealment and anger has been."

"A waste," Simon agreed. "But it was not of our choosing."

It was Henry Stern who had chosen the path of denial and enmity, but surely the passing years had diluted his anger. If his daughter could dance at Leonie's wedding, perhaps the day might come when all of them might sit together around a table, their anger abated. Perhaps they might even speak of Jacob Coen with understanding rather than anger. He looked at Emil, and wordlessly the brothers shook hands, acknowledging the forgiveness it had taken them two decades to achieve.

"Dance with me, Papa," Alice called, and Simon whirled his daughter about the floor in the Texas Two-Step.

The band played a joyous hora, and the dancers joined hands and encircled Leonie and Franz. "Joy to the bride—joy to the groom," they sang in Hebrew and then again in English. The songs and dances of the old world and the new mingled. They formed two lines for Cotton-Eyed Joe and formed squares for the intricate debkas they had danced in the stately ballrooms of Berlin and Vienna, across the meadowlands of Russia and Poland. Hands upon each other's shoulders, they became a dancing chain, moving joyously about the pool, their faces flushed, their voices high and sweet. "Come with me from Lebanon, my bride, my beloved," they chanted as shadows crept across the hillocks of northern California. Leonie and Franz sat side by side, and their chairs were hoisted into the air as voices hoarsened by song and joy shouted *"L'chaim—*To life!"

Franz held his bride's hand. *"L'chayenu,"* he shouted. "To our lives together."

The guests cheered, and Isaac drew Emma close.

"L'chayenu," he repeated. Softly, she echoed his words.

The wedding cake was cut, and Leonie and Franz stole away. Reluctantly, small groups took their leave.

"Such a wonderful wedding."

"What a lovely party."

"Such a special day."

Worlds had blended that afternoon and lives had come together. A community had celebrated its continuity. Thea Coen beamed. The dowager Alice Lilienthal had told her that the reception had style, distinction. Emil and Simon Coen, pleasantly drunk, toasted their niece, their sister, and each other. Brother Timothy embraced Isaac and Johnny Redbird shook his hand. They would travel back to Arizona together on the night train, trading Irish folk tales and Indian lore as they plunged down the Sierra Nevada and across the barren expanse of Death Valley.

"Thank you so much for everything." Barbara Stern held out her hand to Emma.

"Barbara." Emma smiled at the girl, noting for the first time the high cheekbones so like her own. "We thank you for coming. How are you getting back to the city?"

"My father should be waiting at the gate," Barbara said, and a painful blush bruised her cheeks.

"Let me walk down with you," Emma said, and Isaac stared at her in surprise and then rose to join her. It was, after all, a day of reconciliation.

Henry Stern waited at the gate, leaning against the open door of the Daimler. His hand rested on the head of a toddler who slept, face down, against his shoulder. He looked at Emma, surprise widening and darkening his eyes that matched hers. She approached him, slowly, hesitantly, and he, in turn, moved toward her. Barbara and Isaac stood back, still as statues, as though their slightest movement might disturb the delicate balance of the moment. And then the child in Henry Stern's arms stirred and turned his head. Emma saw the thick amber-hued curls, the bright blue eyes, the dreamy set of mouth and high pale brow.

Gregory. Her lips formed the word but she did not speak it. Henry Stern's child, Isabel Cavalajo's firstborn, might have been twin to her own lost son.

She stood still, paralyzed by memory, by a resurgent grief so sharp and painful that she swayed and would have fallen had not Isaac moved swiftly forward to steady her. She closed her eyes because she could not bear to see the child's face as it drifted from drowsy sleep into wakefulness. Would he speak in Gregory's high, sweet voice and sing with tremulous sadness? Isaac held her close, his own breath coming in stertorous gasps. He shared her pain, her grief.

And then a car's horn sounded harshly, impatiently. Barbara pressed her hand.

"Thank you again."

Henry Stern sat in the car and stared straight ahead. His face was locked against her, and he did not look back as they drove off.

Emma and Isaac did not speak of Henry Stern as they walked back to the house, nor did Emil and Simon ask any questions. Joshua, lonely because he was neither boy nor adult, listened as they spoke softly. The lowering sun turned the waters of the San Francisco Bay the color of molten gold, and Emma recalled the narrow canals of Amsterdam, briefly phosphorescent in the glow of the dying light. Simon filled their glasses, and they spoke of how their father had loved to sip Genever on the balcony of their Prinsengracht home at the sunset hour.

Joshua grew impatient. They spoke of the past, and he yearned for the future. He walked out to the lawn and watched Samuel and his cousins dash across the tennis courts. They played wood tag, a family game of their own invention. "Safe!" they shouted as they touched a tree or wooden ballast. Months ago Joshua had played with them, but now the game seemed pointless and he had no interest in safety. It was adventure he craved. He leaped suddenly and swung from the low-hanging branch of an orange tree. The white blossoms drifted about him in a snowy burst, but he found a single, perfect cluster and carried it back to his mother. Deftly, she separated two sprigs and wove them, each in turn, through his lapel and his father's. His heart turned because his father held his mother's hand and the scent of orange blossoms filled the air.

Late that night Emma and Isaac stood together on the balcony of the Lombard Street house and looked down at the harbor lights. Exhausted after the long day, Emma had luxuriated in her bath. Damp tendrils of hair curled about her face, and beneath the flowing white peignoir her skin was the color of sunlight. Isaac drew her close and she turned in his arms. She cupped his face in her hands, and their kiss commingled tenderness and passion, promise and regret.

"We will be together always now," she said.

"Always," he promised, and he led her into the dimly lit room, where the white canopied bed faced the harbor. They did not draw the curtains. They were, at last, at one with each other and with the velvet darkness of night and the pearl shimmer that marked the break of dawn.

Phoenix,
1928

JOSHUA LEWIN stared through the open window of the train at the changing face of the desert as the Santa Fe express hurtled toward Phoenix. He smiled as a jackal darted through a thicket of thorny brush and vanished into an overgrowth of brasada. Spiked blossoms the color of sea coral jeweled the prickled arms of the huge saguaro cacti that cast their velvet shadows across the pale sands. Two Indian boys, astride pie-bald ponies, galloped by and plucked thick-skinned fruits from the flowering plants without slowing their pace.

"My brother and I used to try that," Joshua said to the young woman who sat opposite him. "We usually ended up falling off our ponies."

She looked up from her book, a flicker of annoyance on her face.

"I beg your pardon. Did I miss something?" she asked politely but without real interest. She had read steadily, since boarding the train at the New Mexico border, and her pre-occupation and indifference to the landscape irritated Joshua. The Arizona desert was his passion, and he returned to it now, after a three-year absence, with the heightened intensity and enthusiasm peculiar to those who have yearned for a beloved terrain from a great distance.

He had walked the alpine mountain trails, stared up at the snow-covered peaks of Mont Blanc and Mischabel, and spoken longingly to his companions of the sunwashed desert of the state of his birth. He had made love to a beautiful colleague in a verdant meadow sparkling with delicately petaled gentians, and told her of the grandeur of the barren Arizona mountains, of the haunting beauty of its wilderness and canyons. He had vacationed with a student nurse in Lausanne and walked that city's ancient cobbled streets speaking of the

391

pioneering outpost Phoenix had been in his youth. Always, the young European women had been intrigued by the home-sick American doctor who spoke slowly and dreamily of his home in the West.

"Tell us about the Indians," they begged, because they had seen films of marauding redskins attacking white-hatted cowboys. Joshua had told them instead of his friend Johnny Redbird, of the boys at the Indian School in Phoenix with whom he had played softball on hot spring afternoons, of the large-eyed youths at Brother Timothy's school in Prescott. He wrote home to Johnny Redbird and ordered gifts from the Arizona Experience, delicately crafted jewelry of silver and turquoise, baskets of intricate weave, which he gave as gifts to the nurses and doctors with whom he worked at the Alpine Sanitorium for Tuberculars.

His own room in the hospital dormitory had been deco-rated with Navajo rugs, a Hopi wall hanging, and a painting of the desert at dusk that Rachel Wallach had sent to him as a Hanukkah gift. Often, he had looked at the painting and struggled against a seizure of homesickness so overwhelm-ing that he felt that a weight had settled on his heart. Rachel had painted a desert hawk into the corner of her landscape. The painted bird soared over the parched chaparral, and Joshua had stared at it, shivered in the mountain chill, and wished himself back in Arizona.

And now at last the train was speeding him through the desert, but there was no one with whom to share the joyous recognition, the flood of memories. Already his chance trav-eling companion was turning back to her book, as indifferent to his reply as she was to the passing scene.

"Yes, you are missing something," he said boldly. "In fact it seems to me you are missing this entire journey. That must be a fascinating book."

"It is," she replied coldly, "although I am sure you have not heard of it." She spoke in the clipped accent of the East-ern seaboard. Boston, he thought, or perhaps Washington. His years in Europe had heightened his awareness of regional dialects, a small talent in which he took an odd pride.

"Try me," he said. "I may surprise you."

"It's by a British author—Aldous Huxley."

"Ah, *Point, Counterpoint*—so you like it?" His own copy had been a gift from his uncles' British colleague Philip Sasson and he had read it during the Atlantic crossing, between bouts of seasickness.

"Obviously," she said and resumed her reading, but he saw that his knowledge of the title had unnerved her. She stole a curious glance at him as she turned a page.

"Is this your first trip to Arizona?" he asked companionably.

She rose abruptly, plucking up her jacket and her wicker handbag. "I will find a seat in the next car," she said. "If you will excuse me." Her cheeks were flushed and her hazel eyes glinted.

"I'm sorry. I meant no offense," he said, rising. He had made a tactical error, he supposed. A European woman would have replied softly, hesitantly.

"And no offense was taken."

She moved swiftly past him, her head held high, and he saw how the blond curls formed damp golden ringlets at the back of her neck. She was definitely from the East, he decided. She had not yet learned how to move with slow deliberation through the desert heat. He forgot her as the train cruised through the dun-colored hillocks and arroyo-slatted flatlands at the outskirts of the city. He was at the door and ready to descend as the train pulled into the terminal and the conductor shouted, "Phoe-nix—Phoe-nix!"

The station platform was crowded, but he saw his parents at once, standing beside Leonie's small dark-haired twin daughters.

"Joshua!" His mother and father called his name in unison, and Isaac rushed forward to greet him while Emma smiled and stared up at him.

It always startled Emma Lewin to recognize her sons as the tall self-confident young men they had become. In her thoughts and dreams they remained the small boys who had galloped along desert trails on their ponies and sprawled on the polished wood floor, playing with their puzzles and their maps, moving their toy soldiers from place to place. Life happened too quickly, she thought. It bewildered her, on occasion, to realize that she was the mother of grown children, grandmother to Leonie's large-eyed daughters and the infant boy who slept so peacefully now in the cradle that Isaac had crafted for Joshua.

Joshua strode toward her now and almost lifted her off the ground as he embraced her.

"You're more beautiful than ever, Mother," he said.

She blushed as he stroked her cheek and brushed back the silvering hair at her temple. Her face was relaxed, and her turquoise eyes were soft and peaceful.

"You're right, Joshua," Isaac said. "Your mother grows more beautiful every year. But then she must if she is to keep up with these California granddaughters of ours. Say hello to your uncle Joshua, Rebecca and Sarah." The dark-haired little girls were named for the wife and daughter he had buried in Russia, a decision that Leonie and Franz had made in their quiet thoughtful manner on the day the twins were born. Franz had discussed it with his wife's parents, gently, carefully.

"We believe in continuity," he had said. "And we believe in confronting the past. Names live on in our tradition. You had another life in Europe, Father-in-law. Shouldn't those who were a part of it be remembered?"

"I think Sarah and Rebecca are beautiful names," Emma had said, and she had looked hard at Isaac, willing his consent, his acknowledgment that new lives suborn distant deaths.

He had agreed, of course, and always he thought of Franz's words when he saw Henry Stern sit beside his young son in the synagogue. The child was named for Jesse (still, it was startling, unsettling, that he so closely resembled Gregory), and surely, with each mention of his name, Henry Stern was reminded of his firstborn son, who had died of influenza in a French field hospital. Confrontation and continuity—an odd choice for a man who rejected continuity, evaded confrontation, who still waged emotional war with Emma and her family.

"Now how am I going to tell Sarah from Rebecca?" Joshua asked, and they smiled shyly up at him. "I know. I'll give Sarah the edelweiss and Rebecca the gentian pin I bought in Geneva. Then I'll be able to tell you apart because of the flowers."

"Unless we switch them and fool you, Uncle Joshua," Sarah said, and Rebecca giggled mischievously.

"Where are the pins?" Rebecca asked.

"In my trunk," Joshua said. "Come along now and help me claim it."

The little girls trailed after him as he went to the baggage car and gave his claim ticket to the porter.

"Just a minute now. I got this real big one to see to," the overworked porter said. He picked up a large pigskin valise and hurled it onto the platform. It landed on its side and the lid flew open. Snow-white undergarments, pastel-colored blouses, gossamer-thin nightgowns scattered across the dirt-streaked loading platform. Joshua flipped the valise over and began to toss the fallen garments in.

"Help me, girls," he said, and the twins laughed and scurried about, filling their small arms with clothing. Rebecca giggled as she plucked up a pair of flesh-colored silk stockings, and Sarah perched a navy blue beret on her head.

"Oh, no. How did this happen?" His traveling companion, still clutching her copy of *Point, Counterpoint*, stared down at her possessions.

"Your case fell open," Joshua said. "My nieces here were helping me to get everything back in." He held a peach-colored nightgown, light as a cloud in his hands. Too swiftly she snatched it from him, her face beet-red, her hands trembling, but she smiled faintly when Sarah offered her the beret.

"I must thank you for troubling yourselves," she said and snapped the case shut.

"I'll be glad to help you to your cab," Joshua said, but she shook her head vigorously.

"I can manage, thank you."

She walked off then, staggering beneath the weight of the valise. Joshua watched her ruefully and was relieved when a station redcap hurried up to her and placed her luggage on an empty cart. Then his own large trunk was lowered, and he claimed the crate that contained his surgical instruments and the fluoroscopy equipment he had bought in Switzerland. The twins clamored for their gifts and so he opened the trunk. Kneeling to close it, he noticed a pale blue silk scarf that had slipped beneath the wooden planks of the platform. He thrust it into his pocket and hurried after the porter, the twins trailing after him. He was anxious now to be home, to embrace Leonie and Samuel and to meet Bryna, the girl Samuel would marry that fall. "She fills me with peace and with courage," Samuel had written to him, and he had been at once glad for his brother and envious of him.

The entire family gathered that night to celebrate Joshua's homecoming. Emil and Simon were visiting and Emma was pleased that Leonie and Franz had delayed their return to California after spending the Jewish New Year and Yom Kippur in Phoenix. Franz had reversed the family's tradition of spending the holidays in San Francisco.

"Phoenix has its own synagogue now," Franz had said. "And I think it is important that the children know their family and feel comfortable in the house where their mother grew up."

His own childhood home was inaccessible to his children, and although he wrote often, imploring his parents to come to California, at least for a visit, the grain merchant remained adamant. He still envisaged the American West as a wilderness, undeveloped and sparsely populated, devoid of the cultural life of Vienna. He dismissed Franz's references to Hitler and the National Socialist party. Hitler's hooligans were in Germany, after all, and he was in Austria. *Mein Kampf* was clearly the work of a diseased mind. Those who read Schiller and Rilke, Heine and Goethe, would dismiss it with harsh laughter. And besides, the Jews of Austria knew better than to attract attention to themselves and incite the Gentiles. Franz's fear was irrational. One would have expected a responsible married man, a father himself, to think more clearly. Franz had not yet answered his father's last letter. He wanted to talk to Joshua. Joshua had visited Germany, and his impressions would be valuable, Franz knew.

Samuel and Bryna Markowitz, his fiancée, sat side by side, holding hands. Like Joshua, Samuel was tall and broad-shouldered, with rough, dark hair that had to be combed into place several times during the day. Yet his features were delicate like Emma's, and, like his mother, he was deeply introspective. He had studied economics at the University of

Arizona and then enrolled in a graduate program at the University of Chicago. Always, the inequities of life had disturbed him. Even as a child he had asked Isaac unanswerable questions. Why were some people rich and others desperately poor? Was it fair for his family to live in a large house while he had classmates who lived in one-room adobe homes? He wanted to study economic theory, social philosophy, but even before the semester ended, he was back in Phoenix.

It had occurred to him, as he sat in the library one evening, wrestling with the economic philosophy of Keynes, that he had a unique opportunity to translate economic theory into action. The Lewin Emporium was, after all, an American economic structure in microcosm. He told Isaac that he wanted a job at the Emporium. An entry-level job, he had been swift to specify. He wanted to understand the business on every level, to experience the work of inventory clerks and sales personnel, of stock boys and buyers.

"He is right," Isaac had told Emma. "One day the business will be his, and he will understand it from its roots to its crown."

He was proud of his son and prouder still when Samuel began to institute changes and make suggestions. A profit-sharing plan would increase employee productivity. A Lewin Free Loan Fund would reduce the stress on individual employees. He cited the case of Juan Alvarez, with whom he had worked in the shipping room. The young Mexican had been so worried about paying the medical bills of his ailing mother that his work had suffered. It made sense, Samuel argued, sound business sense, to ease the strain on a valued employee. Isaac agreed. He also agreed when Samuel suggested that a personnel director be hired.

"Someone who understands people and understands the store," Samuel suggested. "We're too big now to run it the way you once did."

Isaac nodded, although he felt a pang of regret for the days when he had known every employee by name.

Bryna had answered their discreet advertisement for the position and had been hired at once. She was a plump, outgoing young woman whose warmth and laughter intrigued the shy and reticent Samuel. He came to her office to discuss staffing problems, the possibility of an employee cafeteria, incentive awards. Always, he came late in the afternoon, and they both pretended surprise when darkness fell and they found themselves together at the dinner hour.

They ate together in Mexican cantinas and the dining room of the Phoenix Hotel. She took him to a small restaurant on the Tempe road where a guitarist strolled through the dimly lit room and played haunting Spanish love songs. He invited her to the house on MacDowell Road for Friday night dinner. Bryna watched Emma place the candles in the tall silver candlesticks. She, too, covered her eyes at the moment of benediction, and Samuel watched the linear lights of the gentle flames scale her fingers. He longed to take her radiant hands into his own, to press his cheek against her smooth dark hair. He asked her to marry him that night, and in answer she lifted his hand to her lips and he felt her breath warm against his palm as she said, "Yes, oh, yes, my darling."

Their engagement had pleased Emma and Isaac. Emma smiled now at the young couple as Samuel laughed aloud at something Bryna said. Bryna was good for Samuel, although it had surprised her that her shy younger son would be the first to marry. It had always been handsome Joshua who escorted the prettiest girls in Phoenix to dances and parties. The servant girls had always blushed when he came into the room. His letters from college and medical school were peppered with the names of girls, with references to cotillions and dinner parties.

But then Joshua had always surprised her. Throughout his boyhood he had spoken of becoming a writer, and then abruptly he had abandoned his journals and expressed an interest in medicine.

"Being a doctor will give me a chance to help people," he had said. "My scribbling won't do that. And besides, I'm not good enough."

Always he had been disarmingly, almost painfully honest with himself and with others, and always he had maintained a clear perspective on his own ability. He had been good enough at medicine. Good enough to gain acceptance to the Baylor University Medical School when he was only eighteen and to graduate first in his class, completing a four-year program in only three years. Good enough to be offered an internship at the Massachusetts General Hospital, a rare achievement for a graduate of a western medical school, especially a Jewish graduate.

"With one admission they get both their token westerner and their token Jew," Joshua had told Rachel Wallach. "I'm not sure I want to give them the satisfaction of solving both their quota problems at once."

In the end he had turned the internship down after spending the summer as a volunteer locum physician on the mesa. Lung disease haunted the Indian population, ravaging men and women, attacking small children. The clear, benign desert air, which attracted tuberculars and emphysema sufferers from all over the United States, failed to benefit native Arizonans.

"Perhaps there is a congenital vulnerability," Brother Timothy speculated. He had watched graduates of his mission school fall victim to the hacking cough, the labored breathing, and he had administered last rites to those who could not gather breath for a final confession.

"More probably we just don't know enough about it," Joshua had replied bitterly.

He stood beside Johnny Redbird when the Indian's teen-aged son was buried. The keening of the squaws tore at his heartstrings, and he cursed himself for his ignorance, his professional impotence. Interesting work was being done in Switzerland, at an alpine tubercular hospital. That fall he had sailed for Europe.

What would Joshua do now? Emma wondered as she watched her elder son whisper a secret into Rebecca's ear. The child laughed and hurried across the room to share Joshua's joke with her twin. He had spoken of a clinic during dinner and speculated about the possibility of a mobile health unit. A preventive ambulance service rather than an emergency one—an expensive investment but a practical one, in the end. His words had been meant to tease his father, Emma knew, to coax the practical businessman into considering a medical problem in terms of debit and credit. He need not have bothered. Joshua could count on their support. She and Isaac would welcome the opportunity to contribute to Arizona, to pay their debt to the state that had welcomed and sustained them.

"Are you sad, Grandma?" Sarah climbed onto her lap and pressed her cheek against Emma's.

"No, child. I'm not sad. I was just thinking of how fortunate we are—how very, very lucky."

Sadness and sorrow belonged to her past. She and Isaac had escaped the shadows; they had been granted a second lease on their lives, a new tenure for their love. She kissed the child and went to the door to greet new arrivals.

Brother Timothy came in, all gray now and slightly bent with the arthritis that had attacked him in recent years. She felt stricken, almost betrayed, because he had aged so quickly, and her hand flew to her own silvering hair. It was true, then, as Emil had suggested only that afternoon, that it was only by observing contemporaries that one became aware of the impact of the passing years.

Natalya and Abner Wallach and their children swept in, laughing and talking, encircling them with their friendship. Joseph and Reuben Wallach were quick-thinking, ambitious young men who had worked at the Emporium even while they were in high school. Unlike Samuel, they were concerned and intrigued with selling and salesmanship. Always they spoke excitedly of new products and new projects. They argued for aggressive sales campaigns, for the mark-down policies that had worked for Filene's in Boston, for Rich's in Atlanta, even for Neiman-Marcus in Dallas. They greeted customers by name and worried over advertising and window displays.

"Damn it, this isn't a social experiment—it's a department store!" Joseph had shouted at Samuel and Bryna when they had insisted that space be taken from the accessory department for an employee infirmary.

They were impatient with their father and with Isaac himself and spoke restlessly of going to California. There were merchandising opportunities in Sacramento and Los Angeles. Herbert Hoover would bring a new prosperity to the country. "The business of America is business," he had said, reiterating Calvin Coolidge, and Reuben had cut the quotation out of the newspaper and pasted it onto his desk blotter.

They shook hands vigorously with Joshua, but their sister, Rachel, smiled shyly and blushed when he kissed her on the cheek. Always there had been a special rapport between Rachel and Joshua. She had written to him through the years of his absence; her letters had been newsy accounts of family happenings and events in Phoenix. It had been Rachel who sent him gifts on his birthday and holidays and clipped newspaper stories that she thought might interest him.

She was slender and sandy-haired, calm and competent, like Natalya, her mother. Although she was younger than her exuberant brothers, she exercised a restraining influence on them, and they responded to her with a loving deference. It was Rachel who reminded them that the Emporium was the property of the Lewin family and that it was Samuel who would eventually assume its control. She encouraged them in their aspirations yet advocated patience. Isaac Lewin would be fair to Abner Wallach's children as he had always been fair to Abner himself. She herself managed the Lewin Link that Emma had opened on her return to Phoenix, but all her free time was concentrated on her drawing and painting. She studied with Isabel Cavalajo Stern, who taught studio classes in the large, wide-windowed workroom that Henry Stern had built for her.

"You look wonderful, Rachel," Joshua said, smiling down at her. "How goes the painting?"

"All right, I suppose. I'm good but not good enough."

"Now, where have I heard that before?" They grinned at each other because he had said as much to Rachel when he had decided to abandon his writing in favor of medicine. She had not changed. She still shared his penchant for honest self-evaluation. He liked the way she wore her hair now—in a pixie bob with uneven sand-colored bangs fringing her high forehead. She had been a plain child who had grown into a plain woman, yet when she smiled her face curved into lines of beauty, and always her dark-eyed gaze was thoughtful and kind.

"It's good to have you back, Joshua," she said and moved across the room to admire Leonie's infant son.

Franz Eisenmann stood beside Joshua, and together they watched Rachel lift the infant in her arms and extend her finger for his grasp.

"Rachel is a rare kind of woman," Franz said. "She is totally herself. She will neither dissemble nor disappoint."

"Like her parents," Joshua agreed. The Wallachs had always been a second family to him, and he seldom thought of Rachel independently of Natalya and Abner and her brothers.

"Do you think so?" Franz asked. "My profession has taught me to tread cautiously when I make such judgments."

"You know, Franz, I attended a lecture by your Dr. Freud in Berlin."

"And what did you think?"

"Very impressive. It was sparsely attended. Apparently the German medical community is not particularly sympathetic to what they perceive to be the eclectic revolutionary theory of a Jewish doctor from Vienna. At least that is what a colleague of mine indicated."

"What was your impression of the situation in Germany?" Franz asked, lowering his voice.

"Unrest. Anger. Beer-hall mutterings about unemployment, lack of land for expansion, inflation. Adolf Hitler telling the Germans what they want to hear—Jewish cowards lost the war for them, and Jewish capitalists are responsible for all the nation's ills."

Franz sighed. "I wrote my father urging him to leave, to get the family out of Vienna." He looked across the room at Leonie and his children. "I can't comprehend his hesitancy. I would leave California at once if I felt my family was endangered."

"But Franz, you have been in California only for a few years. Your father's family has been in Vienna for generations. The Jewish doctors I met at the conference are convinced that Hitler is a transient phenomenon, an evil wind that will exhaust itself. Only one spoke of leaving, but then he admitted that his roots were not in Germany—he had migrated there from Amsterdam. David Deken—a hematologist who read a paper on blood chemistry and tuberculosis."

"Did he know your mother's family?" Franz asked.

"I didn't think to ask," Joshua replied. "I had other things on my mind that night." He smiled, remembering the pretty blond nurse he had escorted home from that meeting. He reflected now that her hair had been straw-colored, unlike the golden curls of the young woman who had traveled with him to Phoenix. He had spread her pale blue scarf across his bureau and wondered vaguely if he would ever see her again so that he might return it. He doubted it. Phoenix was no longer a small pioneer town. It had fulfilled the promise of its name and become a city where chance encounters were unlikely.

"Please, friends, may I have your attention?" Isaac stood in the center of the room, his face beaming. "I have a pleasant announcement to make—good news to share with you."

"What now?" Reuben Wallach asked Joseph.

"A welcome-home speech to Joshua, I suppose," his brother answered indifferently; he frowned when Abner Wallach lifted his fingers to his lips, cautioning him to silence. "Goddamn it—you'd think Isaac Lewin was the king and the Wallach family his courtiers," he muttered, ignoring his father's reproachful stare and falling silent only when Rachel moved to his side and touched him lightly on the arm.

Isaac stood before the large refectory table and unrolled a set of blueprints.

"I have here the plans for Phoenix's Second Lewin's Emporium," he said. "Two weeks ago I took title to the empty lot on the corner of Garden Street. Phoenix is changing—growing and expanding—and Lewin's will also grow and expand. The architect's plans are complete, as you see, and already I have bids from contractors. Within a year, by the summer of 1929, our new store will be open for business."

He stared at them expectantly, and they responded with a faint burst of applause, a nervous exchange of glances. The Wallach brothers moved forward to study the plans, but Samuel and Bryna looked worriedly at each other.

"When did you decide all this, Father?" Samuel asked.

"Not I—*we*—your mother and I. We have been planning this for months. We wanted the plans to be ready tonight—in honor of Joshua's homecoming."

He smiled proudly, and Emma moved to his side. They had planned this new enterprise together as now they planned all things. The partnership she had sought to legislate, had fought to achieve, had become a natural part of their marriage. It was Emma who explained the plans, calling their attention to the enormous basement area ("The final discount center," Isaac explained, "like Filene's and Rich's." He grinned at the Wallach brothers. "You thought I wasn't listening, Reuben, but I listened and then I went to Boston and to Atlanta to see for myself"), the broad aisles on the main floor ("Strictly for the newest fashions—popularly priced lines that won't be available at the other store," Isaac explained), and the way in which the upper levels of the building were carved into self-contained sections ("Boutiques within the heart of the store—we could have a Lewin Link contained within the Emporium just like the Arizona Experience").

Rachel Wallach studied the architect's drawing with an approving professional eye. She admired Isaac Lewin for hiring Albert Chase MacArthur. He had studied with Frank Lloyd Wright, and like his mentor he believed that buildings should blend into the natural environment. The Emporium would be built of tufa stone. Its wide windows would exploit the brilliant desert sunlight, and its graceful cornices would protect passers-by from the fierce heat.

"I don't understand, Father-in-law," Franz said. "Won't your stores compete with each other?"

"No more than I. Magnin and J. Magnin in California compete. The present store will continue to cater to the carriage trade, to the tourists who have money to spend and want to return east wearing the Lewin Look. The new store will satisfy customers who want good, stylish merchandise but have less to spend," Isaac replied.

He had always tried to stock items for his less prosperous customers, but it had been difficult to maintain two profiles. The Lewin image had been established back in the tent store when the governor's wife had bought her gown there for the capital's first ball. The Lewin Look had reinforced the store's reputation for high style, and he knew that working people were intimidated by the mahogany counters, the crystal chandeliers, the elaborate displays. The new store would promote a more egalitarian image, more accessible displays.

"But why now?" Leonie asked. "You and Mama should be thinking of working less. Why take on a new enterprise at this point?" Her father's health worried her. Earlier in the afternoon he had lifted Rebecca and swiftly set the child down, his face pale, his hand clutching his chest. It was just a transient pain, he had assured her. He did not often suffer such discomfort, although Dr. Lashner had advised him to rest in the afternoons, to take long walks. Still, she had noticed the pallid sweat that beaded his brow and the new worry lines that rimmed his eyes.

"We will work less," Isaac responded. "Your mother and I will have nothing to do with managing the new store. That we turn over to Reuben and Joseph Wallach. If they agree, of course." He smiled shrewdly at the two young men, whose faces were already split into smiles.

Reuben leaned over the plans, his fingers tracing the corridors, the architect's delicate delineations of space. Where could they fit a cafeteria? Not a restaurant but a wide-windowed room for snacks with paper placemats advertising the store's specials. They could offer the food cheaply. Losses on coffee and sandwiches would be made up for in the volume of sale merchandise.

"We agree," Joseph said. "Of course, we agree." He did not look at Rachel, ashamed to meet her reproving glance. She had been right and he had been wrong. Isaac Lewin had been fair to his friend Abner, and he was now demonstrating his fairness to Abner's sons. Joseph put his arm around his mother's shoulders and moved forward to embrace Isaac and then his father.

"I just wonder if now is the wisest time to embark on such a project," Samuel interposed in his slow academic's voice. "We are in a comfortable, secure position now. Granted that if the second store is a success we could recoup the investment rapidly and double our income—the question is, do we want that kind of a gamble and do we need that kind of a profit."

"All business is a gamble," Isaac replied. "But there is need and there is want. When your mother and I began the

Emporiums, when we lifted the flaps on the tent store, it was out of need—our need to simply survive, to earn enough money to buy food and shelter and to build a life in this new land. We had both known loss and poverty, and perhaps it was that knowledge that spurred us to success. We build now because we want to build, because there are things we want to do with the kind of revenue the new store will generate. Reuben and Joseph have their dreams as I had mine, and I want to help them. Without the Wallach family the Lewins would not have succeeded so well. But we want money for more than that. Joshua speaks of a clinic for his work—a clinic needs facilities, equipment, nurses—maybe a mobile medical unit to service the reservations, the outlying settlements. Samuel and Bryna come to me each day with new plans to help our employees. Health insurance, free loan funds, even a recreation center. I don't need Abner Wallach's sons to tell me that such ideas cost money—a great deal of money. I am not a doctor or a politician. I can't heal the sick or pass laws to help working people. But I am a businessman. I know how to make money. And I think that I know how to use it for justice, for *tzedakah*. You know in Hebrew there is no word for charity—the word for justice is used instead. The day I became an American citizen I stood before a judge and said the Pledge of Allegiance—'with liberty and justice for all,' I said. I've enjoyed that liberty, and now I want to do that justice.''

He sat down then and clutched the arms of his chair as if the outpouring of words had somehow depleted him and he struggled now to replenish his spent energy.

"But Father, you will have to use reserve capital for the building and stocking of the new store. Is this the best time to make such an investment?'' Samuel persisted.

"Of course it is,'' Emil Coen said confidently. "The economy has never been this good. Simon and I can't find enough ships for leasing to carry exports abroad. You've seen the reports yourself, Samuel—we have a fifty percent increase in foreign trade over last year. Our factories are going into overtime, and the workers need outlets to spend their money. That bastard Ford sells his cars as fast as they roll off his damn assembly line. Real estate is booming. My secretary has a fur coat, drives to work in her own car. I don't even check my broker's reports any more—I know that the stock market is zooming. Skyscrapers are going up all over the country. On the coast everyone is buying, expanding. Why should Lewin's be left behind?''

"I also read the economic journals," Samuel countered. "For every factory that is working overtime, another has shut down. Unemployment is up and the booming economy is based on speculation—a house of cards that could tip over at any minute. I think we are making a mistake."

"Perhaps Samuel does not want the competition of another store—even another Lewin's Emporium," Joseph suggested slyly.

"Joseph." Rachel's voice was quiet yet laced with warning.

"Sorry," he said and turned away. Samuel had always been a spoilsport—the boy who called off a planned softball game because clouds were gathering. He always kept a poncho in his saddlebag. His intentions were good, Joseph acknowledged, but his caution was stultifying.

"All right," Samuel said in a tight voice. "After all, it's Father's decision."

"Of course. And a good and generous one," Joshua said. He clapped his hands. "A toast. Rosa—it's time for the champagne."

Corks were popped and glasses filled.

"To Emma and Isaac Lewin—and to their second Emporium in Phoenix," Abner Wallach shouted.

"To happy days," Emil Coen added.

"Happy days are here again," they sang in unison as Natalya sat down at the piano and pecked out the tune. Franz waltzed Leonie around the room, and Joshua bowed deeply to Rachel and danced her off to the terrace. The twins each took a sip of champagne from their mother's glass and giggled as the bubbles tickled their noses.

Emma sat beside Isaac. Silently, they lifted their glasses, toasting their own good fortune. Joshua was back, and their family and friends were gathered together in their brightly lit home, overflowing now with music and laughter. They had paid past debts and claimed the future.

* * *

Two weeks later, ground was broken for the new Emporium. Crowds flocked to the site and applauded as low-flying airplanes trailed the Lewin banner across the clear blue sky. The barnstorming pilots tossed handfuls of red, white, and blue confetti, and the children scrambled to retrieve the tiny bits of crepe paper and exultantly traded colors. The marching band of the Indian School played "The Star-Spangled Banner" and "Happy Days Are Here Again" in such rapid sequence that the two songs seemed to blend into one. Dignitaries sat beside the Lewin family on a makeshift platform decorated with American flags and the state banner. The mayor of Phoenix spoke, shouting his expletives because this was an election year and the promises of the bright spring day would be remembered that fall in polling booths all over the state.

"With this groundbreaking," he shouted in conclusion, "the Lewins of Phoenix demonstrate their faith in Phoenix and in the prospering economy of these United States."

The audience shouted its approval, and the children waved their paper flags and the red and white flannel pennants embossed with the familiar silhouette of the tent store.

Isaac rose and walked to the podium. He was wearing the state flower, a small saguaro cactus blossom, in the lapel of his tan suit, and he touched it now and again as he spoke. That morning he had given Emma a similar flower crafted of pink gold, and she had pinned it to the wide collar of her champagne-colored silk dress. Her fingers toyed with the delicate blossom, her movements matching his own.

The audience quieted down. Isaac Lewin, they knew, would not shout to make himself heard.

"Over two decades ago, on the day our beautiful capitol building was dedicated, when Arizona was still a territory and statehood seemed a dream, my wife and I hoisted a tent in Phoenix and opened our first 'Emporium'—a canvas enclosure with packing cases for counters. We opened that first store for ourselves. It represented our dream for self-sufficiency, for independence in this country to which we had come as immigrants. The writings of our religion taught us that if we were not for ourselves, we could not expect others to be for us. And so we worked for ourselves, for our own survival. We were fortunate. We grew and prospered. But we did not forget that our rabbis also taught us that we cannot live only for ourselves. We do not want to live only for ourselves. We want our efforts to be for Phoenix, for Arizona, and for these United States, and so we build again— a second Emporium—this time for you!''

The silver shears glinted in the sunlight as he cut the blue ribbon symbolically stretched across the construction site. The crowd clapped and cheered. The band played a medley of favorites, and Isaac and Emma stood together on the platform, holding hands and smiling.

Only Samuel and Bryna sat quietly, although they had clapped dutifully at the conclusion of the mayor's remarks and risen to their feet when Isaac spoke. Their restraint did not surprise Joshua.

''Construction costs are up—way beyond the estimates. We just negotiated a new mortgage on the Emporium to meet them,'' Samuel had said worriedly the previous evening as the brothers sat in the loggia. ''I still think we are moving too fast.''

''Then the whole country is moving too fast,'' Joshua had replied. He had been reading the comics, and he tossed them to Samuel. ''The funny papers do not lie, Sam—even chinless Andy Gump is making a killing in the market.''

Samuel had smiled thinly.

''America wants to believe its comic strips and illustrated magazines. We're like children, Josh. A nation of innocents. Lucky Lindy flies across the Atlantic and the whole country rushes to buy aviation stocks. A radio announcer tells kids to get their parents to buy Dentapeal and the drugstores are sold out. We actually believe in happy days—we'll win all our wars, push back all our frontiers. Sure, we won the war. I just hope we don't lose the peace.''

Joshua remembered his brother's words, and a dark mood clung to him as he made his way through the crowd. Friends and acquaintances surrounded him.

''Welcome home, Joshua.''

''Great to have you home, Dr. Lewin.''

''Josh, your father was wonderful.'' Rachel Wallach

clutched his arm, her eyes bright, her color high. She stood beside a petite dark-haired woman who looked vaguely familiar.

"Yes. I thought he was very eloquent," Joshua said.

"I have never known him to be anything but eloquent," Rachel's companion said. "Has he ever told you of his White House meeting with President Taft? I served on that committee with him, and I still remember how persuasive he was then. He negotiated us into statehood."

"Then you must be Isabel Cavalajo," Joshua said, and he looked at her with new interest. Her black hair, threaded with silver, was coiled into a chignon, and glints of gold flecked her hazel eyes. Her amber skin, leathered by sun and wind as she painted her landscapes, was stretched tight across her delicate, chiseled face.

"Isabel Stern now," she said and smiled at him. She remembered how, during their years together, Isaac had spoken worriedly of his eldest son, concerned always that dreamy, gifted Joshua would not be able to focus his interests, channel his talents. He need not have worried, she decided now; Joshua Lewin, grown to manhood, was handsome and determined, conscious of his dynamic power, his persuasive charm.

"Yes. Of course, I remember." His voice grew distant, and Isabel wondered how much he knew about her relationship with his father. Oddly, she thought of Isaac as a valued friend now, almost a brother. It seemed unimportant that once he had been her lover. Those had been different times, and they had been different people—the passionate, idealistic girl and the lonely man who had sat together on the veranda of the adobe house and watched violent sunsets ravish the desert sky. They had not harmed each other. Isaac had reclaimed his marriage, and she had found a life of her own. A good life, she thought, and wondered what else she could say to Isaac's son, who stared at her so intently, so searchingly. She could not apologize to him for once having loved his father.

"Mama, Mama, I got a flag and a pennant." Her son, Jesse, ran toward them, and Joshua turned, startled by the appearance of the auburn-haired boy, whose high, sweet voice resonated with a familiar sweetness and whose long-lashed blue eyes sparkled with a reminiscent brightness.

"Jesse, this is Dr. Joshua Lewin, a good friend of Rachel's and the son of an old friend of mine."

"Hello." The boy stretched out his hand. Joshua took it and pressed it gently.

"I am glad to know you, Jesse Stern," he said gravely.

The child grinned.

"Are you a real doctor?" he asked.

"I hope so."

"Do you make people better?"

"I try."

"That's good." Jesse was approving and suddenly uninterested. "I'm hungry, Mama. Let's go home."

"All right." Isabel smiled apologetically. "I'll see you at the studio later, Rachel. There should be a beautiful sunset tonight, and I want to use the new water-based oils. It was good to see you, Dr. Lewin."

Joshua nodded and stared after the mother and son. Isabel walked slowly, but the child skipped ahead of her, waving his flag and singing gaily.

"For a minute there," he said, "when I first took his hand, I thought I was looking at Gregory."

"I know. The resemblance is amazing," Rachel agreed.

"Not amazing at all," Joshua replied bitterly. How sad, how wasteful it had been for his parents and Henry Stern to allow their grievances to fester. He felt the righteous indignation of the young at the foolish perversities of their elders. "Goodbye, Rachel."

He turned abruptly and walked on. Rachel clutched her broad-brimmed straw hat and thought of hurrying after him but turned instead and walked in the opposite direction.

Joshua pressed on through the crowd, smiling and nodding, answering questions and acknowledging congratulations. Yes, he had decided to settle in Phoenix, he told his former history teacher. No, his French was far from fluent, he told the girl who had sat beside him in high school French. She was a mother now. A toddler clung to her skirt, and she moved with the awkward gait of advanced pregnancy. Many of their former classmates were married, she told him, and he felt a new restlessness. It was time for his own life to take form, for his own future to unfurl. He walked on, moving quickly now, his eyes raking the crowd, his glance jumping from face to face, although he could not decide who it was he wanted to see.

Walter Larson, a classmate at Union High School who was now city editor of the *Phoenix Gazette*, hurried up to him.

"Hey, Josh, wait up. Give your old pal an interview. When your dad said that this new store would be for Phoenix, did he mean anything specific, or was he just talking about giving our sun city an economic boost?"

"Hi, Walt. You really should be asking my father," Joshua said. "But I guess he won't mind my telling you that he hopes to use some of the profits from the new Emporium to finance a tubercular clinic here in Phoenix. Or, to be more accurate, a facility to deal specifically with lung disease."

"That could be a great story," Walter said. "That's your specialty, right? I don't think publicity would hurt that project, especially an interview with you. You know the kind of thing—'Young Physician Returns to Native City—Revolutionary Medical Program Envisaged!' It wouldn't hurt to get some other Phoenix bigwigs interested—the Goldwaters, the Campbells, the Sterns."

"You haven't changed, Walt," Joshua said. Walter Larson had always known how to promote an idea. It had been freckled Walt, he recalled now, who had hired a camel to lead Union High School's homecoming parade and a barnstorming pilot to drop leaflets congratulating the class of '21 at their high school graduation.

"So how about an interview, a feature story, like they say back east?"

"All right. An interview. A feature," Joshua agreed.

"Hey—Gracia, over here," Walter called. "A new reporter, Josh. We just hired her away from the *Baltimore Sun* with the promise that she could do this kind of feature. Where is she?—I want to get back to the office. Gracia!" He shouted now and gesticulated to a cluster of reporters who were comparing notes.

The young woman who stepped forward, still laughing at

a colleague's comment, was flushed with the heat, although she had rolled up the sleeves of her white blouse and her pale blue jacket was flung over her shoulder. Her golden curls were scooped back and tied into place with a narrow black ribbon, and Joshua was perversely pleased to see that her very white teeth were slightly crooked, giving her an endearingly childish expression. He had not noticed that on the train.

"Sorry, Walt. I was trying to find out if anyone knew anything more about MacArthur, the architect. You can't write much about a hole in the ground, but the plans might be worth a story, especially since they say MacArthur studied with Frank Lloyd Wright and the rumor is that Wright is planning eventually to build a Taliesin West somewhere near Phoenix."

"You can do that story after you take care of the feature I have in mind," Walter said. "This is Dr. Joshua Lewin, who can give you a story on one of the reasons Isaac Lewin is building a second Emporium. Josh, I want you to meet Gracia Curran—Baltimore's loss and the *Gazette*'s gain."

Joshua removed his low-brimmed hat and took her hand. Surprise flooded her face.

"Actually Miss Curran and I have met, after a fashion, although we were never introduced. We did have a brief conversation about literature, however."

"Well, then, Gracia, you'll have no trouble setting up an interview with Dr. Lewin. I have to get back to the *Gazette*." Briskly, he shook hands with Joshua and hurried off.

"Have you finished *Point, Counterpoint*, Miss Curran?" Joshua asked.

"Not yet, Dr. Lewin. I've been rather busy getting settled." She matched his amusement with cool politeness, but he noticed that she twisted her handkerchief into intricate knots as they spoke.

"I suppose that we should set up an appointment for this interview," he said and drew out his pocket diary.

"Tomorrow afternoon at the newspaper office," she suggested.

"I think not. I'm very busy just now myself setting up my

surgery. Tomorrow evening would be more convenient. Shall we say seven o'clock in the Desert Inn dining room?''

"But that's dinner," she said, blushing.

"Indeed it is, Miss Curran. Busy as we both are, we still must eat. I'll see you there." He smiled at the look of confusion on her face as she nodded and walked swiftly away. She was much prettier, he thought, than the beautiful young doctor who had slept beside him in the alpine glade. And he noticed that her shapely legs were encased in the flesh-colored silk stockings that had caused his small nieces to giggle as they scurried about on the station platform.

He walked home, indifferent to the crowd around him. He knew now that he had been looking for golden-haired Gracia Curran.

It rained the next evening, and though he left early he was forced to drive slowly. She was already seated at the candlelit table when he arrived, her notebook open, her pen poised. He slid into the seat opposite her and reached across the table to close the notebook.

"This is a business meeting, Dr. Lewin," she said primly. Her golden hair, loosely brushed and pearled with pellets of moisture, framed her face. She looked, he thought, like an angry angel.

"I do know that," he assured her, "but surely we can eat first and then I can tell you where I went to medical school and why I decided to study pulmonary diseases and why I decided to return to Phoenix."

"Very well."

The curtness of her tone both challenged and annoyed him, and he ordered briskly, consulting the waiter about the piquancy of the salsa, the thickness of the mole sauce on the chicken.

"And two orange juices," he added. "With grenadine, I suppose. I make believe I'm drinking a highball," he confided to her. "This is not for publication, but my father still has a supply of wine and champagne, the remnants of my sister's wedding reception, which he rationed out. I suppose he claimed sacramental privileges to get them."

She smiled, and he noticed that the crooked front teeth were lightly stained now by her pale pink lipstick.

"You see," he said, lifting his glass of orange juice to her, "I can make you smile, after all."

She blushed and lifted her glass in turn.

"A truce, then?" he asked. "A good ending to a bad beginning."

"A truce," she agreed.

"Since I don't have to write anything up," he said, leaning back, "I can ask you questions while we eat, and then it will be your turn."

"And what questions do you want to ask, Dr. Lewin?"

"First, I want to ask you to call me Joshua because I want to call you Gracia. It's a beautiful name."

"It's a family tradition—there has always been a Gracia in any given generation. Ever since the Currans came to Baltimore."

"Where did they come from?"

"They came from England way back—the seventeenth century. My father can give the exact date, and often does. They followed Lord Baltimore and other English Catholics. The first Gracia was born in Maryland—family myth has it that she was named in thankfulness for religious toleration. At least that is what my father has always claimed, and my brother—he's a priest now—has studied family documents and he thinks that's a pretty accurate assumption."

"It sounds right," he acknowledged. "Are you also involved in the Church?"

She lowered her eyes and her face tensed.

"Involved enough so that the first thing I did after I found a room was to find a church. And are you involved in the synagogue,"—she hesitated and then said his name for the first time—"Joshua?"

"Not really. There was no synagogue in Phoenix when I was growing up, although they held services in lofts and storefronts. My folks went, but it was hot and crowded and I was a restless kid, so I never got the habit. My bar mitzvah took place on our front lawn. Of course, there were only a couple of hundred Jews in the city then. Beth Shalom was built a few years ago when more Jews began settling there, and now there's talk of building another synagogue in the valley.''

''Why is that?''

''My father says it's so that every Jew will have a synagogue that he doesn't go to,'' he said, smiling. ''Still, I'll have no problem. The only time I attend services is on Yom Kippur, the Day of Atonement.''

''Because you have so many sins?'' she asked teasingly as the waiter brought their main course.

''Because I have so many interesting sins,'' he replied and showed her how to dip the tender white chicken meat into the dark pools of chocolate sauce.

As they ate she told him of her work on the *Baltimore Sun*. She had studied English at Goucher College and had submitted essays and articles to the newspaper by mail. She signed them G. Curran and concentrated on political subjects. She wrote an analysis of Mussolini's election and an argument against the congressional bill that limited immigration and attempted to exclude all Japanese. When William Jennings Bryan died, she wrote a retrospective review of the Scopes trial, which was printed as a featured article in the Sunday rotogravure section.

''They printed everything I wrote,'' she said. ''Mencken even wrote and asked me to contribute to *The Mercury*. When I graduated, I wrote and asked for a position on the paper, and they wrote back offering me a job. It came as a surprise to the city editor to realize that G. Curran was a woman.''

''But they hired you anyway?''

''Oh, they hired me and assigned me to the woman's page. I spent three years writing up engagement notices and exciting features on ladies' auxiliary bazaars and charity balls.''

''And that is why you decided to come west?'' he persisted.

''Part of the reason. The *Gazette* promised that I could do regular features and political features.''

''And what is the other part of the reason?'' He asked the question with almost professional detachment, as though he were taking a case history but he did not deceive himself. He wanted to know with an urgency and intensity that surprised him.

"I'm afraid I don't want to discuss it," she said, and a look of pain flashed across her heart-shaped face.

"I'm sorry." He was sorry. His light, flirtatious questions had been intrusive. Deftly, he changed the subject.

Over the dessert of guava and kiwi fruits he told her about the journals he had kept since his bar mitzvah.

"For a long time I thought of becoming a professional writer. But in college I decided that I wasn't good enough."

"But you are a good doctor?"

"The best."

"I would imagine so," she said gravely.

"Why?"

"You have such an air of authority, such an incisiveness."

"That sounds almost as though you might even learn to like me," he said, grinning.

"I might."

"Then may I ask you something? Why did you withdraw from me on the train and again earlier this evening?"

She hesitated and then replied in a low, almost fearful tone. "Because you remind me of someone—someone who hurt me."

"The other part of your reason for coming to Arizona?"

"Yes." She drained the last of her thick Mexican coffee and reached for her notebook. "It's my turn now."

Her questions were well paced, well planned. She had researched his family's background, their long commitment to social causes. He told her how Emma and the other Jewish women in the community often prepared kosher meals for the *lungers*—the Jewish victims of lung disease who came to the desert city to recover and recuperate.

"I grew up thinking of Arizona as a haven for tuberculars," he said. "It was a shock to realize that the Indians of the Southwest were themselves victims of the disease. That's when I decided to do my research and began to think about the clinic."

"I know you will be successful," she said as she closed her notebook.

"Thank you."

Their eyes met and they looked at each other for a long moment in the flickering candlelight. Their gaze was intent, unguarded, and when he covered her hand with his own, she remained still.

He drove her to her rooming house, slowly maneuvering along the roads still slick with rain and flooded by the culverts that had overflowed. Riders in the desert the next day would find small animals drowned in brimming arroyos and floating in pools prismed by bright sunlight. Once, he told her, he and Samuel had plucked a small kit fox from a water gulch. They had nursed the graceful animal back to health, keeping it in a small cage in the loggia, and finally they had released it into the desert. Always, afterward, he had searched for it, but although other foxes had skittered across his path, he had never seen that one again.

"How would you know which one was yours?" she asked.

"He had a white tip at his tail and white crescents on his ears. He was beautiful." He had never forgotten that fox, and strangely, he had never spoken of it to anyone else. He walked her to her door.

"Good night." She held out her hand, but he ignored it.

"I think you may have been missing this," he said and drew her pale blue silk scarf from his pocket. "It fell from your case at the station."

"I remember," she said. "Thank you."

She reached for it, but instead he draped it around her neck and, holding both ends, he drew her toward him. She was his prisoner, caught in her own silken lariat. Her golden head was bowed submissively, but he lifted her chin and gently he kissed her on the lips, on the blue-veined lids of her eyes. "Don't," she murmured. "Please."

"Why not?" he asked. "I am not the man who hurt you."

Still she withdrew, her face pale, her hands fumbling for the door knob.

"Gracia, I will call you tomorrow. And remember . . ."

"Yes?"

"Remember that I would never hurt you."

"I'll remember," she whispered.

He stared after her as she disappeared into the house. A single golden hair clung to the sleeve of his blue serge jacket, and he twisted the silken tendril about his finger so that it formed a barely discernible ring.

* * *

He called her the next day.

"Lunch," he said crisply. She had admired his air of authority, and he exerted it.

He showed her the office he had rented on Main Street. It would serve as a temporary surgery until funds were available for the clinic.

"Modest but my own," he said, pacing the empty suite, envisioning his examining table in one room, his files in another, his instrument cabinet just beneath the sink.

"You like things to be your own?" she asked.

"A family quality. My father could not tolerate working for anyone else. That was one reason why he launched the Emporiums."

"And your mother?"

He frowned. "My mother always believed that a woman should be in control of her own destiny. It created conflicts between them when I was a boy—conflicts that I did not understand, that I still don't. Things are good between them now, but my mother had a difficult life."

"All lives are difficult," Gracia said, and he was startled by the bitterness in her voice.

She stood at the unshaded window and closed her eyes against the brightness of the sun, yet she did not move to avoid its searing radiance. He was reminded of a patient at the alpine sanatorium, a young woman who always chose the brightest corner of the solarium because she believed that the sun's rays would burn away the infection that darkened her lungs. He wondered if Gracia believed that the Arizona heat would melt her misery, her sadness.

"You must have window shades," she said. "And curtains."

"What color shall they be?" he asked.

"I can't think now."

"Then you will tell me tonight." He did not offer an invitation. He issued a summons.

"Tonight," she agreed. Acquiescence and submission mingled in her voice.

"We'll meet here at six."

He walked her back to the *Gazette* office and then went to

buy window shades. He whistled as he hung them and smiled as he pulled them down. The empty rooms were webbed with shadows and blinded to life on the busy commercial street below. He went to the Emporium then and headed for The Arizona Experience.

Johnny Redbird himself helped Joshua to select the narrow bright rugs of a cerise weave, the huge leather pillows like those on which tribal chiefs sat at meetings.

"You see how our traditions have become accessories to your lives," the Indian said, and Joshua glanced at him sharply. But there was no bitterness in Johnny's tone, only calm resignation tinged by sadness. "It is as it must be," he continued. "The new world invades the old. Different drums sound in the night. Your dreams are not those of your father, nor will my son walk in my path."

Johnny's oldest son, Joshua knew, had become a Catholic and was on the staff of Brother Timothy's mission school. He seldom visited the mesa, but Johnny drove to Prescott several times a year, although he would not enter the school. Father and son met outside the gates. They were Indians and understood the mystery of defined borders, of separate territories.

Joshua carried his purchases back to the office. He spread the rugs across the newly sanded floors, placed the pillows beneath the windows. He hung Rachel Wallach's desertscape on the whitewashed wall. When he left, he locked the office door for the first time.

At a small grocery he bought an Italian bread, a wheel of cheese, candles, and a bottle of wine. A barefoot Mexican boy stood on the corner hawking cactus fruit, and he bought the entire basket. He grinned as the child ran off, clutching his money without looking back, as though fearful that Joshua would change his mind.

It was dusk when she arrived, but he did not light the candles. She had changed to a light cotton dress that exactly matched her hair, and she moved through the dimness of the room like a shaft of radiance. She admired the rugs, the cushions, and stood for a long time before Rachel's painting.

"Do you like it?" he asked.

"Yes. But its loneliness frightens me."

"Shall I take it down then?" He would protect her from loneliness, from fear, from the vagrant sadness that stole across her face.

She laughed. "No, of course not. I like it."

He spread the food across the rug, pulling the bread apart and cutting the cheese and the fruit with his pocketknife. They drank the wine from the bottle. He licked the rim and tasted the moistness of her saliva.

"You must have blue curtains," she said decisively. "Sky-colored."

"A wicker couch in the waiting room," he added. "These pillows on the window seat."

She leaned back against the leather cushion.

"Did the chiefs really sit in judgment on pillows like these?"

"So Johnny Redbird told me."

Darkness stole across the room, and he reached for the candles, but she touched his hand.

"No," she said softly. "Didn't the chiefs sit in judgment in the darkness?"

"They had fires of mesquite and piñon boughs. When we were boys, my brother Samuel and I would ride into the desert. Sometimes we saw the flames, smelled the fragrance." He thought of himself and Samuel perched on their ponies, watching the distant fires flare against the darkness. They had been lonely boys who fled the tension of their parents' silence; they were at home in the desert, yet always they felt themselves oddly alien as they inhaled the sweetly burning wood scent and watched gray spumes of smoke soar across the night dark sky.

Again he reached for the candles, and again she touched him lightly.

"No," she said. "I don't want any light."

"Why not?" He spoke gently.

"Because I must say what I have to say in darkness."

"All right. But understand—I do not sit in judgment. Not on you. Ever." He lay back then, his head against his own pillow. She leaned toward him, her breath soft against his face as she spoke.

She told him then of her childhood in the large family

home in Baltimore. A gentle, protected life, with gentle, protective parents, for whom Catholicism was more than a religion—it was a way of life. Her parents were daily communicants, attending church together every morning of their lives. Often Gracia and her brother, James, joined them, and the family would walk together through the fragile light of dawn, their hands linked. Gracia remembered how their shadows fell, sometimes forming a penumbral cross on the paving stones. The church girdled their lives, gave meaning to their days. Her senses tingled with its rites—prayers as poetry, softly sung benedictions, the communion wafers so delicate against her tongue, the wine sweetly darkening her lips. She thrilled to the voices of the choir, the resonance of the organ; she welcomed the dark privacy of the confessional, her own voice rising and falling in a melodic tremolo. "Forgive me, Father, for I have sinned. . . ." Her heart growing lighter as she spoke, the grateful reception of penance.

She envied her brother when he left for the seminary to study for the priesthood. She went to a Catholic school, and briefly she thought of becoming a nun. They were so peaceful, so protected. But the nuns who taught her did not offer encouragement. They praised her for her writing, pinned her compositions to the cork bulletin board, and published them in the school paper. "Writing is your vocation," the Mother Superior told her.

She went to Goucher, but all through college she remained devout and always her eyes filled when the choir sang "Ave Maria." And then she went to work for the *Baltimore Sun* and met the feature editor.

"His name was Miles Anderson," she said, and her voice faded. Joshua took another gulp of wine and decided that he hated Miles Anderson.

The editor befriended the young reporter. She was restricted to the society page, but he surreptitiously assigned her to features and published them under an assumed name. He read and corrected the articles she sent to magazines. He stayed late at the office to work with her and walked her home, choosing circuitous routes so that she saw parts of the city that she had not known before. He would have her understand the metropolis in all its terror and all its beauty, he told her. She lay awake at night and his face danced before her eyes, his voice echoed in her ears. One moonless night, he kissed her on a deserted pier.

The next weekend she went with him to a small white cottage on Rehoboth Beach. They slept together on a narrow bed, the windows open to the scent and the sounds of the sea. Her rosary beads were in her purse, and the thin gold cross her brother had given her hung on a chain at her neck. She thought that she prayed as Miles Anderson rode her body, moaned her name. She knew that she had wept in loss and joy as the ocean pounded the shore.

"Why?" Joshua asked softly. "Why did you go with him?"

"Because I trembled when he touched me, when he spoke to me. Because I melted when I looked at him."

Three weeks later he told her he was married. He had assumed she knew. Everyone in the office knew. Only she, the Catholic girl who had wanted to be a nun, had not known. She went to her confessor. She had committed a mortal sin, he told her. She had to leave Miles Anderson, leave the newspaper. She wept then. She could not leave her love; she could not leave her life. The grille of the confessor's booth slammed down. The Church was closed to her.

She lived that way for three years, enduring her gentle parents' silent anguish, her own isolation, her removal from the peace and ritual that had been natural to her since childhood.

"Three years," Joshua said.

"Three years." Three years of stolen weekends and evenings of breathless waiting for phone calls that did not come. Friends at work glanced at her with sly smiles, sympathetic complicity. All the while he told her that he loved her, pleaded for patience, forbearance. His marriage was intolerable. They would yet find a way. And then Miles Anderson's wife had a baby. She chipped in for a perambulator with the rest of the staff. Then she went to see her brother. He was gentle, consoling. The Church was not lost to her, nor was she herself lost. It was James who had encouraged her to leave Baltimore, to accept the position in Arizona. She had rejoiced as the train moved westward, as the distance between herself and Miles Anderson widened. And then Joshua had sat opposite her at the New Mexican border, had spoken to her, and that new fragile peace had been threatened.

"Why?"

"Something about you reminded me of him. Your compelling manner. The authority in your voice. The way you moved."

"I am not Miles Anderson," he said. "I would never deceive you. I would never hurt you." His voice was husky, pleading.

"I know." She took his hand in her own, brought his fingers to her lips.

"Gracia." Her very name was a pledge of her faith. He cupped her face in his hand and lit a candle at last so that he might see her. Her long lashes were stained to a dark gold by her tears, and he wiped her cheeks gently and kissed away the traces of her grief. At last he blew out the tiny flame and they lay side by side in the sweet dark silence, their hands linked, their heads resting on the leather cushions of judgment.

They saw each other almost every day after that. Often he met her for lunch, and they ate swiftly and then shopped. She helped him to buy his office accessories, the prints for the walls, the low table on which she arranged potted plants, which she watered carefully each evening. They ate dinner together in Mexican cantinas where patrons and proprietors greeted him by name, offered him jars of guava jam and hot chili peppers, and asked him about an aunt's indigestion, a grandfather's palsy. He answered each query gravely. The Indians and Mexicans who questioned him about their gaseous stomachs, their swollen veins, came to him accompanied by cousins who experienced difficulty breathing in the night, small nieces with hacking coughs. His reputation as "the doctor who helped people to breathe" grew.

Occasionally, they ate a cold meal in his office, spreading the food again on the woven rugs and washing the dishes in the surgery sink. He read his medical journals as she worked on an article, and they looked up to smile at each other, to duel playfully with their pens. Once he turned the radio on and found dance music; they waltzed about the waiting room with stately grace.

"We are playing house," she said happily.

"No," he replied. "Children play house. We are not children."

They took long walks through the city, sometimes pausing to observe the construction of the new Emporium. A skeletal steel frame had emerged, but there had been delays. Supplies were late in arriving. A contractor who had received advance payment had declared bankruptcy, and Isaac had taken a loan to engage the services of another firm. Samuel was worried, Joshua knew, but then his brother had always been pessimistic.

He took Gracia to dinner at his family's home for the first time on an evening when Brother Timothy was also a guest. Emma and Isaac were cordial, and Isaac questioned Gracia closely about a recent series she had written on Arizona ranchers. She had traveled through the state and interviewed homesteaders and their wives. Many were threatened with foreclosure and spoke of leaving the state, giving up life on the land.

"The only thing that will save them is federal relief," Isaac said worriedly. His account books at the Emporium showed that many farmers and ranchers had overextended themselves. Many, he knew, would never be able to meet their bills. "Once Coolidge is out of office, we'll get a federal farm bill through. Both Hoover and Smith agree to that." He himself would vote for Al Smith, but he had confidence in Herbert Hoover.

"A federal farm bill is like placing a tourniquet on a hemorrhage and expecting the blood to stop," Samuel said bitterly. "The only reason why there haven't been more foreclosures locally is because Henry Stern's bank keeps granting amnesties and extensions. It's a dangerous game, and I don't know how much longer he can play it."

Isaac glanced at Emma. She sat rigid in her seat, her lips tight and her eyes narrowed. Always, the mention of her half brother unsettled her. Only Isaac knew that she timed her morning walk to coincide with the recess hour at the elementary school that Jesse Stern attended. She watched the boy as he ran through the schoolyard, cavorting with his friends and calling to them in the high, sweet voice that might have been Gregory's.

"Samuel has always been the voice of doom," Joshua said. "The Jeremiah of the family. Everyone else sees prosperity around the corner. The stock market keeps going up. Reuben Wallach told me that he doubled his holdings last week."

"Jeremiah did predict the destruction of Jerusalem," Brother Timothy said quietly.

After dinner Bryna walked with Gracia in the garden. She showed her the mariposa tulips that Emma had planted. Gracia threaded a blossom through her hair.

"Your friend is a nice young woman," Emma said cautiously as she stared at them through the window.

"Very intelligent," Isaac added.

"I think so," Joshua said.

"She is an interesting friend for you."

"She is more than a friend."

Brother Timothy looked hard at them, and, as he often did in the confessional, he strained to hear the secrets concealed in their silence.

Rachel Wallach invited Joshua to see her work at Isabel Stern's studio.

"I want you to see my new work," she said in her shy manner. "I am working in watercolor now."

"May I bring a friend?"

She nodded, and he thought it strange that she blushed and turned away from him, walking so briskly that he was discouraged from dashing after her.

He and Gracia drove out to the studio in the early evening. Isabel Stern welcomed them and invited them into the studio.

"Rachel is very talented," she said. "But she is reluctant to have a formal showing of her work."

"Perhaps I could do a piece about her for the paper," Gracia said. "We are beginning to do features on cultural events."

"Then Phoenix has really come of age," Joshua remarked casually and put his arm carelessly about Rachel's shoulders.

"When Rachel and I were kids, a cultural event would have been a local poet giving a reading for the Ladies Cultural Circle."

Rachel moved awkwardly away.

"I don't want you to write about my work," she said. Her voice was harsh and etched with pain.

Gracia glanced at Joshua, who took her hand as they followed Rachel about the whitewashed studio and studied her delicate watercolors, her vivid oils. Gracia admired a sketch of a desert palm shadowing a red rock formation, and Rachel removed it from the wall and gave it to her.

"You must take it," she said. "I insist." They understood that she was apologizing for the harshness of her response to Gracia's offer.

Small Jesse Stern sat on the patio reading and drumming on the wooden table with his fingers as he turned the pages. Gregory had had such a habit, Joshua remembered, and he held his hand out to the child.

"What are you reading?" he asked.

"Peter Pan."

"Oh, yes. My brothers and I used to act it out. I was always Captain Hook."

"I want to be a lost boy and never grow up," the child said.

"Oh, I think you'll have fun growing up, Jesse," Joshua assured him. Again he thought of Gregory, who had also loved *Peter Pan* and who had never grown up.

"All right, then. I'll be a pirate and frighten everyone," the child said equably.

"Why should you want to frighten people?" Isabel asked her son as she set down a tray laden with tall glasses of lemonade.

"Oh, I wouldn't really frighten them. It would just be for fun," Jesse said pleasantly, and he took a glass of the cold drink and went off to read where adults would not disturb him with their foolish questions.

"He's a nice child," Joshua said.

"Yes. We're very lucky. Jesse is our only child. We named him for my husband's son, who died in France."

"Yes. I knew him," Joshua said carefully. He wondered

how Leonie had assimilated the memory of her youthful lover. She was happy now, happy in her marriage to Franz Eisenmann, happy with their children and the Jewish communal work that involved her in San Francisco, but he remembered still the depth of his sister's misery, the sorrow that had crippled her legs and almost restricted her life. Leonie had overcome grief and bereavement; surely Gracia could overcome betrayal and loss.

They left as night fell. Joshua kissed Rachel on the cheek and thanked her for giving the watercolor to Gracia.

"I am glad she liked it," she said. Her reply was faint, and he worried because her face was drained of color and her breath came in stertorous gasps. He would suggest to Natalya that Rachel have a thorough physical examination. He suspected anemia or fatigue.

"Come again," Isabel Stern said, and he promised that they would.

"She is in love with you," Gracia said as they drove back to the city.

"Who? Mrs. Stern?" he asked, laughing.

"No. Rachel Wallach."

"Don't be ridiculous. She is like a sister to me. We've known each other since childhood."

"Children grow up," Gracia said.

He grinned and placed a monitory finger on her mouth, then drew over to the side of the road and brought the car to a halt. Gently, then, he kissed her.

"That," he said, "means that I am in love with you."

She bent her head and did not reply.

"Gracia." Again he drew her to him, but she pulled away.

"Joshua, I need time. You understand that. Surely, you understand that."

"Yes." He cursed himself for a fool because he saw the tears that stood in her eyes, the trembling of her fingers.

He gave her time. The weeks drifted into months. She went home to Baltimore for Christmas and wondered how she could ever live again in a cold climate. Her stay was briefer than she anticipated. She returned to Arizona to celebrate the new year with Joshua. Just before midnight they left a large party and went to his office. He turned the radio on, and slow dance music filled the room. His arms tightened about her and they moved slowly, singing softly together. "My heart stood still . . ."

"Happy 1929," he said and kissed her.

She did not pull away, and they danced on, indifferent to the beat of the music, content to be holding each other close as a year began.

They saw each other every day now, although both were absorbed in their work. His practice grew rapidly, and often he was at his surgery at the break of dawn and was startled when she entered the office at lunchtime carrying a basket of fruit and sandwiches. She raced after stories and met her deadlines. She wrote an impassioned plea against the Boulder Dam, arguing that it would be dangerous for Arizona's water supply to divert the waters of the Colorado River. The day after her column appeared, the attorney general announced his decision to argue against the dam.

"She is a smart girl, your Gracia," Isaac said approvingly. He did not tell Joshua that he had written a letter to his old friend Rabbi Cohen in Galveston, asking him about the procedures for conversion.

Gracia launched a series of articles for the *Gazette* on "The New Arizona and the New Economy."

She interviewed Henry Stern. The silver-haired banker was cordial and candid. He leaned back in his leather chair and answered her searching questions without hesitation.

"Isn't it true," she asked, "that you are refinancing mortgages on farms and ranches even when there is considerable risk?"

"All of business is a risk," he replied. "The bank is not overextending itself, if that is your concern. We have invested in solid growth stocks."

"But stocks are only paper," she said.

Henry Stern took a dollar bill from his wallet. He held it up and ripped it in half. He lit a match and held the two separated strips of currency over the tiny flame. They ignited and became a small torch, which he dropped into his ashtray. Together they watched it smolder into a cloud of ashes.

"Money is only paper, my dear Miss Curran," he said.

"But the people who come to me are flesh and blood. They are hard-working, and their dreams and their families' dreams are bound up in the land, their farms and ranches, the mines that may begin to yield next week or next month or perhaps the month after that. I cannot turn away from them. But I am not a philanthropist. I am a businessman, and I believe that the decisions that I make, the investments that I undertake to sustain these dreams, are in the best interests of my depositors.'' His blue eyes glinted, and patches of scarlet blazed in his cheeks.

Embarrassed, she turned away from him and studied the photographs on his desk—a young man in an officer's uniform, a slender bride, Isabel Stern standing beside the child, Jesse, who was said to bear such a remarkable resemblance to Joshua's brother Gregory.

"His words reminded me of your father when he justifies credit extensions at the Emporium. And his eyes made me think of your mother.''

"I suppose so.'' Joshua was noncommittal yet uneasy and she did not mention the interview with Henry Stern when she had dinner with the Lewins that evening.

She visited Joshua's home infrequently, and although Emma and Isaac were always gracious, she sensed an odd uncertainty in their manner toward her. Once she had asked Bryna about it, and Samuel's fiancée looked at her in surprise.

"Wouldn't your family be a little uncomfortable with Joshua?'' she asked.

"No.'' She would give them no cause to be uncomfortable with Joshua.

Still, she admired Emma Lewin's energy and enthusiasm. Emma had organized a foundation to raise funds for the projected tuberculosis clinic. Committees were in formation and fund-raising events were planned. Cash contributions came in slowly, although pledges were generous. Emma was optimistic. Once the Emporium was built and the loans taken out for its construction were paid off, there would be a new influx of cash income. Prosperity was just around the corner. The ''Great Engineer'' was in the White House, and she agreed with him that the American dream had progressed from the full dinner pail to the full garage. And people with cars in their garages had money to spare—money for clinics like the one Joshua envisaged. Now and again she called Gracia and asked her to place an item in the newspaper about a parlor meeting on behalf of the clinic.

"My parents have always recognized the value of advertising and public relations," Joshua said wryly. He told her then about Teddy Roosevelt's visit to the Emporium and showed her the photograph of the president and Isaac Lewin.

Gracia smiled. She perceived the Lewins and the Coens, the Wallachs and the Sterns, as a special group of American pioneers. They had ventured into the unsettled Southwest and plunged their roots deep into that territory's economic and political life. They had been insiders who tenaciously chose to remain isolated from the majority culture; they had their own traditions, their own religion. Like her own family, in Baltimore, they had sought and found expression for their religion on the western frontier of their new world.

"I have a very close friend here in Phoenix," she wrote cautiously to her parents. "His name is Joshua Lewin." They made no mention of him in their reply. She wrote a longer letter to her brother, who taught now at a Jesuit seminary. She concealed his reply beneath the scarves in her drawer.

Bryna and Samuel set their wedding date for May, and Joshua delivered Gracia's invitation.

"We'll go together, of course," he said in that casually imperious manner that both intrigued and frightened her.

"Of course."

It seemed increasingly natural that they do all things together—sharing meals and weekends. And always he was gentle with her, careful and restrained in touch and tone. She had revealed her fragility, her vulnerability, and he did not abuse that revelation.

She bought a new dress of sky-blue peau de soie for the wedding, and her sun-dried hair formed a gossamer aureole, framing her face in a cloud of gold. She smiled throughout the ceremony because Bryna looked so lovely and Joshua so serious as he handed his brother the wedding ring. Gracia sat beside Leonie and Franz Eisenmann, and she heard Joshua's sister whisper the Hebrew words that Samuel proclaimed in full voice before the congregation as he placed the ring on his bride's finger. Franz took his wife's hand in his own and slowly turned the marriage band, his eyes closed and a smile on his lips.

She danced with Joshua at the wedding party, waltzing across the polished floor with him and laughing when he pulled her into the circle for the wild dancing of the wedding hora. Exhausted, she withdrew and stood aside to watch the dancers.

"Joshua dances well." Brother Timothy stood beside her.

"Yes. I couldn't keep up with him."

"The dance is part of his heritage," the priest said. "His father danced like that in a wooden synagogue in Russia; his mother remembers dancing like that during her girlhood in Amsterdam. They sing the same song they sang then. Isaac told me what the words mean."

"And what do they mean?"

"Our heart is as one heart because the chain remains unbroken. The chain. The chain of their tradition carried from generation to generation from the old world to the new."

Emma and Isaac danced now in the center of the circle as their guests clapped and sang. Their faces were flushed, their eyes bright, but they moved with unerring step, unbroken rhythm.

"Be careful, my child," the priest said.

"Are you afraid for me, Father?" Her voice was cool, although she liked Brother Timothy.

"I am afraid for both of you," he said.

"You needn't be."

She herself was unafraid, newly confident. She clapped wildly as the bride and groom were hoisted into the air on their separate chairs, each holding one end of a handkerchief as their guests whirled in a joyous nuptial dance about them.

Later, when the party was over, she and Joshua drove into the desert. It was the sunset hour, and cumulus clouds rimmed with fringes of flame formed a canopy above them as they walked barefoot across the cooling sands. In the distance, the mountains formed copper-colored fortresses, and slender junipers swayed as they stood solitary sentinel along the serried ridges.

He took her hand in his and she pressed his fingers, one by one.

"I want to marry you," he said. His voice was strained, almost breathless.

"And I want to marry you," she replied.

"Gracia." He pulled her to him, kissed her lips, her eyes, buried his face in her breast. His heart pounded with joy, with sweet triumph. Time had vanquished her pain; his patient love had soothed her hurt. She would be his bride, his own, consecrated to him as that very afternoon Bryna had been consecrated to Samuel.

"When?" she asked.

"Soon. Next month, perhaps."

"But that will not be enough time."

"Time for what?" His cheek rested in the golden cloud of her hair, but he felt her stiffen in his embrace and then draw away.

"Time for you to take religious instruction."

He stared down at her, at once frightened and bewildered.

"Joshua, I cannot marry you unless you become a Catholic." She kept her voice steady, controlled. Certainty gave her courage; faith negated all argument.

"How could I become a Catholic, Gracia?" He smiled down at her. They were caught in a misunderstanding that would soon be dispelled. "I would not expect you to become Jewish. But certainly I could not convert."

"But you said that you don't care about being Jewish. You said that when we first met." Now at last she was uncertain.

"No. I never said that. I could not have said that."

"Yes. You said that you never went to synagogue."

"Still, that doesn't mean that my Judaism is not important to me, a part of me."

"I don't understand." She stared at him in disbelief.

"Then I cannot explain it to you."

The darkness gathered about them, yet they stood apart and stared miserably at each other. She thought that her heart might break. He felt weighted by sorrow. They had no words to offer each other. He knelt and took up a handful of pale sand. Grain by grain, he allowed it to sift through his fingers and fall silently back onto the desert floor.

* * *

She went to see Brother Timothy the next day. He listened to her without betraying surprise.

"I tried to warn you," he said. "I knew you did not understand."

"I don't," she replied helplessly. Her own religion absorbed her, enchanted her with ritual and observance. During the three years the sacraments had been denied her, she had felt herself crippled, isolated. Joshua had no such need, no such commitment. She was angered, suddenly, that he would deny her her religion while not even practicing his own.

"Jews think of themselves as a people—a tribal nation of a kind, linked by language and tradition. Religion is only one aspect of their Jewishness. They identify with each other, with their history and their future. They may never enter a synagogue, and yet they think of themselves as Jews. Especially Jews like the Lewins, who settled in this desert city where there was no center of Jewish authority and yet they struggled to preserve their tradition, their heritage." The priest's hands clawed the air as he struggled to give voice to his thoughts, to explain his own inchoate perceptions to the unhappy young woman who sat before him.

Gracia twisted her blue silk scarf, and her lovely face was knotted in misery.

"What can I do?" Her question was a whisper of pain.

"Perhaps you can reach a compromise. Joshua may consent to having your children brought up in the Church. Still, it will not be easy. Only one religion can rule a household, dominate a home," he said sadly.

She reread her brother's letter. He had anticipated Brother Timothy's compromise. It was, she thought, a solution of a kind. She suggested it to Joshua that night as they sat in a cantina and listened to the strains of a Mexican guitarist.

"I don't know," he said.

"I think it is the only way."

"I need time," he said desperately. Now it was he who bargained for hours and days, for compromise and understanding.

"All right. I will go to Baltimore. To visit my family, to speak with my brother."

"All right." They needed distance, he knew, although he feared her return to her native city.

Two days later he took her to the train and held her close as the departure whistle sounded and the crowds surged about them.

"Come back," he said. "Please, please, come back."

That night he walked with his father in the garden. His mother's tulips wafted like pale ghosts in the gentle wind. A memorial candle burned in the loggia.

"The candle is for Sarah and Rebecca, the wife and child I lost in Russia," Isaac told him, reading the question in his son's eyes.

Joshua nodded. His father seldom spoke of the life he had left behind in Europe, nor did his mother speak of her past. The new world had meant new lives for Emma and Isaac Lewin. The vanished years were shrouded in shadows, illuminated now and again by flickering candles encased in coarse glass that burned for a day and a night.

"Papa, I love Gracia Curran and I want to marry her."

Isaac said nothing.

"She wants our children to be raised as Catholics."

"And you, Joshua? What do you want?" Once again Isaac was the teacher, his question probing, gentle, but Joshua saw the pain in his eyes, the tightness of his lips. "I can only tell you this. All marriages are fragile—two separate lives coming together. Lesser differences than those between you and Gracia divided your mother and myself, created unhappiness between us. You remember?"

"I remember." One did not forget a childhood bounded by constrained silences, slamming doors, taut, clipped exchanges.

"Still, you must decide for yourselves."

"I love her very much."

"I know."

They returned to the house. In the doorway Isaac lifted his fingers to the wooden mezuzah, worn thin by age and touch, weathered by the snows of Russia and the hot, dry winds of the Gila Valley.

"That mezuzah hung on the door of my home in Russia."

"I know," Joshua replied. His father's mezuzah, his mother's candlesticks were the talismans of his childhood, of the Judaism that had formed his life, informed his consciousness. They bore witness to his parents' pasts; they were guarantors of continuity.

Each night that week, after closing his surgery, he rode into the desert and stared up at the starlit sky. He thought of Gracia as she had sat opposite him on the train, as she had stretched out beside him on the cerise blanket in the unfurnished office. Each morning, he watered the plants she had brought him and lightly touched the leather cushions of judgment. He sat in judgment now—in judgment of her life and his own. *Gracia.* Her name weighted his thoughts, anchored him to sorrow.

He did not go home to dinner that Friday night but drove past the house at the sundown hour and saw Emma light the Sabbath candles and cover her eyes with her hands as she invoked the blessings. He thought of how she had done that each Friday evening of her life and how he had watched her from boyhood on, moved by the flames that draped her fingers with radiance as she prayed. He remembered how the tiny Jewish community of Phoenix had gathered together to pray in storefronts and lofts on Sabbaths and festivals, seeking each other out, extending a hand of greeting and welcome. *"Shabbat Shalom.* How fared a Jew this week?" Natalya Wallach had told him of the Sabbath services in Cripple Creek, Colorado, to which Jews had traveled from isolated mining sites, distant homesteads. How thin their voices had been as they prayed, yet the familiar words had soothed them. He had understood their tenacity, their will to survive, their will to congregate. He was the son of a man who had removed a mezuzah from the doorpost of a cabin at the edge of a Russian woodland and of a woman who had carried a pair of silver candlesticks across an ocean. He dreamed of Gracia that night. She stood beside him on the front lawn of his parents' home, before a Torah scroll that floated on the wings of the corporeal desert heat.

* * *

The train that carried her back to Phoenix arrived in the late afternoon. Joshua watched her alight and thought that she had never looked more beautiful. She wore a navy blue suit, and a matching beret perched on her golden curls

He rushed toward her, yet they did not embrace. He took her outstretched hands into his own and studied her heart-shaped face as though memorizing each delicate feature. They stood absolutely still as the crowd surged about them. She spoke, but her words were lost amid the station clamor, the announcements of conductors and the station master, the imprecations of the candy butchers and the Indian boys who pressed silver jewelry and souvenirs upon them.

They drove through the city and parked at last at the construction site of the new Emporium. The skeletal steel girders arched their way blackly across the sky, and gray cinder blocks formed clumsy sculptures on the raw, newly excavated red earth. A fragment of the blue ribbon that Isaac had cut so proudly at the opening ceremonies hung forlornly on the chain-link fence. They walked through the construction rubble and paused at the spot where they had first met. A year ago. A life ago.

He took her hands in his. Her fingers were cold as ice. He kissed her cheek and tasted her tears. He thought that his own heart would break.

"You have made up your mind?" Her voice was very soft. She swayed from side to side, and he moved to steady her, his body becoming a pillar for her own. If they could stand that way forever—their two forms one . . . But they could not. Always they would have to take their separate paths. Her religion was her passion, he knew, and his own was his history—his past and his future. They could not shed their own shadows, strip themselves of their own strengths. Their lives would sour their love. The lesson of his childhood had been well learned. It had taken his parents two decades to reconcile lesser differences.

"Gracia, try to understand. I would be separating myself from my family, from my people." He himself absorbed the pain each word inflicted upon her, but the pain did not obviate the truth.

She wept openly now, huddled in his arms.

"I do understand," she said sadly. "We have no real choices, you and I. I thought we did, but I was wrong."

"Gracia. My darling." His voice was a rasping plea, and his cheeks were hot with his own scalding tears.

She took the handkerchief from his breast pocket and gently passed it across his face.

"We shall always think of each other kindly, Joshua."

"And with love." He cupped her chin in his hand and kissed her.

"With love." Her shoulders quivered and briefly, as though in benediction, she placed her hands on his closed eyes.

Henry Stern awakened at the break of dawn that cool Thursday in late October. He lay still, so as not to disturb Isabel, and watched pale wreaths of aqueous light converge to form a mackereled silver dome as the desert sun began its slow ascent. Always he had loved that quiet hour of the day's beginning when he alone was awake and his family was locked in sleep. As a boy, the eldest son in the household of an absent father, he had charged himself with the morning chores and responsibilities. It was he who had brought Analiese, his mother, her morning coffee, ascertained that the maidservant had filled the furnace with peat and coal, and awakened his brother, David.

He closed his eyes now against the thought of his brother. They had lost contact after the war. David had written from Berlin, offering his sympathy at the deaths of Henry's wife and son, but he had withheld an acknowledgment of culpability. Germany had been a nation at war, and Abigail and Jesse Stern, regrettably, had been victims of that terrible war. Henry's bitter reply had not been answered, and when he wrote David two years later, to tell him of his marriage to Isabel, the letter was returned, stamped "Addressee Unknown." Henry Stern's last link to his boyhood in Europe, to any family, had been severed.

He heard the front door open. Juanita, the maid, was on her way to the bakery to buy fresh rolls for the family's breakfast. Still, he had a while longer to lie abed and allow his thoughts and memories to wander. Oddly, such early-morning thoughts often resulted in decisions that startled his staff or an incident from his boyhood recalled with poignant clarity. Usually, the lazy thoughts of first light were tinged with magic, but on this morning they were darkened by ominous foreboding.

Restlessly, he turned his head on the pillow to look at Isabel and smiled because a streak of ocher paint darted across her palm. She had worked late into the night and washed in the dark so that she would not awaken him. Her new project was a triptych for the lobby of the capitol, tracing the evolution of Phoenix from a Hohokum outpost to the exciting sun-washed metropolis it had become. Always, Isabel thrust herself into her work with the same energy and intensity she had displayed during her campaign for Arizona's statehood, for women's suffrage, and for pacifism. Her passions both enchanted and amused him. She was, at once, his protégée and his wife, his old friend's lovely daughter and his own radiant bride. She had rescued him from solitude and mourning and restored him to vitality and involvement.

"Sweet girl," he murmured and kissed the earth-colored stain on her palm. She smiled in her sleep, and he tucked the light blanket about her as though she were a small child. How fortunate they had been to find each other and build a new life together. It was not possible that their fortunes would darken, that he would be revisited by the pain and deprivation of his boyhood.

He stole out of his bed and went to Jesse's room. The child had fallen asleep while reading the illustrated *Blue Fairy Tale Book,* which Rachel Wallach had given him. The heavy volume lay open on his pillow. Henry Stern closed it and put it on the bedside table. Briefly, he stood over the bed and looked down at his son. Jesse's face, whether wreathed in serene sleep or sparkling with alert eagerness, always filled him with wondrous pleasure. The child's very existence seemed to him to be a miracle of sorts. Isabel's first pregnancy had resulted in a stillbirth, and a year later she had miscarried. The doctor had been grave, monitory. They were not young, and she was such a small, delicately built woman. Still, her pregnancy with Jesse had been strong from the start, and the child had been delivered swiftly and without complications. Now, once again, against all odds, Henry Stern had a son named Jesse with hair the color of burnished copper and eyes as brightly blue as Henry's own.

The sleeping boy stirred restlessly.

"A pony, Papa. A silver pony," he said in a clear, sweet voice that broke forth from the depth of a happy dream.

"Yes. I know that silver pony," Henry Stern whispered. They had seen the dappled pony at a ranch foreclosure auction a week ago, and Jesse had stroked the chubby animal's silver mane, fed him sugar cubes, and scratched his ears.

"If he were mine, I'd call him Silver," he had said. "Lots of boys in my class get ponies for their birthdays, but none of them are as pretty as Silver."

"A pony is a good birthday present," Henry Stern had agreed noncommittally. He had been ill with hepatitis on the boy's last birthday and had neglected to get him a gift. He would make it up to him this year. Quietly, then, he had spoken to the auctioneer. Jesse's birthday was a month away, but the pony would be waiting for him. Henry Stern would not disappoint his son.

Determinedly, now, he returned to his own room, opened the locked door of his desk, and removed the heavy black ledger. He stared down at the neat entries, his brow furrowed and his pencil gripped so tightly that it snapped in half. He did not replace it. The figures were familiar, and there was no need to repeat the addition. He had added the columns so often the previous night that it seemed to him that the numbers had danced through his dreams. Always, the final tally, indicating the actual cash reserve on hand in the bank's vault, was the same. The Salt River Valley Bank would open that morning with just enough reserves to carry it through the day if there was no extraordinary pattern of withdrawals.

Bitterly, he stared at his debit columns. Clearly, he had authorized too many loans, sanctioned too many extensions. Prosperity had conditioned him to anticipate its continuance. He was a frontier banker and accustomed to risk. His own fortune was founded on loans to men who had wrenched silver and copper out of sheer rock and built farms and ranches on wastelands of chaparral and mesquite, expanses of barren desert. Besides, the election had bolstered his confidence. He had operated on the assumption that Hoover was right, that the bull market would continue to soar. Even Isaac Lewin, an archconservative, was expanding his Emporium, building an entirely new store. Herbert Hoover was a man who understood business, an advocate of sound money and balanced budgets.

And, on balance, Henry Stern had done well enough for the bank all that year, buying stocks that soared overnight and then using the spectacular profits to underwrite additional loans, refinance mortgages. The farmers and ranchers, who were suffering reversals, were his depositors, his constituency. It was sound business, he assured himself, that his profits be diverted to their benefit. Ultimately, their welfare meant the bank's welfare.

He had not anticipated the sudden downturn after Labor Day as the market slowly plummeted. He smiled to think that there were those who blamed the decline on the unusual heat. New York, the radio commentators advised, was as hot as Arizona, and Arizonans wiped their brows that fulminating September and reflected that it was probably cooler in hell. Others impugned that damned fool Roger Babson, the economist, who had thought it necessary to give an interview to the *Wall Street Journal.* "Sooner or later," the respected student of the stock market had said, "a crash is coming." He had made that statement during the first week of September, and since then, despite the soothing voices of President Hoover and his economic advisers, the market had been erratic.

Still, Henry Stern had not betrayed uncertainty, nor had he altered his investment pattern. He had, throughout those early autumn days, continued to buy and sell, to guarantee loans, ignoring rumors that heavy investors like Bernard Baruch and Joseph Kennedy were selling their way out of the deteriorating market. Confidently, he had worked the floor of his bank, smiling at patrons, stopping to chat with a miner, a housewife, an Indian craftsman. It was important, he knew, that the public remain unaware of the slow erosion of the bank's capital as the market continued its downturn.

He glanced at his watch and blessed the time difference between New York and Phoenix. It was six A.M. The New

York Stock Exchange would not open for another hour, and news of its progress would not reach Arizona until the afternoon. A reversal was possible. He had time. Fortunately, it was Thursday and there were no payrolls to be met, nor did he anticipate any extraordinary volume. It was true that he was opening too close to the margin, but he would make calls to colleagues at other banks and arrange for short-term loans of ready cash. He had done it himself for others.

Indeed, all that month, messengers had scurried through the streets of Phoenix, carrying infusions of funds to financial institutions that had run short. Occasionally, bankers had quietly turned to merchants whose volume of cash business gave them the flexibility to make short-term loans. Only two days ago the Goldwaters had sent almost fifty thousand dollars, their entire registry intake, to the Phoenix First National. There were firms that would offer him similar help. He took a clean sheet of paper and made a list of retailers who would be likely to accommodate him, gathering optimism as he covered line after line.

It was comforting, he reflected, that the business community had closed ranks, pooled resources. Isaac Lewin, only yesterday, had transferred thousands of dollars from his employees' pension fund in order to demonstrate his confidence in the Arizona Savings Bank. Well, he could expect no help from that quarter. His relations with the Lewins remained as strained now as they had been twenty years ago when he and Emma had first recognized each other. He had initiated the hostility between them, he acknowledged, but Emma had perpetuated it.

Strangely enough, he had thought they were leaning toward a reconciliation after the war. His daughter, Barbara, had told him about Leonie and Jesse. He had felt shame then, because his irrational hatred for the Lewins had so deeply shadowed his son's brief life. He had driven to Simon Coen's Atherton estate on Leonie's wedding day to offer his congratulations to Emma and Isaac, to extend an apology, and to make his peace at last with the Coens and the Lewins. He remembered still how Emma had come toward him as he held Jesse—an infant then asleep in his arms—and frozen suddenly. He had watched her face blanch, become a mask of rejecting disbelief. His overture, offered on that day of her joy, had been rebuffed. He had driven away swiftly, spurred by renewed anger, renewed shame.

He stared down at his list. Clearly, Lewin's Emporium would not help the Salt River Bank. Jabob Coen's daughter could not be counted on to help Jacob Coen's son.

He dressed with special care, selecting a dark suit and a blue and black striped cravat, and ate a full breakfast. It was important, he knew, to appear confident, controlled. He smiled at Juanita as she poured him a second cup of coffee.

"I need a lot of energy today," he said. "The bank will do important business."

Juanita was friendly with maids who worked at other homes. The news of her employer's optimism would spread as far as Scottsdale by midmorning.

Jesse came into the dining room as he folded his napkin and replaced it carefully in the sterling silver ring. He smiled at his son.

"Jesse, your birthday is only a couple of weeks away. I think it's time for you try out that pony you called Silver. Maybe after you've had a chance to ride him around the corral, you'll change your mind about wanting him."

"Oh, Papa." The boy leaped into his arms, entwined his thin arms around Henry Stern's neck. "You're the best father in the world."

"Well, then, come to the bank after school and we'll take a look at Silver this afternoon."

"You'd better hurry, Jesse," Isabel said.

She stood at the door of the dining room and smiled as the boy bolted down his food and dashed out of the house.

"You spoil him," she said.

"It's not such a bad thing for a father to spoil his son," Henry Stern replied easily. Even Jacob Coen had bought his illegitimate sons extravagant gifts, cosseted them in the house in Osdorp. But he was not like Jacob Coen. He would neither deceive nor betray his son.

"I think I'll come to the bank then too," Isabel said. She would take her sketch pad and draw Jesse's joyful face as he mounted the pony for the first time. Other families recorded their lives with the aid of Brownie box cameras, but Isabel

Stern captured her son's youth in charcoal drawings and delicate pen-and-ink sketches.

"Good." Nothing in his manner betrayed the accelerated beat of his heart, the fibrillation of his pulse. He kissed Isabel goodbye. He could not betray his anxiety to her nor to anyone else. He stood alone on this autumn morning, as he had stood alone through most of his life.

Isaac Lewin stopped at the construction site of the new store before going to his office that morning. A full crew sat in the shade of the steel girders as Matt Evans, the foreman, shouted into a field phone.

"What's wrong?" he asked quietly when Matt slammed the receiver down.

"No supplies, Mr. Lewin. We're waiting on shipments of lumber and copper wiring that should have been here two days ago. The lumber's ready, but the trucking company that was supposed to haul it didn't meet its payroll last week, and the drivers walked out. We can forget about the wiring. Kennecott Copper stopped shipping a week ago, but no one let us know. What do I do about the men? Just send them home, I guess."

"No. You can't do that. They showed up for work. They deserve their pay. It's Thursday. Let them finish out the week. Put them to work cleaning up the site, and tell them there'll be another labor call when we get deliveries," Isaac said.

He left hurriedly as Matt blew his whistle. He had acted as fairly as he could, but he did not want to look at the faces of the men when they learned there would be no jobs, no paychecks, the following week.

The phone was ringing when he reached his office, but he did not hurry to answer it. A sign of age, he thought. Young men reached eagerly for a ringing telephone, anticipating excitement, challenge; older men lifted the receiver reluctantly, braced for disappointment, annoyance. He glanced at his messages and drank the tall glass of water his secretary always had waiting for him. On the tenth ring, he finally lifted the receiver.

"Isaac, how long does it take you to pick up that damn

phone?'' Simon Coen's voice was irritable, and the connection from San Francisco was riddled with static.

"We move slowly here in the desert," Isaac said equably. "In San Francisco you're in a hurry. Here, we have time."

"You don't have much time today," Simon retorted. "You own General Motors stock, don't you?"

"You know I do. We bought it together."

"I just sold mine. Get rid of yours while it's still worth somcthing."

"Simon, it's nine o'clock in the morning. It's too early to be in a panic."

"It's noon in New York, and by ten their time they had already dumped twenty thousand shares of General Motors and twenty thousand of Kennecott Copper." ∙

"So it could be a ploy. By closing time they'll stabilize. It's been happening since Labor Day." Still, he drummed his fingers on his desk. Kennecott had not met its shipping schedule and was now plummeting. He didn't need Simon Coen to tell him what that meant.

"Isaac, they've been using bootleg loans. Call money that the companies themselves have been putting up. Today is different. I can feel it. Sell and sell now."

"I'll call you back," Isaac said.

He dialed his broker's office. The girl who answered the phone sounded breathless and harried. His own broker could not be reached.

"Can I ask you for some readings, then?" he persisted.

"I'm afraid I can't help you, Mr. Lewin. The ticker is two hours late. All I know is that there was heavy selling at the exchange in New York this morning, and it's hard to tell what anything is worth."

"I imagine we'll find out soon enough," he said drily and hung up to stare at Samuel, who had entered quietly and closed the door softly behind him.

"So what do you think, my economist son?" Isaac asked.

"I think the New York market is crashing and we're in the middle of a sellers' panic," Samuel replied. "Papa, don't be angry, but I felt this coming since Labor Day."

"I should be angry that you felt this coming?" Isaac asked.

"No. Don't be angry that I sold almost everything two

weeks ago. I called the broker and told him I was acting on your behalf. And I persuaded Abner Wallach to sell. Reuben and Joseph wouldn't listen, but Abner sold his whole portfolio. I knew you wouldn't agree then, but now I know I was right. Are you angry?''

"I'm not angry. Your Uncle Simon thinks you were right. Your Professor Babson thinks you were right. Me—I'm a shopkeeper. Merchandise, I understand. Style and trends, I understand. The rest I leave to you and to your uncles. I'm only sorry that you didn't ask me, but I understand. What did you buy?''

"I didn't buy. I took the cash. It's in the office safe.''

"You didn't buy and you didn't bank the receipts," Isaac said thoughtfully. "How frightened are you, Samuel?''

"Pretty damn scared, Papa. I've been scared for weeks," Samuel said. "Listen.''

He switched on the radio, and they sat in the quiet office, awash now in sunlight, and listened to a special broadcast from New York. Floyd Gibbons's rapid-fire reportage was unmarred by extremism, but he could not controvert his bulletins. Prices were dropping so steadily that he cautioned listeners to discount stock quotes given only moments before. There was word that the city's leading bank presidents were meeting with Thomas W. Lamont of the J. P. Morgan Company. "That's an upbeat item that leads many to feel that the market is on the way up. Stand by for a complete recovery, America," he concluded as he signed off.

"That damn liar. No one in the country feels that way," Samuel said softly, bitterly. "They're playing roulette with a fixed wheel.''

Henry Stern also listened to Floyd Gibbons behind the closed door of his private office. Then he called his assistant, and they went together to the vault.

"All the cash," he said. "I want the tellers' trays to be full, and I want them to lift an excess of bills when they count them out.''

"Work as fast as you can," he cautioned the tellers as he distributed the cash. "We don't want any unusual lines to form.''

He returned to his office and, using a private wire unconnected to the bank's switchboard, he made a series of calls. Briefly, almost cryptically, he spoke to the presidents of Arizona National and the Phoenix Federal Banks. His last call was to his daughter, Barbara, whose husband, Nathan Katz, owned a large wholesale meat business. Their conversation was terse. Barbara had worked in the bank before her marriage. His request required no explanation.

"I understand. I'll speak to Nate," she said.

An hour later, Nathan Katz's office manager was at the bank, ostentatiously counting out a large sheaf of notes.

"Got a big deposit to make," he said loudly to the man who stood ahead of him in line. "My boss will rest easy when his money is in this bank."

"I'm withdrawing myself," the man said grumpily. "You listened to the radio today? Even the New York bankers are shitting in their breeches."

"Rumor. All rumor. We've been doing business with the Salt River Bank for twenty years. I'll believe Henry Stern over any eastern rumor monger."

Two young Mexicans on an adjacent line nodded in agreement. They too were making deposits. Their cash advances against salary had come from Nathan Katz's paymaster, who had added ten dollars to each check on the condition that they deposit their earnings in the Salt River Bank.

Three women, clutching withdrawal slips, looked at the depositors. Two of them withdrew from the line and left the bank. The third hesitated but retained her place. She wore a faded cotton housedress, and her shoes were run down at the heels. She could not afford even the smallest risk.

The messengers from the Arizona National and the Phoenix Federal Banks entered through the rear door, and each left a locked canvas sack and a sealed envelope on Henry Stern's desk. He opened the envelopes and read the enclosed memos without surprise. The sacks contained only half the amounts he had requested. The other banks were also experiencing difficulties with cash reserves, and Southwestern Savings and Loan had declined to send him anything at all. Still, unless something triggered a sudden panic, he could hold out until the normal closing hour. New York had a three-hour time jump on Phoenix. By the time the Exchange closed, a full recovery could be in effect. It had happened before.

He looked at his watch and switched the radio on again. It was one-thirty in New York. The broadcaster's voice was harsh with excitement as he spoke from the floor of the exchange itself.

"Pandemonium down here just now. Richard Whitney, J. P. Morgan's floor man, is approaching the Big Steel trading post, and yes—he has a buy order in his hand. . . ."

Henry Stern unplugged the radio and carried it out to the teller's area. He plugged it in, and the announcer's voice filled the bank. Patrons paused and listened to the New York announcer describe Whitney's activities. Breathlessly, it was reported that he had bought twenty-five thousand shares of Big Steel and was now wandering to other posts, buying large blocks of stock at the last quoted price.

"Others are climbing on the bandwagon. John Rockefeller and his son are purchasing large blocks of common stock. Mr. Rockefeller himself is approaching the microphone. He has a statement for America."

The raspy voice of the ninety-year-old oil baron was impatient and querulous, like the tone of a teacher addressing a class of slow learners.

"Believing that the fundamental conditions of the country are sound, my son and I have been purchasing common stocks."

"This sellers' market is turning into a buyers' market," the newscaster shouted encouragingly. "I can read the board now. Prices are steadying. Yes, the market is definitely rallying. I have a bulletin here from our Washington correspondent, and he tells us that the president is optimistic. Happy days are just around the corner—just around the corner."

The patrons of the Salt River Bank glanced at each other uneasily. Several stepped out of line and left the bank, but others retained their place, clutching their passbooks and their pale blue withdrawal slips.

Henry Stern called Isabel.

"I don't think I'll be able to take Jesse to see the pony today," he said.

"Is everything all right?"

"Yes. It will all work out."

"You're feeling all right?"

He should have known that it was his health that worried Isabel and not the stock market. His last bout with hepatitis had left her increasingly concerned.

"I'm feeling fine," he assured her and glanced at the clock. In two hours the tellers could ring down their grilles and he would be safe. "Leave a message for Jesse at school and tell him to go straight home."

"All right. In that case I'll go out to the studio."

"Good." He was pleased for once that the studio had neither a phone nor a radio. Not that anything was going to happen, he told himself. By next week he would be laughing at his own fears.

He went out to the floor of the bank again, fixing a smile on his face, nodding to his patrons. Johnny Redbird turned to greet him. The Indian came to the bank regularly every third Thursday of the month to make a deposit for the Hopi Crafts Council.

"I hope your people had a good month, Johnny," he said and extended his hand.

"Not as good as we had hoped," Johnny replied. "But the winter should be better if we have the same tourist season as last year. And how is your son?"

"Growing into a sturdy lad. I'm going to get him his own pony this week." He spoke loudly and several men turned and smiled. All of them, he guessed, recalled buying their own sons their first mounts, a rite of passage of a kind for Arizonans. A pony was a symbol of prosperity and independence. And that was precisely the image he wanted to project that afternoon as the clock moved forward with agonizing slowness—the image of an independent and prosperous banker in charge of an independent and prospering bank.

"Mr. Stern, may I speak with you?"

He looked up in surprise at the pale man with thinning hair whose face was streaked with perspiration despite the cool of the afternoon.

"Mr. Eldridge." He greeted the assistant to the president of the Phoenix Federal Savings Bank without betraying his apprehension. "It's good to see you."

"May we talk in your office?"

"Yes, of course."

Still smiling, he led the man into his office and closed the door. "What is it?" He was no longer smiling. He gripped his desk as though to steady himself against an impending blow.

"Southwestern Savings and Loan just closed its doors. It ran out of cash. The word is spreading. We're going to announce an early closing, and we suggest that you do the same."

"But the news from New York is encouraging."

"The ticker is four hours late. That means we have no way of knowing what our holdings are worth. Investors know that. They'll want their cash and they'll want it now," Dwight Eldridge said grimly.

"We're a small bank. My depositors know me and I know them. They trust me. Even today we've managed."

"Can you make it until closing?"

Henry Stern did not reply.

"Don't fool yourself. Close now and salvage what you can. We'll declare a bank holiday and take some time to reassess, recoup. If there is a turnaround in the market—if Rockefeller and Morgan aren't just bluffing—we'll just acknowledge that we acted too hastily. We're bankers, not God."

"I can't close," Henry Stern said. "My people trust me."

Dwight Eldridge shrugged. "You won't make it." He stared through the frosted-glass pane on the office door. "It's starting already. One bank fails and the others can expect a run. The herd instinct. Have you ever seen a pack of jackals at night on the desert?" He laughed harshly.

Henry Stern opened the door. Lines had formed in front of each teller's cage and snaked out into the street. Housewives and businessmen, miners and ranchers, factory workers and shopgirls, pressed forward, their faces grim, furrowed with worry. Mothers grasped small children by the hand, and an old woman's lips moved soundlessly as she read the entries in her passbook. A child, frightened by the tension, began to cry, and two men argued loudly over a place in the queue.

Henry Stern moved through the tellers' area quickly, calculating the cash available in the open trays. Dwight Eldridge
was right. His bluff was over, his resources were exhausted.
The bank clerk moved toward him.

"What are we going to do, Mr. Stern?" he asked.

"We're going to lock the door," he said quietly. "We'll
try to accommodate everyone on the floor, but we can't let
anyone else in. Lock the door from the inside and slip the
bolt into place. Then go to the rear door. We'll let those who
are already inside leave one by one as their business is accomplished."

The guard glanced through the plate-glass window of the
bank to the crowd outside. A line had formed on the sidewalk, and people were running to join it, sprinting across
Jefferson Street in their desperation. Automobile brakes
squealed, and a frightened horse whinnied angrily, but the
crowd surged forward. He went to the door and closed it,
thrusting his own bulk against it, fighting back those who
pitted themselves against the heavy oak as he slipped the bolt
into place. The crowd roared in fury and pelted the door—
the men with their fists, the women with their handbags.

"Our money! We want our money!" Their voices were
shrill, anguished.

Those inside the bank were pale with fright. Henry Stern
stood before them. He knew their names, the ages of their
children; he could estimate the size of their accounts. Jason
Kennedy, a farmer whom he had staked to seed for three
drought seasons running, stared at him through reddened
cyes. The Martinez sisters, whose mortgage he had refi-
nanced only a year ago, clutched each other's hands. Abraham Goldstein, the grocer, whose business had been
launched with a collateral-free loan when he arrived from
Poland a decade earlier, shook his head from side to side.

"Friends," Henry Stern shouted. "You know me. You
trust me as I have trusted you. Let us work together today.
We are Americans, Arizonans. Let us not lose our dream to
the panic of a single morning!"

They looked at each other uneasily. They had worked hard
and saved carefully. Their pasts had been forfeit and their
futures were tenuous, but Henry Stern's voice was strong,

his words persuasive. They came of a pioneering tradition that called for daring and courage. Henry Stern had reminded them that they were the sons and daughters of frontiersmen, arrived now at a new and unfamiliar frontier.

Abraham Goldstein was the first to speak. He had survived a pogrom, the theft of his savings in a Hamburg hostelry, a voyage in steerage to Galveston harbor. Henry Stern's face had been welcoming to a "greenie" newly arrived in this city built on sand. He had not questioned the amount Abe Goldstein needed to start his grocery, nor had he pressed for payments during the first difficult months.

"How do we leave, Mr. Stern?" he asked quietly.

Henry Stern nodded, and the head teller opened the rear door. One by one they left the bank. His breath came easier. There were those who remained in line, but now the tellers too had regained their calm. They processed the withdrawals swiftly, counting the bills with practiced rapidity.

"I want to change the amount," Rosa Martinez said softly. "I want to withdraw only what we will need for essentials this week. Twenty-five dollars will be sufficient."

"Thank you, Miss Martinez." Henry Stern stared out the window. The calm within the bank was offset by the faces of those who waited outside. Men paced and pummeled the air. Women wept and fell upon those who exited, their expressions distorted by anger and fear. He counted himself fortunate that he had forestalled Isabel and Jesse and that they were at a safe distance.

The crowd grew more irate and pressed against the plateglass window, peering in.

"They're getting theirs. Where's ours?" a man shouted.

"It's not fair," a woman shrilled.

Police officers arrived and worked their way to the front of the crowd.

"Back, now. Let's step back," the sergeant shouted. "The bank's closed for the day."

"But what will happen to us?"

The question hovered in the air, and they trembled at the unarticulated answers. Hunger might overtake them. Their homes and businesses might be lost. They would wander the desert bereft of shelter and sustenance, their savings gone, their hope depleted. The sun would beat down on them, and they would be lost in a land whose promise, on this black Thursday, had failed them. Their scattered fears compounded, and their separate voices converged into a roar of fury.

The boy saw the crowd as he approached the bank. He loosened the straps of his schoolbag and stared at them, bewildered but unafraid. Still, their clamor unsettled him as he moved through the clusters of angry men and frightened women with odd agility. Deftly, he ran beneath the arches of their raised arms, scurried past a barrier of bodies before finding small spaces and openings through which he thrust himself in his determined advance.

"Where are you going, sonny?"

An officer held him back briefly, a nightstick extended.

The child stared up at the policeman, his bright blue eyes flashing confidence.

"It's all right, officer," he said in the exact tone he had heard his father use so many times when he took control of a situation. "I'm Jesse Stern. Henry Stern, the president of the bank, is my father."

He dashed forward. He would skirt the plate-glass window that fronted the bank and turn in to the door at the rear. His father needed him. He would not be angry that Jesse had ignored his message and had come to the bank instead of going home. It was like the fairy tale he had read just last night. He was the strong prince sent to aid the besieged king.

Sunlight flashed across the plate-glass window as he ran. The golden letters turned molten. His father's name dazzled him with brightness. Not everyone's father had his name emblazoned in letters of gold on gleaming glass. Now, he was in front of the window, running, running.

"Stern, we want our money and we want it now!"

The man's voice was hoarse, his face purple with anger. He leaped forward, his arm upraised, and a huge stone sailed through the air.

"No!" the boy screamed. A flying stone could break the glass, shatter the golden letters. It was wrong, evil.

"No!" he shouted again, but his voice was lost as the huge

window was shattered. An almost musical crescendo filled the air—the glittering shards scattered with timpanic resonance, glass against pavement, with the shouts of the crowd a shrilling chorus.

He was pushed forward, and he saw the golden letters had, after all, not been shattered although the window was broken. The glass just above them jutted upward in a crystalline jagged splinter with a point so fine that when it plunged into the artery at the boy's neck it sank swiftly and deeply. His mouth opened, but he did not cry out and the blood spurted from his neck in a crimson flow that spattered the blond hair of the woman who stood beside him and drenched the blue denim jacket of the bearded rancher who stretched out his arms to catch him as he fell.

Joshua Lewin and Rachel Wallach walked slowly through the downtown district. He carried his black medical bag, swinging it slightly, and Rachel's sketch pad was tucked beneath her arm. She was glad that they had decided to walk rather than drive. The afternoon was cool and it was good to be out of doors after the hours they had spent in the stifling room of the small Mexican girl. Poor Inez. The large-eyed child had slipped into the sleep of death even as Joshua bent over her, pressing the stethoscope to her chest. Joshua had asked Rachel to visit his young patient because the family wanted a drawing of their daughter.

"Un recuerdo," the weary mother had said tearfully as the father crossed himself. They had accepted their daughter's impending death. They could not accept her disappearance from their lives.

Rachel had agreed without hesitating as she agreed to all of Joshua's requests. Increasingly, since Gracia had left Phoenix (she had accepted an offer to work on a newspaper in Sacramento, Joshua had explained—an offer too good to resist), Joshua turned to Rachel with small demands, spontaneous invitations, pleas for advice. It was as though he were adrift and she were his ballast, weighting him with her acquiescence, her presence. Could Rachel design his visiting cards? Could she accompany him on a trip to a reservation in the South? Did she think the acreage near Camelback was a good location for the clinic?

Dutifully, she designed his cards, packed a picnic lunch for the journey to the South, and observed that the resort hotels on the Camelback road might make the location unsuitable for a clinic. And that afternoon she had sat beside him in the tiny adobe hut and sketched the angular face of the dying child, emphasizing the large dark eyes and the mouth curled into a sweet, accepting smile. The small girl's hair had been matted with sweat, but in Rachel's drawing it fell in two smooth braids, each tied with desert flowers.

"She loved flowers," the mother had whispered when Rachel gave her the drawing. "You are kind, señorita, very kind."

She held the sketch tenderly. The family would place it in a frame, and always their beautiful, dark-eyed daughter would stare out at them, her hair neatly plaited, her wooden crucifix nestled at the cleft of her slender neck.

"She was a beautiful child," Rachel said softly as she and Joshua approached an intersection.

"Sometimes the hour of death has a beauty of its own," Joshua reflected. "I've seen it often—the release from pain—the end of all sadness and loss."

"Joshua." She hesitated. She had thought to ask him about the source of his own sadness, to offer him comfort against loss, but before she could find the words an anguished cry ripped through the afternoon quiet.

"A doctor! Damn it, get a doctor!"

They stared at each other. The shout had come from Jefferson Street, just around the corner, where the old Wormser warehouse and the Salt River Bank stared across at each other. Joshua gripped her wrist and they ran, the dust forming small clouds behind them, their hearts pounding with fear. As they turned the corner, they saw the crowd in front of the bank, heard the low murmur. The men and women stood grouped together, almost motionless, as though shock had frozen them into positions they feared to abandon.

"Dr. Lewin is here. Thank God, Dr. Lewin is here." Rosa Martinez ran toward him.

"What is it, Rosa?" He had treated her for asthma, held

her limp wrist as she struggled for breath, the inhalator pressed against her nostrils. Now she looked at him with relief. He had cured her. Surely he could save the injured boy, the bright-haired son of Henry Stern's mature years.

"There."

The crowd parted as she led him to the spot where Jesse lay, the blood still spurting. He hurried forward.

"Call the hospital. Tell them to send an ambulance," he shouted to Rachel.

Stern bent over his son, his hands helplessly outstretched.

"Help him. Help him." His voice was broken, and he cradled his head in his arms.

Joshua thrust the heel of his hand against the open wound. The blood was warm and thick. He felt its surging power as it struggled to force its way free, to stream forward once again. The carotid artery. That bastard of a bleeder, his lab partner at medical school had called it. He increased the pressure, forced his weight upon the boy. Slowly, too slowly, the flow subsided.

"Give me handkerchiefs," he shouted. "Clean handkerchiefs."

Squares of white linen fluttered down, and he wadded them together and packed the gaping wound with them, not relinquishing the pressure of his own hand. God only knew how much blood the boy had already lost.

A shrieking siren announced the arrival of the ambulance. He lifted the boy in his arms and hurried into it, Rachel and Henry Stern following him.

"I didn't want him to come. I thought he wouldn't come." The banker swayed from side to side, and his lips moved silently now in prayer, in supplication, as the ambulance sped to the hospital.

The child lay on the ambulance cot, blankets piled on his slender form. The small cabin was stiflingly hot, yet he shivered. Shock, Joshua thought. He took his own jacket off and added it to the mound of coverings. They would need a transfusion. The child's pallor was frightening, his pulse dangerously weak.

"Do you know your son's blood type?" he asked Henry Stern.

"Yes. It's the same as my own. B. Rh-negative."

Joshua breathed easier. The type was rare, but Henry Stern was on hand as an immediate donor, and the odds were that a transfusion within the family would be compatible. There would be no antigen or platelet problem.

"You're healthy—no infection?"

They approached the hospital gate. Jesse's skin was parchment-pale; the long copper lashes swept his cheeks. Joshua bit his lip, banished the memory of his brother Gregory. If Jesse spoke, would his voice resonate with Gregory's sweetness?

"I'm healthy," Henry Stern said bitterly. "Hepatitis last year, but I'm fine now. Fine." He would trade his health for his son's life; he would grow weak so that his son might be strong.

"Hepatitis. Goddamn it. We can't use your blood."

Jesse moaned and Joshua took the wet cloth Rachel handed him and bathed the boy's forehead, tested the packed wound. The bleeding had stopped, but they would need blood for a transfusion. His mind raced, jumping from solution to solution. It was unlikely that the boy's mother would have the same rare blood type, and besides, it had already been established that she was at her studio. There was no telephone there, he knew.

"What about your daughter, Barbara?" he asked the banker.

"No. Her type is A. She needed blood when the baby was born, and they could not use mine. But surely the hospital will have access to the type Jesse needs." His voice wavered.

"We need a blood relative," Joshua replied tersely. There was no time for testing, and he could not risk platelet incompatibility. "Do you have any other relations in Phoenix?"

The banker stared at him, and Joshua looked into the turquoise eyes that exactly matched those of his mother.

"Of course," he muttered. Emma had the same blood type. She had been called to donate it often enough during the war. And she was a blood relative. The risk would be small.

"Rachel," he said, "stay in the ambulance. The driver will take you to my mother's house. Tell her what happened and tell her that she must come at once. Only she can save the life of her brother's child.''

Again Jesse moaned and shivered, and Henry Stern covered the boy's body with his own, his lips moving soundlessly as the ambulance shrieked to a halt at the emergency room entry.

An hour later Emma Lewin lay on a hospital bed and stared at the long, thick needle that pierced the vein of her arm. Her blood, the color of wine, coursed through it slowly, steadily, swelling the white silk tubing that stretched between herself and small Jesse Stern. Drop by drop, her blood filled the needle that seemed so large in the child's slender arm; drop by scarlet drop, it flowed into his body, replenishing, repairing. They formed an odd partnership, she and the boy— donor and recipient, his face strangely peaceful, her own tensed with determination, as though by sheer will she might infuse her blood with the sustenance he needed.

The light of the dangling hospital lamp turned the child's hair the color of burnished bronze. She closed her eyes and remembered how her father had sat at his desk in the lamplight and how she, a small girl then (perhaps the same age as young Jesse), had been entranced by the metallic sheen of his thick hair. Her father—young Jesse Stern's grandfather.

How pale the boy was—his skin as white as the translucent shells that pebbled the beach at Galveston, as the ivory sands near the approach to Squaw Peak, as the crust of snow that carpeted the narrow bridges of Amsterdam during the long months of winter. Gregory had not been pale at the hour of his death. Fever had flooded his face with radiance, caused his limbs to glow.

The boy moaned, and Joshua moved toward him, spoke softly into his ear.

"Can you hear me? Can you tell me your name? What is your name?" His voice was gentle yet insistent, authoritative.

Jesse's lips moved. They had lost their pallor. Was it her blood mingling with his own that gave them that gentle rose color? Her life's substance was melded now with his—if he were wounded, her lifeblood would flow. The thought comforted her. That was as it should be. They were bound to-

gether by legacy and lineage, by consanguinity and continuity. Jesse Stern was almost twin in color and feature to her
own lost Gregory. She could not deny him, no more than she
had ever wanted to deny his father.

"Jesse. My name is Jesse." His voice was weak, but he
spoke without hesitating. Emma saw Joshua smile, watched
the wreath of worry lift from his brow.

"What do you want for your birthday, Jesse?" Joshua
asked.

"A pony. A pony named Silver." He smiled but said no
more. He breathed slowly, evenly.

"He's asleep," Joshua said. "That's good."

Gently, he removed the needle from his mother's arm and
then from Jesse's.

"He's all right," he said. "He'll be fine."

"I know."

She sat up and looked at the sleeping boy. She imagined
him stirring to wakefulness. Did he sing sweetly into the
night darkness as Gregory had? A fatigue, at once heavy and
peaceful, engulfed her, and gratefully she leaned on Joshua.
Together they went to the anteroom where Henry and Isabel
Stern, their fingers interlocked, sat opposite Isaac.

Henry Stern rose as she entered.

"How can I thank you?" he asked, his voice breaking.

"There is no need to thank me. Wouldn't you have done
as much for me?"

She stretched her arms out to her father's son, her brother.
They had hovered too close to death that afternoon to deny
their shared lives any longer.

He took her hands in his own, drew her close and then
closer. She moved toward him, and they were locked in embrace—her tears soaking his chest and his own glistening like
dewdrops in the copper and silver coronet of her hair. They
wept for all the wasted years, for the losses of their youth and
the solitude of their lives, for their parents' sorrow and their
own.

Joshua crossed the room and went to stand beside Rachel
Wallach. Through the hospital window they watched the sun
slowly set. The sky was threaded with veins of mauve, lightly
tinged with gold; smoke-colored clouds drifted westward to-

ward the sculpted mountains as light and darkness merged. It was the magic hour of reconciliation, acceptance. The moon, a slender silver crescent, glowed in the gathering dusk. It was Isaac Lewin who offered the prayer, speaking solemnly, softly.

"To Him Who made great lights—the sun to rule by day and the moon and stars to reign at night."

"Amen."

They bowed their heads, thankful that the day was past, that the desert was draped in darkness and that together, as one family, united by blood and by tradition, they would walk into the moonlit night.

A new vigor seized them. Reconciled, the two families worked in concert, energized and revitalized by their own unity. Relief and an almost chimerical rapport melted the constraint of years. Determinedly, then, they fused their new alliance, made their plans.

The bank's survival was their immediate concern. An unofficial "bank holiday" was in effect in Phoenix that Friday—a three-day reprieve to allow time for manipulation and maneuver. Isaac and Henry Stern met for lunch at the Phoenix Hotel. They studied the menu and ordered the same meal. Omelets made with spicy jalapeño peppers and draft root beer served in tall, frosted glasses. Such commonality of taste did not surprise them. Through the years of their estrangement they had consistently voted the same ticket, spoken passionately in defense of the same issues—statehood, women's suffrage, wartime price controls. They dared not form the thought that they had even, in their different ways, loved the same woman, although, as they raised their glasses in silent hopeful toast, each thought of Isabel's face as she had rushed into the Lewin home the previous evening.

Worry lines had tessellated her eyes and fear had dulled their golden gaze. The phone message at her home had directed her to call the Lewins—a strange enough instruction—but the line had been engaged. Instead she had driven to the MacDowell Road house, her foot jammed down on the accelerator, while she bit down on her lower lip so that a ribbon of blood formed.

"Jesse!" She had shouted her son's name, blending hope and terror as she rushed through the door that had for so long been closed to her, without sounding the bell or knocking.

"He's all right. He's fine." Henry Stern had held her in his arms, reassured her, his voice gentle, his large hand encasing the cap of her dark hair. Soothingly, gently, he told her what had happened.

"We were fortunate that Emma was at home, that she came at once. . . ." His voice faltered at the thought of what might have been.

Isabel had turned to Emma then, and the two women had embraced. The past was vanquished and they could at last plan the future. Talk burst forth then; their words collided with febrile urgency. They were like survivors of a long thirst who at last confront a source of water and drink steadily, voraciously. And then the torrent slowed, and shyly, hesitantly, Emma and Henry spoke of Jacob Coen. Henry showed them the faded daguerreotype of Analiese he kept in his wallet, and he studied the photograph of Leonie Coen that stood on the piano. They knew that for a long time they would offer each other fragments of their separate pasts, like segments of a child's puzzle that stubbornly refuse to mesh.

They discovered that they were all exceedingly hungry. Emma and Isabel went into the kitchen together and prepared platters of meat and salad, bowls of fruit and carafes of rich, dark coffee. Joshua arrived home to tell them that Jesse's pulse was strong, his blood pressure normal, and they toasted the boy's health with Genever. Emma noticed that Henry downed his drink in a single gulp, as their father had, and that he laughed with a full and breathless release of merriment, as their father had laughed.

Reunited, reclaiming memories, they were reluctant to part. On impulse they called Simon Coen's home in San Francisco, and the sons of Jacob Coen spoke to each other shyly, pleasantly, their subdued voices mingling regret and relief. Henry Stern thought of his brother, David. Could an overseas operator trace a Dr. David Deken presumed to be in Berlin but unlisted in the phone book of that city? It was unlikely, he knew, and he cursed himself for the anger that had resulted in so grave a loss of contact.

Emma was energized by her own excitement. She glided between Isaac and Henry Stern, touching her husband's shoulder, studying her half brother's face. She urged Isabel to eat, sweetened her coffee, and told her, truthfully, that she had always admired her work. She liked the intense, fine-featured woman, admired the forbearance with which she had accepted Joshua's advice not to rush off to the hospital. Jesse was sleeping and needed his rest. Always, Isabel would place the needs of others above her own.

I understand, Emma thought.

It was clear to her why Isaac had been drawn to Isabel. Like a traveler recalling a distant journey, she looked back across the years and thought of herself frightened and with-drawn, silent and constrained. The betrayals of her past had entrapped her while Isabel had been a free spirit, vibrant and acquiescent. Her need and Isaac's own had melded. They had all been so different then, Emma thought, so needy and so vulnerable. The clarity of her understanding drew her to Isaac's side. She placed her hand in his, and he lifted her arm and kissed the soft white skin just below the crescent of gauze that protected the small puncture in her vein. It occurred to him that he and Emma, Henry and Isabel, had triumphed over their own histories. They had chosen to come alone to this desert state, at a remove from the lives they had known, distant from their coreligionists. It was not chance alone that had brought them together at last but their own courage and generosity, their fortitude, and, finally, their forgiveness.

Isaac thought about that now as he sipped his root beer and looked at Henry Stern.

"How much money will the bank need in order to reopen with a margin of safety?" he asked. It would be economic suicide, he knew, to reopen with limited cash reserves and be forced to close yet again.

The banker scratched tiny digits on the frosted surface of his glass and watched them evaporate.

"Fifty thousand," he said. "At least fifty thousand. On a short-term loan." He had been fortunate. Two of the firms into which he had poured massive investments of depositors' funds had stood firm, surviving the crash, but it would be foolhardy to sell now. "But I suppose it might as well be a hundred thousand. Who has that much in cash, and if they had it, who would risk it?''

"I have it," Isaac Lewin replied quietly, "and I am prepared to risk it. We are family." The word thrilled him, imbued him with a source of power.

On Monday, the Salt River Bank, its plate-glass window repaired, opened for business. Henry Stern worked the floor, smiling confidently. The tellers, in their cages, deftly sorted mounds of currency. Hillocks of single dollar bills, neat piles of twenties and tens, small stacks of fifties, were banded and counted. They shuffled the bills with the skill of card sharps, and they wore rubber thumb guards so that the cash that Samuel Lewin had so prudently withdrawn from the stock market and concealed in the safe of the Emporium would not bruise their fingers. By early afternoon couriers arrived from San Francisco with additional cash. The sons of Jacob Coen would stand together.

Within weeks most of the loans had been repaid. The bank was out of danger, its on-hand currency stabilized, its investments protected. Another luncheon meeting was held, and now the entire family met. It was time to discuss the new Emporium. Construction had been halted for too long. Field mice darted through the girders, and a hawk's nest crowned an elongated beam. Samuel brought out architects' plans, contractors' estimates, and they assessed the work that had been done, the work that had yet to be done.

Grimly, then, they spoke of the mood of the city. The Depression held sun-washed Phoenix in its dark and iron grip. Throughout the city businesses were closing. Other banks had not shared the Salt River Bank's happy recovery. Doors that had slammed shut on "black Thursday" had not reopened, and many Phoenicians had lost their life's savings.

Each day another house went on the market, the *For Sale* signs swinging with forlorn hopelessness. California beckoned, no longer offering the promise of gold but teasing with the hope of jobs at minimum wages, verdancy, and faint hope. Furniture was piled onto the roofs of cars, and what could not fit was often left on the street. Barefoot children played house at curbside, perched on velour-covered sofas, offering each other cups of desert dust served on abandoned gate-leg tables that briefly retained their polished sheens against the glaring sunlight.

Tent cities sprouted on the desert, and the city sent water trucks to the stranded wayfarers and ambulances to carry dehydrated children to hospital emergency rooms. Mines shut down or worked half shifts, and Indian craftsmen squatted on the sidewalks, their wares spread out on dusty blankets as they waited for tourists who did not arrive. The Depression was not conducive to luxury vacations in the American Southwest.

"Is this the time to open another store?" Bryna asked. Like Samuel, she was practical, pragmatic, an efficient businesswoman and a social dreamer. A marriage of the practical and the ideal, Joshua thought, envying his brother and vaguely pitying himself. He had sent Gracia a New Year's card, and it had been returned unopened, marked "Addressee Unknown." She had never been his, yet now she was irrevocably lost to him.

"The Wallach brothers didn't think so," Samuel said.

Reuben and Joseph had left for California, daring and energetic as always. They had heard about a factory foreclosure in Sacramento—a small company that had manufactured radios and had overreached itself in the economic delirium of the roaring, booming twenties. They had gambled the last of their savings on its acquisition.

"What do you know about electronics?" their father had asked. He did not want his sons to go farther west. Natalya was nagged by a mysterious fatigue, and he himself felt the signs of encroaching age.

"About as much as you and Isaac Lewin knew about department stores when you got off the boat at Galveston," Reuben replied with affectionate impudence. "And besides, we speak English."

The brothers shared the cheerful irreverence of first-generation Americans, confident of their language, their birthright. Pioneers themselves, and the sons of pioneers who thought and dreamed in the Yiddish they barely understood, it seemed natural to them that they should push onward to the last frontier. Besides, they were convinced that the future of their country rested on electronics, that one day the radio

(which their own father had contemplated uneasily and re-
garded as a mysterious miracle) would also feature a screen.
Americans would sit in their own homes and watch shows
and the nightly news as they now listened to H. V. Kalten-
born and Jack Benny. There was laughter when they spoke
of it, but Henry Stern did not laugh, nor did Isaac Lewin.
Indeed, both had given the brothers modest checks as initial
investments in a business so young they had not yet thought
of a name for it.

Joshua and Rachel had driven them to the train station,
and Rachel had hugged them and smiled and waved as the
train pulled out. But back in Joshua's car she had wept, and
he had pulled over to the side of the road and watched quietly
until her sobs ceased. Silently, he had handed her his large
white handkerchief, and she had wiped her eyes and folded
it carefully when she returned it to him. They had not spoken, nor had there been any need for words between them.
It had occurred to him that he understood Rachel herself as
instinctively as he understood her paintings. Her daring desert-
scapes and her delicate pen-and-ink drawings reflected both
her undemanding gentleness and a poignant loneliness, an
unarticulated longing. He reached out and touched her hand,
startled at the warmth of her skin and the pulse that beat
wildly at her wrist. He had bent his head then and pressed
his lips against the pulsating blue vein as though he might
still and steady it and thus soothe her pain and loss.

"The Wallach brothers just decided to strike out on their
own," he said now. "But still we must consider if the time
is right to go ahead with a second Emporium." He felt a
peculiar responsibility because he knew his father wanted
the profits to finance the clinic.

"My son, you are a doctor. Never would I give you medical advice. And I am a businessman, and as you understand
medicine, I understand that it is not always good business to
wait for the right time. Who thought it was the right time to
sell ball gowns and ostrich-feather hats from a tent store in
the middle of the desert? But sometimes you make your luck,
create your own right time. Things are hard now, but they'll
get better. I say it is good for Phoenix and good for us if we
build the store. Activity. Recovery. Workers with money in

their pockets to put food on the table with enough left to buy shoes for the kids, a dress for the wife. Sure, we take a risk, but I think we must go forward. We'll build as planned, but we'll start small. Maybe we'll limit departments at first. All that comes later. But for now, I say we gamble again and build.''

''I think you're right,'' Henry Stern said. The Salt River Bank would hold the mortgage, guarantee extensions, refinancing. They were a family unit now, succeeding or failing together.

''It's decided, then,'' Emma said. She smiled at Isaac. ''We go ahead.''

She looked around the table, and they all nodded and one by one extended their hands, palm upon palm, linked in solidarity. Bryna's other hand rested on her abdomen. The new Emporium would be completed in half a year's time if they stuck to their schedule. Her first child would be born that same month—the second generation of Lewins in Arizona. She smiled at the joyous sweetness of her secret and at the mysterious continuity that bound generation to generation.

On the hot July night that Franklin Delano Roosevelt accepted the Democratic presidential nomination, Natalya Wallach died quietly in her sleep. Heart failure, Joshua said, and he was grateful that death had come before the carcinoma so deeply rooted in her womb could spread its malignant foliage and turn her abdomen into a canyon of pain. It was Emma who cleansed the body and prepared it for burial, passing a soft cloth soaked in warm rosewater across the cold, yielding flesh, the rigidifying bones. She brushed her friend's light hair, grieved at the tendrils that broke loose. Natalya had always been so proud of her thick hair, with the peculiar vanity of the plain woman who had a single beautiful attribute. In Galveston she had worn wreaths of oleander blossoms, and in Phoenix she had threaded sprigs of desert laurel through her intricately braided chignon. Emma wept, and her tears fell into the bowl of rosewater so that the cloth with which she washed Natalya's slender ankles was moistened with her own sorrow.

Rachel entered the room carrying the tall white candles

that would burn throughout the long hours of watching on either side of the plain pine coffin. Natalya's daughter was pale, her eyes red-rimmed, but she moved with grace and confidence. Like her mother, she recognized obligations and carefully guarded the parameters of her own grief. She had, that morning, spoken to her brothers in California, breaking the news to them and then reading off the plane schedules, which she had researched before calling them. She had prepared breakfast for her father and sat beside him as he ate, buttering his toast, sweetening his coffee. She was as good a daughter as she would be a mother, Emma had thought as she watched her.

Rachel had covered the mirrors and spoken to the rabbi, showing him the yellowed news clippings from the Galveston papers that described Natalya's heroism during the tidal flood as she had led the children in her care to safety. Gently, she had refused Joshua's offer of a sedative, although she had accepted one for her father.

"Rachel is very strong," Joshua had said admiringly.

"Not too strong, I hope," Emma had replied and turned from her son's startled glance. Strength was deceptive, inhibiting, isolating. *You are so strong,* Isaac had once said bitterly, and she had not dared to tell him that it was her vulnerability, her fear, that forced her into that posture of rigid competence. True strength allowed for the revelation of weakness.

She watched Rachel now as she set the candlesticks down and looked down at her mother.

"She was so good," she said, and her voice broke.

Lightly her fingers touched the bloodless lips, so oddly curved into that familiar smile of happy reminiscence. Had Natalya died then in the midst of a happy dream? Had she glided into death remembering the June evening when she had first danced with Abner Wallach on the Galveston green, when a happiness she had never anticipated had found her?

"She was very proud of you, Rachel," Emma said.

She put her arm about the girl's quivering shoulders and led her from the room. The men of the synagogue who came to stand guard over the body and to recite the psalms of consolation which Natalya, the daughter of a Vilna rabbi and teacher of Hebrew, had known by heart, would light the candles.

"And *I* am proud of you," she added as they sat together in Natalya's small sewing room.

She took Rachel's cold hands into her own. A sudden urgency seized her. There were things she had to say to her friend's daughter, hard-earned kernels of knowledge that she would share in this quiet hour when a life had ended and they were mindful of a future that stretched before them like an unshaded narrow road threaded with mysterious and dangerous turnings.

"You must be proud of yourself—of what you can give, of what you can share. Don't be afraid to speak of what is in your heart, to make your feelings known. I lived in fear for so many years, Rachel. I wasted so much time."

Rachel looked at strong, tall Emma Lewin and saw that she wept. She understood that her grief was not only for Natalya but for herself and that her tears were at once a confession and a warning.

"I am afraid that if I speak to Joshua of love, it will mean the end of friendship," Rachel said. Her voice was clarion-clear, as though the words had broken free at last and rang true, released from strangulating fear and doubt.

"Joshua needs time," Emma said. She pleaded now for her son as once she had been afraid to plead for herself. She, too, had needed time and had feared to confess her need. Precious years that could not be reclaimed had been lost. *You must say what you feel,* Leonie's wise Franz had told her as the fog obscured the San Francisco Bay, and these words, too, she had offered to Rachel. She reached out to the young woman who loved Joshua as once Analiese had reached out to her.

"But he would have to be ready to hear what I feel," Rachel said. "And he is not ready."

Emma did not answer. Rachel had inherited Natalya's instinctive wisdom, her gentle forbearance. Joshua was not ready. Gracia was gone, but her shadow lingered, and he was imprisoned still in that penumbral loss.

"What will you do, then?" she asked.

"I want to study in Paris. Isabel thinks that I have talent, that I need training. My mother wanted me to go. I think—I hope—she would have been glad.''

Now, at last, she cradled her head in her arms and allowed the grief to well over her, to absorb her, to lock her into its unremitting throes, its terrible finality. Her mother was dead, but Rachel herself was alive, and her life would move forward, and that, too, was at once terrible and wonderful.

She wept, and Emma Lewin comforted her, smoothed her fair hair, and softly spoke the words of solace which, at that moment, neither of them could believe. It was the knowledge that Emma, too, had sustained loss, traversed loneliness and sorrow, and in the end had triumphed, that comforted Rachel. She gripped Emma's hands, her nails carving small arcs of blood into the older woman's flesh—the stigmata of grief.

Joshua, who opened the door of the sewing room just then, saw the two women, in their dark dresses, sitting together, their hands clasped, their heads bent low. Quietly, he closed it again and, for the first time in many years, he went to join his father at the morning prayer quorum.

Berlin,
1934

BRYNA LEWIN glanced at the résumé on her desk and sighed. She was pregnant again and felt the nagging fatigue that had haunted her first pregnancy. Small Nathan was an active toddler now, and Bryna treasured those days when she arrived home early enough in the afternoon to watch him pedal his tricycle busily up and down the path, alighting now and again to toss his large red ball at her with the dictatorial instruction "Mommy, catch!" Today, she acknowledged, would not be one of those days when she would leave her office at a reasonable hour and sit beneath a palm tree while she watched her son at play.

One crisis after another had imposed itself upon her since early morning, and she had dashed from the "old" Emporium to the "new" to sort out employee schedules, deal with a shipping mishap and meet with a grievance committee. The Lewins themselves had at last succumbed to the Phoenician nomenclature for their two stores. Their customers, from the days of the second Emporium's festive opening, had referred to the "old" and the "new," and all advertising efforts to change that perception had failed. Finally even Isaac, who had vainly tried to call the second store "Lewin's on the Square," began to speak of the "old" and the "new."

Bryna supervised personnel and inventory control for both stores, but it was now clear that someone would have to be hired to share her responsibilities. Initially, the sluggish economy, mired in the Depression, had precluded hiring additional staff. The family had proceeded cautiously, mindful always of the risk they had taken in opening a new establishment when so many businesses were declaring bankruptcy. Still, they had survived, and slowly the new Emporium was gaining a personality and reputation of its own. Its more modestly priced line of merchandise attracted customers whose strained budgets could manage the off-the-rack suits and ready-to-wear dresses. Isaac had instituted a layaway plan and arrangements for time payment contracts.

Now, three years after its opening, the new store had finally showed a narrow profit margin. "Paper profits," Samuel had warned, but Isaac spoke again of the clinic he still planned to underwrite, and occasionally he and Joshua visited prospective sites. Bryna had begun to interview candidates for the position of manager. She hoped fervently that the man she was to interview that afternoon would prove qualified and scanned his résumé again. It had been sent to her by the Hebrew Immigrant Aid Society with the notation that the applicant was knowledgeable about the retail business and had worked in the field in Berlin.

She lifted her phone.

"Please send Mr. Grossmann in," she said.

The middle-aged man who entered her office radiated an aura of confidence. His smile was cordial, his handshake firm, yet she noted a strange wariness in his gaze, a minatory control in his stance. His well-cut brown tweed suit was clearly too heavy for the sultry Arizona climate, and he had lost weight since it had been fitted so that it hung too loosely. She noted too, with the attention to seemingly irrelevant detail which Samuel claimed was among her professional strengths, that the collar of his starched snow-white shirt had recently been turned and the faint odor of carbolic clung to his heavy silk cravat.

"You are familiar with the operation of a relatively large department store?" she asked.

"Yes. I owned my own store on the Kurfürstendamm in Berlin," he replied.

"I should think that you would perhaps be interested in opening your own business here in America," she said, relieved that his English was fluent enough to preclude any difficulty.

"I had to sell my own store at a fraction of its worth," he replied curtly, and she did not press him.

She turned the conversation to matters of personnel and inventory. Werner Grossmann was knowledgeable about staff rotation and record keeping. His Berlin store had utilized a system of inventory control that had been remarkably efficient.

"It could be applied here with comparable success," he said. "I noticed, for example, unfortunate duplications in your haberdashery department which my system would avoid." He had, very sensibly, spent the hour before his interview wandering through the Emporium, and his small pocket notebook was filled with his astute observations.

Bryna listened carefully. It was possible, after all, that she could cancel her other appointments and leave early that day. Werner Grossmann was clearly the right candidate for the position.

"I think that we can certainly come to an agreement," she said. "But of course, I should like my husband and my father-in-law to meet you. They leave tomorrow to visit our other stores. Could you come in again next week?"

"I'm afraid not," he replied. "If you are undecided, then I will go on to California, where I have good contacts with the Magnin stores. I must have an immediate decision. My family has been so long unsettled." His voice was cool, but his eyes narrowed and she discerned his nervousness in the tight clasping and unclasping of his hands.

"I see." She did see. He pressed her because he himself was pressed. He would exert the same pressure on suppliers and employees, and he would gain results. "Perhaps you could come to my in-laws' home for dinner this evening," she suggested. "Nothing formal, I assure you. Only family. My sister-in-law and her husband who are here on a visit from San Francisco."

"I should be delighted." Werner Grossmann's tone betrayed neither surprise nor relief, but she noticed that when she shook his hand at her office door, his palm was damp to her touch.

It was an informal dinner, and, as Bryna had anticipated, Isaac and Samuel immediately recognized Werner Grossmann's qualifications. Although the terms of his employment had not been discussed, even before dessert was served Emma offered advice on a school for the Grossmann children, and when Henry and Isabel Stern arrived for coffee, they were discussing housing. Henry advised the German to rent rather than buy.

"We don't know what Roosevelt's New Deal economics will do to mortgage rates," the banker said. He had voted for Franklin Roosevelt, but he knew that the president's first priority would be to reverse the train of events that had been set in motion that black Thursday when the window of his bank had shattered and his life had taken a new turning. It was difficult to know how that reversal would affect property values and interest rates.

"In any case I would not be able to buy a home," Werner Grossmann said bitterly. "I could not afford to do so."

Isaac looked at him in surprise.

"Surely your store was a valuable property," he said.

"It was," the German replied. "But I was obliged to sell it for a fraction of its worth, and the same was true of the sale of my home. Our savings were exorbitantly taxed, and much of my capital went to help my relations and Jewish employees leave Germany."

"But why did you have to sell so cheaply?" Emma asked.

It was Franz Eisenmann, who read the German papers regularly, who replied.

"Mr. Hitler's anti-Semitic theory translates into action. Discriminatory taxation of Jewish accounts coupled with a kind of economic terrorism. Either a Jew sells his business at a deflated price, or that business may be vandalized or burned to the ground. I suspect that Mr. Grossmann here considers himself lucky to have sold at whatever price and to have gotten himself and his family out of the fatherland."

"I do. I am alive and I am in a free country. My body was not found in the Spree like that of my brother. Wherever I live in Phoenix, I do not think my windows will be broken because my home is the home of a Jew. There will be no swastika chalked on my front door. My children will not be attacked on the streets as they walk home from school. You cannot imagine what it is like for Jews in Germany now. And it is only the beginning. It will get worse. If you have family there, advise them to leave. At once." He spoke dispassionately, but his coffee cup rattled against the saucer as he set it down, and beads of sweat stood on his high pale forehead.

The family looked uneasily at each other. They had had intimations of the situation in Germany, both in newspaper accounts and through Rachel Wallach's letters. She had spent several weeks in Berlin at a seminar on the Bauhaus artists and had written despairingly of the overt anti-Semitism—epithets scrawled on Jewish shops, the shattered windows of synagogues. She had been glad, she wrote, that she had not been alone but with a fellow art student, a young man named Etan from the Bezalel Academy in Jerusalem. Joshua had noticed, with restrained irritation, that Etan's name appeared more frequently in her letters.

Isaac turned to Werner Grossmann. "We are pleased that you have found your way to Phoenix," he said. "And even more pleased that you will be joining the staff of the Emporium."

"I, too, am pleased." The German stood and bowed formally from the waist. He left shortly afterward, and the family sat about the refectory table in silence. The evening was warm, but Isabel Stern reached for her shawl, and although there was no sound from the stairwell, Leonie went upstairs to check on her sleeping children.

"My brother—*our* brother—David is in Germany," Henry Stern said in a strangulated voice. "I've written him care of Poste Restante in different cities over the past several months, but the letters have all been returned. I even contacted the American Embassy, but they cannot help except to confirm that he is not listed in any German phone directory." He looked around the table as though in search of advice, absolution. Were there other paths of inquiry he could follow? Had he exhausted every course of action?

"He is a physician. Perhaps we could trace him through the various medical societies," Franz suggested. "What do you think, Joshua? We place a query or an advertisement asking for any information about a Dr. David Stern. . . ."

"Not Stern," the banker interrupted. "Stern was my mother's maiden name, which I adopted when I came to America. David kept her husband's name, Deken. He is known as Dr. David Deken."

"David Deken?" Joshua leaned forward excitedly. "But - I met him. He spoke at a conference I attended in Germany just before I returned to America. And he is to deliver a paper at a symposium I've been invited to in the spring. I never made the connection.''

''Of course not. How could you?'' Henry Stern's voice quivered with excitement. He turned to Emma and gripped her wrists. ''What do you think? Is it possible? Can it be possible?''

''Who are we to disbelieve in the long arm of coincidence? We found each other against all odds. Why should we not find David?'' She spoke with confidence, and her determination became electric. Hope brightened their faces. They leaned forward. Henry Stern remembered, suddenly, his brother's habit of clapping his hands when he laughed. Did he do that still? he wondered.

''We must find him and persuade him to leave at once,'' she continued more soberly. ''Even if he must abandon his home, his practice.''

There was urgency. Werner Grossmann had spoken of bodies floating in the Spree, of broken men and frightened children. Here, in this whitewashed room, he had fleshed out the skeletons of fear that had haunted Franz Eisenmann for years and given pained voice to Rachel Wallach's grim observations.

''That is not something you can put in a letter,'' Franz said. ''I am certain that incoming mail, particularly letters addressed to Jews, must be read.''

''Someone must go to Berlin,'' Isaac agreed. ''One of the family.'' He smiled bitterly, recalling that when he had left Hamburg for Galveston, there had been those who had tried to dissuade him. It was madness, they thought, for an educated man to leave civilized Germany (''We have no pogroms here,'' they had asserted proudly) for the untamed and unsettled American Southwest. In the end they had marveled at his courage. Now it required courage to go to Germany.

''I will go. I can present my paper at the symposium and make contact with David Deken there. It would arouse no suspicion, involve no danger,'' Joshua said. A sense of excitement, an aura of adventure, enveloped him. Mentally, he juggled itineraries, priorities, thought of himself racing for trains, crossing borders, holding clandestine conferences. He

would travel to Berlin via Paris and see Rachel. Three months
had passed since she had last written him, although she had
sent him a series of pen-and-ink sketches for his birthday—
delicate drawings of the primrose blossom they both loved
and which once, during an odd winter, they had observed
tenaciously blooming during a Flagstaff snowfall. Rachel had
marveled then at the flower's tenacity, its power to break
forth without the nourishment of either sun or earth. Emma,
who understood flowers, had told them afterward that it took
its strength from its roots and sustained itself. Rachel's drawings traced a single blossom from its softly enfolded bud to
its slow opening and its final sensual flowering.

Joshua had framed the drawings, but he had not hung them.
Instead, he kept them in the drawer of his bedside table and
studied them now and again with a strange intensity, as
though seeking a solution to an elusive and important puzzle.

"Yes. Of course. It is best that Joshua go," Emma said.

She smiled at her son and looked at Isaac. Their family
was no stranger to danger and daring, to the crossing of
oceans and continents, the spanning of deserts and mountains.

"But Joshua, you will be careful," Franz Eisenmann said.
His tone was grave, almost ominous. He was, after all, a
man who understood history and saw into the darkness of
men's hearts.

Joshua walked slowly down the Rue Jacob and lifted his face
gratefully to the pale sunlight and hesitant warmth of early
spring. Lacy white blossoms fringed the chestnut tree that
stood in front of Rachel Wallach's boarding house, and he
wondered if she sometimes lay abed and sketched the graceful, flowering branches. He had not written to tell her that
he was coming to Paris, nor had he told his family of his
intention. It would be a surprise, he had told himself, and
felt again the exhilaration of adventure.

He knocked at the door, and a stern-faced woman, wearing the black dress and black stockings of a mourner, opened
it a bare crevice and stared out at him.

"Mlle. Wallach?" He smiled engagingly.

The landlady did not smile back. *La mademoiselle amér-*

icaine was not at home, she told him with an air of sour satisfaction. She was enjoying *les vacances de printemps* with her friend.

"Ah, her friend." Joshua smiled knowingly and nodded, hoping that the landlady would invite him in so that he might leave a note for Rachel.

"Yes. Monsieur Etan. He is also an art student. From Jerusalem," the woman said and smiled as though she derived pleasure from mentioning the name of the holy city. Grudgingly, she accepted the note Joshua hurriedly scrawled, giving Rachel the name of his hotel in Berlin.

He thought about Rachel as he made his way to the Gare du Nord to await the evening express to Berlin and acknowledged the depth of his disappointment at not seeing her. He wondered, too, about Etan. Was he Rachel's friend or lover? The thought was unsettling, and he wondered suddenly why, in all the years he had known her, Rachel Wallach's name had never been romantically linked with anyone. Certainly, she was attractive. In fact, when she smiled she was quite beautiful. He paused and his heart turned as he remembered the shimmering, mysterious beauty of Rachel Wallach's face when she smiled.

At the station, he bought a magazine, but although he turned the pages, he did not read it. He thought instead of the trio of drawings she had sent him, seeing them in his mind's eye with perfect clarity and a new understanding. In that segue of pen-and-ink sketches, she had revealed herself to him—her emergence from that enclosed bud, a slow and languid flowering and at last that full-petaled, open blossom, long-stemmed and honey-hearted. He rose abruptly and phoned the boarding house, ignoring the landlady's acid displeasure, and instructing her that it was in fact urgent that Mlle. Rachel Wallach telephone him in Berlin.

It was raining when he arrived in Berlin, and he took a cab to the hotel just off the Friedrichsstrasse that Werner Grossmann had recommended. It was centrally located and moderately priced, the German had said, but more important, the proprietor could be relied on to guard confidences and even offer aid.

"If you tell him that you are a friend of mine, he will understand," Werner Grossmann had added.

The veiled warning had irritated Joshua. He acknowledged that there was some risk, but there was no need for elaborate intrigue. He was an American doctor, attending a medical conference to which he had been invited by an august committee. Still, he found the huge colored posters of Hitler in full uniform standing beneath a swastika banner strangely disturbing. Even more unsettling were the graffiti he had glimpsed from the window of his taxicab as they passed a clothing store. *Jude verrecke. Jew, Perish.* He averted his eyes now from the swastika insignia the pale hotel clerk wore in the lapel of his uniform.

"Are there any messages for me?" he asked coldly.

The clerk handed him several envelopes, and he tossed away the invitation to the dinner launching the symposium, which he had missed because of his detour in Paris. He felt a pang of regret. Surely David Deken had attended the dinner. They might already had initiated their arrangement for his leaving Germany. Carefully, he read the note inviting him to a cocktail party that evening. Deken would surely be there.

"Please have a basin of hot water sent to my room," he said.

"Of course," the clerk replied indifferently. "Heil Hitler." He thrust his arm forth in a salute, which Joshua ignored.

The basin of hot water did not arrive. Joshua shaved with cold tap water and went to the cocktail party.

There were no photographs of Hitler, nor were there any swastika banners in the elegant ballroom where the cocktail party was held. There was a profusion of champagne, an elaborate buffet and the rustling of taffeta, the whispering of organdy, as beautifully gowned women circulated. They smiled constantly, their faces glowing, as though ignited by the radiance of their husbands' brilliant achievements. The physicians and scientists, in their well-cut dinner jackets and snow-white dress shirts, discussed current research on lung disease, articles that had appeared in international journals, and, in lower voices, academic appointments. Joshua greeted colleagues. He himself had recently published a study of the influence of diet on tubercular patients, using two different Indian control groups, and his findings, while speculative by his own admission, had attracted wide interest. He answered questions affably, asked many of his own, and searched the room for Dr. David Deken. He had seen his mother's half brother only once, but he was certain that he would remember him.

The beautiful Italian doctor with whom Joshua had had a brief affair during his residency in Switzerland approached him. Dutifully, he kissed her on the cheek. She was married now and happy, *very* happy, she told him too many times. (He wondered if he would ever see Gracia again, and if he did, whether she would tell him that she was happy, *very* happy. It surprised him that he hoped so.) He smiled at Theresa and told her that he could tell she was happy because she was more beautiful than ever, while he noted with wry satisfaction that she had gained weight and that in a few years' time she would be a very fat woman.

"Have you seen Dr. David Deken, the hematologist?" he asked.

"I remember him from the conference we attended together. He gave that brilliant paper on blood chemistry." She did not add that she remembered, too, that she and Joshua had slept together that night. "But no. I haven't seen him at all. He was not at the dinner last night."

"Odd."

Joshua walked on. He recognized an Australian hematologist who was absorbed in balancing two glasses of champagne and a plate of sausage.

"Ian, let me help you with that." He relieved the Australian of a glass of champagne, grinned, and drank it himself.

"You Americans—always joking. How are you, cowboy?" At the last conference the Australian had been intrigued by Joshua's description of Arizona. "Not too different from my territory, then," he had insisted, cheerfully and drunkenly equating Indians and aborigines, the vast American desert and the seemingly endless outback. Joshua had not disabused him.

"Fine. Good. Have you seen David Deken? He's scheduled to be on a panel with you, isn't he?"

"He was. His name was removed, which is a damn shame. It was his paper I really wanted to hear."

"Why?" Joshua asked. "Why was his name removed?"

The Australian led him to a corner and lowered his voice.

"The bloody huns. More of their Jew hating and Jew baiting. Just look around the room. Plenty of faces missing. They say that Karl Rosenstein sent his regrets and that Elias Kirsch couldn't fit us into his schedule. But I know for a fact the Deken planned to be here. He wrote me a note about some research of mine and said as much." He downed his own champagne as though ridding his mouth of a bitter taste.

"Then he won't attend the conference at all?" Joshua asked.

"I shouldn't think so. Most of our Jewish colleagues are staying prudently out of sight." He blushed then, remembering that the tall, breezy American, so muscular and suntanned, was himself Jewish. "Sorry. Don't think of you as Jewish, you know."

"Yes. I know," Joshua said drily.

He walked on. The champagne had made him lightheaded, and the large room seemed too bright, too crowded. On impulse he strode over to the conference organizer, Dr. Hans Hoffmann of the Pulmonary Diseases Department at the Wilhelmsstrasse Research Center.

"Ah, Dr. Lewin, we missed you at the dinner and thought that perhaps you had changed your plans," Dr. Hoffmann said.

"I hope my arrival does not disappoint you," Joshua replied with an amiable smile.

"You Americans—always joking." The German coughed appreciatively. "I am looking forward to your paper."

"I had wanted to discuss my research with Dr. Deken, but I am told that he will not be presenting at this conference. Where can I reach him?" Still smiling, Joshua opened his pocket notebook.

Dr. Hoffmann pursed his lips.

"He is no longer at his clinic. I'm afraid we have no current address for him. He may have left Berlin. It is difficult to know."

"And difficult to find out?" Joshua persisted.

"Regrettably, almost impossible." Hans Hoffmann bowed, keeping his shoulders rigid, and hurried away. The next time he passed Joshua, he did not greet him.

Joshua approached two other colleagues. Neither of them had any knowledge of Dr. David Deken.

"You might call the medical society," a Danish scientist suggested.

"I'll do that," Joshua said, but he knew that when he called he would be told that somehow the records of Dr. David Deken had been misplaced.

Dejected, he walked slowly back to his hotel. It was a warm evening, and the windows of the apartment buildings along Friedrichsstrasse were open. Drapes flared in the gentle wind, and the sounds of a subtle string quartet mingled with the static-marred resonance of too many radios. A man's voice shouted in a hysterical staccato rhythm his belief in the supremacy of the German race and of the nation's need for land. The rasping words rose and fell in emotional crescendo, and passers-by paused and listened. Joshua, too, stood still.

"That's Hitler speaking," he thought. He wondered if any psychiatrists were listening to the speech, analyzing the desperate cadence. His brother-in-law, Franz Eisenmann, would surely recognize the symptoms of hysterical paranoia in the German dictator's voice. He felt frightened now, fearful for himself and for David Deken.

"You've never heard him before?" Ian Holmes, the Australian hematologist, who was staying at a neighboring hotel, stood beside him. "Frightening, isn't it?"

"Yes," Joshua agreed.

"Deken said as much in his letter. Or at least hinted as much."

"Ian, you've been in correspondence with him?" Joshua cursed himself for his stupidity.

"I told you so at the reception."

"Then you have his address?"

"Of course I have his address. He lives in Charlottenberg." The Australian reached for his address book and read it off, struggling with the German. "Sorry I haven't the phone number."

"Just as well," Joshua said.

He would not phone David Deken even if he had the phone number. He understood now that Werner Grossmann's cautions had been neither frivolous nor overly dramatic. They had been warranted.

The next morning he took Werner Grossmann's advice and introduced himself to the proprietor of the hotel.

"I hope I will be able to help you," the balding, sad-eyed man said. His wife, he revealed, was half Jewish and distantly related to Grossmann, who had always been kind to them. They spoke very softly, their heads bent over a map of the city, as though directions to an obscure street were being offered rather than dangerous confidences exchanged. The frosted-glass door was closed, but Joshua saw the thin-lipped clerk glance at them now and again.

"There is a rear entry, which I will leave unlocked this evening. It leads to a stairwell with an exit almost at the door of your room. It will be open all night, until the daytime staff arrives. Anyone who enters or leaves—and it is not necessary for me to know who that might be—must do it between those hours." He waved his pencil above the outstretched map, and Joshua bent his head even lower.

"You understand that I am operating on instinct. I do not even know for certain that my uncle is in danger or whether he will want to leave. But I thank you in advance for your kindness and for your discretion," he said, reflecting that it did not seem unnatural to call David Deken his uncle.

"We must all operate on instinct in these times," the proprietor said. He did not add that his own instinct had caused him to apply for visas to England for his family. A half-Jewish wife meant that his children were considered non-Aryan, he had recently been advised by a friend in the Nazi party, who had also told him, in the most casual way, of two mutual acquaintances who had recently divorced their Jewish wives.

Joshua took a taxi across the Kurfürstendamm but dismissed the driver before reaching Charlottenberg. He walked the rest of the way, aware of the profusion of swastika flags flaring in the morning breeze and conscious that despite the pleasantness of the day, drapes were tightly drawn across the windows of the large villas. In Phoenix windows were flung open to the brilliant sunlight, and voices resonated on such a street with greeting and openness. But Berlin was a city where people spoke cryptically, keeping their voices low, and where ordinary families shielded their lives from scrutiny.

David Deken lived in a red brick house on a quiet residential street. As Joshua approached it, he noticed a man leaning against the lamppost on the corner, glancing impatiently up and down the street. Instinctively, he slowed his pace and paused as though to study a house number. The man made no move. Joshua walked on, keeping close to the curb. He remembered how Johnny Redbird had advised him always to follow the edge of a trail. He was almost at the red brick house, close enough to see the drapery at the second-floor window part slightly and fall back into place, when the man moved toward him. Suddenly a young woman dashed across the street. Her high heels clattered across the cobblestones and the hood of her light blue cape dropped to her shoulders, revealing thick folds of sand-colored curls.

"Joshua!" Joyously, she shouted his name, threw herself into his arms, her lips pressing against his and then her voice soft in his ear.

"Kiss me back. Hard. He's watching."

Bewildered but obedient, he held Rachel Wallach in his arms on the quiet street and kissed her with an unfeigned passion that soared, even as his wonderment grew.

"Hold me close. Laugh. Whisper in my ear."

He held her close. Her skin smelled of sandalwood; her breasts were soft and yielding against his chest. He heard the wild beating of her heart, saw the throbbing blue pulse at her throat. He laughed and was startled to discover that his throat rasped painfully.

"What are you doing here?" he whispered to her. "What is going on?"

"Just follow my lead"—the phrase of their childhood when they had gathered in the loggia for dramatic improvisations. Her breath was moist against his ear and her body trembled in his embrace, and then she tossed her head petulantly and drew away, rubbing at her eye.

"What is it?" he asked, his voice loud. They were playing for an audience, he knew.

"A cinder in my eye."

He glanced up, saw David Deken's shingle at the second-floor window.

"We're in luck, then. Here's a doctor's surgery."

"Oh, let's not bother him." She pulled away.

"Don't be a baby. It won't hurt," he persisted.

As they bickered, the stranger glanced at them irritably, shrugged like a man whose time has been needlessly wasted, and turned the corner.

Swiftly, she drew him up the steps and into the building. The door to David Deken's surgery stood open. Rachel pulled Joshua into the dimly lit room, and David Deken rose from his desk, closed the door, and dropped the chain into place.

David Deken sat behind his desk and stared at them. He resembled Emil Coen, Joshua thought as he studied the lean-featured face, the tense, coiled posture. David Deken had been writing when they entered, and he sat very still, one hand still gripping his pen, the other splayed across the lined sheet of paper on his desk.

"You have a good reason to be here?" His question was cautious, noncommittal, and his deep voice was startlingly similar to that of Henry Stern.

Joshua turned to Rachel.

"I'll explain," she said. Her voice trembled, and he understood that she had been frightened, although she had not betrayed her fear. She sank into the leather chair opposite the doctor's desk.

"I am Rachel Wallach. I am an art student in Paris, and I work with Etan."

"I hope Etan is well. I expected to see him today," David Deken said. "I have his medical forms ready." His voice was tense, questing.

Joshua moved forward, held his hand out. "We met some years ago at a medical conference."

"Joshua Lewin," David Deken said. "I thought I recognized you." Relief crept into his voice. He dropped his pen, took Joshua's outstretched hand.

"Please let me explain," Rachel said. She turned to Joshua. "Your mother wrote to me that you were coming to Berlin. She gave me the name of your hotel and told me that you were here to see Dr. Deken. I knew his name at once because of my work with Etan."

"What work?" Joshua asked. He felt bewildered, disoriented, an outsider who had stumbled into a meeting without knowing its purpose, denied its agenda.

"The work of Youth Aliyah," David Deken said. "Arrangements are being made for German Jewish children to leave this country and go to Palestine. Etan is one of a group of Palestinian Jews who is helping to organize this operation. Of course the National Socialist government creates all sorts of obstacles, asking for tax clearances, family histories, endless releases and medical forms. They want to see vaccination certificates for everything from smallpox to the bubonic plague, and the families have had great difficulties producing these forms. Aryan physicians are either frightened or reluctant. Government offices discover an amazing shortage of certificates."

"But art students like myself have discovered that we have some talent for creating rather authentic-looking documents," Rachel said. "Still, we needed doctors to provide sample forms and fill them out. German doctors so that the emigration officials could check them against a medical register."

"But wouldn't that place them at considerable risk?" Joshua asked.

"We are all at risk, in any case," David Deken said wryly. "We are, after all, Jews."

"Still, we did not want to take unnecessary chances," Rachel continued. "The Nazis began to study our medical documents too carefully, and last week they arrested a Jewish physician in Leipzig who had worked with us. We became concerned for the other doctors. My friend Etan was told to travel to Germany from Paris to try to warn them. I came with him so that I could see you, Joshua." Her voice, so direct and forceful as she spoke of her work, grew shy and soft when she spoke his name.

Joshua smiled. He had been jealous of a journey which she had, after all, undertaken on his behalf. She had ventured into danger to see him. *She is in love with you,* Gracia had said all those years ago as they drove through the desert. He had laughed, dismissed the idea. He would not dismiss it so easily again. He studied Rachel's face as she told her story. Once he had thought her beautiful when she smiled, but now he saw the strength of her features, the vivacity of her expression, the softness of her eyes. Like the desert primrose of her drawing, she had assumed full and tender blossom, drawing from the depths of her own strength, sustaining herself. Her sensuality was derived from courage and generosity, her strength from the same tenacity that enables a flower to flourish in drifts of snow. He wanted to cross the room and take her in his arms, to curse himself for his blindness and obtuseness. Instead he sat and listened as she finished her story.

"This morning Etan and I came to Charlottenberg. We saw at once that this house was being watched. The man on the corner, other men waiting in a car nearby. Our courier often came at this hour to collect forms from Dr. Deken. We waited at the bus stop, and then I saw you, Joshua. I was afraid that they might think that you were the courier—a man by himself, a foreigner walking too slowly down an unfamiliar street. We know that the Nazis act first and ask questions afterward."

"And so you staged our little love scene, including the cinder in your eye," Joshua finished for her. Beaming, he leaned forward and gripped her hand. "Bravo, Rachel. I always knew that you were the best little actress in Phoenix."

"Phoenix. Phoenix, Arizona?" David Deken's voice quivered with excitement. "Coincidences converge. My only brother lives in that city, although we have not been in contact since the war."

"There is no coincidence," Joshua said gently. "Henry Stern is your brother, and my mother, Emma Coen Lewin, is your half sister. They asked me to come to Berlin to persuade you and your family to leave Germany and come to

Phoenix.'' Briefly, succinctly, he traced the family's turbulent history, told him of their reconciliation and their yearning to be reunited with the Deken family.

''Will you do it?'' he asked. ''It's possible to leave now. It can be arranged.'' His mind raced forward, sorting out possibilities. The Deken family could enter the hotel through the unlocked rear door and wait in his room until morning. A Paris-bound train left the Potsdam terminal at the break of dawn. Both Werner Grossmann and the hotel proprietor had told him that American dollars in appropriate denominations, slipped between the pages of a passport, effectively erased any irregularities.

David Deken stood. Tears glittered in his eyes and then streamed, unheeded, down his cheeks.

''A miracle,'' he said. ''In a single morning I have found my family and my freedom.''

Joshua rose then and moved toward his uncle. A siren shrieked in the street below, and Rachel went to the window, peered out, and then drew the drapes even closer. In the dimly lit room, Jacob Coen's son and grandson reached their arms out to each other and embraced.

That afternoon Rachel and Joshua climbed the Kreuzberg. Hand in hand, they stood at its summit and looked down at the city.

''Do you remember how we climbed Squaw Peak when we were children?'' he asked.

''Yes. I cried, and you and my brothers laughed at me,'' Rachel said. She smiled as though amused by the image of herself as a child, timid and awkward, climbing the desert mountain like a clumsy fawn.

''I would not laugh at you now,'' he said gravely.

''What would you do now?''

In answer he pulled her toward him. Again, he inhaled the scent of sandalwood, pressed his lips against hers, and drank in her sweetness. He passed his hand across the satin-skinned nape of her neck, and his fingers were blanketed by the thickness of her sand-colored curls.

''I would protect you,'' he whispered into her ear.

''Only that?'' she asked. ''Is that all you would do?''

Danger, he saw, had made her daring, and he understood that she was no longer the compliant playmate of his boyhood, the patient, comforting friend of his young manhood. It was Rachel the woman, teasing and challenging, at once demanding and yielding, whom he held in his arms.

"And I would love you," he added. "As I love you now. As I will love you always."

In reply she thrust her fingers through his dark hair and drew him so close that he could feel her lashes beating against his cheeks, and he could hear the timpanic, triumphant beating of her heart.

Epilogue,
1940

EMMA awakened early and watched the dull gold motes of first light float across the room. A lark, perched on the orange tree just outside her bedroom window, sang with a piercing sweetness and then flew westward. She took the song as an omen for the happy day ahead and smiled. Beside her, his sleep unbroken, Isaac turned, and lightly, almost imperceptibly, she touched his iron-gray hair. His lips curled, as though a vagrant dream amused him, and she pulled up the light blanket and covered his shoulders, pleased to minister to him as he slept because when he was awake her gestures of solicitude often irritated him.

"I'm fine," he insisted when she protested that he was working too hard.

She did not argue, nor did she speak of the heart seizure that had overtaken him the previous spring. Joshua, skilled in the euphemisms of his profession, called it a "warning incident," but Emma was not deceived. Instead, she monitored Isaac's phone calls, quietly declined invitations (No, Mr. and Mrs. Lewin could not attend the fund-raiser for Liberty Bonds, but they would be pleased to make a pledge; they were unable to attend the Hadassah dinner for Youth Aliyah but would be delighted to be listed as sponsors), and arranged for Leonie's family to visit more often so that Isaac was spared the journey to San Francisco.

But she had not protested the ceremonies that would be held that day to mark the opening of the clinic. The dedication, she knew, would not exhaust Isaac but invigorate him. She had worked with her usual intensity to prepare the invitation lists, arrange accommodations for guests, and coordinate the program. She had undertaken the floral arrangements herself, carefully selecting the large planters fashioned by the Indians of the Acoma Pueblo and filling them with the sturdy and tenacious wildflowers of the desert.

Slowly now, so as not to awaken Isaac, she eased out of bed and walked through the house. It pleased her that every room was occupied. Family and friends had journeyed from every part of the Southwest to share the day with them. Simon's sons were awake, and she heard them laughing, their deep voices reminding her that they were no longer boys but young men, as old as Emil and Simon had been when they left Amsterdam.

The door to the room where Leonie's twin daughters slept was slightly ajar, and she saw that Sarah and Rebecca slept with their arms encircling the soft rise of their breasts, their dark hair fanned out across the pillows. Sarah murmured aloud in her sleep and stretched her arms toward a shaft of sunlight that ribbed her flesh with radiance. She was newly in love, Leonie had confided to Emma. The boy was a senior in high school, and too often he did not call Sarah when he had promised that he would.

"She will have to learn for herself," Leonie said gravely. As she had learned for herself. As Emma had learned. The lessons of girlhood became a woman's legacy of strength and wisdom.

But now, Sarah was caught in the net of her dream, and she smiled, her eyes closed, her long lashes damply sweeping her cheeks. Rebecca, beside her, whispered a single word then lifted her finger to her lips.

It seemed to Emma that her house overflowed with the dreams of its sleepers and with the laughter and soft talk of those who had awakened to watch the day begin.

She went down to the kitchen and saw that preparations for breakfast were under way. Pitchers of freshly squeezed orange juice were ranged on the refectory table, flanked by golden mountains of toast and mounds of sweet peach preserves that the Weinglasses had brought from their factory. Through the window, she saw a plump grapefruit shimmering in a dark-leafed branch, and she went to the garden and plucked it, marveling, as she marveled anew each day, at the warmth of its thick skin, at the miracle that such a fruit grew in her own grove.

Isaac was awake when she returned to their room.

"Good morning." He sat propped up in bed, reviewing the speech he would make that day, but he watched her as she moved purposefully, busily. Always, Emma's energy bemused and mystified him.

"You are a witch," he said teasingly as she unbraided her hair and brushed it vigorously. "You have forgotten to grow old."

"I can't grow old," she replied and studied herself in the mirror. "There is too much to do."

"And you must do it all."

"No. *We* must do it all."

"We." The word was sweet upon his tongue, and she came and sat beside him. He lifted her hair, silver-gold now and lustrous from its brushing, and kissed her gently on the cheek.

"What are you thinking?" he asked.

"Not thinking. Remembering."

Memory gripped her still as she watched her family gather in the large dining room for breakfast. The doorbell rang, and Henry, Isabel, and Jesse Stern came in, followed by David and Lina Deken and their daughters. The Deken girls, so swiftly Americanized, slid into place beside the twins and giggled wildly at something Rebecca said. Emma watched Joshua and Rachel feed their small son a sliver of toast while Samuel grimly reprimanded his own children and glanced imploringly at Bryna, who had wisely chosen to sit at the opposite end of the table.

"Proud?" Franz Eisenmann stood beside Emma and smiled down at her. There were those who thought it odd, he knew, that his mother-in-law should also be his close friend and confidante. He did not find it odd. It was Emma, after all, who had guided him toward Leonie, just as she had, in the end, guided Joshua toward Rachel. Recently, he had attended a professional conference at which a colleague had presented a paper on family dynamics. Each family, the presenter had hypothesized, had its own catalyst, one family member imbued with energy and insight, who energized and motivated the others. Franz, always conservative, had been restrained in his acceptance of the theory, but clearly, Emma served as catalyst to her family.

"Proud," she agreed, and because he had initiated her into the mysteries of his profession and taught her to pursue thought and feeling, she continued, "And happy and, perhaps, a little afraid."

There was danger in too much happiness, she knew. A Mexican maid had told her of the haunted *danados*, people who had been harmed by the evil eye cast by the envy of others. She had marveled then at how closely it paralleled the *ayin hora*, the evil eye that even her cultivated English cousin Greta Anspacher had feared. She understood now that such fears were universal, and she perceived them as a kind of preparedness against the malicious vagaries of fortune.

"Oh, always afraid," Franz agreed. "You are too wise not to be afraid."

He was a doctor. He understood the body's vulnerability, the arbitrariness of illness—the laughing, playful child overtaken by a mysterious fever, the strong man subdued by racking chest pains. Daily, he read of cars going out of control, of trains crashing, of airplanes plummeting. Calm seas within minutes became raging maelstroms, and the small girl who had come to the shore to gather smooth stones was swept away by angry waves. And now the dangers were multiplied. They lived at the edge of war. Each hour they listened to the radio and wondered how much longer Franklin Roosevelt would, or indeed should, keep them out of the war that engulfed half the world.

He studied Emma and marveled at how little she had aged since they had walked together on the Embarcadero. Still slender, regal and controlled in her bearing, she moved with a studied grace. Laugh lines nestled at her eyes, creased the corners of her mouth, but her turquoise eyes had not lost their igneous sparkle, and her laughter was generous and full-throated. In that, he acknowledged, she had changed. When he had first met her, Emma Lewin had laughed very little, if at all. The love that she and Isaac had at last recognized and accepted, the warmth of the family reclaimed and reunited, had released her gaiety, her natural vibrancy. In the fullness of womanhood, she had discovered the spontaneous

joy, the careless pleasure, she had denied herself during her
youthful years.

Laughing, she hurried her family through breakfast. They
could not be late for their own party, she reminded them.
Senators and congressmen, the governor of the state and the
mayor of their city, awaited them.

They had scheduled the dedication ceremony for midmorning, hoping to avoid the searing heat of high noon, but
when they left the house they stepped into the golden blaze
of a drenching sunlight and felt the scorching breath of desert
heat. Still, they lifted their faces to the cloudless cobalt sky
and shielded their eyes against the radiance they both cursed
and loved.

The pebbled pathway that led to the clinic site was shaded
by palm trees, planted long years ago by an aging eastern
millionaire. It was said that he had thought to build a desert
pleasure palace for his young wife east of Phoenix, where
the sands were the color of ocher and the coarse, pale blossoms of the yucca plant strained skyward. The young wife
had hated the heat and isolation. She had fled the unfinished
house, and it was rumored that her husband had shot himself
in an upstairs bedroom. He had pitched forward through a
windowless frame, and his body had fallen onto the sand,
which swiftly and neatly absorbed his blood. The house had
stood empty for many years, unfinished and decaying, plundered by scavengers, inhabited briefly by the dispossessed
wanderers of the Depression years until Isaac Lewin bought
the entire property for the clinic. He had razed the existing
structure and cleared the path of detritus. His family walked
up that path now, toward the makeshift platform that had
been erected for the ceremony. Slowly they made their way
up the crude stepway, glancing at the small plaque of hammered copper that stood at the center of the platform. It was
covered by a gauze veil, across which a ribbon had been
stretched.

"The scissors. Did you remember the scissors for the cutting of the ribbon?" Isaac asked.

Emma nodded. "There, on the podium."

He relaxed. He should have known that she would remember, that he could, as always, rely on her.

He glanced approvingly at the flowers she had arranged in the graceful jars unique to the Acoma Pueblo. Johnny Redbird had helped her to select them, and she had chosen designs that intricately blended black and a rich earth red, imposed on creamy white. She had filled them with the snow-colored flowers that the Indians called Queen of the Night and the honey-hearted pink blossoms that they referred to as Living Rock. These she had plucked, with difficulty, from the micaceous crags so strangely planted on the desert floor. She herself carried a bouquet of the white mariposa tulips that grew in her garden.

"It's wonderful," she whispered to Isaac, "that so many people came."

Isaac peered into the audience and nodded. He saw that Johnny Redbird and his family, proudly dressed in their brightest rebozos, wearing necklaces and bracelets of silver and turquoise, hammered copper and blended gold, sat in the first row. Brother Timothy had come from Prescott with a contingent of his "boys." The little priest had grown fragile with the passing years, and each summer, as the heat engulfed them, he spoke of asking for reassignment to the East. But both he and Isaac knew that he would never leave Arizona. He was bonded to the desert, and even in reverie he had difficulty remembering the Irish coast of his boyhood.

The Weinglasses had come from Monterey, and Rabbi Cohen, bent with age, had journeyed from Galveston. Reuben and Joseph Wallach, married to twin sisters, each petite, dark-haired, and bespectacled, had driven all the way from Sacramento. Natalya would have approved, Emma thought, and she felt light-headed suddenly, bewildered to think of all the lives they had touched, the loyalties they held close and cherished, of all they had gained and all they had lost. She lifted her eyes to the undulating slopes of the mountains, and her lips moved in silent prayer. Isaac took her hand.

"Shall we begin?" he asked.

She nodded and fingered the turquoise pendant at her throat, straightened the skirt of her pale blue dress of watered silk.

He lifted his hand in signal, and they stood as the band of the Indian School played "The Star-Spangled Banner." The

Dekens, who had become American citizens only weeks before, stood at attention, enunciating each word. David Deken's voice trembled when he sang "the home of the free," and his wife moved toward him, leaned against him.

Isaac moved to the podium and spoke briefly.

"The clinic that will soon rise here is my family's expression of gratitude to the people of Arizona since our arrival. Here we were reunited. Here our hopes rose in flames and became our lives." Briefly he was silent, and the audience waited. He introduced the codirectors of the clinic—his son, Dr. Joshua Lewin, and his brother-in-law, Dr. David Deken.

Applause welled up as Joshua and David came forward to speak of the work they hoped to accomplish at the clinic. They were familiar figures in the community, accessible and compassionate, respected for their knowledge and their dedication. And then Jesse Stern approached his aunt Emma, and together they stood before the plaque. The tall youth smiled, and the sun turned his bright hair the color of burnished bronze. He lifted the scissors and cut the ribbon. The gauze veil fluttered to the ground.

Emma's voice, clarion-clear, rang out, reading the inscription.

"This clinic is named for Leonie and Jacob Coen—and for Analiese Deken."

Again applause broke forth, and now her brothers rose—Emil and Simon, David and Henry. The sons of Jacob Coen stepped down, and each in turn lifted the shovel that rested where the cornerstone of the clinic would be set. The desert earth was dry and yielding, yet they perspired heavily as they worked. Emma stood beside them. Gravely, she gave each of her brothers a tulip. Soundlessly, the white flowers fluttered into the newly dug earth. It was Emil, ever watchful, who saw Emma drop the sliver of shimmering green sea glass, which she had plucked so long ago from the pathway of the Prinsengracht mansion, amid the pale petals. He looked down and saw that it glittered as it caught the light of the brilliant sun. He understood then that Emma had left it as a pledge of a kind—in its fragile lucency, cradled by red earth and white flower, the old world and the new were mysteriously merged.

GLORIA GOLDREICH has created characters with the rich complexity and unforgettable passion her readers have come to expect. Her bestselling novel *Leah's Journey* won the National Jewish Book Award, and she won the Jewish Federation Arts and Letters Award for *Four Days*. Her essays and stories have appeared in many major magazines.